Oceanside Public Library
330 N. Coast Highway
Oceanside

D0457230

LOST RIVER

ALSO BY DAVID FULMER

The Blue Door

The Dying Crapshooter's Blues

Rampart Street

Jass

Chasing the Devil's Tail

LOST RIVER

DAVID FULMER

HOUGHTON MIFFLIN HARCOURT

BOSTON • NEW YORK

2009

Oceanside Public Library
330 N. Coast Highway
Oceanside, CA 92054

Copyright © 2009 by David Fulmer

All rights reserved

For information about permission to reproduce selections from this book
write to Permissions, Houghton Mifflin Harcourt Publishing Company,
6277 Sea Harbor Drive, Orlando, Florida 32887-6777.

www.hmhbooks.com

Library of Congress Cataloging-in-Publication Data
Fulmer, David.
Lost river/David Fulmer.—1st ed.
p.   cm.
1. St. Cyr, Valentin (Fictitious character)—Fiction. 2. Police—
Louisiana—New Orleans—Fiction. 3. New Orleans (La.)—Fiction.
4. Prostitutes—Fiction. 5. Creoles—Fiction. I. Title.
PS3606.U56L67 2009 813'.6—dc22 2008012619
ISBN 978-0-15-101187-2

Text set in Sabon
Designed by Cathy Riggs

Printed in the United States of America

DOC 10 9 8 7 6 5 4 3 2 1

3 1232 00837 7113

JAN 0 7 2009

15

In memory of Randall D. Stephens
1934–2002.
My teacher.

I stand on one side of a lost river
And you are on the other
I can see you clear
But I can't reach you there, my

Fragment found during renovations in 1939 at the Louisiana State Hospital for the Insane.

LOST RIVER

ONE

No one called him Buddy. No one called him Kid. No one called him King. They called him *Charles,* if they spoke to him at all. That was his given name: Charles Jr. When the attendants in their frocks and the doctors in their white coats spoke his name, that's what they used.

Though more often than not, he didn't hear, his mind resting in a blank and serene place. Except for those rare moments when lightning would flash, the thunder rumbled, and a blue luminance glowed along the horizon of his memory. Then the pictures would come to life: a curve of brass glimmering off hot lights, the wild and hungry faces, then bodies of midnight black, fair brown, and light coffee writhing in electric animation, as others stretched all languid on divans draped with shawls embroidered with flowers and vines and exotic birds. He could hear the crazy dervish dance of the horns, the treble slap of the guitar, the hollow thump of a bass fiddle, percussion knocking and jangling along, and behind it all, the shouts of all the drunken dancers.

Go, Kid, go!

How they loved him! Loved the way he prowled the stage, loved the delirious flash of his eyes under the red lights, loved the fast train he drove through the bell of his horn, loved the way he filled the night with sound and motion so loud and busy that they'd never forget.

They did, though. Yes, they did. Forget. The noise would fade into silence as the light shifted to a pale midday gray, and he'd find himself alone again.

Passing so unnoticed, all but invisible, he overheard voices that carried secrets, read the stories in curious charades, saw mischief in the way eyes shifted and lips curled. The patients and their guests and the hospital people didn't know they were putting on a play for an audience of one. Much of what he saw and heard was wallpaper and stale air, anyway, foolish words falling down as thin and dry as so many leaves on an autumn breeze.

Then, later one evening, a name emerged from the noise. His ears perked as the name was repeated, followed by something about being *gone and not coming back no more.* Feeling the gaze of dense black eyes, they stopped talking and turned his way.

Don't worry about him, the patient said. *Man don't hear nothing. Don't see nothing. Don't remember a damn thing.*

He did, though. He did. Remember. So he held fast to the name after they'd moved away, and momentarily he spoke it out: *Valentin.*

TWO

In the autumn of 1913, the view from the trains pulling into New Orleans' Union Station was the panorama of Basin Street, the mainline of the red-light district that went by the sobriquet of "Storyville."

It was a beehive all through the week, more so on weekends, as cars disgorged eager customers by the hundreds, and carriages and touring cars turned the corner to deposit the higher rollers onto the same banquettes.

The kitchens in the grand mansions and the better saloons simmered with heat and motion while bottles and glasses clinked as merrily as bells. Smoke filled the air of every room, mingling with the aromas of whiskey and cheap perfumes. Walls echoed with music, chatter, and laughter. Behind it all were sly looks and thin smiles as the chickens were plucked, one after the next.

Storyville was an economy of sin, and a good two-thirds of the devil's wages arrived between Friday afternoon and Sunday morning. With the paid services of two thousand prostitutes, the sales of liquor and food, and the take at the gambling tables, "the District" generated a small fortune every weekend.

Friday nights were raucous with the release of energies that had been pent up through the workweek. Saturday morning brought more business, mostly country lads off the early trains.

Late afternoon took a small pause, a collective breath. Men with families rode the streetcars home to dinner with their wives and children. The rounders who had lolled away the daylight hours with a favored sporting girl now took their time dressing for the evening's drinking and gambling, done up in the finest—suits and vests with gold chains—that those same women had paid for. A straight razor or small pistol and a card of hop or envelope of cocaine disappeared into this pocket or that. Meanwhile, the day cooks and maids and invisible others who worked backstage at this tawdry carnival got to lay their burdens down for a few blessed hours.

The sporting girls at the better houses usually joined the madam for an early dinner, after which they would bathe and douse their bodies with powder, perfume, and paint, readying themselves for the first visitors. Because most of the customers chose to appear at twilight, the women liked the autumn and the spring months the best. It was still warm enough to keep it busy, and they could get an earlier start.

The women in the Basin Street bordellos could count on the fingers of one hand the number of gentlemen they would host. The prettiest of the octoroons and quadroons might entertain only one fellow all night long. Some especially well-heeled types kept a woman on retainer for weeks or months at a time. A lucky, lovely few got to leave for good and become the lifelong mistresses of men of wealth.

That only happened to doves at the best addresses. The deeper into the District, the faster and cheaper the action, until it reached rock bottom with the Robertson Street crib whores, those filthy, drunken, degenerate sluts who would do anything for a price.

All the while, the money dropped like steady rain until dawn on Sunday, when the last of the customers went away and the whole of the District heaved a long, weary sigh.

———

The madam had gone by many names. Presently, she was using Mary Jane Parker. She had been a fair prostitute until she lost an eye and some of her scalp in a fight with a jealous, razor-toting rival. Now a madam, she was burdened for life with a patch and a variety of colorful wigs to hide the wounds of that epic battle. Her rival fared worse, as dead as the fellow who lay at the precise center of her fancy parlor floor rug.

The day maid had come barging into her room a little past five. The girl had been on her way to open the front door for the couple who did the cleaning when she happened to glance into the parlor. She took a half-dozen steps forward, then did a quick backpedal. Leaving the Negro couple on the gallery, she scurried upstairs, rushed into the room without knocking, and shook the madam awake. Miss Parker's good eye flared and she was about to treat the stupid girl to a healthy slap when something about a man lying dead in the parlor broke through the babble. The madam rolled out of bed, drew on her dressing gown, and went down to see for herself.

She stood in the archway and gazed at the body of Mr. Allan Defoor for a fretful half minute. He was a small-boned and dapper fellow of middle age who sported a delicate mustache, pointed beard, and thin blondish hair cut short. He was dressed in his usual sober three-piece. In one outstretched hand, he gripped a silver cane at a jaunty angle, his dead fingers folded into the crook. The wound was apparent, a hole directly above his heart, about the size of a .22-caliber slug.

Though not a man of wealth or importance, Mr. Defoor had been a regular and a decent spender in his own quiet way. Miss Parker vaguely recalled some gossip about family money, most of it gone. The victim did not have a reputation for abusing drink or dope and had always been a gentleman with the girls.

Not that it mattered anymore. Staring up at the chandelier with blue, unblinking eyes, Mr. Allan Defoor appeared calm, as if ending up dead on the carpet came as no surprise. For her part, the madam *was* baffled; she had no recollection of seeing him on the premises that evening.

Her first thought was that something had gone wrong, that one of the girls had done the violence. It happened; all she had to do was look in a mirror to be reminded that sporting women in even the finest bordellos could be vicious. Though Mr. Defoor wasn't exactly the type they'd fight over.

Stepping closer to stand over the body, she noticed that the blood that had stained Defoor's coat, vest, and shirt was dry. Indeed, not a single drop had splotched her fine rug. In the next instant, she realized that the poor man hadn't met his end there at all; at least not in her parlor. He had been killed elsewhere and then dumped.

She called to the maid, who had remained in the foyer, too spooked by the corpse to draw any closer, and sent the girl upstairs to rouse the rest of the women. It took another ten minutes to rouse the six sleepy carcasses from their beds. One by one, they appeared on the stairwell, grousing curses until they saw the body. Three of them crossed themselves and the other three whispered prayers.

"You see Mr. Defoor?" Miss Parker demanded once they were all assembled. "That's right, he's dead." The madam made an impatient sound. "Come on, now. What happened?"

The women on the stairs looked at each other.

"He wasn't in at all," Mary, who was the oldest of the staff, volunteered. "He ain't been around in maybe a week." The others murmured assent.

"He—," Miss Parker began, and then stopped, her good eye glaring as she went from one face to the next. She detected nothing devious, and her thoughts turned to which vile bitch in which other house hated her enough to pull such a macabre stunt. After fuming for a few moments more, she sent the girls back to their rooms, ordering them to stay in unless they were called. No one needed urging.

Once they were gone, Miss Parker beckoned to the maid once more.

"Run down to Basin Street," she whispered. "Go to Antonia Gonzales's and see if they can tell you where to find a Creole fellow, name of St. Cyr." She said the name the American way using *saint,* rather than the French *sawn-sear.* "The one used to work for Tom Anderson. Him."

"Yes, ma'am."

"You find him and tell him I need him here. Right quick."

The maid gave a hurried nod and bolted, only too happy for an excuse to vacate the premises. After the door slammed, Miss Parker bent down and folded the carpet over poor Mr. Defoor's body, then went into her office to call the police.

It took another forty-five minutes for two patrolmen and a detective to arrive on the scene. The coppers milled about, accomplishing nothing save to drink every drop of coffee in the kitchen. The detective, whose name was Weeks, studied Defoor, examined the wound in his chest, and questioned the madam, all without much interest. This was no Basin Street mansion.

When Miss Parker pointed out the dried blood, the detective gave an absent shrug and told her that a wagon would be around later to pick up the corpse and carry it to the morgue.

It was another two hours, the sun was coming up, and the body was still there and getting ripe when the maid finally arrived back.

The madam was in a state. "Where in God's name have you been?"

The girl was all out of breath. "I had to rouse them at Miss Gonzales's, and they, they told me go down to Spain Street. And then I had to wait for the—"

"Did you find him?"

"Yes, ma'am."

"Well? What did he say? Is he coming?"

"No, ma'am," the maid said. "He say to find someone else. He say he don't do this no more."

THREE

When Valentin couldn't get back to sleep, he reached for the hem of Justine's nightdress and found her willing, as always. Afterward, they lay across the bed letting the breeze through the window cool them. She dozed. He ended up tossing and turning with such agitation that she muttered and then poked a finger into his ribs to make him stop.

The clock on the bedside stand was turning seven when he gave up and rolled out from under the sheet. In the tiny kitchen, he splashed water on his face and set the coffeepot to boil. He plucked a breakfast apple from the basket on the table on his way to the narrow balcony that overlooked Spain Street.

It was the time of day he liked best, still and quiet, and he often spent his early mornings there with a book or newspaper, or just watching the sun rise as his little corner of the city came to life, first in gentle eddies, then in a chop of busy noise and motion. He was pleased to take no part in the break-of-day rush.

Though on this morning, his thoughts were in a stir. The maid had stood in the doorway, explaining that a Liberty Street madam named Miss Parker had sent her. Valentin didn't recognize the name, but such women came and went all the time.

Apparently, this one didn't know that he hadn't played the role of the Storyville detective for some time.

He recalled how the maid had squinted as she tried to guess in what category he belonged—"American," Creole, one of the shades of Negro, dago, or even Arab—so she'd know how to address him. He was used to it.

The girl kept her voice muted in case he was white and relayed the message from Miss Parker, describing a man lying dead on the parlor floor. Unnerved by his gray eyes and his silence, she prattled on, recounting the scene in too much detail until he cut her off with a curt refusal.

Her eyebrows hiked as the last word died on her tongue, and she stood unsure of what to do next. He had to get short with her. *Tell her I don't do that anymore. That's all!*

The girl gave a start, stuttered an apology, and made a kowtowing retreat down the stairs. Valentin closed the door and stalked back to the bedroom, annoyed that he had barked at a poor servant.

Before the sound of her footsteps had faded down the stairs, he found himself pacing as he imagined the scene she had described: the parlor cast in the dim amber light from the tasseled lamps; the heavy furnishings and Persian rugs; the madam and her sporting girls standing around in their kimonos and nightdresses staring at the body that had appeared from nowhere; the bullet hole in the victim's chest but not a drop of blood anywhere except on the body.

It was a peculiar tableau, and not so long ago he would have thrown on clothes and rushed to get to the house before the police made an official mess of the scene on their way to sweeping the crime under the fancy rug.

That was back when Storyville was his territory. Nowadays, he felt as if his career working as a private detective for Mr. Tom Anderson belonged to someone else, and far in the past. He had quit before, had been fired, had even escaped the city, only to come wandering back like some lost mongrel finding his way home.

He left this time because he had frankly grown tired of ghosts dogging him through his days and nights. He hadn't caused all of their deaths, but he hadn't been able to save them, either, and their haunting eyes accused him. Neither drink nor dope would keep these haints at bay, and he had come to understand that they'd be constant company as long as he stayed in Storyville.

When it got to the point that they were invading his dreams, he gave up. He knew he couldn't explain to Anderson, Frank Mangetta, Lulu White, or any of the others, so he told Justine it was time to pack up and go. She didn't need to hear it a second time. She wanted out worse than he did. Even on Spain Street, the District was a little too close for her comfort.

Though it was true that New Orleans in the year 1913 was not such a bad place to live. The summer had passed into fall without a fearsome hurricane like the one that had blown through the year before and torn up half the city.

He and Justine were getting along. They had forgiven each other their betrayals and had come to an unspoken agreement that as long as he stayed with his current vocation, she wouldn't go back to her former life, either. One day he woke up and it was settled.

He had found rooms over an import-export office and every now and then, an odor redolent of some faraway port would drift upward like incense, and they'd fall a little drunk and dreamy on it. Other than that, their lives were so common and domestic that Valentin sometimes swore she was building a nest. So the red-light district was the last place she'd want to hear about.

His mind was drifting back in that direction when he caught a whiff from the pot in the kitchen. He was pleased to have the diversion of the morning's first cup of chicory coffee, which he would douse with cream and honey. That and one of his books would take his mind off the maid's visit and the dead man on the parlor floor, the kind of bizarre and bloody drama that could only happen in Storyville.

Tom Anderson was up just as early and heard about the body in the Liberty Street sporting house from one of the local gadabouts who seemed to have no purpose in life other than to sweep bits of news and gossip from the banquettes and carry them to his Poydras Street doorstep.

By the time the maid had served him a breakfast of scrambled eggs and fresh fruit, he had learned more, including the interesting news that the madam had in her panic sent a girl to find Valentin St. Cyr, and that the long-absent Creole detective had run the girl off. He was not surprised.

Meanwhile, the police arrived at the bordello and bumbled about for a while before carting the body away. Mr. Defoor was carried to the morgue and the next of kin were notified. It was all done quietly in order to spare the family shame, a traditional courtesy whenever a man died in the District, whether he expired from an excess of amours or a bullet lodged in his chest.

There was one other curious detail: Those on the scene were saying it appeared that Defoor had been shot dead somewhere else and then carried into Miss Parker's house, all without being detected. The local wags would be snickering; Anderson didn't see any humor in it. But his mood was gray that morning, in spite of the misty sun that was casting a golden glow over the New Orleans streets.

He took a last sip of the coffee that he'd laced with a hefty shot of brandy and rose from the chair with a soft groan. A substantial man, of late his bulk had begun to drag on him. Sometimes his bones ached and he found himself short of breath. There was the gout, the itching rashes on his skin, fevers that came to stay. His appetite had faded, and not only at the dinner table.

Since his earliest days as a street Arab and the police department's most able stool pigeon, Tom Anderson had been able to perform with the ladies like a regular stag, slipping from one steamy bed to the next. Not so many months ago, he'd had his most recent wife and three or four other scarlet women hissing at each other like alley cats. But Gertrude, a former Basin Street madam whose true last name was Hoffmire, now regarded him as if he was a tired old hound that wouldn't worry a mouse. Some days, he reflected with a doleful sigh, she wasn't too far off.

He carried his coffee cup through the silent first-floor rooms of the house, Gertrude having toddled off to Canal Street to meet a friend for breakfast and shopping. Or maybe she was on her way to see a lover of her own. He didn't know and didn't care. In any case, it would have been a perfect opportunity for him to spend a half hour dallying with the maid, a young quadroon who was round, cheerful, and ready for some work in the bedroom to start the day. He wasn't in the mood.

His advancing years—he was now sixty-two—and a more general weariness had him feeling low. Though managing the red-light district had never been easy, it also had always been filled with pleasures. Lately it felt like tiresome, alien territory.

And now, playing the part of a doddering old fool, he couldn't seem to make up his mind whether the death of poor Mr. Defoor was serious. He had once been able to sense anything amiss in any corner of Storyville, as if the twenty-block square was an extension of his own nervous system. Not so much anymore; especially without the services of a certain Creole detective at his disposal.

He heard the maid calling from the kitchen and came out of his funk to find himself standing in the middle of the living room, staring at nothing at all.

"What's that?" he called back.

"Said the man's bringin' the car around. He'll be out front in a minute." It was rude for a servant to be yelling like that, but he couldn't scold her, because . . . well, just because.

Instead, he muttered, "All right, then," and spent a moment fumbling to find a place to set his cup. On his way out the door, he decided that he was going to seek out a doctor who could prescribe a tonic for what ailed him, and sooner rather than later.

Justine had been drowsily aware of the knock on the door before the break of dawn and Valentin rising to see what it was about. She heard him mutter something she couldn't catch. The door closed and he was back in the bedroom.

"Who was it?"

Sounding gruff, he told her it was a girl who had been sent by a Storyville madam named Parker. He lay down, curled into her, and in the next moment lifted her nightdress. He came on her hard, rougher than usual, though she wasn't about to complain. They rattled the bed frame for a little while, and then it was over and she dropped back to a brief, sweet slumber that was interrupted by tossing and turning that ended when he got up again.

She came awake to the rich scent of coffee and chicory. The sun, slanting through the window, was the color of pale butter behind curtains that undulated in the breeze. She lay back to savor the moment, spreading languid arms and legs and thinking about how their lives had changed, welcome after her career as a prized Basin Street sporting girl and his as a detective in the employ of Tom Anderson, "the King of Storyville."

Three years before, he had investigated a string of murders of well-to-do citizens that included some of the richest men in New Orleans. Though he lingered for another year or so afterward, the case seemed to have taken something out of him. So he walked away, leaving Tom Anderson and his scarlet battalions to get along without his special services. He surprised Justine by showing up on Miss Antonia's gallery to humbly request that she come with him to the rooms he had taken over the import business on Spain Street, not far from the river. She considered his offer for a little less than a minute before stepping back inside to pack her things.

She cut all the strings to her past, save for the posing she did for a class of student artists. She was happy and at least once a day stopped to utter a small prayer that it would last.

Valentin appeared with a cup of coffee, one of the little things he did for her. She sipped and watched him dress. Like her, he was of mixed blood, though his was an odder gumbo. She could detect his Sicilian father in the olive cast of his skin, the Mediterranean curve of his nose, and his slender peasant body; and his Creole mother in his gray eyes, curly hair, and African lips and cheekbones. Depending on the way the light struck him, he could appear to be anything from Negro to dago to white or any selection in between.

For years, and without trying, he had passed. Those who knew the truth either kept it to themselves or didn't care, because he was so good at what he did and because he had been Tom Anderson's man. Though every now and then she noticed in those eyes a hint of a longing for his former life, he had stayed put, and she was grateful.

William Brown lay on a bed in a rented room in a house on the corner of Bolivar Street, watching the dust drift in a swath of thin morning sunlight that poured in through the window. A door slammed, echoing along the hallway, startling him. He didn't know exactly how long he had been lying there, transfixed by the drifting, sparkling particles. His shirt and trousers were damp in the stuffy room, and he sat up, feeling a sticky sheen on his skin and the mild buzz of a headache. His mouth was dry.

When he swung his thin legs off the bed, he noticed dark spots splattered on his trousers above the knees and more trailing down the front of his white shirt. He got up to shuffle to the mirror over the washstand to study the dots on the drawn and grayish flesh of his face for a few puzzled moments before pouring some tepid water from the pitcher into the bowl. Using the ragged cloth, he scrubbed until he couldn't see the splotches anymore.

He lay back down on the bed and closed his eyes, reaching into the shadowy corners of his brain for some clue to how his clothes and flesh had been soiled, and a gradual pantomime came to life.

The fellow had turned around, startled. A pistol cracked and in the next instant his eyes flew wide in shock as he staggered and then went down in a heap. In a few gasping seconds, it was over. There was some odd comedy about getting the body into a house and leaving it on the parlor floor. William remembered sneaking back into the night and looking up to see one blazing star in an indigo sky—a good sign.

He opened his eyes and the images fluttered away. Maybe it had been a dream. He had those, wild with colors, shrieking images, and bizarre, clownish characters. Maybe so; but he wasn't imagining the stains on his clothes.

In a spike of alarm, he stripped down, rolled the greasy trousers and shirt together, and hurried to stuff the ball in the back of the closet. His pulse calmed when he closed the door, and he wandered pale naked to the window, where he stood running an absent finger over the scar on his torso. The squalid box of a room offered no view to speak of, just the flat roof of the next building, and beyond that more buildings, and more after that, shades of gray and brown, all the way to the river.

William could see a small stretch of the Mississippi, wide and olive colored, polluted with oil from the ships and barges and foul wastes of the sewers, and loud with a racket of clanging bells, screaming whistles, rude honks, and low moaning horns, all carried along on the slap of the dirty water.

There was more filth on land. The streets were crowded with automobiles, trucks, hacks, and carriages, the gutters awash in horse manure. The whole city smelled of rust and decay and the sour sweat of humanity. There were too many people, and too many of them stared with eyes that made it hard for someone like him to hide.

He knew that if he pushed his mind, he could make this world dissolve and he'd be back on the ward, gazing out over the rice fields that rippled like a gentle green ocean. On the far edge of the last verdant plot was a line of trees. Far beyond that was a ribbon of river that he remembered vaguely as a placid curve of silver that meandered from one horizon to the other as if lost.

A whistle shrieked, tearing a hole in the canvas, and William once again was surveying the dirty panorama of New Orleans. There would be salvation, and soon. Once his work was done, he could leave it forever.

Valentin descended onto Spain Street to the hooting of the barges out on the river as they floated their tonnage to the Mandeville Street wharf, not a quarter mile away. He strolled at an easy pace, enjoying the bright early autumn day. At the corner of Esplanade, he stopped at a newsstand for the morning *Picayune* and stepped outside just in time to climb on the northbound car.

The run up to St. Claude took only a few minutes, and he kept the newspaper folded under his arm until he transferred to a westbound car. It was fifteen jostling, stop-and-start minutes to the beginning of St. Charles, and he took the time to look over the front page.

The top story was the trial of several defendants in the dancehall shoot-out at the 102 Ranch six months before. Valentin remembered hearing about the gunplay and feeling a tug in his gut. He knew at the time that had he been around, he probably could have cooled the action and saved some lives. As it was, the popular saloonkeeper William Philips and a rival named Harry Parker had died and three others had been wounded.

In the aftermath, there had been grousing up and down the Storyville streets that they were falling back into the Wild West days of decades past, when such violence was a nightly occurrence, before Tom Anderson had hired an ex–New Orleans policeman named Valentin St. Cyr.

Turning some pages to find lighter fare, the detective noted that Joe Borrell (*né* Borelli) had knocked out Harry Lewis in five rounds for the middleweight title. The last few paragraphs were a compilation of other boxing news, including Jack Johnson's attempts to have his conviction for white slavery overturned so he could return to the ring.

A few more pages into the local news, Valentin came upon a small item about a Negro boy named Louis Armstrong who had been arrested for shooting off a pistol on Carondelet Street. According to the article, the boy was being placed in the Colored Waifs' Home. Valentin wondered if it was the same Louis who had roamed the streets with the kid who went by "Beansoup" for several years. The age was about right. The detective recalled that all the kid ever wanted to do was eat and ask endless questions about Buddy Bolden. The boy had heard stories and had to know if they were true. Valentin told him what he could and still spare his tender ears.

He read on, feeling guilty that his eye was wandering for any items from the District. It was a harmless vice. Hadn't he just the night before refused to travel there and help a madam? Still, he felt like someone was looking over his shoulder and whispering in his ear that Storyville was no longer his business.

The law firm of Mansell, Maines, and Velline was located in a two-story building of new brick on the corner of St. Charles and Girod. The street doors were tall and plated in brass that shone with such a polish that they always made Valentin imagine the gates of heaven. At this time of morning, with the sun up over the river, those same portals positively glowed so that he could see his reflection, a blur cast in hazy gold.

Compared to those gilded doors, the lobby beyond them held all the charm of a mausoleum. The walls were lined with shelves

of law books, portraits of distinguished gentlemen from generations before. The attorneys and law clerks padded about in near
silence, their faces dry and sober.

The legal work undertaken on the premises was just as arid,
mostly the contracts, mergers, deeds, and other legal documents
that kept wealthy New Orleanians that way. The occasional law-
suit added some spice, and delicate confidential matters arose just
often enough.

Human beings were weak, no matter what their station.
They made errors in judgment and fell victim to vices. The firm's
clients could not afford their good names to be tarnished, their
reputations to be dragged through the mud, their mistakes to be
exposed on the pages of the daily newspapers or scandal sheets.
And so their attorneys sometimes required the talents of a man
like Valentin St. Cyr, now stepping up to the front desk, where a
stiff-backed, blank-faced woman of middle years barely nodded
a greeting, disapproval pinching her face so tightly that it almost
folded.

The office at the end of the long corridor was occupied by
Samuel Ross, one of the junior partners. Valentin knocked once
and opened the door to find him standing behind his desk, fanning through a sheaf of legal-size papers as he murmured into an
ornate telephone.

Ross had contacted him over a year ago about a husband and
father by the name of Mayson, whose family had connections to
the New Orleans diocese of the Catholic Church. Mr. Mayson
had disappeared, and there were whispers that he had gone crazy
and was holed up with a low-down Storyville harlot. The lawyer
offered Valentin a sizable reward for locating the errant soul and
returning him home.

In less than twenty-four hours, the Creole detective knocked
on the door of a stifling Conti Street attic and found Mayson and
the crib whore. Though the girl, a child of no more than sixteen,
was thin as a stick, dog ugly, and foul smelling, Valentin saw the

dreamy look of ardor in Mayson's eyes as he gazed upon his trollop. It was actually touching in a sordid way.

Touching or not, the romance was over. The girl screeched
like a cat when she saw how meekly her patron surrendered to the
Creole detective. Though her mouth snapped shut when Valentin
fixed his stare on her, and then curved into a ghastly, gap-toothed
smile once he handed her a twenty-dollar gold piece—as much as
she could hope to make in a month working in a crib.

Valentin had a touring car idling in the alley behind the
building, and within the hour, Mr. Mayson was delivered to the
Louisiana Retreat, a private sanitarium located on Henry Clay
Avenue on the west end of the city.

The detective learned some weeks later that his name had
been passed to Ross by Miss Anne Marie Benedict, the daughter
of one of the victims in the last major case he had investigated. It
was a surprise, because he hadn't heard a word from her since the
matter and their personal affair had ended. Justine knew what
had gone on between him and the wealthy white woman, so he
had the good sense to lie about who had recommended him for
the job.

In any case, the Mayson family was relieved and Samuel Ross
delighted. He referred Valentin to another attorney at the firm,
this one with a well-to-do client who had suspicions about how
his wife was spending her mornings. When that led to yet another job, a door to another career opened, and he decided to
walk away from Storyville.

It was an abrupt departure, badly managed, and he left injured feelings in his wake. Once it was clear that he was gone for
good, he was as much as shunned. Except for the occasional message from the saloonkeeper Frank Mangetta, he hadn't heard a
word from anyone in the District. Not until Miss Parker's maid
showed up at his door.

The attorney now laid the handset of the telephone in the

cradle, pushed his papers aside, and peered over wire-rimmed glasses at his visitor.

"Good morning," he said.

Samuel Ross was a short, round man, as bald as an egg, and, unlike the other attorneys, a pleasant fellow. Never one to look down his pudgy nose at the detective, he seemed to take odd pleasure in his clients' more ridiculous scrapes. He also exhibited a never-ending fascination with the red-light district. He was the only one at the firm who knew about Valentin's past there and took full advantage.

Is it true what goes on at the Circus? he'd whisper. *Are there really houses over there just for women? Is Tom Anderson as sharp as they say?* And so on.

"Do you want anything?" Ross asked him. "Coffee?"

Valentin shook his head and produced a notebook from his jacket pocket. Flipping it open, he proceeded to share the information he had gathered on two matters. The first concerned the young wife of a bank manager. As the detective described it, the affluent home life that Margaret Renard enjoyed did not keep her from visiting the dirty back room of a certain Chinese herb shop in an alley off Common Street.

"It's definitely an opium den, and she's been there more than once," Valentin said.

Ross frowned. "What the hell? Why doesn't she send one of the maids? Isn't that what most of those women do?"

"She wants to hide it," Valentin said.

"So she smokes her pills on the premises?"

"She's spent most of several afternoons."

"How many times?"

"Three that I know of. Probably more. I have someone watching the place."

The attorney pondered the information, his fingers caressing his shiny pate. "What can we do about it?"

"I'll tell the chink who runs the shop to stop selling to her," the detective said. "I guarantee they don't want a white woman there in the first place."

"But won't she just find another shop?" the attorney said.

"I'll put the word out," Valentin said. "They'll all heed it. No one will want the trouble."

"And what about her habit?"

"The only thing you can do is tell Mr. Renard about it," Valentin said. "Tell him he's not going to cure her overnight. He can send one of the servants from now on. It's better than having her wandering around the wrong part of town. He can threaten to have her put in an icehouse if she doesn't agree. Or he can just go ahead and have her locked up right away."

Ross nodded thoughtfully. They moved on. "All right," he said. "What else? Tremont Vines?"

Valentin came up with a small smile. "Mr. Vines's partners can stop worrying. He's not up to anything having to do with the business. I'd be surprised if he's taken an extra dime. He has a mistress, that's all. That's his secret."

They were finished, and Valentin started to close his notebook. The attorney held up a hand. "Wait a minute," he said. "I've got something else."

Valentin waited, hoping that it was something halfway interesting.

"Do you know the name James Beck?" The detective did but couldn't place it and gave a slight shrug. Whatever it was already sounded boring. "He's a state senator. Very powerful, very wealthy, and a very important client. It seems that his son James Jr. and some of his friends paid a visit to Storyville last weekend."

The detective gave Ross a blank look. Young men from good families were regular features around the District. Some lost their innocence there, delivered by a father or uncle to an able sporting girl. It was quite the ritual in certain quarters.

"Apparently there was trouble," Ross went on. "One of the senator's friends in the police department contacted him about it."

"What kind of trouble?"

The attorney shifted in his chair. "The word is that a woman was assaulted. And that James Jr. and his pals were involved."

"Where did this happen?"

Ross glanced at a slip of paper. "On Claiborne Avenue."

The detective cocked an eyebrow. Claiborne and Robertson, the District's lowest rungs, were warrens of cheap, ugly, and mean-tempered whores, a filthy and violent place after the sun went down, and far too rough for rich white boys any time of day.

"How bad is it?" the attorney said.

"It's not good. The woman was assaulted how?"

"I don't have any details," Ross said. "The senator asked that we find out what happened and if there's a problem, fix it."

Valentin thought for a moment. "You want me to go to Storyville?"

"Well, yes, you'll have to." The attorney regarded the detective curiously. "What's wrong? You still know the territory, right?" Valentin answered with a brief nod, and Ross said, "If this is anything at all, make it disappear. We understand we might have to pay. But a man in Mr. Beck's position can't afford embarrassment. And if we don't stop it now, someone could get hurt."

Valentin knew that by "someone" Ross meant one of the boys rather than whichever whores they might molest. "Can't these people control their families?" he said.

"That's what they pay us to do," the attorney said crisply. "The young fellow has a future, and his father wants him corralled. Do whatever's necessary. Just so it's quick and quiet."

Valentin didn't need to hear this last bit; it was the standard order. He put his notebook away. "Anything else?"

"That's all for now," Ross said. "But there'll always be more. Isn't that right?"

"Yes, sir, it is," Valentin said, and stood up.

The attorney waved him out of the office and went back to his papers.

Valentin walked away from the heavy doors feeling a stitch in his gut. Though Samuel Ross was a pleasant-enough fellow, Valentin didn't care a bit for the firm's clients. He didn't give a good goddamn about the welfare of James Beck, his band of louts, or the father who couldn't manage his brat of a son. Because of them, he would have to travel to Storyville after avoiding just such a visit only a few hours earlier.

He walked a half-dozen doors down the avenue to the second of the three law firms that currently employed him. Inside, he stepped to the front desk and collected two envelopes; one was a scribbled note from one of the attorneys asking him to check on a client's fiancé, a certain gentleman who was making claims of European royalty, and the other contained a bank check for his monthly retainer of seventy-five dollars.

He signed for the check, thanked the dour-faced clerk, and went outside to catch a car back into town.

It didn't take long for the word about the dead man on Miss Parker's floor to make its way along Basin Street. Though the madams down the line uttered shock over the incident, each one also let out a sigh of private relief that it wasn't her parlor where Defoor had come to rest, and even more privately wished that if he had died on Basin Street, the curse would have landed on French Emma Johnson. Let the evil witch explain *that* away.

Honore Jacob, the landlord of the property, made an appearance and a proper fuss. Red-faced and flustered, he sweated his way up the gallery steps to demand to know what the hell was going on. *A dead man on the floor? Who was he? Which one of your good-for-nothing whores shot him?* All Miss Parker could do was shrug. The exasperated landlord left, shaking his head in bewilderment.

Other than that, the odd happenstance was brushed aside. Corpses were a fact of Storyville life. Usually, it was some poor fellow whose heart couldn't take the strain. Women were murdered by lovers, and vice versa, sometimes with such tragic drama that local musicians wasted no time in turning the incidents into song. Suicides were not uncommon among the ranks of the sporting women. So the death of Allan Defoor raised few eyebrows.

Antonia Gonzales was not so complacent. Sitting at her kitchen table, sipping a lukewarm cup of coffee, and gazing out at the back garden, she thought the other madams were a little too eager to shove the strange incident out of sight. There was something wrong about it.

Not so long ago, she could have gone upstairs, tapped on Justine Mancarre's door, and, finding Mr. Valentin there, asked him to look into it. And he would have solved the problem just that directly. That was why Tom Anderson had kept him on, in spite of their regular quarrels and the detective's mixed blood. St. Cyr had been good for Anderson and for the District. And yet the King of Storyville had let him walk away.

Two blocks down on the corner of Iberville Street, a white Packard Victoria pulled to the curb. Tom Anderson opened the passenger side door, put a foot on the running board, and clambered down with a soft grunt of discomfort. The springs of the automobile replied with a mocking squeak of relief.

Standing on the banquette, he surveyed the world he had created. Even with his ills, the mere sight was a balm. The mansions that fronted the street were the showcases, with ornately furnished downstairs rooms for relaxation before and after the more lurid diversions of the upper floors. These houses employed the finest of the sporting women, known for their beauty, amorous skills, and wit. Some well-traveled gentlemen claimed that they ranked with the courtesans of the high-class bordellos of Europe.

That was the main line. To the north lay Franklin, then Liberty, Marais, and Villere, and each avenue was a step down a slope that ended in the nightmare alleys of Robertson and Claiborne. When it came to fornication, Storyville offered something for every pocketbook and taste.

Though quiet at this early hour, around noon the District would come to life, yawning and stretching like a harlot worn out by too many rough nights, and yet ready for service. The daytime hours were businesslike, as men of modest means were ushered in, sated, and sent back out the door, an assembly line of quick and cold joy.

Later, though, when the sun went down, Storyville would apply its paint and perfume and turn on its lights to become a fantasy world dedicated to pleasures of the body. Men drank, caroused, drank some more, listened to the professors at the pianos, caroused once again. Finally, they went home, leaving piles of gold behind.

It was all part of the grand machine that had been devised by the heavy-framed gentleman who now waved off his driver, then watched absently as the Packard chugged away in the quiet morning light. Stepping beneath the colonnade that stretched along two sides of the building as the etched-glass doors of the establishment opened wide, he muttered a good morning to Ned, the old Negro janitor.

"Coffee's ready, Mr. Tom," the Negro replied, and the King of Storyville passed inside and enjoyed another rush of pride.

As a premier drinking, dining, and gambling establishment, Anderson's Café and Annex occupied almost half the city block and anchored Basin Street. Anderson had opened it fifteen years before as a modest restaurant, then expanded it by steps until it dominated the District. The decor, from the tiled floor of Italian marble to the brocade on the walls to the chandeliers overhead, had been inspired by the great casinos of the Riviera. The food and drink were the best to be had, and all the games were straight up. There was even a salon for ladies tucked away behind a curtained archway. It was a grand room by any measure.

Now the proprietor of the address leaned at the end of the long bar to observe the crew going about their chores.

"You hear 'bout what happened up at Miss Parker's?" Ned said.

"I did." Anderson eyed the janitor. "Is there anything else going around?"

"Jes' that they done took the man away," Ned said. "Police is all gone now. It's over with." His white eyebrows arched and he said, "Someone say Miss Parker sent for Mr. St. Cyr, but that he wouldn't—"

"I know about that," Anderson interrupted gruffly.

Ned shrugged, stepped behind the bar, and picked up a rag to resume polishing the brass fixtures. Anderson walked slowly down the length of the room to his favored table near the end of the bar.

He helped himself to a cup of coffee from the urn and settled into his usual chair, facing the door. As the morning passed, he would attend to paperwork, direct his staff, and address the mundane details of his day. Only after his lunch would he make his way upstairs to use the telephone set and doze in his big leather chair. Later in the afternoon, he would greet visitors on more delicate and confidential errands: local politicians, merchants, landlords, certain high-level criminal types, the occasional madam. He'd listen and then dole out advice, orders, and justice. When the sun went down and the streets came alive, he'd be back downstairs to host his most important guests.

At the very end of this long workday, he might slip away to a private room in one of the better houses to enjoy the attentions of a special young lady. Otherwise, he would call for his car and go home to bed. Lately, that's how most of his nights ended.

The body of Allan Defoor was placed in a locker in the Parish Prison morgue, along with the other white unfortunates. It was late morning when the police brought the victim's eldest son, who provided a hushed identification before being escorted back out, ashen faced and shaking. The police sergeant on hand informed him that the investigation would likely be closed and the body released to the family by the end of the day.

The official review was cursory. The coppers made quick rounds to ask about the victim. When these efforts came up empty, they dropped it.

After Defoor's son hurried home to deliver the sad news, the police went back on duty and the morgue attendants locked the doors, hitched the horses to the hack, and rode to North Peters Street to collect the body of a drowning victim. On the way back, they stopped at their usual place on Perdido Street for an early lunch, leaving the waterlogged corpse outside.

When they returned to the morgue, they found a police officer waiting. Detective James McKinney had been given part-time leave from street patrol and was eager to cover every detail. If his captain gave the word, he'd talk to the family and friends and see if he could puzzle out how and why the man had been murdered. It was unlikely he'd get that far. No one appeared interested, least of all Captain Picot, who seemed to harbor the belief that any death in the red-light district was well deserved.

The senior of the two attendants, a callow-faced mulatto named Royce, told their visitor that one of the doctors from the medical examiners' office would be around later and that maybe he should come back then. The detective requested instead that they fetch the body from the cooler and wheel it on a gurney into the examination room so he could have a look. The two attendants exchanged an annoyed glance. They were used to having a nap after lunch and weren't much in the mood to work. McKinney got his way, though, and within a few minutes stood viewing the denuded corpse from head to toe and taking notes on a little pad. The younger attendant wandered out of the room, and the mulatto perched atop the desk, with his back against the wall, his arms crossed and head drooping.

McKinney found Defoor's wound to be precise: a hole the size of a Liberty dime, over the heart but doing enough damage to put an end to the victim in a matter of seconds. While there were no powder burns in evidence, the precision of the shot meant that it had come from at most a few feet away.

The detective searched the body further.

"What's this?" he inquired presently, interrupting a rattling snore.

Royce raised his chin, blinking. "What's what?"

McKinney pointed. "Right here."

Huffing, the mulatto pushed himself off the desk and stepped close to the gurney. "What?"

McKinney directed his attention to Mr. Defoor's forehead.

Royce squinted. "What?"

"He's been cut," McKinney said.

The cop pointed to the faint pinpoint line that started over the victim's right eyebrow, crossed the bridge of his nose, and ended on his left cheek. Officer McKinney treated the dull-faced mulatto to an absent glance.

"Now why would someone do that?" he said.

FOUR

The fellow had been lying dead for a day and a half and had grown so putrid that the smell was noticed even among the cribs that lined Robertson from Conti to Bienville streets. The call went out around midmorning. It took another two hours for the police to arrive, first a pair of beat coppers, then a detective from the precinct attached to Parish Prison.

The sergeant and the rookie patrolman in their blues and round-topped helmets ambled along the litter-strewn banquette in opposite directions, canvassing for witnesses. They came back to report to the detective that the whores on both sides said the crib had been vacant for at least a week, and none had a recollection of the woman who had rented it last.

So the officers had the body of a white man in a plain suit and that was all. The victim had been shot in the back of the skull, from the look of the entry wound a single bullet from a .22, and then dumped on a filthy, lice-riddled mattress in a foul Robertson Street crib. A few more of the harlots were paraded by the door for a look at the poor fellow. Not one of them could identify him. This was no surprise; the men who visited that part of Storyville rarely lingered for long. And even sober, the sluts who served them saw so many faces that they all blurred into one.

The detective sent the women away, and he and the sergeant strolled off to Marais Street to find a saloon with a telephone so they could call the precinct for missing persons reports and enjoy a draught beer or two while they waited to hear back.

The patrolman, whose name was Casey, was left to stand by until the wagon came for the pungent corpse. It wasn't his first visit to the raw edge of the red-light district, though like most New Orleans policemen, he hoped it would be his last.

Even now he could feel hard eyes glaring from other doors. Business was already bad; having a copper standing around made things worse. A corpse in a crib was a regular occurrence, and the whores were used to quicker service. They wanted the body and the policeman watching it gone, so that they could go back to selling pieces of themselves to whichever citizens were desperate enough to pay the ten cents.

After a half hour, Casey got bored and, with a glance up and down the banquette, stepped into the crib for a closer look.

The room was the usual size, ten feet wide and eight deep, with a low ceiling, and appointed with the usual iron-framed bed and washstand. It reeked of sweat, sour whiskey, urine, New Orleans' special bouquet of damp rot, and the odor of flesh decaying.

The dead man was lying on his back on the greasy and stained mattress, his eyes open and fixed on the ceiling, his arms flung wide as if he was trying to fly away. Though his suit was the kind offered in the Sears catalog for a dollar, it was clean and buttoned, quite prim for that dirty and disheveled place.

Though this didn't signify. Casey had been around enough to know that all sorts of men found their way to Robertson Street, drawn for reasons he never understood to the filthy trollops who populated it and the lewd acts they performed.

As the patrolman stood studying the body and pondering the odd tastes of some men, the light through the doorway shifted and he noticed what appeared to be a scratch on the victim's forehead. Edging closer, he bent down to see more clearly a clean and simple line from the right cheek to the jawline on the left side, scrawled with something so sharp it had barely broken the skin.

He was still peering at the wound when he heard the familiar creak of wagon wheels. Straightening, he stepped outside and into the relatively fresh air as the hack pulled up.

With the casual efficiency of veterans, the mulatto driver and his Negro helper climbed down, carried their stretcher in and the body out, loading the cadaver in the bed alongside two others. They were hooking the clasps on the gate when the detective and the sergeant ambled up, their eyes a bit glassy.

While the sergeant filled out the form the attendant produced, the detective stood by the hack, gazing morosely at the three bodies. Officer Casey stepped up to explain about the odd cut on the victim's face, then pulled down the sheet so the detective could see. The detective glanced at the wound, gave an absent shrug, and walked away to join the sergeant, who had finished with the paperwork. The two senior officers crossed the street, climbed into the Ford runabout, and chugged away. The men from the morgue fastened the rear gate of the hack, pulled themselves up into the seat, and drove off to their next call, leaving Officer Casey standing alone on the Robertson Street banquette.

After a leisurely bath and a half hour dressing before her mirror, Evelyne Dallencort called down for Malvina to tell her eldest boy, Thomas, to fetch the automobile and bring it around front. As she descended the stairs, she stopped to listen to the son snickering as he told his mother about a body found on the floor of a bordello in the red-light district. From the sound of his voice, Thomas was taking a giddy delight in recounting the details.

"Woke up and there he was lying dead on the floor," he was saying. "And ain't nobody got no idea how he got there."

She heard Malvina mutter something in response.

"How the hell you manage somethin' like that?" Thomas went on. "I mean, what a goddamn lark!"

Malvina snapped back at the cursing. Thomas produced another blunt laugh as he let himself out.

After a light lunch, Evelyne put on a Floradora hat with a veil attached and went out the front door, throwing back something breezy about shopping and then being expected for tea. She would telephone when it was time for Thomas to come carry her home. From behind his *Picayune*, her husband coughed, dabbed his dry lips, and nodded gravely. Malvina stood by with the blank face of a woman who knows much and says little.

Outside, the Winton, nicely turned in deep burgundy with brass and wood appointments and black leather seats, rolled up to the curb. The sixteen cylinders chattered gaily, and Thomas squeezed the horn bulb for a merry honk.

He was slow about climbing down to offer Evelyne a hand up, just shy of insolent. She knew this was because he was in livery, which he hated. It annoyed her. The young sport got to drive a fine automobile, one of the first touring cars to feature an electric starter. This meant that unlike other chauffeurs who had to bend down clumsily to turn a crank, Thomas merely closed the choke and slipped a switch on the dashboard to bring the engine to life. A body would think he'd appreciate that.

Though his attitude could use some work, he was an able driver, and his touch was sure as he pushed the automobile around the corner and down St. Charles at a good twenty miles an hour. When they reached the corner of St. James Street, she returned his discourtesy, snapping out an order to take the car back to the house and wait for her call. She knew when he was on his own, he liked to race around the Negro parts of town, showing off for the girls, and she was letting him know there wouldn't be any of that today. She stepped down from the Winton without his help and, lifting her skirts, crossed the banquette.

An attendant leaped from behind the glass to push wide Mayer Israel's heavy double doors.

The store clerks would recognize her as one of the Garden District wives who spent their days shopping and socializing while the colored help did the housework and raised the children. These women all appeared to have been cut from a mold, hair swirled and pinned in Parisian style, and dressed in the latest fashions from the Continent by way of Mayer Israel's racks.

Most of the ladies had enjoyed a privileged upbringing that had led to a privileged marriage. Evelyne was the wife of Benoit Dallencort, a scion of one of the city's best families, with a lineage of wealth and prominence going back over a hundred years to the time when New Orleans was still a French city. Claiming this pedigree, she had assumed her wifely duties with a placid grace. She bore her aging husband two children and managed their Perrier Street mansion. She arranged social events and made appearances at the charities at the Opera House. Indeed, she performed with such skill that no one considered that a serpent lay coiled in her breast.

As she began the transformation from common girl to woman in her Mississippi hometown, she realized that she had a special gift for changing shape to suit her environment. First it was a matter of survival; later a way to serve her pleasures. She had turned being "ruined" to her advantage by blackmailing the rich older gentleman who had deflowered her. She used his money to escape her lowly origins for the city of New Orleans, where she promptly remade herself into a woman of class.

Possessing a patrician face, admirable figure, and the brazen confidence to match both, Evelyne slipped smoothly into her new role as a society woman, using the secret that fine trees sometimes had crooked roots to her advantage.

She could demur when asked about her people, knowing that immense fortunes had begun with horrors like trafficking in slaves. Other families had betrayed their own by dealing in criminal schemes such as trading with Yankees during the blockade. And some others were descended from characters like the pirate Jean Lafitte.

Indeed, Evelyne believed that bandit blood ran in her veins; or perhaps that she was kin to Marie Laveau, the octoroon woman who had grown rich, famous, and feared by all of downtown New Orleans in the first half of the last century. Like Marie, whose ghost was said to still haunt the city streets, Evelyne possessed a devious, devilish intelligence. Also like that queen, she had grand plans, and this morning's visit to Mayer Israel's, the finest department store in New Orleans, was part of her most audacious design of all.

On the second floor, she was greeted by a quadroon girl named Delia, who escorted her to one of the private changing rooms reserved for special customers. Delia was not only her favored dresser, but a useful spy. In addition to what she overheard from the other rich men's wives, she ran with rounders, keeping up with sordid news from the darker corners of the city, places like Rampart Street and Storyville. The girl never failed to deliver useful information.

Now down to only a camisole of fine silk, Evelyne patted her hips and stomach. It was still a good figure for a woman of thirty-six. The lines and the sagging had only just begun, and her profile was still comely.

Delia rapped on the door and stepped in with three fine dresses draped over her tan arm. She knew what was expected and, before they got to the business at hand, spent languid moments fussing over the older woman, murmuring about her choice of clothes and caressing various parts of her body with a gentle touch, lingering on her breasts and buttocks, until Evelyne's breath came short and her flesh fairly glowed.

Delia helped her into the first of the dresses, and she spent a pleasant quarter hour trying that one and the other two, enjoying the sight of herself done up so. She would be a vision at the

Christmas balls. Then she thought, *No, no Christmas balls this season,* and laughed quietly.

Delia said, "Ma'am?"

"Oh, nothing," Evelyne said.

She took all three dresses, and Delia carried them out to the counter. They'd be delivered at a later hour, proof of her busy day of shopping.

Now the second act of the comedy began. Evelyne remained in the changing room, as giddy as a child playing hide-and-seek. Five minutes went by and Delia reappeared, slinking in with a feline grace and holding a garment bag under her arm, from which she drew a common day dress, along with a slouch hat, white stockings, a pair of brogans, and, for a final touch, a wig of auburn curls.

Delia set to work preparing the older woman, helping her wriggle into the dress and pull on the stockings. She helped her with the shoes, then went to work getting the wig set just so, using pins she plucked from her own braided hair. She ducked out again and came back with a coat, knee length and a size too large. Once the wrap was draped, the wife of a rich and prominent local citizen had been replaced by a washerwoman.

A few more touches here and there and Evelyne was ready. Delia scurried from the dressing room to scout any of the other Garden District ladies who might be lounging about. Any such women would be steered aside by other helpful clerks. It was a service the girls traded, since many of their clients were involved in affairs that required delicate choreographies.

This morning it was clear sailing, and Delia hurried her charge out of the dressing room, along the back wall, and through the set of doors onto the upstairs landing of the back stairs.

Evelyne pushed a gold Liberty dollar into the quadroon's hand, whispered a thank-you, and made her way down the two flights of dark steps to the employees' entrance in back. If she happened to meet one of the Negro stock boys coming up, she would just brush past, and the boy would know to avert his eyes.

As usual, Delia had carried out her instructions to the letter, and a yellow Hudson OC was waiting when she stepped out onto Common Street. The driver would have strict instructions to mind his own business and not speak a word to his passenger. So, with her head bent and hat pulled low to avoid any chance of detection, Evelyne Dallencort was whisked away into the New Orleans streets.

Riding along, watching the crowds, she chuckled quietly to herself. If only the peasants knew!

They slowed for an intersection, and the pedestrians stared at the fine automobile, tracing it from the gleaming radiator cap to the spare tire mounted in back. Their gazes passed over her, seeing a poor nothing, a nobody like themselves who happened to have the luck to get a ride across town in some downtown family's touring car. At that moment something bitter rose in her throat that made her want to lurch to her feet and shout for them to turn their eyes away.

She bit her tongue. It wouldn't be long before her name was on lips from one end of the city to the other. They would all find out soon enough. Once she finished shedding her skin, no one would be able to deny her.

Tom Anderson spent the morning working his way through the stack of papers on the table before him, stopping now and again to refill his coffee cup and talk over minor business matters with various characters who passed in and out of the Café. Just before noon he got up to stretch and to fetch a small shot of grappa to settle his stomach, something he had learned from St. Cyr—or, actually, *Saracena,* which was the name that was on the Creole's birth certificate.

He used the telephone set behind the bar to call the offices of *The Blue Book,* the pocket-size guide to the two thousand prostitutes working in the District. Billy Struve, the publisher and a regular source of uptown news and gossip, came on the line. The King of Storyville, an old-fashioned sort who distrusted telephones for private matters, asked Struve to stop by as soon as he had the time to spare. He dropped the hand piece in the cradle, topped his coffee with grappa, and went back to work.

After he made his rounds of the law offices, Valentin bought a boudin sandwich and a cola from a street cart and sat down on a bench in Lafayette Square to eat. He didn't have much of an appetite, and fed the pigeons with what was left of his lunch. He had skipped a visit to Sam Ross. Not that he'd be able to avoid the attorney for long. Ross would already be expecting a report on James Beck Jr. Which would require that a certain Creole detective make a visit to a certain red-light district.

A lucky bird got the last crumb, and the detective decided to go and get it over with. It was still early, and he could be in and out in no time. He'd be less than a minor distraction on those sorry streets, and they'd likely forget about him as soon as he was gone.

Still, he prudently crossed over far up on Canal to reach Claiborne Avenue, stopping for a moment to make way for one of the familiar creaking hacks from the city morgue. The narrow thoroughfare was lined by rows of brownstones in much need of repair, a selection of low-down saloons, a grocery store or two, and the odd Chinese laundry. From what he could see, nothing much had changed in the three years since he had last seen it.

This back boundary of the District was the lowest rung on the scarlet ladder, so far removed from the broad thoroughfare of Basin Street with its grand bordellos, fine dining establishments, high-dollar saloons, and gilded music halls that it might have been in another country.

Though not a few of the women who rented the cribs for a half-dollar a day and served men for a dime a trick had once boarded in those same mansions. Once pretty, with firm bodies and all their teeth, they had fallen victim to drink, narcotics, and evil men. Other trollops were cursed from the start and never rose any higher than these foul corners. No matter how they started out, the lot of them tended to ugly and vicious, as derelict as the city had to offer.

The streets were so bad that the police rarely patrolled after sundown and then only in pairs, and any man who ventured there was on his own. The women—whether drunk, addicted, diseased, or mad—were only the most recent edition of the vicious bawds who had populated the section for decades, the type who considered it sport to lure a man into a hovel, knock him unconscious, and steal everything he carried or wore. They sometimes fought each other in fierce bouts that left puddles of blood in the middle of the cobbled streets and provided an extra bit of Saturday-night entertainment. Many ended up dead in a crib, either murdered or finished by their own hopeless hands.

The two streets should have been closed down years ago, but for all the filth and violence, they still generated plenty of cash. Not to mention that the city fathers preferred the scourge not spread to any other part of New Orleans. Like any sewer, it was better to have it contained.

The earliest-rising birds of the Quarter were up and about, and Valentin stopped every few doors to talk to a girl. It didn't take him long to pick up bits of the story, one more piece at each stop. He had only done it hundreds of times before, and he slipped back into the routine as if he'd never been gone at all.

By the time he reached Bienville Street, he'd heard several versions of a tale of young louts assaulting a woman the previous Saturday evening. There was also some chatter about a fellow carted out of a crib one block over, but that meant nothing to him.

Finding the victim of the malfeasance turned out to be easy; everyone knew Essie Gill. The detective was directed to a decrepit house halfway down the block between Conti and St. Louis, one of the structures that were cracking apart as a bad foundation settled further in the soggy New Orleans earth.

Valentin heard her first, the voice ripping through the early afternoon quiet like a rusty saw blade. She was standing halfway up the rotting steps of the house, dressed in a Mother Hubbard, once white, now stained and mottled. When he called her name, her head came around in a slow glare. Then her eyes went wide with surprise and her gap-tooth mouth stretched.

"Well, god*damn*!" she cried out, clapping clumsy hands and then pointing a finger. "Is that Mr. *Valentin* right there?"

Her cry echoed along the street and Valentin winced. Stopping at the bottom of the steps, he said, "How are you, Essie?"

Essie said, "Whatchu doin' 'round here?"

"I came to see you."

The woman blinked, dazzled by this news. "Issat right?" She hobbled unsteadily down to the banquette, bringing the odor of her unwashed body with her.

Essie was a well-known character around the streets. Once a decent-looking girl, plain featured but with a pleasing smile and good eyes, she had worked in one of the better houses, not a first-rate Basin Street address, but only two blocks back on Liberty. She might have stayed or even moved to a house down the line, save for her unfortunate problem with drink. One sip led to a second, then a third, and continued on from there.

Many was the night she shuffled to a temperance meeting at Deliverance Baptist and swore before God and the other wretches that she would imbibe no more. The pledge lasted until she encountered a bottle that held liquor. And then it would all go 'round again, a slow whirlpool of Raleigh Rye. The more she drank, the more it affected her, and she would go out of her mind on a few short glasses.

The madams tired of her, tired of opening doors on a drunken Essie and a half-dozen men, all taking their turns at her and not one paying a dime. They lost patience with her wild diatribes as she stood at a window, screeching foul curses at the neighbors and innocent bystanders alike. Time and again, she was told to pack her things and go. Each dismissal took her one step farther north and another rung down the ladder. Soon she wouldn't even be able to keep herself in a crib and would end up working on the street, which meant bending over or scraping her knees in whatever alley or entranceway was handy, lucky to earn a nickel for each act.

Her clothes were often torn from falls and spotted with spilled drink and other stains that got laughs from some and disgusted others. She bathed rarely, didn't bother to douse herself with perfume, and so appeared to be just another worthless, falling-down-drunk slut on a fast train for the bughouse or the cemetery.

Valentin had dealt with her a few times, back when she had first arrived. She had been determined to get into one of the Basin Street houses and wouldn't take no for an answer. Even then she had a wild streak that frightened the madams. They did not want the likes of her around their well-heeled customers and left it up to Valentin to deal with her.

He handled it, directly and to the point, banishing her from any decent house until she learned how to behave. Though furious over the treatment, she still appreciated the Creole's honesty and accorded him a grudging respect. For his part, he soon learned that she had an odd ability to sweep up information from the street and recall it precisely, even when she could remember little else. He had used her talents dozens of times.

She now regarded him with curious, though bleary, red eyes. "Whatchu doin' back 'round here? I thought you was long gone." Her breath reeked of sour whiskey.

"I came to see you," Valentin repeated.

Essie cocked her head. "Me?"

"I heard you had some trouble the other night."

"Trouble?" Then: "Oh, you mean with them *white* boys." She cackled. "Jesus Christ almighty!"

"What happened?"

Essie let out another raw laugh and plunged in. The way she told it, the four young men had come knocking at her door early Saturday evening.

"They come inta my crib and they say, 'We here to have some fun, and we heared you was a good sport.'" She winked, an aside. "Everybody know that. Yes, sir! Then they tole me to take off my dress, and I figgered they was wantin' to take turns, or maybe go two at a time, like that." She took a leering pause that was meant to be dramatic. "But that wa'n't it at *all*!"

A few stragglers, alerted by her screeching voice, stopped to listen.

"You know what they done?" Her voice swooped. "They dragged me out to the corner without a goddamn stitch on! You believe that shit? In the middle of the fuckin' banquette and in front of the whole goddamn *world*!"

Her bloodshot eyes widened. "One of 'em pull off his belt. I thought he was gonna give my bare ass a whuppin'. But that wa'n't what they wanted. No, sir." Pointing a shaky finger along the banquette, she said, "They went and strapped me to the fuck-in' *lamppost* down there." She let out a whoop and another couple pedestrians stopped. "That fat fuck of a copper, what's-his-name, the one walks the beat 'round here, he was 'cross the street. He saw what they was doin' and just stood there laughin', like it was the funniest goddamn thing he ever saw." She stopped, sniffed mightily. "And you know what they did next?"

Valentin did know or at least could guess.

Essie said, "The one boy went into his pocket, pulls out a firecracker. You know what a 'sixteen' is? It's one of them big fuckers, six, seven inches long, and about this big around." She made a circle of a dirty thumb and index finger. "They all thought it was so damn funny, 'cause it's right 'bout the same size as they yancies. That's what they said. They *wish* it was!" She cackled again, then sobered. "The one little bastard done stuck that thing right up in my pussy, way up in there. Then another one struck a lucifer and lit the goddamn fuse! I couldn't get loose, and I was screaming and crying, but they just kept laughin'. And none these bitches out here'd help, not one bit."

Valentin said, "What did—"

"That fuckin' fuse was burnin' down!" she screeched. "I could sho'nuf feel it on my leg and I seen it smoking. Now I was cryin' like a baby, 'cause I thought they was gonna blow up my cunt. And I was prayin' to Jesus that it went ahead blowed me up all the way!"

Valentin opened his mouth, then closed it. She wasn't going to stop.

"I hear them go, 'fi', fo', t'ree, two, one,' and I jes close my eyes. And then they all start to cheer." She let out a raw shriek. "It was a goddamn *blank*! Nothin' but the tube and the fuse!" Now she coughed up a gob of phlegm, which she spit into the gutter. "I was still cryin', 'counta I was so scared, and then I was laughin' 'cause I still had my stuff left."

Valentin said, "Then what?"

Essie stopped and eyed him. "What?"

"What did they do then?"

"Oh. Then they untied my hands and took me back to my room. The people on the street be cheerin' like I won a prize. The one boy told me to blow 'em all, and I was glad to do it, just so they would get gone. I done one at a time, whilst the others watched. When I got done, they say 'You a good sport, Essie,' and left out without givin' me a goddamn nickel!"

Valentin waited an extra moment to make sure she was finished. He hated hearing such stories. He said, "You know the boys?"

Essie's gaze shifted. "No, but if I seed 'em again, I bet I would."

"What about names?"

"The one was called 'James.' Didn't hear no others." She was silent for a few seconds, then peered at him blearily. "'My in some kinda trouble, Mr. Valentin?"

"No, you're not," the detective said. "Thank you for the information." He went into his pocket and handed her a Liberty half. "And they won't bother you anymore."

Essie grinned, showing the gaps of missing teeth once more. It was a gruesome sight, and Valentin thought about young boys from good families making cruel sport of this poor slattern.

He thanked her and started back the way he had come. It had been a safe visit. He found out what he needed, and as far as he knew, no one aside from Essie had recognized him.

When he reached the next corner, he stopped to gaze across the avenue at the whitewashed wall of St. Louis Cemetery No. 2, known as "the City of the Dead" and the final resting place of those uptown citizens who could afford it. How many characters he could name resided inside those walls? Too many to count, a parade of the deceased, reaching all the way back to his childhood, beginning with the barely remembered faces of his brother and sister, taken by the yellow fever epidemic they called "Bronze John"; his father, murdered by a mob and followed by a string of villains and their victims. It was some grim procession he had left behind.

Now he felt a flush of guilt. He could say the same about whoever was still alive in Storyville. He had abandoned all of them, from the madams in their Basin Street mansions down to the poor wretches like Essie Gill.

Thinking these thoughts, he ambled south, took in the sights, finding the streets in a general state of disrepair. Tom Anderson had always made a point of keeping the District tidy, as if to belie the debauchery upon which it thrived. The banquettes were cleaned, the garbage collected, and the gutters washed, if Anderson had to pay the crews himself. Now it all seemed soiled and worn around the edges, as if someone wasn't making the effort.

A half block on, he passed a woman in a common dress, cheap wig, and a hat pulled down low. Old habit had him steal a glance. The keen planes of the woman's face and the hawk-sharp light in her eyes made a startling contrast to her tawdry shirtwaist and mess of fake hair. She returned his glance, and though it was only a flicker, he was startled by a cold hard light, as if a photograph had jumped into focus.

Then she had hurried past, and he looked over his shoulder, puzzled by what he had seen. Something was wrong about her, but he couldn't settle on what that might be. In the next moment, he considered how long he had been gone from those streets and how much he'd forgotten.

Evelyne moved off at a good clip. She sensed the man she passed casting his eyes on her and stifled her own urge to turn around. She couldn't imagine what he was doing there, in that place, at that time. And though they'd never met, she had heard enough to be able to identify him on sight. The good news was that he didn't recognize her, but it wouldn't have mattered much if he did. They'd meet up soon enough.

The door to Mangetta's Saloon on Marais Street stood open to allow cool air inside. Valentin had barely stepped over the threshold when he heard a voice call out in a whoop of surprise.

"Managg'! Non lo credo! Look who's here!"

Frank Mangetta hurried from behind the bar, his teeth flashing with a pleasure that lit up his round peasant face as he raised his arms in a Sicilian welcome that embraced the very air around him. The three customers at the bar, the first of the day, were used to these operatic displays and smiled before returning to their lonely drinks.

The saloonkeeper crossed the floor to throw one thick and affectionate arm around Valentin's shoulders and steer him to the booth in the back corner.

Valentin sighed and settled back into the old leather. Mangetta's was a Storyville landmark, a building divided in half with a grocery on one side and the saloon on the other, the two large rooms connected by an archway. The store opened early and closed at sundown to serve the red-light district and the Italian community beyond it. At noon the saloon began serving drinks and light meals and in the evening transformed into a music hall with the best jass players New Orleans had to offer.

It was in fact Frank Mangetta who had first brought musicians across Canal from Rampart Street, throwing Negroes, Italians, Creoles, Frenchmen, and Americans together on one low stage. While there was a long-standing tradition of colored "professors" playing piano in bordello parlors, this was something else entirely.

The saloonkeeper, a violinist of little talent himself, hadn't asked permission, and before anyone thought to stop it, the wall had been breached. The music was just too fine and the crowds that filled the house nightly too eager to spend their dollars. Within another year a half-dozen saloons were offering bands that mixed races on a regular basis, and no one blinked an eye, all thanks to the rotund, mustachioed fellow who now wore an eye-twinkling grin of delight as he made his way back to the booth, a bottle and two glasses in hand.

He slid onto the cracked leather seat, poured the wine, and handed a glass to Valentin. *"Salud."*

Valentin murmured a response and slouched deeper. Frank Mangetta was family, a cousin of his father's from the old country, and *compare* to Valentin in New Orleans. Frank had known him all his life, had witnessed the tragedies that had befallen the family, had kept a close watch as *Valentino* grew to manhood and switched careers from petty criminal to policeman and then to private detective. One of the rooms over the grocery had been his home for a while. In the Sicilian tradition, Frank stood as substitute father, and Valentin had always been grateful for it.

Though not at this moment, because the substitute father was treating him to a glittering stare and a lip that curled in reproof.

"*Come sta?*" he muttered tightly, belying the courtesy of the words.

"*Sta bene,*" Valentin said. He'd lost most of his Italian; at least he remembered that much.

Before the saloonkeeper could continue the scolding, a cook came out of the kitchen, carrying a plate of black olives, prosciutto, and provolone, along with a half loaf of bread. He put the food on the table and went away. Though the detective had eaten only a couple hours before, he fell to nibbling hungrily.

"So, you still hiding?" Frank said.

Valentin smiled slightly and shook his head.

"What then?"

"Busy, that's all."

"Oh, *busy.* I see. *Capisco.* I'm busy, too. But not too busy to come over to see you on Spain Street, what, five, six times a year? But, you, you're too *occupato* to visit one time in three years?"

Valentin felt his cheeks reddening. "I just—"

"Then why you come by today?"

Valentin said, "I . . . I had something to work on over here." He fumbled. "*Sto . . . sto lavorando.*"

"Oh? You working? Well, that's all right, then."

Valentin made an empty gesture. It was true; he had no excuse, and he didn't want to try and explain.

A moment passed and Frank relented. "What kind of something?"

The detective took a sip of his wine and told Frank about the Claiborne Avenue escapades of James Beck and his friends. Frank listened, faintly amused, and then got annoyed again. He sat back and folded his arms.

"That's what you come over here for?"

Valentin, embarrassed, said, "*Zi'* Franco, I'm—"

"Don't give me '*Zi'* Franco,'" he said. "Why you working for those people?"

It was a plaint that Valentin used to hear every time he had wandered too far from where he belonged, at least as the saloon-keeper saw it. As before, he couldn't think of an answer that made sense. The little pander of using the Italian for "uncle" hadn't helped.

At the same time, the detective didn't take *Zi'* Franco's insulted frown too seriously. "Is this what you want to talk about?" he said.

Frank shook his head slightly and gave a sad half smile, Storyville's own Pagliacci. "Drink your wine," he said.

He asked after Justine, and Valentin inquired about some of the characters from around the District, and what new musicians were worth a listen. He heard a few good stories about women who did not risk having their private parts stuffed with firecrackers. All in all, he heard nothing remarkable.

The saloonkeeper said, "Then there's that thing down on Liberty Street . . ."

"You mean that fellow they found?" Valentin didn't mention Mary Jane Parker's summons, but Frank was eyeing him as if he knew all about it.

"There's something not right with that."

"I don't see it," Valentin said.

"You ain't around to see anything," Frank retorted. He picked up an olive, chewed for a pensive moment. "You visit Mr. Anderson lately?"

"No, why?"

"He don't look so good. People say he ain't doing so good."

"Is he sick?"

"He's something, I don't know what. Just not the same."

Valentin lifted his glass and put it back down again. He didn't drink much these days, and the wine was going right to his head. "Maybe I'd better head home," he said.

Frank smiled laconically. "You just got here," he said, and poured more wine into Valentin's glass.

The cook who came in early to ready the kitchen for the evening rush at Anderson's Café fixed a late lunch for Mr. Tom, which Ned then brought to his table. He was eating when Billy Struve wandered in from the street, stopping at the bar to have the janitor fetch him a short glass of whiskey. It was not his first of the day; Anderson could tell by the wide arc of his steps as he crossed the marble-tiled floor.

After Valentin St. Cyr turned his back on the District, Struve had stepped in as the King of Storyville's right-hand man. Though there was no comparison between the sharp-eyed Creole detective and this happy-go-lucky gadabout, Struve was loyal and dependable in his own small way, and that was something.

Anderson looked up from his plate and used his fork to point his red-faced, bleary-eyed visitor to the opposite chair. Struve sat, helped himself to a slopping sip of his drink, and let out a relieved sigh.

"So?" the older man inquired.

Struve ran down the list of Storyville gossip and scandals, failing as usual to notice his host's impatience. He had always been a useful spy, gathering up bits of dirt from the streets, what this madam was saying about that madam and what they were both saying about the King of Storyville; what city official had taken a shine to what sporting girl; or which pious church elder preferred the company of men. Anderson had once delighted in hearing these sordid details, as much for their entertainment value as for the usefulness. Now it mostly just irritated him. After almost twenty years, what did he care about such nonsense?

He longed for the likes of St. Cyr, who always appeared on time, stone sober, and with the information he needed, nothing less and nothing more, and every bit of it valuable.

But St. Cyr had gone on the payroll of a set of rich down-town lawyers, doing their dirty work, and no one had come along to replace him. Certainly not Struve, who, having quaffed his whiskey, was now waving to Ned for a refill. The janitor looked at Anderson, who gave a slight shake of his head. One more drink and the man would be worthless.

"What about Liberty Street?" he asked. "Any more news?"

Struve blinked his wet eyes. "Liberty . . . oh, that . . . No, nothing more. Coppers don't know how the body got there. Or who killed him, none of that. Pretty damn funny, if you ask—"

"Is the family making any noise?"

"Not that I know of." Struve laughed loosely. "Honore Jacob showed up mad as hell."

Anderson pursed his lips in frustration. Jacob was a parade of rude noise on two feet. "Is anyone else talking?"

Struve was watching over his shoulder as Ned retreated to the other end of the bar.

"Billy!"

The head came back around. "What's that?"

"I asked if anyone else has anything on that dead man."

"If they do, I ain't heard it."

"Well, keep your ears open."

"You know I will," Struve said. He picked up his glass and stared at it morosely.

The King of Storyville sighed at the state of things lately. "Ned," he called out. "Mr. Struve will have another whiskey over here."

FIVE

Detective McKinney stood in the doorway. At twenty-four, he was on the tall side, his face Irish ruddy and sporting a mustache that was a splendid orange-red and matched his bristling hair.

By contrast, Captain J. Picot was short and lumpish, his flesh a shade shy of swarthy and his hooded eyes the color of old copper. Sensing a visitor, he looked up, then gestured for the young officer to speak his piece.

McKinney said, "I went over to that house on Liberty Street, the one where Mr. Defoor was found."

"And?"

"And I didn't get anything more than they reported the other night. Sometime between the time the occupants went off to bed and when the maid got up, someone carried the body into the house and left it in the middle of the parlor floor."

The captain gazed at his subordinate for a second, then let out a sudden bark of a laugh as his face went all rubbery.

"That's about the funniest goddamn thing I ever heard!" he chortled. "Whoever did it must have a bad case with that madam. Or maybe got a bad case off one of her *girls*!" Noticing that McKinney didn't get the humor, he stopped laughing and resumed his scowl.

"All right, what else?" he said.

"I went to the morgue to have a look at the body."

Picot drummed thick fingers on his desk blotter. "What for?"

McKinney shifted his feet. "I wanted . . . I was completing the investigation." He wagged a clumsy hand at his chest. "The bullet struck him over the heart," he went on. "He would have died instantly."

Picot nodded and yawned.

"And he had a cut on him."

The captain closed his mouth and blinked like a turtle. "A what?"

McKinney drew a slash in the air. "A cut." He used the same finger to cross his face at a rising angle. "Right here."

"Cut with what?"

"A blade of some kind. A sharp knife or—"

"I don't get it."

"I don't, either, sir. But it was fresh. So I believe the murderer did it."

Picot gave him a blank look. "So? Don't make that poor fuck any less dead, does it?"

"No, sir, but I—"

"They release the body?"

"I asked them to hold it for twenty-four hours."

"What the hell for?" The captain's eyes sharpened in annoyance. "Family's going to want him back. I don't need them calling to complain."

"I was just making sure there was nothing else," McKinney said.

"There ain't, or we would have heard by now," Captain Picot said. "You get back down there and tell them to let him go."

The younger officer hesitated for the briefest instant, then said, "Yes, sir, thank you." He exited the office, stepped into the hallway, and made his way back to the morgue, where he signed the form releasing the body of Mr. Allan Defoor to his grieving family.

Once she was certain that the man she'd encountered wasn't tailing her, Evelyne stopped to catch her breath. She settled herself and continued walking the District from Basin Street to Villere, traveling up one street and down the next and taking it all in from behind her disguise. She viewed women hawking themselves from windows, from doorways, even right out on the banquettes, and the men eyeing the goods as if making market for cuts of meat; smells that gyrated from heavy perfume to animal droppings, and in between a mélange of animal, vegetable, and mechanical scents; finally, the sounds that began with women already tired of trying to entice buyers for their services and ended with the sweet and sad notes of a professor's piano through an open window.

She spent nearly two hours on her exploration and arrived back at the corner of Iberville and Basin streets, directly beneath the facade of Anderson's Café and Annex. The Hudson was waiting, but before stepping aboard, she turned to survey the Café and then the mansions down the line one more time, fixing it all in her mind like a photograph.

The attendant of the colored ward lowered his voice to mutter in the woman's ear. She listened, her eyes widening in surprise. The Negro assured her that he had heard it correctly.

She found the patient standing by a window, his favorite, the one that looked out over the rice fields. After a few moments' silence to allow him to adjust to her presence, she murmured, "Buddy?"

It took him a half minute to get around to clearing his throat. When he spoke up, it was just as the Negro attendant had described it.

———

The Hudson pulled to the curb at an address on Royal Street in the Vieux Carré, and Evelyne tossed a dime onto the front seat before stepping down to the banquette. Fishing in her purse for a brass key, she opened the wrought-iron gate and crossed the tiny brick courtyard to the French doors. She found Louis inside, lounging on the brocade sofa in the studied slouch of a young man of leisure.

As she expected, he uncoiled and tried to get fresh with her, helping her off with the old coat and using a kiss on her cheek as an excuse to caress her neck. When he reached for the top button of her day dress, she brushed him away as if he was an annoying insect.

She took his place on the sofa and made an impatient gesture. He spent a few moments nursing his hurt feelings as he went about pouring her a glass of brandy, then brought it to her with the satisfying carriage of a servant, his eyes downcast and back bent slightly. He retreated, and she allowed herself a cool smile as she nodded for him to speak up.

"People are talking about that body on Liberty Street," he began.

"Is there an investigation?"

Louis waved a vague hand. "The coppers gave up on it right away. There was this one detective on it, but he's—"

"What detective?" Evelyne said.

"Name's McKinney. He walks a beat during the day."

"Oh. A *police* detective." She sat back.

"Yes, but he's off it now. They dropped the whole thing."

Evelyne smiled slightly. "And what does your father have to say about it?"

"Well, he's in a state, that's for sure." Louis paused to glance her way. "He swears someone is out to get him."

"Well, it would make me wonder, too," Evelyne said.

"He wants to go see Tom Anderson to make a complaint,"

the young man went on. "I'm to pick him up in a little while and carry him over there."

Evelyne's eyes fixed on him. "I want a report on what they say. Especially Mr. Anderson. You understand?"

"Don't worry," he said, and treated her to a wink and his best sly smirk. "I won't miss a thing."

Briefly enticing, his affectations now only rankled her. She didn't need his viperish charm; and she wasn't some schoolgirl who could be swayed by his looks. What she did need was information. It was his part of their bargain, and he knew damn well that he'd better provide.

She signaled brusquely for him to continue, and he started to pace as he talked. Much of what he said was useless, so she listened with only half an ear.

She had discovered Louis when he invited himself to one of her social events, picking out his striking profile from across the room. Once she cornered him, it took no time at all to punch through his little charade. Who better than she to spot such a crude gambit?

Crashing her soiree was foolish, and if she had exposed his pretense, those gilded doors would be the last ones he'd ever breach. But he was so desperate about staying and such a pretty young man that she let it pass. She made an arrangement to meet, then allowed him to bed her. That he was at least fifteen years her junior made the experience all the more wicked.

Though deliciously handsome, he wasn't near rugged enough for her. When he realized that she was bored with him, he tried to hold her interest with gossip he'd picked up about some of her rich friends, but she already knew all those stories. She was just about to send him on his way when he mentioned Storyville, the twenty square blocks of uptown New Orleans where, for the last sixteen years, sin had been permitted by way of local ordinance.

Intrigued, she pried deeper, and in the manner of a confession, he admitted what she already guessed: that he didn't come from money in Baton Rouge or anything close to it. His last name wasn't "Jakes" but Jacob, with the French emphasis on the second syllable. Two generations back, the family had been respectable and of considerable wealth, but Louis's uncle had thrown most of it away on one foolish scheme after another. It was a grim tale his mother repeated as a bedtime story. Now all that was left was a handful of properties in the red-light district—bordellos, in fact.

Evelyne had never paid too much attention to Storyville, regarding it as nothing but a crude carnival. Now she grew fascinated by this opening into the scarlet realm, and as he pumped away at her, she pumped him for all sorts of banter about the blocks just beyond the French Quarter but a world away from the quaint Vieux Carré.

For his part, Louis was ashamed of his family background and the knowledge of the red-light district he had gathered over the years he'd worked in his father's office. At the same time, he saw that Evelyne had grown entranced; it was, in fact, the only reason she kept him around. So he told her everything he knew and more that he simply fabricated.

As Evelyne listened, an odd notion took hold of a far corner of her brain. Day after day, through long afternoons in the bed and on the sofa in this same private house, he drew her deeper into Storyville's bizarre economy of sin. It took no time at all for her to absorb the District's complex mechanisms.

When he told her about how badly things had been going lately, with business on the decline and the legendary Tom Anderson unable to turn the tide, the notion began to sprout tentacles. Her first daydreams were so crazy that she let them roll about as idle fantasies. But Louis talked on and one corner led to another, one angle turned into a second and then a third, and she began to believe that the ploy she had concocted could actually work.

She knew that decent ladies did not imagine such schemes, let alone put them in motion. But it was well into a new century and things were not the same anymore. The day of women who served at the pleasure of their men was showing signs of wear.

She was faintly astonished by her skill at working such a fiendish construction. Then Louis told her all about Miss Lulu White, and she understood that some women just had the skills, no matter what the men of the world pronounced.

Louis discussed other characters, too, including the madams of note, certain skilled whores, and some of the better-known sports, each of them boasting a colorful name: Ace High, Johnny the Jake, Little Blue, Slow Moe. He described the vile French Emma Johnson, who operated a live show called "the Circus" that featured lurid sexual acts on display for any gentlemen who could pay the price of admission.

She had to see firsthand, and took to visiting the District incognito. No one knew about these trips. Indeed, this day's encounter on the street was the closest she'd come to being detected by the man she recognized as Valentin St. Cyr.

In the course of regaling her, Louis eventually got around to mentioning the Creole who had been Tom Anderson's right-hand man for years until he went away, leaving the King of Storyville without his best asset. That was all he could tell her, and so she availed herself of other young men to find out more. She enjoyed the fringe benefit of these spies' energies beneath the sheets while completing the private detective's biography. And then, without warning, he had appeared in her path.

Reclining on the divan, distracted by her musings, she was barely aware that Louis had finished his latest spiel and was readying to leave. She asked him to repeat the important points and found nothing more she could use. There was little new from his mouth these days, and she realized that he was fast losing his value to her.

Momentarily, she thought of something he could do and gave an instruction that brought back his cloying smile. He left, locking the door behind him.

As the pattern of the game stretched out in her mind, she settled down into the soft cushions and unbuttoned the cotton dress from neck to knees. She thought about the exotic-looking detective St. Cyr. He didn't resemble Louis Jacob or any of her other young men, with cameo profiles that would make only silly girls swoon. St. Cyr was another creature entirely.

She lay there imagining the drama to come, and as she reached the part that the Creole would play, she dropped a hand between her legs and began to caress herself with gentle fingers.

Valentin let Frank keep him in the saloon for another two hours, listening to stories that he had missed, some comical, though enough that were not so.

Finally, he managed to drag himself away and rode the streetcar south, arriving home in a soft wine haze just as the October sun was beginning to dip over the river. He trundled up the stairwell, stepped inside, and locked the door behind him. Draping his jacket over the back of a chair, he wandered to the kitchen to find Justine standing over the stove. The smells of filé and peppers drifted to his nostrils as he leaned in the doorway. With her hair tied back with a ribbon, her well-worn shift, and bare feet, she looked like nothing so much as the country girl she had been not so long ago. He smiled fixedly at the way her body shifted under the thin cotton.

She glanced over her shoulder at him. "Where have you been all day?"

Instead of answering, he reached out to grasp her lightly by the wrist, take the spoon from her hand, and lay it aside. Backing up, he pulled her through the parlor and into the bedroom and laid her down. She turned pliant and let him lift the shift over her head. She wore nothing underneath. As the evening breeze lifted the curtains, they fell into a familiar dance.

Valentin never got over his infatuation with her body, down to the tiniest crease and corner. He knew she had been with more than a few men; it had been her profession, after all. And yet he thought of her as his territory, over the years to be claimed, reclaimed, and held.

He knew that she had been waiting for him to speak up for her person, to put his name on the line and take her as his wife. At the same time, she couldn't make a demand, any more than he could on her. They had betrayed each other in the past, had repelled and attracted, and much of what drove the passion between them was the exquisite tension.

For her part, Justine sensed that he was afraid that changing the equation between them would burst a delicate bubble and that surrendering to her would somehow weaken him. But he always thought too much.

Except in moments like this. Time stopped as they entwined, sculpted beneath the cotton sheet. Valentin knew how to make her vibrate, and he pushed her ahead of him in a mounting arc of heat and noise, feeling the tension rise beneath her *au lait* skin like current running through a wire, working her faster and harder until he all but ground her into pieces.

When it was over, they lay for more minutes, not speaking. She gazed blankly toward the open window, watching night come on as he half dozed, worn down by the work and the wine. She smiled and stretched to kiss his cheek, then got out of the bed, pulled on a kimono, and stood over him.

"So what were you doing up there?" she inquired.

He should have known it wouldn't get past her. She had probably smelled it on him, the special Storyville aroma. Or maybe she caught something in his eye, that predator look that he carried when he worked the streets.

For a brief moment, his scoundrel self made an appearance and he considered lying. He could tell her he tried to find one of the other investigators to go, only to discover that they were all at the Fair Grounds. But he knew it wouldn't be worth the trouble it would cause, and anyway she was too sharp. So he explained in a few short sentences about James Beck and his friends and poor Essie Gill.

She said, "And that took you all afternoon?"

"I stopped to see Frank while I was over there."

Her expression softened slightly. As badly as she had wanted out of Storyville, she missed some people, and the Sicilian was one of them.

"How is he?" she said.

"He's fine," Valentin said. "He asked about you."

He could tell from her blank expression that the explanation didn't sway her. She stood with one languid hand resting on the bedpost and her kimono hanging open, watching him with her dark eyes. She looked so lovely in that posture that he had to wonder what kind of fool he could be to risk her ire. He made a stab at an expression of contrition.

She, however, was not inclined to throw him even the thinnest rope. She lifted her hand from the bedpost, tied the sash, and headed off for the kitchen and the dinner that she had left simmering on the stove.

Valentin reclined in the veiled light, wondering if he really was that much of a fool. Most men would not want much more than what he already had: a good woman, a decent job, a safe home.

New Orleans was full of private coppers. He could have found one to talk to Essie Gill and taken it from there, avoiding the District altogether. And once he did go, he shouldn't have lingered to encounter the woman with the strange green eyes and then to drink wine and reminisce with Frank Mangetta. He knew it had been a mistake; because he had spent more time in that place than he had in three years, and now part of him wanted to go back again tomorrow.

By the time Valentin left Storyville for home, the word that he had visited Mangetta's Saloon had already begun dribbling in the direction of Basin Street and the ears of several of the madams of the high-toned mansions.

The talk also found its way to the police precinct at Parish Prison, where Captain Picot received it with a grunt of irritation. Though it had been a good long time since St. Cyr had gone away, the captain was one person who did not believe that he was done with Storyville, or vice versa.

Though it was true that much had changed for Picot in those years. Thanks to a chance stumble upon a revolting bit of information involving a member of the police board and a dead woman, he had received a promotion and another bar on each shoulder.

Then-Lieutenant Picot had handled the affair with a sly hand. He whispered the right words to the right people and certain involved parties were paid for their silence. He had played his hand just right, and within a few months, his promotion orders came down. When the announcement was made, he claimed to be as surprised as anyone.

The gossip that he had found a way to blackmail someone important made the rounds, nodded over as one of those things that happened to even the most undeserving louts, like ne'er-do-wells who made big winnings at the track. The months passed, and the grumbles from the other officers stopped.

Along with a fatter pay envelope came a larger piece of the graft money and more power. So life had been mostly pleasant for the new captain, right up until the moment he heard the talk about St. Cyr reappearing in the red-light district. He and the Creole detective had tangled for the better part of ten years, and if Picot had learned one thing, it was that St. Cyr wasn't about to walk away from Storyville, not for good, and probably not until they carted him off in a hoodoo wagon.

The streetlights along the main line flickered and then glowed a steady pale yellow. From his office window, Tom Anderson looked down on Basin Street, wondering if the foot traffic was that light or if his mind was playing tricks on him again.

He had spent almost two decades as the King of Storyville, though it was in fact Alderman Sidney Story who created the District by way of a city ordinance. Prostitution was deemed legal there; more precisely, it was pronounced *illegal* everywhere else in New Orleans.

All Tom Anderson did was step into the breach with a vision of Storyville's glorious possibilities and the energy to connive, wheedle, battle, and buy it into reality and then keep it rolling along like a smooth-running machine.

A smooth-running *money* machine, in fact. Something like a quarter million dollars was generated in the bordellos, cribs, saloons, and music halls every month. There were more workers under Anderson's sway than Henry Ford employed in his largest plant. He had hobnobbed with senators and presidents, men of enormous wealth, the royalty of foreign lands, beautiful women. He had no doubt that had he been born in some other time and place, he would have been a political powerhouse or a captain of industry. And yet as Storyville's lord and master, he was quite famous in his own right, afar and at home.

Though his admirers would not be so impressed if they could see him now. Always a thick man, his waistline had advanced with the years. His hair and extravagant mustache, both once a reddish blond and both parted precisely, had gone gray and thin. He had been known for a gaze that was now often weak and watery behind wire-rimmed spectacles. Everything about his body felt slower, like a clock winding down.

Indeed, this evening had just begun and he was ready to go home. But what would he do there? Listen to the birds singing in the eaves?

He turned away from the window and crossed to his desk, a solid affair of good oak that was adorned only by a blotter, a brass reading lamp, a ledger bound in fine leather, and a pen-and-ink set. He kept it that way, as a simple and powerful statement that Mr. Tom Anderson did not need crass symbols of power. As a side benefit, it was simpler to clear when he was in the mood for a quick and breathy dalliance with a compliant young lady.

Settling back in the throne-size chair, he tried to remember the last time the desk had been pressed into that service and could not.

As he mused over how things had changed, his thoughts turned to Valentin St. Cyr. So, the Creole had visited the District that afternoon. The word was that after chasing down some vague business on Claiborne Avenue, of all places, he had stopped to see the Sicilian saloonkeeper Mangetta. He had not paid the King of Storyville the same courtesy.

Tom Anderson was not a man who indulged petty slights and did not take this one to heart. St. Cyr had too much history fending off crooks of every stripe, thieving and murdering sons of bitches, crazy whores, and crazier madams, all on the King of Storyville's behalf. Who could blame him for moving on to other work? At the same time, he was the one person who could be trusted with the arcane inner workings of the District.

The lord of that piece of real estate blinked out of this reverie, aroused by the sound of footsteps on the staircase. He sat forward and flipped open his ledger to October 15. There was nothing entered for that hour, and he frowned, wondering what had slipped his mind. The footfalls drew closer: two people, one heavy, the other lighter.

At the sight of Honore Jacob, Anderson felt a small pain in his temples. Jacob was the landlord of several houses in the

District, including Antonia Gonzales's and, more significantly, that Liberty Street house where the body of the Defoor fellow had been found. No doubt it was the reason for the visit.

That was bad enough; add to it Jacob's habit of complaining constantly, and mostly about money, about the coppers, about the madams who rented his properties. He never left home without carrying along a grievance of one sort or another. So the next few minutes promised to be unpleasant. With a quiet sigh, Anderson stood up, placing his palms flat on either side of the blotter.

Jacob was not alone this night. A young man entered on his heels. He was of medium height and lank, with ash-blond hair with the slightest wet curl to it. His cool green eyes and perfect nose were set on a feminine oval of a face. In contrast to his father's loose, rumpled suit, he was done out in a well-tailored coat and trousers of eggshell cassimere. All in all, he cut a striking figure and, from the smug way he cast his eye about, seemed to know it. He studied the King of Storyville with a blank sort of curiosity that lacked regard for so eminent a personage.

"Mr. Tom," Honore Jacob said. "I'm sorry to interrupt your evening." He gestured. "This is my son, Louis."

Anderson nodded to the younger Jacob, and Louis responded with the barest movement of his own head, a gesture just short of insolent. Anderson felt a jab of ire. But what did he expect, that the young fellow would bend a knee? He decided to overlook it and waved the two visitors to the chairs on the other side of the desk.

Jacob asked for an appointment every other week or so, though Anderson was at a loss to understand why. The man rarely made specific demands, preferring instead to roll out a litany of complaints that seemed never to vary: the police were too greedy; the city inspectors too harsh; the madams always trying to cheat him; there were rats everywhere; and there was never, *never* enough cash.

The Jacobs had once been among the better of the city's old-line French families, until Honore's brother, also named Louis, squandered a fortune that included whole blocks of the red-light district by bungling every business deal he laid his hands to and then dropping dead from a bad heart before the damage could be repaired. A few modest properties were all that was left.

Anderson had a tray with two glasses and a bottle of brandy waiting at all times, and he now added a third glass from the cabinet behind his desk. As he poured, he glanced up to see the younger man gazing idly around the room as if checking for anything that might amuse him. Honore Jacob, meanwhile, stared fixedly into space, likely cataloging his complaints for the hundredth time.

The attentions of both returned when Anderson handed over the brandies. The two older men raised their glasses and sipped. Louis hesitated, frowning into the golden liquor as if there was something wrong with it. The King of Storyville now counted a second strike, and the visitors hadn't been in the door five minutes.

He sat down again. "So, how can I help you this evening?" He addressed the father, keeping his voice neutral.

As if he'd been waiting for this signal, Honore Jacob hunched forward.

"You hear what happened at my property on Liberty Street?" he said.

"I did," Anderson said. "Very unfortunate. Is there any more news about it?"

"Not that I heard." Jacob shook his head dolefully. "The police don't have a thing. But I don't think they're trying. Don't think they give a goddamn."

The King of Storyville shrugged calmly and took another sip of his brandy. If he was lucky, Jacob would realize that there was nothing he or anyone could do and move on.

"It might not be Basin Street," Louis said. "But it's still Storyville."

Both Anderson and Jacob turned their heads. The cool and prickly note in the son's voice had bordered on the surly. Anderson returned a gaze that was even cooler and waited, expecting the junior Jacob to flinch under his famous gimlet stare. He was surprised that Louis did no such thing, instead turning lazy eyes in the direction of the open window, broadcasting an elegant boredom. The King of Storyville decided that was strike three for this dandy.

The father, sensing a sudden change in the air in the room, spoke up hurriedly. "Sorry, Tom, I should have explained. I'm showing Louis some of the ropes. I mean, in terms of my business affairs . . ." He tried a short laugh. "We're none of us getting younger, and, uh . . ." He laughed tensely again. It seemed he'd lost his place.

Anderson drew his stare off Louis and placed it on the father, cutting the son out entirely. "I understand the police are continuing the investigation at Miss Parker's," he said brusquely. "Let's just wait and see what happens. It won't go to make trouble where there isn't any." He produced a tight smile from beneath his mustache. *"Comprenez?"*

Jacob smiled in return, though uneasily. *"Je comprends, oui."* He finished his brandy and placed the glass carefully on the edge of the desk, still fretting over his son's disrespect. Anderson was ready to dismiss both of them and stood up. Honore Jacob rose in kind.

Louis, however, remained slouched in his chair, his almost-girlish face distracted by some thought. "Perhaps Mr. St. Cyr could be of service," he murmured.

Anderson took pains to not look startled as he gazed at the younger man. "Pardon me?"

"That Creole detective." Louis's lips curled into a mocking smirk. "The one who used to work for you."

The King of Storyville continued to bite down on his bafflement. "I'm sorry? Do you know him?"

"I've heard about him," Louis offered. "I heard he's a very talented fellow when it comes to crimes in this part of the city. Perhaps he can help."

Anderson wanted to say, *Help with what?,* but kept quiet.

The elder Jacob frowned, trying to catch up. "But St. Cyr . . . he's not around anymore, is he?"

Anderson shook his head. "No, he's not. He still lives in the city. But he has no business in Storyville."

A moment of terse silence ensued. Then Louis uncoiled and rose to his feet, his expression distant, as if he'd already lost interest in the subject at hand. Tom Anderson studied him for another few seconds before returning his attention to the father.

"You don't need to worry, Honore," he said, and waved a hand toward the window and the street-lit panorama beyond. "Look out there. It's calm. We have these incidents now and then. But things go back to where they belong." As soon as the words were out, he wondered if his guests could hear the hollow note in his voice.

He brought his gaze back to the landlord, who nodded, then performed a bow that was thinly sincere. Louis crossed to the door without as much as a look back, and his father cast an apologetic glance over his shoulder. Anderson was not mollified. Three wives and several other women had given him enough children to have lost count. So he knew misbehavior when he saw it and now produced a cold frown that said, *Next time, leave your brat at home.*

The Jacobs made their exit along the short hallway and down the stairs. The King of Storyville refilled his brandy glass and crossed to the window to gaze on Basin Street and the eddies of men traveling to or from this or that sporting house or saloon. Momentarily, he saw Jacob, elder and junior, appear on the banquette. The father's hands wagged about as he lectured his son about his disrespect for the King of Storyville.

Who now paused to consider how odd it was that the younger man had thrown out St. Cyr's name like that. He wondered if the fates were trying to tell him something. Not that it mattered; he had never turned to anything or anyone but his own instincts to make his way. Save for the Creole detective, that is.

He pushed all these thoughts aside. Night had fallen, and once again Storyville was coming to life.

SIX

William Brown paced the floor of his room a hundred times over, left and right, up and down, at severe but exact angles. He wanted to leave but couldn't, not until he received his orders. So he walked until he swore he could look down and see where his soles had worn a ditch in the hard wood.

He found himself at the washstand, staring into a mirror so cracked and tinted that he could barely make out his features, but beholding a pale, smallish man with an oval head shaved clean. His eyes were too large, his nose too long, and his lips jutted like a Mississippi carp's. He knew if he kept staring into the dirty glass, all these features would grow larger and then larger still, until he was one of the grotesque ogres in the carnival parade.

Some moments passed before he realized that he was holding his straight razor in his right hand. He opened it long enough to gaze upon the glinting edge of the blade, so delicate and hideous that it made his gut twist.

The razor clattered to the floor at the sound of a cream-white envelope being pushed under the door. William hadn't heard anyone approach, and he didn't move a muscle until he was sure no one was lurking outside. He edged to the door and bent down to pick up the envelope. Sliding a yellowed fingernail along the fold, he opened it to find a single sheet of paper and a gold coin, which he rubbed as he read through the half-dozen words written in a tight hand: a name, an address, a time.

He laid envelope and paper aside. Kneeling to the floor, he lifted a short board and retrieved from between the joists a Liberty .22 seven-shot that was small enough to fit within the span of his hand. Once he had replaced the board, he stood up and dropped the pistol into a coat pocket. He donned his derby hat and stepped to the door.

Downstairs, he exited the back door of the hotel into the alley and began his journey beneath the earth to Basin Street.

It was the dead of morning, that empty pocket between the dark of night and the light of day, and Storyville had fallen into an uncommon quiet as a wispy fog draped the streets in shreds like worn cotton.

Little stirred. Here and there, the invisible wings of a waterbird snapped with the *fit-fit-fit* sound of a flag flicking in a breeze before fading back toward the river. In the yard below Union Station, a train whistle played a mournful note as steel wheels, rising from metallic sleep, groaned into motion. Somewhere down a side street, a nag snorted, a man's voice muttered, and a woman laughed—a tinkling of thin bells. Then it got quiet again.

After some moments, the front door of a mansion halfway down the block between Bienville and Iberville streets opened in a swath of yellowish light, casting the silhouettes of a slender young woman and an older man. The woman took the form of an angel, her dressing gown wafting as the night air stirred, while the gentleman stood as stout as a judge.

They lingered until an engine coughed to life at the corner. Their faces met in a chaste kiss and the gentleman drew away to descend the steps to the banquette. The breeze swirled once more and died, and the hem of the gown fell. The girl, who went by Clarice, raised a listless hand in farewell, and in the manner of an actor after the curtain comes down, stepped wearily over the threshold and closed the door behind her.

Mr. Burton Bolls stood on the banquette, humming a light bit of melody as he waited for the idling automobile to pull up and carry him home to the Irish Channel and his wife and children. He'd enjoyed a lovely night with Clarice, a well-earned diversion from the demands of his life.

He thought he was alone on the street with his agreeable thoughts until he heard someone speak and jerked around to see a man standing a few feet away, hunched in a suit coat that was too thin for the brisk air and a derby hat pulled down low in front. Bolls had not heard his approach and would have been alarmed had he not been standing directly in front of a mansion on the main thoroughfare of one of the most renowned red-light districts in the world. From up the street, gears rattled as the motorcar set to noisy motion.

"What's that, sir?" he inquired politely, expecting the fellow would now ask for a handout and preparing a rebuff.

The voice came from beneath the brim of the derby, as sharp and jagged as broken glass. "Evil gets as evil gives."

Bolls cocked his head, puzzled over the muttering. He was thinking how odd it was for someone to be wearing gloves at this time of year when he saw the barrel of the pistol pointing at him. The hammer clicked back.

The Paterson touring car was fifty paces along Basin Street when the sleepy-headed driver, peering over the folded windshield, saw the tiny blue flash. He watched, stunned, as Mr. Bolls reeled on top-heavy legs and toppled off the banquette and into the gutter, and another, smaller figure appeared, bending over the body. The driver gaped and coughed up a shout that was lost in the noise of the stuttering engine.

The sound and the light sent the figure spinning around and lunging away to fade into the narrow space between the houses behind him.

With another yelp, the driver pushed the accelerator handle, and the Paterson lurched forward until a jerk on the brake brought it to a sliding stop, the fat tires bouncing off the curb. He leaped onto the running board and down to the street to find Mr. Bolls lying flat on his back with his legs on the banquette, staring blindly up at the stars in the New Orleans night. The hole in his chest was bubbled over his shirt and vest. His limbs quivered and his eyes fluttered. He let out an agonized groan and went still.

The driver rushed across the banquette and ran up the gallery steps just as the front door flew open.

Miss Antonia Gonzales stretched out on the divan, her hop pipe in hand. The first crooning notes were wafting from the horn of her Edison Victrola when she heard what sounded like the pop of a firecracker. Then came a rude shout, followed shortly by a ruckus outside her sitting-room door: a chatter of voices, the scrabbling of feet, and one of the girls calling her name in a panicked voice. The madam let out an exasperated curse, laid the brass pipe aside, and went to see about the fuss.

Three of her girls were huddled in the foyer, talking all at once. Pushing through the gaggle, she stepped onto the gallery, where she found Clarice with the house driver, a skinny character with a sparse mustache and slicked-back hair who went by the moniker Each.

"What's wrong?" she demanded.

Clarice threw a wild hand toward the street. "It's Mr. . . . ." She couldn't seem to catch her breath. "He's . . ."

"He's what?" The madam peered over the banister and was shocked to see the body of Mr. Bolls slumped over the curb and into the street.

"Good lord!" she said. "What happened?"

"He got shot," Each said, his voice thin with strain. "I saw it."

The madam said, "Shot? Shot by who?"

"Didn't see," Each said in a rush. "I come up from the corner, and he was, uh, he was going down. The one what done it run off."

Miss Antonia turned on the girl, her black eyebrows hiking.

"I saw him out and he was fine," Clarice said. "I just closed the door when I heard the shot and . . ." She started to shake a little.

Miss Antonia's mouth drew into a tight line. This was going to be trouble. Mr. Bolls was a good customer, an upright citizen who spent freely and was not peculiar in his tastes, the kind of guest any Storyville madam would welcome. Not to mention that he was a man of some importance, the owner of two successful retail stores. In the next moment, she thought about the fellow they'd found on Liberty Street. This was far worse; a gentleman like Mr. Burton Bolls wouldn't just go away with the morning light.

The madam heard voices and glanced toward the next corner to see that the usual worthless yardbirds had already started to gather, peering and pointing.

She made a quick decision. "Go call the police," she told Clarice. The girl gave a sickly nod and hurried inside. Miss Antonia turned to Each. "And you drive over to Spain Street and fetch Mr. Valentin back. I'll call ahead and tell him you're on your way."

Each was startled. "He won't come."

"Just go," the madam said.

The telephone at the police precinct at Parish Prison chirped noisily, and the desk sergeant jerked awake and snatched up the earphone. The two patrolmen who had just brought in the drunken whore snickered between themselves. The girl, a scraggly blond whose thin face was scarred by smallpox, paid no attention, singing softly to herself in a wavering voice.

The sergeant grunted into the mouthpiece and then listened for a few seconds, rubbing his face with his free hand. He dropped the receiver in the cradle and addressed the coppers.

"Basin Street between Bienville and Iberville," he said. "We got a homicide."

The girl stopped her off-key singing. The officers hitched their belts.

"What about her?" one of the officers inquired, jerking a thumb.

"I'll take care of her like she was my own little girl." He shooed them. "Y'all get on over there. We can't have no dead body on Basin Street."

Valentin heard the bell flutter and came awake, confused, wondering who was rousing him at such an hour. He had managed for years without the annoyance of a telephone set, until Tom Anderson, exasperated at having to send a street rat every time he needed to pass a message, ordered him to buy one. So he gave in, had the device and the wiring installed, and heeded the warning not to toss it over the balcony into the street the first time it sounded. Now he wished he'd done just that.

With a curse, he swung his legs off the bed, lurched into the front room, and crossed it in a few strides to grab the handset from its cradle.

"Valentin?" Though the connection was poor and the sound tinny, he knew the voice right away: Antonia Gonzales. Without a moment's pause, the madam blurted the news about a guest shot dead at her front door. The fellow was lying out in the gutter. The police had been called. And Each was on the way to collect him.

It came out in such a clipped rush that Valentin stood holding the handset against his ear, staring dumbly out the front window at the half-moon that was perched over the river.

"Mr. Valentin?"

"I'm here."

"Please, I need your help."

Valentin knew he was supposed to say, *I'm sorry, no. I can't* . . . Instead, he whispered, "All right, I'll be waiting," and dropped the handset back in the cradle.

He stood there for a silent moment, wondering why the hell he hadn't just spoken the *no* that was on the tip of his tongue. He could get the operator to ring her back, of course, but Beansoup—no, it was *Each* now—might be rolling down Spain Street any minute.

A more immediate problem was waiting in the bedroom. Even if Justine had slept through the jangling of the telephone, she'd find soon enough what had transpired.

Soon, indeed; he found her propped slightly against the headboard, her arms crossed.

"Who's calling you in the middle of the night?" she said.

For a wild second, he thought about running back out the door. "It was Miss Antonia," he said.

Justine frowned. "What does she want?"

"She wants me to come to the mansion."

"When?" she inquired, drawing out the torture.

"Now. Bean—I mean Each is on his way with her car."

"Why?"

"So I won't have to walk or take a street—"

"You know what I mean." She gave him a scathing look. "Why the hell does she want *you* at this hour?"

"One of her customers was murdered. Right outside the door."

That caught her, though just for a heartbeat. "Which customer?"

"She didn't say."

The putter of an automobile engine rounding the corner from Chartres Street distracted her and she glanced toward the open window. "He's driving now?"

"Yes. He works for her."

This information brought her attention back to the subject at hand, and she watched him, waiting.

"I told her I'd come," he said.

She kept staring, her eyes opaque. The automobile rattled to the curb in front, and the engine coughed and died. Springs squeaked, a door creaked, and footsteps clopped up the stairwell. Finally, the rap of knuckles on the jamb.

Valentin made a clumsy gesture that was followed by a clumsy escape into the front room. Justine knew it was a coward's trick to allow Each to get inside rather than go to the balcony and tell him to wait on the banquette. She had always been fond of the kid.

She got up, pulled on a kimono, and stepped into the bedroom doorway. Each was standing in the middle of their living room. Now as before, he appeared abashed at the sight of her, unable to settle on friend, sister, mother, or object of desire. He had known her as a bit of each over the years.

She yawned prettily, and began talking to him. She hadn't seen him in over a year, and marveled at how he was finally losing his childish gawkiness on his way to becoming a man.

His real name was Emile Carter, and he now went by "Each," a mangling of his initials. As "Beansoup," he had been a fixture on the Storyville streets, one of the urchins who ran errands for the sports and rounders for nickels while working their own small games. Along the way, he had appointed himself Valentin's assistant and ended up spending more than a few nights snoring on the couch in the detective's flat on Magazine Street.

Though he had grown up, he still exhibited the same faintly baffled eyes and jittery bounce that had marked him as such a local character when he was a kid. Now the law said he had reached majority and could step into any of the Storyville saloons or music halls and order a drink of whiskey. He could sit at a table and gamble his money on a roll of the dice or turn of a card. He could pay for one of the nearly two thousand women who worked the houses along the twenty square blocks, though the last Valentin recalled, he had been hooked to a young maid who worked for the Benedict family of Esplanade Ridge.

The detective would ask him about her, and while he was at it, about the pistol that was clearly weighting one pocket of his threadbare jacket. Each with a weapon was trouble waiting to happen. All that would wait. The detective ducked back into the bedroom to throw on some clothes and take a jacket down from a hanger.

As they went out the door, Justine offered the kid a pointedly sweet good-bye and ignored Valentin completely.

Outside Each cranked the engine of the Paterson, and they climbed up and sped away. Valentin was faintly astonished by the kid's nimble skill at the steering wheel and hand controls as he maneuvered the touring car down the block to Esplanade and turned north, picking up speed. The wind and road noise made it hard to talk, but he needed something to take his mind off the expression on Justine's face, and so he had Each tell him what had happened on Basin Street.

The kid had been on the scene and described how it had developed from the moment he'd left the corner.

They had to stop for a horse-drawn hack at the corner of North Rampart. Valentin said, "So you actually saw the shooting?"

"What I saw was a muzzle flash," Each said. "Then the man—Mr. Bolls—just fell over."

"And the fellow who ran off?"

"I didn't see his face. Just that he was small and kind of thin. Wearing a derby. It happened really fast, and . . . I didn't see nothing else . . ."

The hack clopped out of the way, and Each pushed the accelerator handle. As they traveled on, the detective changed the subject to inquire about Betsy, a young mulatto maid Each had met while helping Valentin on the Benedict murder case.

Each blushed a little. "I don't see her so much anymore."

"But you do see her?"

"Now and again."

"And how is Miss Benedict?"

Each kept his eyes on the street. "I guess she's doing all right. Last Betsy said, she was engaged to be married."

"I see." They left it at that.

A few blocks on, Each maneuvered the Paterson around the corner from St. Louis onto Basin Street, then slowed and stopped. Valentin could make out a gathering crowd just beyond the Bienville intersection, with figures shifting about in the deep gray light.

He pointed and Each pulled to the curb. Laying a hand on the kid's arm, he said, "Leave the pistol under the seat."

Each started, made a face, then did as he was told. They climbed down and approached the scene, keeping to the shadows of the banquette. Valentin picked out the police contingent, four uniformed officers and two detectives. He didn't see Captain J. Picot among their number, always good news.

On the other hand, none of the officers on the scene had recognized him. One of the detectives who was helping the beat coppers chase away the onlookers stopped to poke a finger into his chest. "Move back, fellow."

"What's your name, detective?" Valentin said, keeping his voice even.

"Weeks," the cop huffed. "Not that it's any of your goddamn business. I believe I just told you to move back."

Valentin was obliging when a second detective stepped up, the first one who looked familiar. His name was McKinney and he had been a patrolman when they'd last met, over three years ago at the scene of another murder. At the time McKinney had been little more than an apple-cheeked boy, a greenhorn. Now he had traded in his blue uniform for a detective's street wear: tight-fitting suit, overcoat, leather gloves, dark derby.

The tall detective ticked a finger to the brim of the hat in greeting. "Mr. St. Cyr," he said, smiling slightly.

"McKinney, correct?"

"James McKinney, yes, sir."

"You're a detective now?"

"Third grade," McKinney said. "But only part of the week. I still walk a beat down in the Ninth Ward." He smiled curiously. "What are you doing here?"

"Miss Antonia sent for me."

McKinney turned to his partner and said something in a low voice. Weeks shrugged, gave the Creole detective another glance, and moved away.

Keeping his tone deliberate, Valentin said, "What do you have?"

McKinney took a glance around, then reported as if St. Cyr had a right to know.

Twenty paces away, Detective Weeks was pulling Each aside to ask him about St. Cyr. The kid explained quickly that the detective had been on the force years ago, then left to serve as right-hand man to Tom Anderson. He mentioned the Benedict case that had started on Rampart Street, the killings of the jass players, and what they had called "the Black Rose murders." There were a dozen lesser cases that the Creole had handled before deciding to walk away and leave it all behind.

"So what's he doing here?" the cop demanded. Each shrugged.

The object of their attention was at that moment crouching over the late Mr. Bolls, noting the fatal wound in his chest, and the curiosity of the shaky cut running from below the orbit of the right eye down to the thick chin. McKinney explained that Bolls was a well-to-do businessman, a family man from the Irish Channel, and a regular visitor at Miss Antonia's, one of those dozens of polite and respectable middle-aged fellows who happen to enjoy the physical favors of the young women at that address.

Valentin pointed to the slice across the victim's mouth, cheek, and chin. "What's this?"

"I don't know. The girl said it wasn't there when he left out. I guess it could have happened somehow when he fell, but . . ."

Valentin caught a hitch in McKinney's voice and glanced at him. "But what?"

McKinney said, "Well, I don't know if it means anything."

"Go ahead."

"You know about the body that turned up in the house on Liberty Street the other night?"

"I heard about it."

"I saw it at the morgue. And there was the same kind of cut. Thin like that." He drew a line across his face.

Valentin's eyes narrowed. "So whoever shot him could have been cutting this one when Each drove up."

"What for?"

"I don't have any idea." The Creole detective stood up. McKinney followed suit, and they gazed down at Mr. Bolls's body. He looked like a pleasant fellow; and a wealthy one, in a new and very fine suit.

"Was anything taken?" Valentin asked idly.

The cop shook his head. "He still has his cash and all. And we didn't find nothing on the street." He turned to spit a thin stream of tobacco juice into the gutter.

Valentin noticed the crowd edging close again and said, "You want to cover him now."

McKinney turned away to tell one of the patrolmen to fetch a sheet. The two detectives shook hands, and Valentin moved away, recalling that all the time he was working in Storyville, the police had standing orders to steer clear of him. And yet there had always been a few who chose to treat him with respect, as McKinney had on this night. He hoped it wouldn't curse the officer as it had some of the others.

He found Each standing on the banquette with Detective

Weeks. As soon as he approached, the cop backed away, then went about directing the uniformed officers who were herding the onlookers who had spilled across the street. Any gathering back-of-town was an excuse for a party, and bottles had already appeared. If the police didn't move them along, they'd soon be dancing.

Valentin crooked a finger and led Each into the narrow gap between Miss Antonia's and the next house. They took turns lighting lucifers. It was no surprise to find the killer's escape route all but ruined by the coppers tramping in and out. A dozen footprints were scattered in the soft dirt, with no way of telling which ones might belong to the one who had murdered Bolls. Just to be sure, they worked the passageway all the way to the back of the house, then covered the garden, too.

They arrived on the street by way of the alley and skirted the crowd to mount Miss Antonia's front steps. The girls were crowded at the windows, watching the spectacle, and Each grinned and winked at them like a regular rounder until Valentin plucked his sleeve.

They found the madam inside. Without a word, she nodded toward the sitting room. Each closed the door behind them.

"What a hell of a thing this is," Miss Antonia said.

"Tell me about the victim," Valentin said.

"He never caused any trouble. He didn't mind spending his money. All the girls liked him fine. He spent most of his visits lately with Clarice."

"And tonight?"

"He came in around nine o'clock, like always," the madam said. "He had a drink in the parlor, and then she took him to her room for the rest of the evening. When they came downstairs, I had the boy go fetch the car. I was in the sitting room when I heard all the noise. I went out on the gallery and saw him lying down there in the gutter."

"No one else saw or heard anything?"

She tilted her head toward Each. "Just him."

Valentin said, "All right, call the girl, please."

Clarice had been told to wait in the parlor and now stepped into Miss Antonia's office, looking frightened. After a few questions, Valentin ascertained that she knew nothing of value. She wasn't faking, just another simple country girl who had come to the city to make her way.

Valentin guessed that Mr. Bolls was the first of her customers to die. He wouldn't be her last. He dismissed her with a thank-you, then turned back to the madam.

"This wasn't random," he said. "That fellow was lying in wait to get him. And if that's the case, it has nothing to do with you."

"Except that he died on my doorstep," the madam said.

"It could have happened anywhere."

"It happened here."

"A few days, and it'll be forgotten."

Miss Antonia heard the dismissive note in his voice. She said, "Did you know that just the other night a man turned up dead in a house two streets back?"

Valentin almost smiled. Of course, she'd heard about how he treated the young maid who had appeared at his door. "You think that's got something to do with this?"

"I don't know. Maybe someone should find out."

"That's not my—" He stopped, resumed. "That's Mr. Tom's job."

"Mr. Tom is asleep at the switch," the madam shot back in a low voice. Her stare was black and direct, and the message was clear.

"Miss Antonia . . . ," he began, and then stopped. They both knew she was stepping over a line. Their friendship and this night's one favor didn't change the fact that he no longer worked in Storyville. Things were different now. At the same time, he couldn't just brush this good-hearted woman away. They'd known each other a long time, and she'd shown him kindness over the years.

"I'll keep an eye out, in case something else happens. I can do that."

"Something else like another body turning up?"

His gray eyes went cool, and the madam realized she had pushed him as far as he'd go. She relented, whispering a thank-you. Valentin nodded to Each to go out ahead of him.

More police had arrived on Basin Street. A horse-drawn hack was parked at an angle to the curb, along with a police sedan, effectively shielding the view of the four coppers lifting Mr. Bolls's body and sliding it onto the bed of the hack. The tailgate squeaked closed, and the driver climbed into the seat. A snap of the reins, and the hack creaked away over the cobbles.

Valentin told Each he preferred to walk home, then descended the steps and wandered around until he found James McKinney.

Tilting his head to the cop's ear, he said, "Check the morgue again." McKinney hiked an inquisitive eyebrow. "Just in case," Valentin said.

McKinney nodded and said, "All right, sir. I'll do that."

The detective had just reached the opposite side of the street when a new Buick 10 rattled by and came to a sudden stop. A squat man in a suit that was too tight for his frame clambered down and scurried into the thinning throng. He made such a fuss pushing through that Valentin paused to watch. It took him a few seconds to recognize Honore Jacob, one of the Storyville landlords and the owner of Miss Antonia's mansion. He was in a fluster, and Valentin heard him babbling angrily.

"That's two bodies!" he cried to no one in particular. "Two, goddamnit!" The cops who were standing by treated him to blank stares, which inflamed him all the more. He threw up his hands and mounted the steps to Miss Antonia's gallery. Following him at a lazy pace was the young man who had been driving the Buick. In a perfect suit and riding cap pulled to one side, he rounded the crowd as if to keep from getting something foul on his person.

Valentin turned for home, knowing that Justine would be waiting. He'd need the whole walk to compose his speech.

Once the excitement had died down, Mr. Honore had gone away, fuming in frustration, and the police cleared the street and made their exit. Miss Antonia returned to her sitting room, her opium pipe, and her Victrola.

She closed the door, and so didn't see Clarice pick up the telephone, wait for the operator, and then whisper a number. Minutes later the telephone rang in the foyer at the house on Perrier Street.

SEVEN

Tom Anderson felt as if he had just dropped off to sleep when his wife shook him awake to tell him he had a telephone call.

He let out a weary groan. "Now what?"

"It's Billy," Gertrude said. "Something about somebody getting shot."

Anderson threw off the sheets, lurched from the bed, and in his nightshirt padded along the hall and down the staircase to the foyer to snatch up the telephone. "Billy?"

"Fellow got shot dead on Basin Street." Struve's voice was breathless and a little giddy. "Front of Antonia Gonzales's."

"Who was it?"

"One of her customers. Fellow named Bolls."

The name sounded familiar, though Anderson couldn't quite place it. "Who did it?"

"No one knows. Whoever it was ran off." Struve described how the victim had been met by a miscreant with a pistol. The killer had been interrupted before anything valuable could be lifted. What happened after had been a small mob scene on Basin Street. "And listen to this," he continued in a stage whisper. "St. Cyr was up there."

Anderson's brow stitched. "Up where?"

"At Miss Antonia's," Struve said. "She sent for him and he came. Took a look at the body, talked to the madam and the cops on the scene, all that."

"And then what?"

"Then? Well, I suppose he went home. I don't know about that part."

The King of Storyville muttered under his breath, then said, "Is there anything else?"

"That's the news for this night." Struve cackled gaily. "Though I guess I might have—"

"Billy?" Anderson cut him off. "Go to sleep." He dropped the phone in the cradle. His hand rested on it for a moment, then he lifted it and waited for the operator. It was late and took some long moments for her to come on the line.

"Number, please?" the woman said.

Anderson said, "Sorry, never mind," and put the hand piece back. He turned around and started up the steps, then stopped and gripped the banister, assailed by a wave of weakness.

A good citizen had been shot dead in front of a Basin Street mansion. St. Cyr had been summoned and appeared on the scene. A whole drama had played out, and he was the last to know. A moment later he felt his gut sink with the realization that Miss Antonia's landlord was none other than Honore Jacob. So whatever was happening wasn't just a run of bad luck. There was menace afoot.

He stood there, fuming, and didn't snap out of his funk until his wife called to him from the top of the stairs.

"Come back to bed," she said.

"Yes, yes," he said, and began the climb, knowing he wouldn't be able to sleep a wink.

Valentin took his time getting back to Spain Street, stopping along the way to buy a morning *Picayune* from a kid hawking on the corner of St. Claude. He studied the front page, doing his best to pull his mind off the scene on Basin Street. It was no use. If only McKinney hadn't told him about the cut in another victim's flesh. It kept circling back around, the kind of curious thread that in the past had led him to something more sinister. A black rose, for example.

Then he turned the corner from Royal Street and saw Justine. She was standing in profile on the balcony, a coffee cup in her hand, gazing in the direction of the river. Once again, he wondered if he was bug crazy to risk riling her, just so he could play detective.

She caught his approach in the corner of her eye and turned to watch him. From the look on her face as he drew close, he could tell she wanted badly to pour the contents of her cup on his head, and only for the lack of something more lethal. She didn't say a word before stepping back inside.

The official report of the incident on Basin Street was waiting on Captain J. Picot's desk when he arrived at 8:00 A.M. Reading through the crabbed notations, he learned that Detectives Weeks and McKinney had been at the scene. He called the two officers into his office, then made them wait while he pored over the page one more time.

When he finished, his olive-green eyes flicked between them. "No suspects?"

Weeks shook his head. "He was shot while he was waiting on the banquette for his ride. The perpetrator fled back into the alleys. That kid who drives for the madam came up just after, but he couldn't make much of a description."

Picot peered at the paper again. "What kid?"

"Name's Carter. He goes by 'Each,' I believe. He's—"

"Used to call him 'Beansoup'?" The captain looked up. "That one?"

"I believe so, yes, sir."

Picot frowned absently and rattled the page. "So this wasn't a robbery?"

"Nothing was taken," Weeks said. "But the automobile scared the fellow off before he could have gotten anything."

The captain perused a few more lines of the report. "The one shot did the job?"

Weeks thumped a light fist to his chest. "Right to the heart. He was probably dead by the time he hit the street."

"What about a weapon?"

"Nothing yet. The beat coppers will be looking out for it. We ain't got the report on the slug back from the morgue yet. Looked like a .22, from what I could see."

Picot laid the report on the desk. "Was this Bolls from money?"

Weeks nodded. "He's pretty well-off, yes, sir. Owns two stores."

"Well, that's good news," the captain commented crabbily. "I can expect the chief will be calling any damn minute." He glanced at McKinney, who had kept silent. "Anything else, detective?"

McKinney said, "No, nothing to add, sir."

"I see." Picot studied the junior detective closely. Again, he noticed something just a little too guarded about him.

He found out why that was a moment later when Weeks spoke up. "Oh, yeah, that Pinkerton or whatever he is. What's his name, St. Cyr? He was there."

Picot's ball of a head snapped around. "Was where?"

"At the scene. The madam of that mansion called him." Weeks tilted his chin toward the taller McKinney. "The detective here was talking to him."

Now Picot's cool gaze settled on the junior officer. "Talking about what?"

McKinney felt his ears getting hot. He, like the rest of the department, knew that Picot had always despised St. Cyr. "He just asked if I knew anything about the homicide. That's all."

"And you said what?"

"I said I didn't. Other than what the kid told us."

Picot's ears perked, listening for a kind of hitch in the detective's voice. That he didn't hear one didn't mean there wasn't something wrong. Especially when Valentin St. Cyr was mixed up in police business.

He sniffed with irritation. "That Creole don't work Storyville no more," he said, looking between the two men, but mostly at McKinney. "He ain't Tom Anderson's man, and he don't take care of any of the mansions. I don't know why the hell Miss Antonia called him in the first place. Anyway, don't neither one of you talk to him about anything, especially police business. Understood?"

He dismissed the detectives with a sharp wave of his hand, then swiveled in his chair to stare balefully out his window and over the New Orleans rooftops.

Valentin sat on the edge of the morris chair, keeping his head bent to his newspaper and his mouth shut as Justine banged around their little kitchen, fixing his breakfast. The morning had dawned gray, with an occasional shaft of sunlight breaking through the hanging clouds. Out on the river, the horns of the barges, freight ships, and tugboats played the notes of a mournful dirge.

Rather than call his name, she stood in the kitchen doorway and stared until he felt the sting of her black eyes. He folded his *Picayune,* stood up, and marched forward.

He was relieved to find that she hadn't taken her anger out on his meal. She pushed a plate of eggs scrambled with cheese, with a fat chunk of sugared ham and a heel of French bread that she had toasted over the stove, in front of him, along with a cup of chicory coffee. It smelled wonderful and his stomach yawned. She made up a second plate of smaller portions and sat down across the table. He watched her and waited.

She kept her angry eyes down. "Go ahead," she said. "Tell

me why after three years, you've been back in Storyville two days in a row." She speared a piece of ham with such force that it tipped her plate. "Well?"

"Miss Antonia needed me."

It was a weak point and her head rose with a hard look. He knew his only chance to escape that blade of a gaze was to pull her into the story, and so he lurched ahead, drawing a picture of the rich man stepping down from the gallery and meeting the stranger who shot him dead. No one knew who had done the deed or why. Lowering his voice, he described the cut on the victim's face and mentioned what McKinney had said about another body marked the same way.

He felt like a rat taking her in like that, even more so when he told her that Each had been the sole witness and came within seconds of landing right in the middle of the violence. At that, her eyebrows pinched in worry.

It worked. She had barely touched her breakfast, and the acid in her stare dimmed. He closed the story with a dismissive shrug. "But that's all there was to it."

She caught the false note in his voice and peered at him. "Oh? And what if there's another dead man tomorrow? They'll want you back. What then?"

The way she stared at him, he could tell that either she didn't expect an answer or already knew what it would be. They finished breakfast in polite silence. Valentin escaped to the bedroom to catch a few hours of sleep before he had to go to work.

By midmorning the telephone lines were sizzling as word of the shooting on Basin Street made the rounds. The Bolls family, represented by the victim's brother, had gone railing to their alderman, who in turned railed to the mayor and the chief of police. There were closed-door meetings at City Hall and in offices on the floors above Parish Prison. From all of this hushed conversation came yet another loud agreement that something had to be done about the red-light district, though no one stepped forward with any suggestions.

The one place that wasn't in a state of agitation was Storyville itself. The deed was done, the body had been taken away, and Miss Antonia had sent a man out with a bucket and brush to wash the blood off the cobblestones.

The sun had been up for hours, and William Brown hadn't slept at all, no matter how many times he lay down on the greasy mattress. His mind would not stop replaying the scene in front of the house on Basin Street. Everything had been going perfectly, and he had been bending over the dying man to finish his work when he was startled by the racket of an engine and then was caught in the glare of headlamps. At least he'd kept the presence of mind not to look up and instead turned away to scurry into the space between the houses.

How many times had he heard the words *And don't get caught*? And that's exactly what he had almost done. Another few seconds and the driver of the automobile would have been in the middle of it. That would have meant a second shooting, and then what? A third, a fourth, a half dozen? He imagined a frantic run and then being cornered by the police in some lonely alley, feeling their cold cop stares and the colder touch of their pistols pointing at his heart . . .

If they didn't kill him on the spot, they'd put him back where he came from or someplace worse, a cage that would hold him forever. At the thought of it, his brain went into a jagged tilt, and he rushed to jerk open the window, fighting the urge to throw himself to the cobblestones two floors below and make it all stop.

The raw moment passed and he settled. His heartbeat fell back to normal, and the flush in his face faded away. There was no damage done. He would make up for his one mistake. He would do better next time. It would be clean and quick with no one even close to a witness. The next time it would be perfect, like a design.

He took the pen and pad of paper from the top of the dresser and sat down on the bed to draw. As always, it calmed him, the repetition of the lines soothing his fevered mind.

Late that morning Valentin stepped through the gilded doors of Mansell, Maines, and Velline and into the funereal silence of the reception area.

Sam Ross was waiting in his office at the end of the hall. The attorney waved him to a chair and got right down to business. "What about Storyville?" he said.

It took a moment for Valentin to realize that Ross was referring not to Burton Bolls but to James Beck.

"I found the woman James and his pals assaulted," he said. "She's a crib whore. A poor wretch, wouldn't harm an ant. Couldn't. They played a prank on her. But it wasn't funny."

He related the story simply, keeping to the essential details like the cop he had once been. Still, it was some cruel little tale. When he finished, Ross stared at him for a moment, as if waiting for more, then said, "So the woman wasn't injured?"

"Yes, she was."

"I mean hit or bruised or—"

"Beaten?" Valentin felt his throat tightening. "No, they didn't beat her. What they did was strip her naked, drag her out onto the street, tie her to a lamppost, shove a six-inch firecracker inside her, and light the fuse. When they were done, they dragged her back inside and made her go down on her knees and give them French, one at a time, while the other ones watched."

Ross sighed in impatience at the rehash. "But isn't that all in a day's work for someone like—"

"And after all that, they didn't give her a goddamn nickel."

Valentin's voice had gone brittle, and the attorney stopped to give him a probing glance. Then he said, "All right, all right, so we'll hand her a few dollars and tell her to keep her mouth shut. That's simple enough. My concern here is James. I want to make sure he and his friends aren't back over there getting in more trouble tomorrow." He paused for a reflective moment. "Especially over there. I heard some fellow got shot dead right out on Basin Street last night."

The detective was caught off guard by the change in direction and was briefly astonished by how quickly the news had traveled.

"That can't be good for business," the attorney commented.

"It doesn't help," Valentin said.

"And it's no place for these kinds of boys."

"What kind is that?"

"From good families." Ross clearly didn't like the detective's tone. "Important families. Our clients' families. That's what kind. Can you take care of it or not?"

"I can," Valentin said.

A chill passed through the room as he unfolded from the chair and made his exit.

Tom Anderson was attending to paperwork without much success, as his mind kept drifting to the death of Mr. Burton Bolls. He had stifled an urge to take a walk down Basin Street to have a look at the scene. It would only draw more attention to the crime. On the other hand, he might go unnoticed; the shadow cast by the King of Storyville didn't seem to reach so far these days.

He was staring at a sheet in the accounts book without seeing anything when Ned called him to the telephone. Leaning on the bar, he snapped it up, then closed his eyes in distress as one of his spies, a scribbler for the *Picayune*, whispered that another reporter had run down the recent havoc in the District for the afternoon paper, and that what came out wouldn't be pretty. Mr. Anderson all but threw the hand piece into the cradle. He would have a few hours of blessed peace before the afternoon papers hit the streets, and then it would become one hell of a bad day.

———

The downtown wags claimed that the Friday newspapers always came out early so that the lazy sots who wrote the drivel could get an early start on the weekend's drinking. So it was before three o'clock when the pages were pinned inside the frames on the side of the *Picayune* building and the newsboys sent up a chorus of yells as they spread like speedy mice through downtown, the Vieux Carré, and Storyville.

The article made page three under the title "MAN SHOT DEAD IN DISTRICT."

> Gentlemen looking for an evening of pleasure ought best consider a destination other than Storyville, according to sources in the "demimonde." In less than one week, two murders have occurred, and sources surmise that both are the work of one felon.
>
> So far, neither Mr. Tom Anderson, nor the New Orleans Police, nor any other party has been able to ascertain the first clue as to the identity of this dastardly criminal or the reason for the crimes.
>
> Sources state only that each body has been marked with a similar cut, a sure sign that all were committed by the same person.
>
> Mr. Anderson and Capt. Picot at the police precinct at Parish Prison were unavailable for comment.

The last word in the story had barely left Captain Picot's lips when he was barking an order for his detectives. Weeks appeared, along with a slovenly junior officer named Trevel.

"This damned scribbler"—he snapped a glance at the newspaper—"Packer. Him. I want him arrested."

Weeks said, "On what charge, sir?"

"I don't care," Picot snarled. "Everybody's guilty of something in this damned town. If you can't think of anything, grab him and hold him for questioning."

The two policemen exchanged a look of dismay.

"Well?" Picot's voice climbed. "Get moving, goddamnit!"
Weeks and Trevel vanished.

Within a half hour, a copy of the newspaper with the article circled
in black ink was placed at Mayor Behrman's elbow. Before he
reached the last period, he was calling for the chief of police. Chief
Reynolds arrived directly and closed the door behind him. After
a few heated minutes, he was on his way again and the mayor
was sending his secretary to find his special assistant Mr. Lutz.

The King of Storyville was staring at the article and muttering to
himself when the call came. The man on the line identified himself as Mayor Behrman's secretary. Anderson did not miss the
slight. In times past it would have been the mayor himself or at
the very least a member of his senior staff.

The secretary passed along a clipped and efficient request
that Mr. Anderson be available for a visit at his place of business
at four o'clock that afternoon.

"A visit from who?" Anderson inquired, forcing an offhand
tone.

"Mr. Roland Lutz, the mayor's executive attaché."

Anderson made a point of pausing and then clearing his
throat before saying, "I'll be available to meet Mr. Lutz at five
thirty." Anything less of a countermove would have been pathetic.

As if he had expected this gambit, the secretary responded
prissily. "Very well, five thirty at Anderson's Café and Annex,"
he said, making it sound like someone else owned the place. The
King of Storyville hung up the phone without another word.

Evelyne watched her husband stare forlornly into the bowl of
broth before him as if he saw something grim reflected there. His
bent head appeared as fragile as an eggshell, and she considered
how easy it would be to crack it. She had spent more than a few

idle minutes considering how best to dispatch him, though it was all in the spirit of an exercise. For the time being, she needed him; rather, she needed his money, but only until the time when her plan bore fruit. Then his shock at the realization of what she had done would be enough to kill him. She hoped so.

Malvina broke into her thoughts by laying a copy of the *Picayune* at her arm. She glanced up at the maid, wondering if the gleam in those dark eyes held some meaning. Malvina moved off before she could discover anything, and she opened the paper.

She took her time, in case the maid was lurking and watching, perusing the news on the front page, then murmuring over the Mayer Israel's display advertisement that took up most of the back page. Presently, she happened on the article about the murder in Storyville and shook her head over the bumbling of the police and Mr. Tom Anderson. It was a true wonder that the red-light district had not collapsed into chaos years ago. In any case, it was beginning to look like it was on its way there now. *So be it,* she mused.

She heard the phone ring. A few seconds later, Malvina appeared in the doorway.

"Mr. Jakes is calling for you," the maid said.

Evelyne flipped a hand. "Not now," she said.

It was four o'clock when Detective Weeks reported to Captain Picot that they had roused the *Picayune* reporter named Packer.

"He's outside," Weeks said, and jerked his head.

Picot shifted so he could see the bench near the door where suspects were held. A pudgy, greasy-looking character sat staring morosely at the floor.

"He looks unhappy."

"We pulled him out of a saloon."

"Big surprise," Picot said. "All right, bring him in. And leave him with me."

Weeks fairly shoved the reporter through the door. Packer— round of head, round of middle, round of bottom, bald, red-faced, and sweating—looked scared. This was a good thing; it meant the captain didn't have to waste time browbeating him.

He still started with a cold-eyed glare. "You're on my bad side," he began, his voice down low. "That's a place you don't want to be." He picked up the article from his top tray. " 'Unavailable for comment'?"

"Well, you weren't," Packer said sulkily.

"Then you didn't try hard enough," the captain snapped back. He paused for a glowering moment. "I could stick you with the niggers in the hole downstairs and let you stew there while we make sure you haven't committed any malfeasance." He stopped again, this time to let the reporter think about it. "But I won't. On the condition that you do me a favor."

"What favor?" Packer said, his miserable gaze still fixed on the floor.

"You'll know that when I tell you. In the meantime, you can consider me a source of information at the department." He waited until the reporter met his eyes, then said, "Your *only* source for the time being. You understand?"

Picot could tell that Packer didn't like it. Too bad for him.

"Detective Weeks?" he called out. Weeks appeared in the doorway. "Please escort Mr. Packer out of the building."

Anderson knew the visit from the mayor's man was going to be delicate business and made the climb to his office carrying a cup of brandied coffee. Turning on the ceiling fan, he opened the windows wide for the air and spent a moment gazing down the line. Basin Street looked so peaceful; and yet it wasn't the first time evil had festered beneath its facade. He was recounting some of those instances when floorboards creaked out in the corridor.

The gentleman who appeared in the doorway brought a small pain to his temples and a larger thump in his chest. Though Roland Lutz had worked for Martin Behrman since the mayor had first gained his office, the man's precise duties had never been explained to the King of Storyville's satisfaction. St. Cyr had investigated and reported back that just like Tom Anderson, the mayor kept a handful of trusted aides close by. While on the payroll, they had no titles and their offices were in a rarely visited wing of City Hall.

Behrman and Lutz were both sons of German immigrant parents, and after three terms at the mayor's side, Lutz was the most senior of the mayor's aides. At least Anderson could take some comfort that Behrman hadn't sent the dogcatcher.

As always, Lutz held himself with the hunched posture of a furtive buzzard. Dressed in black even on the hottest August day, he never seemed to sweat and his demeanor remained as icy as a cadaver's. Though he reminded Anderson of a funeral director, he was in fact more executioner than mortician, sent to do the dirtiest work: threats, petty blackmail, and banishments from the inner circle at City Hall. Some men who answered his knock were said to have fallen to their knees and prayed for mercy, even though Lutz would never deign to do brute violence. A severe and fussy gentleman, he delivered sentences that were more like pinpricks laden with poison.

Of course, he had no power over a man like Anderson, and so his towering presence had no such effect. And yet his eyes were cold glass when he said, "Mr. Anderson," in his craggy voice.

Anderson said, "Mr. Lutz," in return. They had known each other for over ten years and had never advanced beyond this stiff formality.

The King of Storyville made a gesture of invitation, and Lutz settled in the chair on the other side of the desk. He offered coffee; his visitor refused politely. Anderson quaffed half the contents of his own cup, then sat down.

"Thank you for seeing me this evening," Lutz said.

"Always a pleasure," Anderson said without an ounce of conviction.

They spent a few moments trading insincerities until the

King of Storyville grew impatient and said, "What can I do for you, sir?"

Lutz folded his hands into one another and said, "What's your opinion of the current state of business in the District?"

Anderson was momentarily thrown. He had expected to be grilled about the two killings. The mayor's man was on a whole other subject.

"We've had better years," he said carefully. "We've had worse."

"Most people would say better," Lutz said.

Anderson's blue gaze flicked and his cheeks reddened slightly, a reaction he would have never shown in the past. He bit down on his temper. "Is that correct? Who are 'most people'?"

Lutz backed up. "The mayor's concerned, sir. Revenues are down. Tax receipts have been in decline. The suppliers say that the District isn't doing the business it's done in the past. The mayor hears these complaints daily."

The King of Storyville didn't know whether to laugh or bark. They both knew the real subject at hand was the decline in graft money. From the lowest beat copper up to the chief, there was less payoff money this year than last. Feeling the pinch, the brass was squeezing him, so he sent this scarecrow of a man to squeeze Tom Anderson.

"And now we have these men being killed," Lutz said, his eyes unblinking. "It's a terrible situation. The mayor is concerned. We're wondering if it's time to make some changes."

Anderson had been expecting his second shot. The mayor had chosen to attack while he was weakened by the two dead bodies turning up in his territory in the space of the week. That Behrman hadn't called or made a personal visit was a way of twisting the knife.

Roland Lutz watched these thoughts brew in the King of Storyville's eyes, and, for the first time since he had crept into the room, seemed to understand that he might have crossed a line.

He opened his mouth to amend his comments; Anderson got there first.

"Who is *we*?" he said in a voice that was clipped with annoyance. "And why haven't I heard this before now?" He jerked a rude thumb at the window at the street beyond. "Nobody's starving out there. The District has been a goddamn money farm for fifteen years."

Lutz swallowed and said, "The mayor didn't mean—"

"I know exactly what the hell he means." Anderson's voice got louder as his face turned a deeper shade of red. "Certain parties are worried they're not going to get any richer off the women. Maybe there won't be as much for the hogs at the trough. Well, maybe it's time for everyone to shut their damned mouths and appreciate what they've got!"

The mayor's man shifted in his chair, gazing narrow eyed from under his sharp brow at the King of Storyville, who was now huffing with the exertion of the tirade. For his part, Anderson knew he had blundered by losing his temper and wished he could go into his desk drawer for the cheap Japanese fan to cool his flushed brow. He couldn't, though; not in front of a hawk like Lutz. He could all but imagine the man pecking at his flesh.

He slouched back in his heavy chair, tilting his head slightly, to catch at least a bit of a breeze from the ceiling fan that whispered overhead. After a few seconds, his calm returned.

"Those murders . . . ," he said. "They're terrible, it's true."

"Now it's two," Lutz rejoined. "What if tomorrow it's three?"

"It won't be," Anderson said sharply. "I'll take care of the matter."

His visitor's cold lips pursed. "How, exactly?"

The mayor's man's tone was accusing, as if his host was spouting an empty boast. Before the King of Storyville knew the words had left his mouth, he'd said, "I'm bringing St. Cyr back."

One of Lutz's eyebrows made a slow arc. "Oh? I thought he quit this place years ago."

"He did," Anderson said, doing his best to sound cryptic. He leaned forward and changed tack before Lutz could interrogate him further.

"Listen to me," he said. "Storyville has been good for everyone for a long while." He tapped his broad chest with a forefinger. "Why? Because of me. Because I've spent my career taking care of the police and the city officials and the businesspeople and everyone else. I keep the women clean and their customers safe. It's been some time since we've had any serious trouble. Now we have a problem, but it's getting fixed. As to the revenue . . ." He shrugged. "It's a slow year, that's all. And if there are *changes* needed, I'll make them."

Lutz waited to see if there was anything else, then nodded his head deeper into his hunched shoulders and said, with no conviction whatsoever, "The mayor will be glad to hear that."

The King of Storyville drew himself up. "Tell him that if he has any more concerns, I have a telephone right here." He nodded toward the ornate box and fixed hard eyes on his guest.

Lutz rose from the chair, a weird display of angles. "Thank you for your time, sir. We'll all hope for a speedy resolution of the crimes. And for the District to get back on sound footing."

He turned away, and his footsteps receded along the short corridor and then down the staircase. With a grunt of relief, Anderson reached for the brandy bottle with one hand and the telephone with the other. Once the operator came on the line, he surprised himself by repeating St. Cyr's telephone number from memory. Then he cut the connection before anyone could pick up.

EIGHT

Sunday morning brought a mist of rain that huddled the city in a thin gray blanket. The moisture muffled the air, so the tollings for early Mass had a hollow, faraway sound, like echoes of the bells on the barges and freighters far down the river. Shapes moved through the mist, singly and in pairs, up this street and down that, congregating at churches marked by crosses that seemed to float like buoys in the dull fog.

Many of the doves went to Mass; indeed, not a few clung to Jesus, Mary, and all the saints as drowning souls might clutch at broken branches. Others took comfort from the sonorous, incense-laden rites. The break of dawn was quite a bit to ask of these women, though, and most saved their prayers for the evening services. The rounders and sporting men were generally beyond any hope of salvation, and sprawled snoring and unsaved in rooms from Iberville to St. Ann. Storyville was as quiet as it got all week.

It was curious, then, to see the silhouette of a woman in a Sunday cloak and broad hat passing over to Basin Street's scarlet banquette and then turning north on Iberville. A sporting girl watching out her window might dream of one of the special an-

gels reserved for whores making the rounds to watch over her ruined daughters.

The woman stopped when she reached Marais Street and
hesitated as if lost. She looked up and down the street until she
picked out the facade of Mangetta's Saloon and Grocery, still
veiled in wisps of the dawn's haze.

Mangetta's. She remembered that name. It had been one of
his places. Stepping onto the cobblestones, she crossed over at a
gentle angle.

Frank Mangetta delighted in the noisy jass that shook the walls
and rattled the windows of his saloon through the long, rowdy
nights. He was as enthralled as a poor *paisan* at the opera by the
musical swells of chatter that animated his grocery when it was
filled with customers. And he adored the clattering symphony of
Marais Street in the middle of a busy Saturday afternoon.

Just as well, he loved the silence around the first light of the
morning, when everything stopped to allow a few hours of
peace. Even if he had been up all night in the saloon, he would
make his way to early Mass and then come back to spend a few
hours tidying up on both sides of the archway.

It was the one time he knew he'd have the place to himself.
It was his habit to make a light breakfast and brew strong coffee, to which he'd add a drop or two of grappa or *anisetta*. He
might pore over the books, then spread a copy of the *Picayune*
or the *Sun* on the bar and read through the city's sundry dramas.
Or, cup in hand, he would stand at his front windows and re-
flect on his life. Which included Valentin St. Cyr's most recent
visit.

The Sicilian's musings were traversed by the figure of a
woman emerging from the mist and drifting along as if carried by
a slow current. She moved down the opposite banquette from
Iberville with hesitant steps, then stopped and gazed over at the

facade of the saloon. After peering up and down the empty avenue, she crossed over.

Frank could tell at a glance that she was no trollop stumbling home from a night of sin. This one was dressed for church, an odd presence stepping up to his front window to put a hand up and gaze inside. She gave a start when she saw the man standing there, a coffee cup in hand, regarding her in turn with blank curiosity.

For a moment neither of them moved. Then Frank settled his cup on the nearest table and stepped to the front door, which he unlocked and held open.

The woman—fair brown, short, and of medium build, with a round, grave, and pretty face—gave him a tense smile, lifted her skirts, and stepped over the threshold. Frank closed the door behind her. She was acting as nervous as a sparrow, clearly the type who didn't spend much time in saloons.

"Can I help you?" he said.

"Excuse me, I'm . . ." She caught a breath. "I'm trying to locate Mr. Valentin St. Cyr."

"Valentin?"

"I heard he kept a room here."

Puzzled, Frank raised a finger toward the ceiling. "Upstairs. But not anymore. Not for a few years."

Her pretty face pinched with vexation. "Do you know where I can find him?"

"He comes around now and then," the saloonkeeper said guardedly.

"I need to reach him."

When Frank, in true Sicilian fashion, kept his mouth closed, she said, "It's very important," and then told him her name.

The telephone shrilled, dragging Valentin out of the darkness. The bed creaked as Justine got up. The ringing stopped and he was falling back when he heard her call his name.

"What is it now?"

"It's Frank," she said from the bedroom doorway. "He wants to talk to you right away."

Even dead tired, Valentin could hear the edge in her voice. It had been two days and she was still angry. It wouldn't do to ignore her, so with a soft groan, he rolled out of bed and straggled past her and into the front room. Snatching up the hand piece, he said, "What is it, Frank?"

"Tino?" the Sicilian said over the crackle of static. "Can you come to the saloon?"

"What time is it?"

"Just past seven thirty."

"What's so important? Is this about—"

"Somebody here needs to see you." Frank cut him off. His voice dropped down to a whisper. "It's Nora Bolden, Tino. Buddy's wife."

The saloonkeeper pulled two chairs to a table and got her settled. He brewed fresh coffee and made a light omelet, even though his guest protested that she had eaten at home. They sat and nibbled and sipped. Frank, who had never met the woman but remembered plenty, avoided any mention of her husband. She in turn was curious about the saloon and grocery, and he told her some stories that were fit for tender ears.

As they talked, Nora stole curious glances around the room. It was the first address where Buddy had played once he crossed over from the Rampart Street saloons. His horn had echoed off these walls not long before it had been silenced. She felt a wave of sadness come over her and turned her mind away from these thoughts.

They were running out of things to talk about when a jitney pulled up to the banquette out front. The front door swung open and Nora rose to her feet.

"Mr. Valentin," she said, and smiled shyly.

She looked so much the same that Valentin's first glance brought with it a swirl of memories. It had only been six years, and yet she seemed a visitor from a murky past.

He stepped up to take her hand. "Nora. How are you?"

"I'm fine. Thank you." Her voice was as he remembered it, too, low and sweet. She sang in the choir at First African Baptist.

Nora took a turn studying him as he settled in the third chair. His face held lines that were gaunt, and yet he was still a handsome man in a strange way. She remembered having thoughts about him, especially during that awful time when Buddy was falling to pieces. He always seemed so solid and sturdy, and she had been mortified to find herself in little fits of jealousy whenever Buddy talked about the Creole's lovely quadroon.

At this moment, though, that same Creole looked worse for the wear, pale and unshaven, his gray eyes a bloodshot mess, and she sensed something unsteady about him. Watching his weary face, she began to feel bad about rousing him. She had counted on the cord that connected him to her husband, and he hadn't let her down. He did not, however, seem unhappy to see her.

"What brings you here?" he said.

"It's Buddy."

Valentin flinched and braced himself. "What's wrong?"

She said, "Oh, nothing's *wrong*. I mean, nothing new. He's the same. He'll always be the same." She stopped for a moment, her lip tightening. Then she said, "I know you haven't gone out to see him for a while."

Valentin felt his face getting warm.

"It's all right," Nora murmured. "There's nothing to see." The moment passed and she smiled again, bringing a bit of light to the shadows on her pretty face.

Valentin knew Bolden had picked her for his wife because she had been such a young beauty and because she offered stability. She had given him a daughter and had made him a decent home where he could anchor his rocking ship. Not that it had saved him in the end.

Frank stepped up to place a steaming cup at the detective's elbow before retreating to the bar, still close enough to overhear the conversation while he pretended to study his morning newspaper.

Valentin sipped his coffee and waited.

"You know he pretty much stopped talking," Nora was saying. "The truth is, he hasn't said more than a few words in six years." She looked at him, her eyes clouding. "But . . ."

Valentin said, "But what?"

"He's speaking your name."

The detective's hand stopped in midair. "Doing what?"

"He's been saying your name."

Valentin didn't understand. "He's . . ."

"I think he's trying to tell me something."

"Tell you what?"

"That he wants to see you, Mr. Valentin."

She had left her daughter, Bernedette, now nine, with her mother and said she needed to get home to First Street. Valentin walked her to the corner of Canal and waited with her until the streetcar appeared out of the lingering morning mist. Along the way, she told him that Bernedette was growing into quite the young lady. Her smile dimmed when she came to the part about how much she looked like Buddy.

The car slowed to a creaking stop, the wires crackling overhead. Without looking at him, she said, "What are you going to do?"

He said, "I don't know, Nora."

She nodded slowly. "Well, just so you understand. Going out there probably won't do any good. He might not remember you, no matter what he's been saying. Most of the time, he doesn't even know me. Doesn't see me or hear me at all. I wanted to tell you about this, but it's up to you whether or not you want to go. Either way, I'll understand." She offered a smile of farewell as she pulled herself onto the step.

The car rattled away. Valentin jammed his hands in his pockets and began retracing his steps along Marais Street, feeling like another stone had been added to his load.

He had given up on going to the hospital after the first few visits. It was too heartbreaking to see Bolden that way, and it served no purpose. Buddy no longer recognized him as his childhood friend from their days on the streets around First and Liberty. Or as the Creole detective who had followed his elusive trail during the Black Rose murders. They had become strangers.

Now, after all that, his long-suffering wife had come to announce that from some cranny of his crazy mind, he had pulled Valentin's name.

The detective understood that whatever was happening with Buddy was most likely a passing event, lightning flashing inside a dark cloud, sharp and random and signifying nothing. He was relieved that Nora hadn't pleaded with him to make the trip. She had simply delivered the information as a duty to the man who had been her husband, shared her bed, and fathered her child.

Valentin looked up to find that instead of heading for Spain Street, his footsteps had delivered him back at Mangetta's.

The saloonkeeper poured two more cups of coffee, these laced with *anisetta*. "Some week you're having," he commented as they returned to the table.

Valentin agreed.

"*Ora che cosa?* Are you back to work over here?"

The detective shrugged tiredly. In a few short days, his life had taken a hard turn. Two men were dead, he had placed himself in the middle of the mess, and Justine was ready to kill *him*. Before he could catch a breath, the wife of the childhood friend he had lost to madness had appeared to tell him that there was unfinished business there, too.

He stopped to consider that Justine had been right all along: They should have moved farther away, certainly beyond Spain Street. She was also correct that he didn't have any promises to honor in the District. He could turn his back on it anytime.

So why, he wondered, did he feel an urge to climb the steps to his old room on the second floor and drop into the iron-framed bed with its thin gray mattress? He felt as if he could sleep for days, not rising until the fragrances from Frank's kitchen seeped through the floorboards and awakened him to find that the drama had ended, the killer put away or dead, Justine over being angry, and Buddy back where he belonged, standing still and silent as he gazed out a window at the world that he had left behind.

"So what now?" Frank repeated, this time in English.

Valentin lifted his cup. "Now I finish this and go home."

The Sicilian considered for a few seconds. "Are you going to go see him, Tino?"

Tino. That's what Buddy had always called him. "I don't know."

Mangetta eyed him wisely. "You will," he said. "You have to."

It didn't take long for the news about Valentin's return to Storyville to revive a whole history. From one end of Basin Street to the other, the stories were taken down and dusted off for fresh readings. The women in the mansions gabbed about how the Creole detective had gone about ridding the District of this villain or that, pickpocket to murderer. They recalled his delicacy in handling affairs between certain harlots and men of position and wealth. And they recounted the convoluted drama between the detective and Justine Mancarre, once a sporting girl herself.

Whatever the tale, the Storyville veterans would finish with a sigh and a murmured *I knew he couldn't stay away.*

––––––––

It was Tom Anderson's custom to enjoy a meal at Germaine's on Ursulines after church on Sunday. He would invite three or four important guests from around New Orleans, and these feasts, which began around noon and ended at two or later, had produced some rousing good conversation and the sort of connections that the host believed fortified his business and political interests. He had stolen the idea from an article about salons that he had read in a magazine.

The restaurant kept a special table reserved, a circular affair that was placed in a corner of the main dining room, yet still in sight of anyone who walked in the door. That Anderson was regarded as the devil himself in some quarters hadn't kept some of the most powerful men in the city and beyond away. He had long been too exalted a presence to ignore.

For his part, the King of Storyville found that the dinners invigorated him. A good meal in the company of three or four gentlemen of import seemed to have a magical effect on his constitution, as well as his profile.

When he arrived on this Sunday, however, he found that two of his four companions invited to the weekly meal were absent. A message was waiting from Father O'Rourke, begging off due to a sick parishioner. John Miles, who among other holdings owned one of the three automobile dealerships in the city, simply failed to show. That left only Laurence Deveaux, a pianist who had traveled from Philadelphia for a production at the Opera House and decided to stay to become a fixture at downtown New Orleans social events, and Charles Auberge, a fellow of idle means who, with a partner, owned a stable of horses that ran at the Fair Grounds.

Though Anderson greeted the two men cheerfully, he was dismayed. Once in a while a guest didn't show. Never two. Though neither man seemed to mind the expanse of empty table laid out before them, looking forward to the extra time with the King of Storyville.

Anderson understood that while savvy politicians and businessmen considered him a man of influence, others regarded him more as an exotic, the leading player in a crude pageant. He never minded that role; it fanned his vanity in a different way.

Spying the empty chairs, the headwaiter sprang to the rescue, creating a flurry of activity as he scrounged two businessmen who had been dining together on the other side of the house and installed them at the table. The two were astonished to find themselves in the company of the notorious King of Storyville and delighted to be treated to the best fare the chef had to offer.

Across the room one of the women at a table of society ladies observed all this, from the delicious moment when Tom Anderson realized that he had been jilted until the two befuddled strangers were hustled up to the table and seated. She smiled and dropped her absent gaze.

More eyes flicked and other mouths whispered, and by the end of the afternoon, the word of Anderson's humiliation was making the rounds at tables at other restaurants, in the smoking rooms in men's clubs, and in the quiet parlors of Basin Street mansions like Mahogany Hall and the Arlington.

William Brown had spent a fevered forty-eight hours as crazed as one of the monkeys in the Audubon Zoo that had been locked up for so long that it had lost what little was left of its mind. He knew he could leave his cramped confines at his will, either by taking the steps down to the street or crawling out the window onto the fire escape and descending to the alley. He wouldn't, though, not without his instructions.

He clung to the missives that were pushed under his door by an unseen hand, as if they were messages in bottles washing up on the shore of a desert island. They gave him purpose and direction, the map by which he charted his days. Otherwise, he would wander aimlessly until he did something wrong and then end up back in a true cage, trapped in an unending nightmare, complete with bars and populated by a mad gaggle of screeching, howling, pissing, shitting, fucking creatures that could be called human only by the kindest definition. He would never be free.

So he waited. He had his bed, his window, his dark, cracked mirror. He had a bag of apples and a loaf of heavy bread to fill his stomach. In an hour or a day, another envelope would appear, and he would have someplace to go and something important to do.

As he began to shift his feet this way and that, the thought suddenly crossed his mind that soon he would perform the final task and then could escape for good. He had a promise.

Valentin went to bed while Justine was at afternoon Mass. When he woke up, he found that she had changed from her Sunday dress to a frock and was reclining on the end of the couch with her bare feet curled beneath her, reading a book. She sat very still, and in the misty light filtering through the curtains, made Valentin think of an old painting.

There was no gleam of anger in her eyes as she raised them from the page. He settled on the opposite end of the couch. She regarded him for a quiet moment, as if trying to read something in his face, then closed her book and said, "I'll fix you something to eat." She stopped to kiss his forehead before moving away.

The package arrived later in the afternoon. William had been dozing and heard neither the footsteps nor the whisper of the envelope under his door, and he turned his head to catch sight of the square of bright white. He swung his legs off the bed to retrieve it.

Once he deposited the coin in a pocket, he drew out the sheet of paper and read the simple words printed there. Closing his eyes, he whispered a prayer of thanks that he would be one step closer to the end.

NINE

The sun was long down over the roof of the house on St. Louis Street. The shutters were closed, so that from inside it was impossible to know when daylight was actually gone, and the front door was shut and bolted, presenting a sober and silent facade. Visitors entered by way of the side entrance that led down three concrete steps, through a dimly lit basement, and up wooden stairs to a first-floor hallway. Deliveries were left on the back gallery. The vendors had their instructions and were paid extra to heed them.

Behind the shuttered windows was another world entirely. The downstairs rooms were adorned with fine French furniture and Persian rugs. Good works of art, or at least good copies, hung on the walls. By day and night, men of means lounged in the golden glow of light from tasseled lamps and crystal chandeliers. The linen in the bedrooms was changed after every visit.

There were no women on the premises: not in the parlor, nor in the kitchen, nor in any of the upstairs rooms. For this was a secret society, reserved for citizens with special appetites. There were other such houses in the District, in the Quarter, and beyond, but they were slipshod affairs that popped up and then closed down when something went awry. Most denizens of

Storyville knew about the address, and yet no one gave it much thought. Like the French houses in the District that were, curiously, staffed by lesbians, it was just one of those things.

The St. Louis Street quarters were quiet and elegant, a sanctuary that was left to its own devices, mainly because important persons paid visits at one time or another, and the two partners who kept the house in operation had the goods on these individuals. It so happened that the owner of the house, Honore Jacob, cared not a whit who did what on his properties, as long as the rent was paid on time.

After sharing a Sunday dinner in the company of a deflated Tom Anderson, Laurence Deveaux spent the afternoon entertaining a group of ladies at a mansion in the Garden District. They lauded him like a prince, fawning at his every word and movement, treating him with coffee and sweets from the best patisserie in the neighborhood. He delighted them with a few chamber pieces on the piano.

At seven o'clock he called for an automobile to carry him uptown to a Basin Street that was quiet under a passing shower. The driver gave him a chum's wink when he stepped down from the touring car at the corner of Bienville.

Laurence strolled along, the brass tip of his walking cane clicking on the banquette, as the automobile swung about in the middle of the street and rattled back toward Union Station. He stopped when he reached St. Louis Street, took a thin cigarette from a silver case, and lit it, glancing about to make sure there wasn't some miscreant following him. Turning north, he moved at an even pace, enjoying his smoke and thinking about poor Tom Anderson with only him, a greasy racetrack maven, and two nervous strangers to keep him company at Sunday dinner.

He stopped in front of the solid brick house that was just past Villere Street. As he tossed what was left of his cigarette into the gutter, he glanced around again and saw only one solitary soul far down the block. The muted tinkle of piano keys from inside the dark house caught his ear, and he quickly ducked into the walkway alongside the house and hurried to the doorway that was cast in the glow of a pale electric light. He rang the bell and a few seconds later was ushered inside.

After dinner Valentin and Justine took an evening stroll south to the river and sat on the levee over the Port Street wharf, gazing at the silhouettes of ships and barges out on the water. Justine wore a plain shirtwaist and skirt, which she hiked up over her knees once they were settled. Valentin smiled, knowing how much she despised the fashions of the day: skirts that brushed the floor, collars drawn tight at the neck, and all the accoutrements underneath. She wore the absolute minimum, choosing to dress more like a servant girl than a lady. Valentin guessed that she would go through the world naked if she could.

For his part, he had donned a pair of worn gray trousers that were held by suspenders over a white cotton shirt that he left collarless. They both removed their shoes, and he his socks and she her stockings, and they relaxed under the starry sky.

He never talked much, but he fell even quieter whenever they visited the levee overlooking the Mississippi. Justine had learned to respect these silences. She didn't understand what he drew from these interludes, though she guessed he was stirred in some fashion by the river's mystery. He was the same way about trains and about roads that led to nowhere.

Or maybe, she reflected in wry moments, he was thinking about all the ways he could escape her.

They stayed for almost two hours, then made a slow amble back along Spain Street in the cool and quiet autumn night. Justine noticed that he had settled into the gait that made him appear almost motionless. She was never sure if he did it by intention, but it always affected her the same way, and she began thinking about what would happen when they got home.

Upstairs, she went into the bathroom to get ready for him,

then slipped into one of her camisoles. She stepped out to find that he had turned off the lights. He was waiting in the bedroom, undressed down to his trousers and undershirt, his features muted in the amber light of the gas lamp. She waited and he came to her.

All the men she had entertained had gone faceless and forgotten, as if they existed in Valentin's shadow. And for all the women he'd enjoyed, he kept coming back. He hadn't yet tired of her; indeed, he seemed to delight in the way she had matured from a lithe whip of a bayou girl into a more womanly presence, still slender, yet with deeper curves and more weight in her hips and chest. Even so, she knew that most men got bored with one companion and wandered off. Not Valentin. Not yet.

Over the years he had learned his way around her body. Tonight he went from slow and tender to hard and vigorous, and she was glad that the import office downstairs was closed so they couldn't hear the mattress complaining, the bedposts pounding the floor, and the noises that spilled from her throat. But for all her passion, she couldn't shake the niggling notion in the back of her mind that his zealous efforts had something to do with taking her thoughts off Storyville.

It was near midnight when Laurence made his crooked way down the steps, through the basement, and into the walkway, his mind adrift of opium and champagne, taken in equal doses, a delicious balance.

The darkness in the dark alley seemed to undulate. The few lights of Basin Street that he could spy were glaring, and he decided to slip through the back garden and into the alley and make his way to his hotel by the back streets. It was a pleasant evening, with a caressing breeze wafting from the lake to the river.

Before he took the first step, he leaned his cane next to the door and went into his silver case for another cigarette. The lucifer cast a sudden flare of light, and in the corner of his vision, he thought he saw a shadow come to life, taking the form of a child's hurried scribble. Though when he looked, he saw just another dark patch that all but got lost in the gray palette. He had just sighed out a first fragrant plume when he was startled by a muttering voice. Turning, he saw a figure rise from a shadow and heard a faint click.

Valentin was in the front room pouring two short glasses of brandy when the downstairs door squeaked and quick footsteps pounded up the staircase. He reached the door just as Justine appeared from the bedroom, wrapped in her kimono. It wasn't Each this time, but a kid who could have been him five years before. The boy didn't say a word as he handed Valentin a slip of paper.

Opening it, the detective found an address on St. Louis Street on top, the name "McKinney" on the bottom, and a diagonal slash of ink across the middle.

It took twenty minutes for the first of the police automobiles to arrive. By that time the house was almost entirely empty. Only the young boy who ran errands and an older fellow named Mr. Thorpe, one of the men who managed the house, remained behind. Those policemen who didn't already know about the address soon found out by way of the whispers and snickers.

Because Laurence Deveaux's body lay in the narrow space between two buildings, it was easy enough keeping curious onlookers at bay. The police wagons and the uniformed officers were there for all to see; but without a body in clear view, the men passing by assumed it was just some small matter and moved on.

James McKinney had been at the precinct when the call came in. He hurried to the scene and was allowed back to see the body. Borrowing a lamp from one of the coppers, he bent down and saw what he expected; this time the line was scrawled from the temple to the jaw, slicing thinly across the dead Mr. Deveaux's cheeks and mouth. McKinney could tell that the wound had been made by a hurried hand.

He straightened and returned the lamp to the officer. Back on St. Louis, he asked around in a low voice until someone was able to tell him that St. Cyr lived on Spain Street, between Royal and Decatur, over an importer's office. It took no time at all for him to whistle up one of the dozen of street Arabs who were always in earshot and hand him a scrawled note.

Even though it was Sunday night—Monday morning, to be exact—and as quiet as it got in the District, the police stood by helplessly as the news of another killing, the third in a week, made a furious sprint up and down the streets and then beyond.

Laurence Deveaux's body had been discovered at 12:30 by another gentleman leaving the premises, and by two o'clock every madam on Basin Street had been roused with the news. Only a few saloons remained open, but the story hopped from one to the next of those that were, finally reaching the ear of Billy Struve, who stumbled to a phone to call Tom Anderson.

Within minutes of the 2:30 bells, a cast of characters had materialized on St. Louis Street. Captain J. Picot stalked about, wearing his usual mask of annoyance. A white Packard Victoria touring car arrived, and the King of Storyville, looking tired and rumpled, climbed down from the passenger seat. Each had arrived and was wandering around, trying to look important. Detective McKinney went about assisting at the scene. None of these men spoke to or even looked at each other. Though anyone watching would have noticed that the four kept stealing occasional glances to the south end of the street and in the general direction of the river, as if they were expecting someone.

Valentin surprised them all by coming in from the direction of Franklin Avenue. Before he did that, though, he spent some minutes standing in the darkness of the alley behind the house and watching the activity in the walkway. He could not see the body from that angle, only the officers, whose faces were cast in the glow of the hand lamps.

Each noticed him first and ambled over to give the detective a rundown in a few clipped sentences. Valentin was startled to learn the victim's identity. He had read about Deveaux in the *Picayune*. The man was known in all the right circles around the city. His recitals at the Opera House were major events, and he had played for J. P. Morgan, the king of Spain, and several governors.

Valentin felt Each nudging him and looked up to see Tom Anderson standing on the banquette, his driver on one side and a dazed-looking Billy Struve on the other. Anderson was staring in his direction, and the two men exchanged a nod. Turning his head, he saw Detective McKinney, and the policeman stopped writing on his pad to shake his head slightly. And as if the worst had been saved for last, Valentin felt a cold glare that could only come from Captain Picot and caught sight of that familiar glowering countenance not twenty paces away.

All the players seemed to be waiting for the Creole detective to make a move. The King of Storyville broke the impasse, crooking a finger in one direction to beckon Valentin to his side and then in the other to summon Captain Picot. The two men joined him on the banquette. Anderson spoke first to the captain, who listened, then gave a nod that seemed to have been wrenched from his neck with pliers. He turned and murmured to Valentin, who nodded in kind.

Walking away, the detective waved a sharp hand for Each to join him and treated McKinney to a quick glance that wasn't quick enough; Captain Picot, who by now had steam blowing from his ears, saw it and grimaced.

Each strutted past the coppers to join Valentin, and the two of them made their way along the walkway between the houses.

In spite of the forlorn business at hand, the portable gas lamps cast a glow as welcoming as a campfire. The detective noticed the line cut across Deveaux's smooth and regal face. It was the work of one man claiming a third victim.

Valentin was assailed by an unsettling sense that he had a chance to turn around and walk away. Justine would be waiting for him to do just that. This grisly business was truly none of his affair.

After a final moment's hesitation, he stepped forward and bent down over the corpse of Laurence Deveaux.

TEN

Justine didn't have to ask to know that Valentin was going against her wishes and risking the good deal he had with the St. Charles Avenue lawyers to heed the call of the scarlet streets of Storyville. She had seen the look in his eye when he raced out the door in the middle of the night, a glimmer that broadcast that he was on the prowl. She knew that while she couldn't turn him around, she wasn't about to let him go on his merry way, either.

She wanted him to suffer, so when morning came, she made him sit at the kitchen table and stutter out an explanation for his errant actions. He did a poor job. Caught up in the moment, he had hurried off to the scene of the third crime at a special house for men who preferred the company of their own gender. Justine wasn't sure if that was supposed to sway her in some way. What did she care about people's tastes? Her concern was what sort of reason the Creole detective who sat across from her could provide for defying her so rudely.

She leaned against the sideboard with her arms crossed and expression taut, waiting with forced patience for him to explain why any of this was more important than the good life they had been assembling. He squirmed like a misbehaving schoolboy until her impatience turned into exasperation.

"You said you wouldn't go back."

"I'm not going *back*," he said. "Not exactly."

She wasn't having any of it. "And what do you expect me to do? Shall I go back, too?"

He looked startled, which satisfied her. Let him think about the weight of his actions. He said, "Don't do that."

"Why not?"

"Because—"

"You can say no," she snapped. "You don't owe any of them anything."

Valentin sighed and said, "I know."

"Then why are you doing this?"

He looked at her directly for the first time since he'd sat down. "Because I'm the only one who can," he said.

Ned the janitor didn't say a word when Mr. Tom stepped through the front door. He merely raised one white eyebrow and tilted his old head slightly. Anderson peered down the length of the bar to see Honore Jacob pacing, his hands clasped behind his back in a posture of overfed aggravation.

The King of Storyville let out an audible sigh that must have carried in the empty room, because Jacob wheeled around with an agitated grunt of his own. Though it had been almost five days, it seemed like the landlord had just left and now was back. Anderson was relieved that his rude spawn wasn't along for this visit.

"I've been waiting for you," Jacob said, as if it wasn't obvious.

At that moment Tom Anderson wanted nothing so much as to call to Ned for a stiff brandy. But he knew what kind of picture that would present, especially to a fussy and suspicious soul like Jacob, so instead he asked the janitor to fetch him a fresh cup of coffee and refill his guest's. With a tug at the lapels of his jacket, he lumbered to the table. He made a gesture, and the landlord sat down.

"This is a fine damned mess," Jacob said.

"It's a terrible thing," Anderson agreed soberly.

"A terrible thing? Dead men turning up on my properties? I'd say that's more than a *terrible thing*. It's a goddamned calamity, is what. Good lord! What are you going to do about it?" The King of Storyville drew back, stung and annoyed. Jacob retreated, though only slightly. "For Christ's sake, Tom. You think anyone needs this kind of trouble? Especially now?"

Anderson cocked an eyebrow. "What do you mean, *now*?"

The landlord posed a petulant look. "Everyone's talking, saying Storyville's coming apart at the seams. It's all I hear. The madams say they can't pay rent because they don't have enough business. So there's no money to keep up appearances. And they can't give the coppers the usual amount, so the damned criminals have the run of the place. The whole District is falling apart. The mayor's on the warpath. And now this!"

Jacob had taken the tone of an adult scolding a child, his voice climbing the scale from grouse to grate, and Anderson, feeling the heat rise in his chest, bristled.

"You be quiet and listen to me." He leaned forward like a dog pulling at its chain. The landlord, sensing he'd gone too far, blinked nervously. Easing the edge in his voice slightly, the King of Storyville said, "We're having hard times. We've had them before. Things go poorly, then they get better. As for these killings, I know it's serious. I'll take care of it. Whoever's responsible will be stopped. Dead or put away. That's a guarantee."

At that moment Ned stepped up with the two cups of coffee, left them, and moved off, though he kept his ears wide open. In the tense pause that followed, both men took a first sip of coffee, and the King of Storyville was pleased to discover that the old janitor had read his mind and spiced his cup with a stiff shot of brandy.

Frowning puckishly, Honore Jacob placed his cup in the saucer. "You're sure?"

Anderson settled back as the brandy calmed his nerves. "You just watch and see," he said.

Louis Jacob steered the Buick to the Basin Street curb just as an ancient darkie pushed the doors open for his father to pass through. Though the daylight cast the interior of the restaurant in shadow, he felt Tom Anderson peering out at him, like a crusty old alligator half submerged in swamp water, battered but still dangerous.

His father performed a noisy climb up and flopped into the tufted passenger seat with a heavy gust of breath. He whipped out a handkerchief to mop his brow, then waved it in the direction of the French Quarter. Louis shifted the transmission into gear and pushed the accelerator handle.

By the time they arrived on Royal Street, he had heard his father's rendition of the meeting with Anderson three times. The King of Storyville had made promises. It was a terrible situation but not hopeless. Just a madman running loose. Valentin St. Cyr had come out from wherever he'd been hiding for the past few years to take care of it.

Louis smiled slightly at the mention of the name. Honore let himself down to the banquette in front of the building.

"You can take the car to the garage," he said.

"I will," Louis said. "First I have a small errand."

Justine and Valentin were equally relieved that Monday was her day to make market. She dressed in silence, and the kiss she delivered as she left their rooms was suited more for a distant cousin than the man with whom she shared a bed.

Once the door had closed behind her, Valentin felt a small butterfly of panic in his chest, a twinge of dread that in some small way he had lost her. It was a good thing that he was exhausted from lack of sleep, the long walks to and from the District, and tangling with Justine before and after the fact. He went into the bedroom, undressed, and crawled in under the sheet.

Tired as he was, sleep didn't come right away. Gazing up at the cracks in the plaster ceiling, he wondered frankly if his pride was leading him to a terrible mistake. Even so, it didn't change the fact that someone was slithering around Storyville under the cover of night, murdering men and taking the trouble of cutting into their flesh, a lunatic to be sure, and a danger to the streets.

The question he had posed to Justine was not just a retort. Who else could bring down such a killer? The police? Not with Captain Picot in charge. Tom Anderson might once have been able to rouse the entire department with a few words whispered into the right official's ear. But not anymore, and so Picot could drag his feet even more than usual and hope for the worst.

The French Market on North Peters Street had for over 120 years been a daily celebration of New Orleans' palate. The market, located on the edge of the Quarter, opened well before dawn and went full steam until around one o'clock, when traffic began to wind down. Up to that point, it was a beehive of the noise, color, and motion of commerce that rang with old echoes.

Working-class women and maids from homes in the Garden District, Esplanade Ridge, and the Storyville mansions assembled to forage and haggle. The male contingent was represented by chefs who insisted on selecting their own foodstuffs, servants in various shades of brown, and hapless husbands who found themselves traipsing like pack mules behind their busy wives. On the intersecting streets, hacks and automobiles waited to help carry the women and their purchases to kitchens all over the city.

Justine loved the market and spent a good part of her Mondays grazing. Her mother had taught her to cook a bit, and she learned more on the road, including how to make a feast out of next to nothing.

For the rest of the week, she shopped with a bucket and rope. The produce hawker would roll along the curb, and the lady of the house would call down her needs and lower a bucket with coins at the bottom on a rope. Once filled, the bucket went up and the wagon rolled away, and on to the next address.

Justine much preferred the market, and loved to wander alone up and down the aisles, taking in the colors and the scents. It was like strolling into the mouth of a cornucopia.

On this day, though, her thoughts were on Valentin and how he had maneuvered his way back into Storyville. The betrayal wasn't so blatant that she had him cornered; he was too clever— or maybe lucky—for that. She knew as well as anyone how he could work the streets. Still, he was breaking his promise to her.

She was so absorbed in these thoughts that three times she had to go back to vendors she had passed by mistake. Walking away from the third, she topped off her morning by running directly into the chest of a man coming the other way. The basket over her arm tipped, and oranges, onions, sassafras, peppers, limes, and garlic came tumbling out. The other half of the collision muttered an apology and immediately bent down to grab what he could, even scuttling part of the way under a stand to chase down an errant orange.

When he crawled back out and straightened up, she found herself looking into a face so striking that her breath caught for a moment. The unblemished flesh had a slight tan cast set off by a near-perfect nose, full lips, and chiseled cheekbones. The eyes were the pale green color of Riesling wine. Dark blond hair, longish and straight, was carefully combed and oiled. He looked like nothing so much as a cameo, and she guessed that he took much care to create the effect. Along with this, he smelled good; the obvious benefit of a cologne, and not one that many men would employ.

With all this, there was something predatory about him, and he gazed openly into her eyes as he brushed the dust from the sleeves of his day coat. She stuttered apologies, stumbling over her words and making no sense whatsoever. Gently, with a small smile, he dropped the last orange back into her basket.

"I'm so sorry," she said for the fifth time.

"It was my fault. Please forgive me."

"No, really, I wasn't watching . . . I was . . ." She got lost again.

His white smile stayed in place and, tilting his head, he said, "Will you let me buy you a cup of coffee?" The small café with the bakery counter was only a few paces behind her. He caught her eye again and served up a deeper smile. "Please."

With one smooth motion, he cupped her elbow in one hand and swept the basket from her forearm with the other. He steered her out of the foot traffic to the recess of the café and then to a table. She was relieved when he stepped away to fetch their refreshments; she needed a moment.

In the years since she had been "ruined," it had been the rare man who could rouse her. She knew them too well. The kind ones bored her, and the dangerous types were more like thieves in the night. So it had always required a particular touch to get through her defenses. Valentin had possessed it, and one day she woke up to find he had breached her wall. She hadn't been able to shake him, even when he wandered away or she had to put him out.

This handsome fellow who was now turning away from the counter with two cups had the same sort of wicked charm, but his came more in ebbs. Justine took hold of herself. She had no intention of falling for some charmer's play, though she didn't mind the attention at all. Let Valentin see her now; how she wished he could . . .

By the time her new friend reached the table, his progress marked by a dozen other female eyes, she was ready. He put her cup down, settled himself, and resumed his study of her face. She wondered for a moment if the French Market might be his turf, a place to hunt pretty women, looking for his next free ride.

"I didn't ask your name," he said, giving her a dimpled smile.

She was trying to recall if she'd ever met a man who was so feminine and yet brashly male at the same time. Keeping her cool, she gave an absent shrug. "And you haven't said yours."

He bowed slightly, like a true gentleman. "It's Louis," he said. He was clearly some snake, his tongue all but flicking into the air around her, and she guessed that he had sunk his fangs into the flesh of more than a few helpless young creatures.

Her vanity was pained to realize that she was too old for him. He couldn't be more than twenty-one. Still, she was flattered, more so when she noticed the looks from the ladies at other tables, as if they had discovered someone who could make their romantic dreams come true—unlike their husbands or even their secret lovers. Justine knew better. Still, she couldn't ignore the stares being cast her way.

The young man across the table did not seem aware of the attention as he fixed his clear green eyes on her. She decided he was one of those who treated seduction as an art.

Even so, she wasn't about to fall for his wiles. Flattered or not, she wasn't angry enough with Valentin to betray him by slipping off to a private room with some handsome fox.

She considered that there were sporting girls and maids from mansions on the premises, and one or more might carry the little scene at the French Market back to Storyville on the tip of her wagging tongue, and from there it might find its way to Valentin's ear. So he wanted to run off and play detective on the streets of the red-light district? Let him think she might engage in some sport of her own.

This went through her head as she sat half listening to Louis talk—about himself, mostly, which didn't surprise her a bit. First it was about his home, then the schools he had attended, then his family, old French and moneyed. And so on. Score a point for Mr. St. Cyr, who didn't speak that much at all, especially not about his life. She dropped in at the middle of something about his plans for the future.

". . . an academy," he was saying. "With a literary salon and a music conservatory and an art studio. And"—he smiled—"it would be reserved for women."

"So you could have your pick of the flock?"

He ignored the quip. "You don't believe that women can create? Be artistic? I think that's been proven wrong. Why, just think of . . ." And on he went. He knew what he was doing, fairly oozing sincerity, and she threw up a shield to deflect him.

"And where will you get the money for this academy full of young women?" she interrupted.

Louis stopped to steal a lazy glance around the room. The reaction from the other tables resembled a pack of dogs going on point.

"Oh, I have some ideas." He shrugged. "Now tell me something about you."

It was almost noon when Valentin woke up. Justine was not back from the French Market, and he rolled out of bed, took a quick bath, dressed, ate a biscuit with a slice of ham, and hurried out the door. In true coward fashion, he cut down Franklin Avenue to avoid running into her. As furtive as a rodent, he rounded the park and entered the District by way of North Rampart Street, circling behind Union Station and crossing over to duck under the colonnade of the corner building.

He knocked on the heavy doors and waited. A dark face peered out through the leaded glass, and the bolt cracked.

"Well, look who we got here," Ned said, pushing the door wide. "Ain't seen you in what, a few years?"

Valentin stepped inside. "How are you, Ned?"

"Day older and a dollar shorter, that's how." The janitor's grin took a crooked turn, and he lowered his voice. "I believe the man's been waitin' for you," he said.

Valentin made his way along the familiar marble-topped bar with its brass rail and rolling ridges of liquor bottles. The chandeliers glistened overhead, and though the spittoons gleamed roundly every ten paces, the carpet held more stains than he remembered, and many of the floor tiles that it intersected were cracked. The bandstand was empty, and any sound brought back a lonely echo. It all looked a little worn out, and yet the Café was by far still the grandest room for dining, dancing, drinking, and dicing in the city of New Orleans.

Tom Anderson did not look up from his papers at Valentin's approach. The detective stopped to help himself to a cup of coffee from the copper urn at the end of the bar, the chicory rising to his nostrils, a local perfume. It was a ritual he had performed a thousand times, and in that instant more months dropped away.

When he turned around, he found the King of Storyville peering at him over the tops of wire-rimmed spectacles. Anderson smiled slightly and waved him to the opposite chair.

Ned came along the back of the bar and stepped to the urn to refill his employer's cup. Valentin was surprised; Anderson had always made a point of serving himself and his guests the morning coffee. Never one to demand kowtowing from the help, he was in fact often criticized for treating the darker races too kindly. Indeed, his right-hand man for the better part of ten years had been a Creole.

That same Creole sat waiting for the King of Storyville to pour a bit of sugar and a drop of cream into his cup.

Stirring idly, Anderson said, "How are you, Valentin?"

The detective said, "I'm well."

"You're still on Spain Street?"

He nodded. Of course, Anderson knew this. The game had begun.

"And your work with those attorneys? How are you getting along there?"

"All right. It pays well."

"I can imagine."

They went around in this dance for a few minutes. Since Valentin was the one who had walked out, he knew he was responsible for the patchwork. Anderson was waiting, so at the next silence, he said, "The murder of this Bolls fellow . . ."

"Yes?"

"Miss Antonia asked for my help."

"And you agreed."

"I told her I'd see if there was anything I could do."

Anderson's eyebrows arched politely; he hadn't lost his flair for exaggeration. "And so?"

"And so I've come to ask your permission to go on with the investigation. And to ask for any help you can offer."

The King of Storyville regarded him steadily, and Valentin could all but hear the gears churning behind the blue eyes. Though Anderson would appreciate the gesture, there was no way he could greet the detective's return with open arms, no matter how much relief it brought.

Valentin said, "Or I could let the police handle it."

Anderson shook his head slowly and gave out a short laugh. "Not while Picot's sitting in that office." He sipped his coffee, sobering. "We need this creature stopped."

Valentin understood that this was as much as he was going to get by way of a welcome back and moved on to the business at hand. "Is there anything you can tell me?"

"I can tell you that Honore Jacob thinks someone is out to get him."

"Because the three bodies turned up at properties he owns?"

Anderson nodded. "That's correct."

Valentin said, "Then I'll need to talk to him."

"Who, Jacob?" Anderson snickered. "You can try. He'll do the talking."

"Does he keep an office?"

"Yes, down on Royal Street. If he's not there, you'll likely find him in the bar at the Lafayette House."

Valentin stole a glance at the clock over the bar. "I'm sorry." He rose from his chair. "I have an appointment."

The King of Storyville gave him a wry look. "What do you think those lawyers will have to say about you working here again?"

The detective sighed and said, "I'm about to find out."

"And here we all thought you were gone for good," Anderson said.

"So did I." Valentin thanked the King of Storyville for his time and made his exit.

Justine allowed Louis to escort her out of the market. He carried her basket and offered her a ride in his red Buick 10. She accepted the help to the street but refused the ride, assuming that like most men, this one was after something. He should have been easy enough to fathom, except that the look in his eye, as if he was amused by a private joke, kept throwing her off. That, and what seemed an honest attraction to her.

He wasn't incensed that she refused his offer. Shrugging agreeably, he shook her hand with a slight bow, then let his gaze rake over her one more time, from the hem of her dress to her face, before backing away.

She fell into the crowd waiting for the streetcar and watched him saunter off. The engine of the gleaming Buick started on one crank, and Louis hopped behind the wheel and spent a few seconds pulling on driving goggles and a pair of fine leather gloves. From his posture, it was clear he knew that she—or at least some woman—had her eyes on him. With deft hands, he released the brake and engaged the transmission. The roadster stuttered away from the curb and zoomed down Decatur Street, leaving a faint cloud of smoke, just as the streetcar came grinding to the stop.

Justine thought about him as she rode along and pictured Valentin on the balcony watching as she rolled up and was helped down from the seat of that fine red phaeton. Or if he wasn't home, one of the neighbors seeing and reporting back. The daydream brought a smile to her face, and she wondered if she should have accepted the ride after all, if nothing else for a chance to put Mr. Valentin St. Cyr in his place.

The Creole detective stopped at the doors of Mansell, Maines, and Velline, undecided about mentioning the business in the District. Though Valentin had not signed a contract with the firm, Sam Ross had been good to him, and the least he could do was tell the attorney that he was about to go soiling the cuffs of his trousers on the banquettes of Storyville. Since he had already traveled there on Ross's behalf, he might even be entertained.

This was not the case. Once they finished the day's business, Valentin announced in an offhand way that he would be taking part in an investigation of the murder of Burton Bolls.

The attorney's brow went into a furrow. "You can't do that."

"Pardon me?"

"You can't do that," Ross repeated in a sharper tone. "We can't have someone employed by this firm working for the likes of Tom Anderson." He laughed without a trace of humor. "My God! What the hell were you thinking?"

"I'm not employed by the firm," Valentin said carefully. "And I'm not working for Mr. Anderson. I'm not working for anyone. I'm just . . . I'm doing a favor."

"For who?"

"One of the madams. Her name's Miss An—"

"A madam!" Ross shot a glance at the door and lowered his voice a notch. "In one of those bordellos?"

Valentin wanted to say, *No, fool, in a grocery store.* Instead he said, "Yes, but she's—"

"I'm sorry, no." The attorney was abrupt. "We have a police department to handle crime in this city. Including Storyville."

"They don't do a very good job. *Especially* in Storyville."

"That's too bad. But you can't be on our books and work in that place, too."

"I told you, I'm not work—"

"Yes, yes, I heard. You're doing a favor. It amounts to the same thing. And we can't have it. It's Storyville, for God's sake!"

"Then what about James Beck?"

"That's different. We sent you. An unfortunate necessity." Ross tapped his pen. "By the way, have you settled with that woman?"

Valentin ignored the question. "The victim of this murder was a good citizen."

The attorney shrugged, clearly annoyed that they were still on the subject. "But not one of *our* good citizens." He waved a dismissive hand. "Just tell this madam that you're not available. She'll find someone else."

The detective spent a few seconds fidgeting in his seat as he digested this. Then he said, "I can't do that."

"Excuse me?"

"I promised her I'd help."

"Promised a madam." The attorney's voice was flat.

Valentin felt a prickling beneath his skin. "That's right."

Ross sat back, regarding him with vexation. Momentarily, he said, "Do the other firms know about this?"

Valentin shook his head. "Not yet, no."

"Well, I can promise they won't stand for it any more than we will," Ross said. "They represent important people, too."

"Yes, I've seen plenty of them. In the bordellos, having a high time."

The attorney's round face pinched at the sarcasm. "Doesn't matter. That's another subject entirely."

"Unless one of them is the next victim."

Ross tossed his pen aside and stood up, cutting a brusque hand through the air. "We're not going to have a debate here," he announced. "You can't work for this firm and in Storyville at the same time. It's that simple. If that's your intention, you might as well resign right now. And it'll be the same at those firms down the street. You can count on it." He tapped a hard forefinger on his desk blotter. "Is that what you want?"

Valentin paused for a few seconds, then said, "No."

Ross relaxed and nodded with sober relief. "Good. You're making the right decision. Let them handle their problems over there, and we'll handle ours."

The detective got to his feet.

"Keep me apprised on your cases," the attorney said.

Valentin walked out of the office, down the long hallway, through the golden doors, and onto the banquette. Fifty paces along, he stopped, turned around, strolled back into the building, and made his way to the office he had just left.

He rapped on the jamb. The attorney looked up from his papers.

"I meant to say yes," Valentin said.

"What?" Ross's face reddened in ire. "You better think about this. You're making—"

"And tell Senator Beck that if his son and his pals show up in Storyville again, they won't be in a condition to walk back out."

Samuel Ross stared as the Creole detective gave a short wave of farewell and disappeared from the doorway.

All the way home, Justine wondered if Louis was following her. It would be easy enough, a simple matter of swinging his beautiful car around and tracking the streetcar until she stepped down. Idly curious, she moved all the way to the rear and, standing next to a foul-smelling Negro, peered out the window. That she didn't see the automobile didn't signify. She knew men and could see through their ploys. Now her gut told her she'd encounter him again, if not this day, then some other.

Walking along Spain Street, she glanced back several times,

the last when she reached the street door of their building. Once upstairs, she put him out of her mind, knowing that the sly and handsome fellow who seemed so taken with her was likely at that very moment sniffing at some younger and prettier female. With distance, he became more of a frivolity, a butterfly that had flitted about her for a lazy hour. She had a more serious man to manage.

Valentin caught the St. Charles Line car to Canal Street. He stepped down and headed directly to Mangetta's, where he found the Sicilian getting the saloon ready for the day's business.

"*Gesu, sguardo che è qui,*" Frank exclaimed when Valentin walked through the door. "Twice in two days."

The detective stopped in his tracks. Was that true? It seemed like his visit with Nora Bolden had happened a week ago.

"I hope it's not too early for a drink," he said.

Frank put his broom up and went to the well to fetch a bottle. Valentin leaned an elbow on the bar and watched the Sicilian pour two glasses full. He downed his in one long swallow and held out his glass.

The saloonkeeper refilled it. "What happened?"

"I quit my job with the attorneys."

"When?"

"About a half hour ago."

"All of them?"

"She's going to kill me," Valentin moaned.

Frank laughed a little. "Eh, she'll understand. Tell her you'll be spending more of your time around here."

"She knows better," Valentin said, brooding. "She told me that if I come back, that means she can, too."

"Oh." Frank pondered gravely for a few quiet seconds, then sighed. "That's a good woman right there."

Valentin said, "I know." He sipped nervously under the watchful eye of the older man. "Maybe if I can get it cleaned up in a hurry, I can get hired on again." He took another shaky sip. "I've already got a good lead."

"What lead?"

"Do you know Honore Jacob?" Two Sicilian eyes rolled to the ceiling. "What?"

"He's *cafone,* that's all," Frank said. "What about him?"

"The killings were on his properties. All three."

The saloonkeeper said, "Well, that's a start, eh?"

"I hope so." As cool as it was in the room, Valentin felt himself starting to sweat.

"So maybe you should go to work," Frank said.

Valentin finished what was in his glass and set it down, his expression doleful. "I have to go home first."

Each had learned some things over the years he had trailed the Creole detective, and as he came closer to filling the shoes of a regular rounder, he'd picked up his own set of spies from among the small army of Storyville street urchins. He had been talking to a rounder in front of Fewclothes Cabaret when one of them ran by with the news that Mr. Valentin had been spotted back at Mangetta's. It could only mean one thing, and so he was waiting across the street from the saloon when Valentin stepped out the door. He fell into stride with an ease honed on much practice. The detective gave the younger man a sidelong glance and a brief nod that was just as casual.

Though it wasn't all the same. Each had grown up and fancied himself some kind of a player now. That was one thing. More to the point, he had also been a witness to one of the crimes. Valentin wondered if the kid realized that he might be in danger. For all any of them knew, the killer thought he'd been caught in the act. Valentin experienced a twinge of anxiety, as if Each was Beansoup again, the snot-nosed street rat who had slept on his couch and eaten at his table all those times. Each might think himself an operator, but he didn't have the wiles or taste for violence to fend off a maniac with murder on his mind.

The detective considered mentioning this to Justine, as a way to get her to let go of her anger. Then he was ashamed at the thought of using someone she cared for in such a manner. Was he truly that much of a coward?

Each left the detective to his thoughts as they sauntered south out of the District. From the look on his face, Mr. Valentin was wrestling with something serious, and he knew to wait. They were crossing Liberty Street, a block down from where the first body had been discovered, when the silence ended.

"How did you know I was over here?" Valentin said.

The kid shrugged. "I heard."

"I told Miss Antonia I'll see what I can do about these murders," the detective said in an absent way.

"I know about that, too," Each said.

The detective sighed and shook his head. His business was in the street. When they reached the next corner, he stopped to gaze across at the white walls of St. Louis No. 2.

Each went into a pocket of his jacket for a white envelope, which he handed over. "She said I was to give you this," he said.

Valentin felt the weight of the gold coins inside the envelope and understood. Accepting the payment made it official. He tucked the coins away. He could always give the money back.

Each hitched his shoulders manfully and said, "You going to need any help?"

Valentin said, "Tomorrow. Meet me right here at eleven o'clock." He gave a short wave, stepped into St. Louis Street, and headed home.

Just as Tom Anderson had his Sunday dinner, the Basin Street madams had fallen into the habit of a regular luncheon on Monday afternoons, and always at one of the better French Quarter restaurants. Lulu White, by far the most infamous of the lot, had begun the tradition long before Anderson started his, and though the other ladies were loath to fuel her vanity, all agreed that it was a good idea, if nothing more than to present a unified front. Each madam had a measure of clout; when they acted as a group, they were formidable.

On this date Miss Lulu was joined by her archrival, Josie Arlington, Countess Willie Piazza, Miss Antonia Gonzales, and Gipsy Shafer, who had recently moved into the circle by virtue of the patronage of a certain figure in Louisiana politics.

Even though Germaine's was closed on Mondays, the dining room had been opened for the occasion, and a chef came in on his day off to treat them to a small feast. They took the same corner table that Tom Anderson and his guests had occupied the day before; though George the headwaiter had thoughtfully removed the chair that the late Laurence Deveaux had used.

They maintained an unspoken agreement to lay aside whatever feuds and grudges they might be nurturing for these hours, making for a pleasant interlude, a rest in their daily battles. The luncheon usually began with idle casual bits of news shared over beverages and salads, then moved to weightier subjects through dinner and dessert. On this Monday, however, they wasted no time with trifles. Even before the wine had been poured, Lulu White looked around the table and said, "We have a problem."

"Three men dead in the space of a week," Miss Antonia said. "Yes, I'd say so."

Josie Arlington gave a cool shrug. "But only one on Basin Street."

"One is enough," Miss Lulu retorted. "And I can spit out my back window and hit any door on Liberty and that house on St. Louis, too. It doesn't matter. Anything that scares away the customers hurts everyone."

Except for Miss Josie, who wouldn't give the madam the satisfaction, the women nodded and murmured sober agreement. Though over the years, some of the things Lulu White had said and done had been nothing short of crazy, there was also no denying that she had a remarkable head for business. Her skills were not to be taken lightly.

Antonia Gonzales tried to cut into the ice between madams White and Arlington. "I heard they found a body on Robertson Street, too."

"Robertson Street!" Miss Lulu rolled her eyes.

"In a crib owned by Mr. Honore Jacob." That brought a silence. Miss Antonia continued, "If it's true, that's four dead men found on his properties."

"Then *he's* the one with the problem," Josie Arlington said dryly.

Countess Willie Piazza had kept silent to this point. Now she said, "What about Mr. Valentin? He's been away for a long time. Do you think he can take care of it?"

"If Justine lets him," Antonia Gonzales cracked, and the women shared a laugh. They'd all had occasion to follow the drama between those two characters.

As the discussion went around the table, it was agreed that even with St. Cyr back on the scene, each house would add security. There were more than enough unemployed Mississippi toughs lounging in the District that they could each hire one who was not quite as dumb as a tree stump and could be trusted to see customers out the door and to their waiting vehicles without letting them be murdered.

That matter addressed, the madams took turns reporting on the business at their mansions. Each described a slow spring and summer, a serious decline from the previous year. They didn't need any more reasons for customers to stay away.

Though, as Countess Willie Piazza correctly stated, "Where else would they go?"

Even as they all chortled, they realized it was no joke.

"What about Mr. Tom?" Gipsy Shafer said.

"What about him?" Josie Arlington sounded just a little

prickly. She had carried on an eccentric affair with Anderson, supposedly secret, though everyone in the District knew about it, including the King of Storyville's current wife, the former madam Gertrude Dix.

It was Lulu White who answered, looking Miss Josie squarely in the eye. "The question is, what's he doing about this? Why was Miss Antonia the one who brought Valentin back? Where was Anderson?" She plunged on heatedly before Josie could answer. "This is no time to kowtow to his damned pride. If he can't help, he needs to move out of the way."

It was fortunate timing that their entrées arrived, and with no small relief, they dropped the grim talk and went around the table, taking turns sharing the week's most delicious gossip.

It was late on Perrier Street when Malvina called Evelyne to the telephone. Though she kept her eyes averted, she noticed that the white woman did not speak a word after her initial greeting, only that she appeared pleased by what she'd heard from the caller.

"Mr. Jakes" called at least once a day. Whoever he was, he sounded young, and the maid assumed that Miss Evelyne had a lover. She would have been surprised if that hadn't been the case. Mr. Dallencort was twenty-some years his wife's senior and as frail as lace. His body was almost gone and his mind was not far behind. Why wouldn't a full-blooded woman of middle years want someone to pleasure her? Since her own husband had passed away, Malvina had her own gentleman friend who did just that.

Except that she never heard Miss Evelyne coo sweetly or giggle like a schoolgirl when this fellow called. Most often she was terse, whispering a few curt sentences and then clicking off. Without the slightest bit of hard evidence, Malvina understood that something strange was afoot.

This time whatever was discussed on the call put the lady of the house into a foul mood. After the call ended her mouth went tight and she paced around in silence. The maid knew better than to try and speak to her at times like this. Some minutes passed, and Malvina heard her let out a little snicker of surprise and blink as if something had just occurred to her.

With a bright smile, she said, "I'd like wine with dinner this evening, Malvina. The best bottle of burgundy in the rack."

When the word about Valentin St. Cyr made it downtown to police headquarters, the reaction was predictable: furtive whispers in hallway alcoves and behind closed doors, and none of it happy. The Creole detective was a thorn that everyone in those quarters thought had been plucked. One pillar of Tom Anderson's power and influence had been effectively removed, only to reappear, though it was true that this time St. Cyr was not in the King of Storyville's employ. Still, that he was on the scene, snooping and sniffing around, was quite enough.

For his part, Captain J. Picot threw a fit that sent his detectives and patrolmen ducking for cover. When he repeated the command that no one was to cooperate with St. Cyr, he made a point of singling out Detective McKinney with a stare of his dirty-penny eyes. Stalking back to his office, he slammed the door, rattling the windows.

The air was only slightly less tense on Spain Street. Valentin had arrived home to find Justine finally back from making market. The look she gave him when he walked in was blank, nesting somewhere between sad and angry. At least she was still there, ensconced in piles of green, red, and brown foodstuffs, and surrounded by garden smells of her country cooking. That was something of a good sign, unless it was to be his last meal.

The tension eased as they sat down to eat and then spent the evening hours idly, him reading and her sewing. They brushed past the subject of Storyville as if there was nothing to discuss. When it came time to go to sleep, he didn't have to be told to keep his hands to himself.

She knew what he had done, and he guessed that she now might be making a plan of her own. She might escape and she might stay put. Either way, she wasn't about to give him a clue. She had been a top-drawer sporting girl, which meant she was a good actress, certainly skilled enough to keep him guessing until she made her move.

ELEVEN

William Brown greeted a sunny Tuesday morning with the relief of a man taking the final steps of a perilous journey. Once it was over, he would spend his dawns somewhere far away, hundreds of miles from there, maybe more, depending on how the trains ran east and west through the night. There was nothing but water to the south, and he wasn't about to go north. It would suit him just fine if he never saw that damned river again. Or another city, either, with the noise and filth and staring faces.

He imagined the dry flatlands to the west, and he considered the low hills of Mississippi and Alabama. Finally, he thought about the deep piney woods of north Georgia and decided that would be a fine place to disappear, now and forever. He would go up on a mountaintop and never come down again.

The same orange sun cast its rays over the town of Jackson and through the east-facing windows of the colored ward of the State Hospital. The warm patterns of light creeping up the wall as the earth turned roused one patient, then the next, and on down the ward until the noise and motion had them all up and stretching and shuffling.

Charles went to the window, as he did every morning, feeling his way along with a brush of his fingertips, first on his bedsheets, then on the cold steel frame, then to the side table, finally on the windowsill. Gazing out, he scanned the horizon, again in vain, for the silver thread that led back to New Orleans. But the river was too far away.

If Valentin thought the worst was over, he was mistaken. He got up from what seemed a chilly bed, made the coffee, and began working on scrambled eggs diced with peppers, ham, and cheese. As soon as he heard Justine stirring, he threw the mixture into the cast-iron frying pan and began stirring with a wooden spoon. It was one of a few dishes he made with skill.

She appeared in the kitchen and took a seat at the table without a word, barely looking at him, though she did whisper a cool *thank-you* when he served her.

Over the next half hour, it dawned on him that she didn't want him there. She wore the same look on her face that she had the night before, a mask from behind which she sent out a slightly veiled message: She would prefer he cool his heels elsewhere. Making her breakfast hadn't mollified her; she saw it for the ploy that it was.

So he got dressed and out the door by nine o'clock, though he had no particular place to go. Most of uptown was still in bed. And except for Frank Mangetta, any friend he might have visited had left town. Ferd LeMenthe, or "Jelly Roll Morton," as he chose to be called, was off in Chicago playing his music and wooing the girls with his fancy-man charm. Bellocq the photographer had fallen ill and was in the care of his brother, a priest in Metairie. And, of course, Buddy Bolden was locked away in Jackson.

The thought of Bolden brought another flush of guilt. What to do about him? What if, for reasons Valentin couldn't fathom, his old friend was waiting for his visit? Common sense and past history told him that couldn't be, but still it niggled. Why now, after almost six years of silence?

Walking on, the detective decided that whatever the reason, it would have to wait. There were too many other troubles resting in his lap. He'd get to the hospital and Bolden soon enough. Or so he told himself.

He strolled to Chartres Street and stood on the corner watching the morning traffic, the streetcars and hacks and an ever-growing swarm of bouncing, rattling, smoking trucks and automobiles. In years before, when he had lived in the flat on Magazine, and during the months when he had stayed in the room over Mangetta's Saloon, he would start his days with a cup of coffee and the morning paper in a café or in one of the parks, a small ritual.

Now he'd feel uneasy doing even that; it would be an admission that he had surrendered what little was left of his former life. Though if Justine didn't let up on him, he reflected gloomily, he might as well move back to Mangetta's.

So he walked, one habit from the past that did not stir any guilt. Over the years he had easily paced off the entire city of New Orleans, from the river to the lake, from Metairie to Gretna, and more than once. When that wasn't enough, he took the ferry to the other side and walked some more. The only places he avoided were the First and Liberty neighborhood where he had grown up and the town of Algiers, where he had shot a man dead seven years before. That the cardsharp and gutbucket player McTier had deserved it didn't signify.

As the morning warmed, he continued west, in the general direction of Jackson Square, where there was bound to be something to divert him, even at that early hour.

Evelyne stepped into the small office off the foyer from where she ran the affairs of the home and closed the door behind her.

Malvina had placed the last two days' mail in a neat stack on the rolltop desk, and Evelyne sat down and began working through the pile. She knew without looking that most of the envelopes contained invitations to this event or that: a charity ball, an afternoon tea, a concert at the Opera House followed by a reception. There were nearly a dozen of them, and she dropped each one into the wastebasket. She would not be attending any events and wasn't going to bother with RSVPs, either. By the time the affairs rolled around, none of the upstanding ladies hosting them would want her anywhere near. She would be a pariah, shunned—this time by choice.

She imagined how their faces would pinch, aghast with disapproval. They would gasp, hands to their breasts, barely able to stutter out the volumes of gossip! *I always knew there was something about her. She never belonged . . .*

Well, they were right about that part, and she would give them more than enough reason for scorn. She would serve it up on a platter and she hoped they'd choke on it.

Lifting the hand piece from the cradle of the telephone box, she gave the operator a number, then waited. When the voice came on the line, she mouthed a quick set of instructions and just as quickly hung up.

Justine had changed from her nightdress into a white cotton shift that was now worn so thin it was near transparent, so much so that it outlined every curve and dimple on her body. No one except Valentin had ever seen her in it, and he loved the sight. She put it on sometimes when she wanted him in bed, and it never failed to rouse his attention. She wished she had thought to put it on before he left, just to torture him.

She opened the French door to the balcony to allow a breeze inside, then ambled back into the kitchen to wash the dishes. As she stood there, with water dappling the front of the shift, she heard the sound of an automobile engine gurgling from the corner of Dauphine Street. She knew instantly that it was him and stood perfectly still as the puttering grew louder before dropping and dying.

She felt an urge to go to the balcony and peek, but she stayed put, staring at nothing. Then she heard the street door open and footsteps start up the stairs, and realized that she was not dressed, not really, and was wearing a garment that would be indecent to anyone except Valentin.

The footsteps drew closer. She told herself that if she stayed still, he wouldn't know she was in. She thought about rushing to the bedroom to throw something on over the shift. She did neither. When the knock came, she laid the sopping dishcloth on the sideboard and padded barefoot to the front door.

She took him by surprise. Framed in the doorway, all but naked beneath a sheath of thin and sheer cloth and regarding him with dark serious eyes, she was the very image of a peasant girl, as exotic as a creature in the wild.

Justine noted with satisfaction that he actually took a step back and stopped breathing for a moment. Then he collected himself, and his eyes settled as they traced her from hips to chest before reaching her face.

"Good morning," he said. She didn't respond, one hand languidly draped on the doorknob. Louis held out a single rose, blushing peach. She accepted it without moving her eyes.

He said, "May I come in?"

She stared back at him, letting the seconds hang, and wondering if he had any idea what would happen if Valentin happened to come back and find him there. Bemused, she shook her head and said, "No."

He didn't appear surprised. With a curious smile, he said, "Well, then," and turned to descend the stairs, taking his time in case she changed her mind. She stood listening until the street door opened and his steps clicked on the banquette. She waited but did not hear the sound of an engine coughing to life.

Valentin arrived at the corner of St. Louis Street to find Each pacing up and down the banquette. The morning's long stroll had settled him down a bit. Maybe it really would be a simple matter of picking up a trail that would lead directly to the guilty party. If it turned out he was that lucky, he could lay the matter to rest and rush off to beg first Justine and then Sam Ross to forgive him his trespasses. He'd go down on bended knee and swear he'd never do it again. He would even promise to stay out of Storyville forevermore.

The thought had barely crossed his mind when its construction fell apart. He had burned the bridge to St. Charles Avenue. And fixing matters with Justine would not be simple.

As they made their way along Basin Street, Valentin explained briefly what he planned to do and what Each's part would be.

When he finished, the kid laid a hand on his arm and said, "I got it." His eyes shifted in such a sneaky cut that Valentin almost laughed. "You go ahead."

The detective nodded gravely, keeping in the spirit, and turned and walked away. Each idled, letting Mr. Valentin get a block or so on. He sauntered along in his path, his eye out for a tail, just like he'd been told to do.

The French Quarter was as peaceful as could be. Only a few blocks from the red-light district, and yet a world apart. This was the Vieux Carré, the old city, and they had long ago chased the madams, harlots, pimps, sports, and the clientele upon whom they preyed to the other side of the basin that had been dug for dirt to lift their fine homes out of the muck of swamp that had been downtown New Orleans.

Strolling through the Quarter, Valentin mulled the business with Honore Jacob. It was hard to accept that three men murdered at his properties was a coincidence. Though it could be so. Maybe Jacob's dice had come up snake eyes. From what he'd already heard, it was also possible that it was part of some macabre joke.

Valentin reached the corner and scanned the intersection until he saw the office on the upstairs floor over a ladies' hat shop, the windows painted with "H. Jacob & Son" in decorative letters. He lingered beneath a wrought-iron balcony across the street until he saw Each appear on the corner a block north, then cross over without as much as a glance in his direction. Valentin smiled; the kid had learned some things.

He found the street door unlocked and stepped inside to climb a staircase that had seen some use. On the second floor, he found a suite of three offices, along with a storage room in the rear. A woman of middle years and graying hair sat behind the desk in the first office.

She said, "Can I help you?"

Valentin stepped inside. "I'm here to see Mr. Jacob," he said, and received a questioning look. "It's in regard to the incidents in Storyville."

"Oh, that." The woman's face pinched. She stood up, said, "I'll be with you in a moment," and stepped around him and into the hallway.

Valentin heard a door close and, for the next half minute, the sounds of an argument. The woman's voice went one way, and a man's another, before winding down to a studied silence. The woman reappeared. Barely nodding toward the hallway, she said, "He'll see you now."

From the doorway Honore Jacob watched with terse eyes as Valentin approached. He waved the detective inside, and the two men shook hands. Jacob's grip was damp.

Everything about him was sweating, in fact. It was early on a fall morning, the ceiling fans were turning, and yet spots of perspiration had seeped through the front of the man's shirt and created arcs under his arms. His forehead was beaded, and Valentin spotted at least two rivulets from under his scalp that were heading in the direction of his cheeks. A damp handkerchief lay crumpled on his desk blotter.

Valentin had seen the landlord at a distance a few times, and
Jacob of course knew St. Cyr's reputation. And yet for all their
time in Storyville, they had never crossed paths. Now the landlord stared across the desk as if regarding some peculiar animal.

"You're back working for Anderson?" he said to open the
conversation.

"No, sir. Miss Antonia asked me to see if I could help out."

"Car. you?"

Valentin was amused by the directness. "That's why I'm
here," he said. "All the victims were found on your properties.
Three men dead and—"

"Four," the landlord said.

Valentin blinked. "Four?"

"You didn't know? They found a fellow on Robertson Street."

The detective took a few seconds to digest this. "So you own
cribs, too?"

"A few, yes." Jacob appeared only slightly abashed. "Anyway,
they dragged a body out of one of them the other day. That
makes four. Now what the hell do you think of that?" It was a
general expression of exasperation.

"Do you have enemies?"

"I got certain citizens I don't get on with," the landlord said.
"Everyone does. That's business. This is something else. I think
some maniac is trying to destroy me. By murdering people. God
almighty!"

Valentin, watching for signs of phony rage, saw none. Jacob
was clearly distressed. At the same time, his frustration did not
earn him any sympathy. Valentin had taken a dislike to the man
the moment he walked in the door. Jacob exhibited all the features of a sneak: eyes that flicked constantly, jowls that quivered,
a loose mouth, and a spike of a nose, ready-made to stick into
other people's business. His voice went in and out of a whine that
was like a train passing through a tunnel. That didn't make him
an automatic fake.

Behind the plaintive tone was a refrain the detective had heard before. Jacob's family had come from money, old French money that had been squandered away. Though he had become rich again, he was one of those who believed the world owed him the repayment of the fortune that his ne'er-do-well brother had lost. From the talk around the District, he tried to make up for some of it by gouging his tenants on one end and shorting them on the other.

Valentin would have avoided this bellyacher, except that now Jacob's trouble was Storyville's. So there he sat, listening to another stanza of mournful blues. On and on it went.

"So you have no idea who might want to harm you this way," he cut in, as much to get the landlord to stop talking as to move the discussion forward.

"I don't," he said. "I run a fair business. I pay my help the same as everyone else."

Valentin dropped his voice a notch. "Anything personal?"

"Personal?" The hooded eyes blinked. "What do you mean?"

"Such as a woman. Gambling. Dope. Anything like that."

Jacob drew back, incensed. "No, nothing."

The detective believed it. Jacob didn't strike him as one who might dally, other than perhaps the once-a-week attentions of a girl in one of the houses. Storyville landlords often received such services as part of the rent. Though it could be a dicey arrangement. Properties had been lost by way of the machinations of a crafty madam and a few skilled harlots.

Not Honore Jacob, though. He seemed not to share the French gene for pleasure and was more the kind of money-grubber who would be too cagey about his riches to fall for such schemes. The Jacobs had already lost too much.

Valentin realized shortly that the landlord, plainly baffled by the horrible turn of events, didn't know a thing that would help him. He waited for Jacob to take a breath, then excused himself and rose from the chair.

"I'll need a list of all your properties," he said.

Jacob stopped to eye him warily. "What for?"

"I want to make sure they're secure. If I can do that, and we have a murder somewhere else, then maybe it's not your problem after all."

The landlord considered, then flicked a hand toward the front office. "My wife has all that."

His *wife;* that explained the arguing. Without offering his hand, he thanked Jacob for his time.

"So you'll get this fellow?" the landlord said anxiously. "I mean get rid of him?"

Valentin said, "He has to be stopped. For everyone's good." He paused to note that for all his troubles, Jacob had not offered as much as a dime to speed his efforts.

Mrs. Jacob turned over the list of addresses, making her disapproval of the entire matter plain. Valentin thanked her and made his exit. When he got to the banquette, he could feel eyes resting on him from the window above.

Each did his part and stayed out of sight all the way to the corner of North Rampart Street.

"So?" he said.

"So now we go to work."

The kid winked and grinned with delight.

They first visited Mary Jane Parker's house and spent a half hour questioning the madam and her girls about Allan Defoor. Valentin listened closely, and Each ogled the doves in their kimonos as Miss Parker described Defoor as a regular customer who never caused any kind of a stir. He was one in a thousand, and there wasn't one remarkable thing about him.

Valentin turned his attention to the four women now lounging behind the madam's chair in various states of undress. It was still early for them.

"Did Mr. Defoor ever mention having trouble with anyone?"
The girls all shook their heads solemnly.

"Problems with gambling? Or dope? Maybe some woman?"
One of the girls snickered. "He wasn't that sort."

Another one said, "He'd just have a drink, come upstairs, and then be on his way."

"He was always *quick*," a third said, and the others laughed.

Valentin asked that the girls be sent away so he could speak to the madam in confidence. Miss Parker could not name anyone who had a personal grudge against her. Indeed, she was a God-fearing woman who attended Mass at St. Ignatius every Sunday and paid her bills on time.

She regarded Valentin in turn. "You ain't got any idea why this happened?"

"I do," the detective said, hedging. "I just don't know enough right now." He shifted in his chair. "Speaking of bills, how do you get along with Mr. Jacob?"

Miss Parker shrugged. "He ain't no worse than the others. He won't do much unless I make noise. I ain't seen him in a year. Someone comes by to collect the rent the first of the month, that's all."

Valentin thanked her for her time, and he and Each went out onto the banquette.

"Now what?" the kid said.

"Now we pay a visit to Robertson Street."

Each groaned in disgust.

"We have to," Valentin said, and explained about the body that was found there.

It was still early enough that few of the crib girls were working, and the ones that were hadn't started drinking or smoking or whiffing, so they didn't have the energy for more than a feeble "Hey, sweetheart . . . Come on over here . . ."

Valentin and Each strolled along, stopping now and then to question one of the girls, dropping a Liberty quarter or two to help loosen a tongue. Except for their filthy flesh, information was all they had to barter, and the Creole detective had always found the Robertson Street banquette a good place to learn things he didn't know.

Not this time, though. It was true there had been a body, but no one knew the dead man and there had been no witnesses to his killing. There were some whiskey-laden whispers about more information for sale, but Valentin divined that the harlots were only angling for more coins. Before they left, he thought to put out the word that he was to be alerted if any gangs of white boys from the good side of town came around.

St. Cyr was on the prowl, and Captain J. Picot sent orders down the line for the officers in that precinct to report in. By early afternoon he knew that the Creole detective had spent a half hour at Mangetta's, sharing an early drink with the proprietor. He had been spotted some time later crossing over in the French Quarter with the kid who called himself Each.

Picot guessed that St. Cyr had visited Honore Jacob's place of business. Then came word that the pair had reappeared in Storyville, first stopping at the house on Liberty, then heading for the filthy bottom on Robertson Street, where they walked up and down the banquette, questioning the girls about the man found dead in one of the cribs.

The captain could see what St. Cyr was up to and accorded him a moment of grudging respect. The Creole hadn't forgotten his lessons and was building his investigation one careful piece at a time, leaving no stone unturned. If only Picot had a man as good. The only one who showed any promise was McKinney, and he was far too loose a cannon to be trusted. The day would come when that young officer would find himself without a badge. Picot would see to it personally.

He pushed that notion aside and fixed his attentions on the killings. The likelihood that Jacob had roused someone's wrath had not escaped him. If not, why dead bodies at four of his properties in the space of a week? Picot had never paid much attention to the landlord, other than to send a sergeant around when Jacob "forgot" to pass along his operating fee, the graft due the police precinct. The officer collecting would always relay how much Jacob complained, as if for some reason he should not have been required to offer a contribution to the men who protected him and his properties.

Gazing out the window, Picot grew inflamed, a more or less constant condition when St. Cyr was about. None of his detectives had any suspects or motives in the killings, not even McKinney, and he knew the Creole could break the case wide open in no time. Storyville had been St. Cyr's territory, and he knew it down to the last cobblestone. It would be another black eye for the police department if he ran this murdering bastard to the ground. Picot wondered again if St. Cyr had been put on earth to make him look bad.

He let out a sigh of frustration, a man who knew he couldn't match an adversary but still had to climb in the ring.

He turned away from the window and went to the office doorway. Detective Weeks sat at his desk, plunking laboriously on a shiny black Remington typing machine. Picot looked around the room.

"Where's McKinney?"

Weeks hit a key and stopped. "At the morgue, I believe."

"What's at the morgue?"

"A body that turned up in that crib on Robertson Street."

"Who sent him down there?"

Weeks looked at the captain. "Didn't you?" he said.

The morgue attendants exchanged an eye-rolling glance when McKinney stepped through the door. The cop had become a regular visitor, and every time he showed up, they found themselves working harder than they were used to, rolling gurneys in and out of the cold locker like valets attending to some Garden District matron who couldn't decide which dress to buy for the ball. McKinney wanted to see every male victim of violence brought in during the last twenty-four hours. Each one had to be checked top to toe, front and back, for any telltale cuts.

If they thought McKinney's visit was an annoyance, it got even worse when the door opened and a man of just under medium height with olive-tinged skin and cool gray eyes walked in, trailed by a short, skinny fellow with a faint trace of a mustache above his lips.

James McKinney looked up from the body with only minor surprise. "Mr. St. Cyr."

"Detective," Valentin said.

The attendants came to attention. They knew the name and the reputation.

Valentin ignored them and nodded toward the cadaver. "Who do we have here?"

McKinney said, "Body that was discovered in a crib on Robertson Street."

Valentin stepped up to the gurney and gave the victim a once-over, his eyes drawn immediately to the line on his face.

"Just like the other ones," McKinney murmured.

"Except that it's straight across."

"Does that mean anything?"

Valentin said, "I don't know." Though he had never been one for sharing information with the police, he felt he could trust this particular cop. With a glance over his shoulder, he said, "The crib where he was found was owned by Honore Jacob."

The officer raised an eyebrow. "He owns the properties where Defoor, Bolls, and Deveaux were killed, too."

"Seems someone has it in for that man," Valentin said.

McKinney kept his eyes on the corpse. "You got any idea who this fellow might be?"

"Not yet," Valentin said. "But I will soon enough." He knew

McKinney was dying to ask how exactly he'd manage that but couldn't get up the nerve. For Valentin's part, he wasn't sure where the new detective's loyalties were lying at the moment and kept his own counsel.

As if he had read these thoughts, McKinney said, "You know Captain Picot would have me skinned if he knew I was talking to you."

"Well, no one's going to say anything about either one of us being here." He made sure it was loud enough for the two men in the corner to hear him.

They spent a few minutes more examining the body. Each hung back. He had seen enough dead people in the last few days. There was nothing new anyway, and no way of telling if he had been killed in the crib or placed there after the crime, and it didn't matter.

McKinney asked if he had visited the scene.

"I went by," Valentin said. "There was nothing. Just another crib."

He stepped away from the gurney to join Each near the door. Detective McKinney pulled the linen sheet over the victim's face and signaled the attendants that he was finished. The younger of the two stepped up and pushed the gurney into the cold locker.

Valentin addressed the other fellow. "No one's come to claim the body?"

"Not when I was here."

The Creole detective turned to McKinney. "And no missing persons reports?"

"None that fit him," McKinney said.

"Well, there was that one fellow."

The three men looked over at the junior attendant, who was standing in the locker doorway with one hand on the gurney.

"What's that?" Valentin said.

"Some fellow come by yesterday morning. He opened the

door, but he didn't come in. He said, 'You got a body out of a crib in here?' And I said, 'We brought this one off Robertson Street.'"

The attendant glanced at his partner and received a hard look.

"Describe him," Valentin said.

"I really don't remember," the attendant said vaguely.

Valentin paused, then unwound from his slouch against the wall and walked over to the senior attendant. He went into his vest pocket for a Liberty dollar and handed it over.

"There's something there for both of you." He faced the other man. "Describe him."

The attendant waited for his partner to nod to say, "He was about my height. White man, but not pale. Red-faced, like he been out in the sun some. Dark hair. A mustache like this." He drew a curve over his lip from one jawline to the other. "Don't recall anything else."

"How was he dressed?"

"Regular clothes. Shirt and trousers. Oh, yeah, he wore spectacles."

Valentin waited to see if there was more. The attendant shrugged. "Thank you for the information," he said. He produced another half-dollar and flipped it through the air. "You don't tell anyone we were here. Understood?"

"No, sir, no one," the older attendant answered with a greasy grin that said he would probably do exactly the opposite.

The three men filed out the door, along the damp stone hallway, and up four steps into the cobbled alley. There, in the autumn sunlight, Valentin had a strange sense of stepping back into a role that he had played often before. It was comforting and troubling, all at the same time. Whether or not it was connected, he was feeling ravenous and thought about the restaurants in that neighborhood.

He wanted to ask McKinney to join them, but knew the policeman would have to decline. Still, he had an ally, all the better

because the officer worked directly under Picot. He made a point
of shaking McKinney's hand and saying, "Thank you," in a voice
anyone within a hundred feet would have heard. Leaning closer,
he said, "I'm going to have a man on every property that Honore Jacob owns. Starting tonight."

He released his grip. McKinney saluted with a finger to the
brim of his hat, turned, and strolled out of the alley and onto Tulane Avenue.

Valentin looked at Each and said, "Where can we get a good
dinner around here?"

The kid winked wisely and crooked a finger for the Creole
detective to follow him.

They found a table at a diner on Common Street and ordered
from the simple bill of fare.

Each said, "Guess that was a waste of time, then."

Valentin said, "Not really. Sometimes it's what you don't find
out."

The kid's mustache twitched. "What's that mean?"

"I can say for sure that the victims don't matter. It has nothing to do with them, except bad luck to be in the killer's path. It
has something to do with Jacob. But he says no one's got any
kind of grudge against him."

"You believe that?"

Valentin said, "Not really. A landlord? I'm sure more than a
few people ain't going to care for him."

"But you got no idea who it could be."

"I don't. Only that he doesn't care what he does. And that
he's had good luck. But it doesn't matter. It's already gone too
far. I have to stop him."

"How you going to do that?"

Valentin thought for a moment. "I'll have to set a trap."

Over plates of shrimp, boudin, chicken, and rice, the detective
explained what he wanted to do and the part Each would play.

The kid puffed with self-importance, and Valentin once again entertained a moment of worry that he could be putting him in the path of a dangerous man. He had done it once before, and it was only by chance that things hadn't gone worse. In fact, Each—Beansoup, then—had come out of that bloody drama a hero. It had been, what? Six years ago? Seven? Valentin shook his head over the time that had slipped by.

Meanwhile, Each was thinking out loud as he ran down names of street Arabs he could call on for help. "Little Hand . . . Boozoo . . . Tony the Wop . . . Black Jimmy . . ."

"Now, listen to me," Valentin said, taking a short pencil from his inside pocket, along with the list of Jacob's properties. Flipping the paper, he drew a quick map of Storyville, a grid of five vertical and six horizontal lines that defined a twenty-block square.

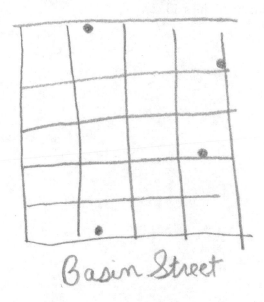

He placed a dot near Liberty Street between Conti and St. Louis, a second on Robertson, a third on Basin Street, and a last one on St. Louis past Villere. "These mark where the bodies were found." He studied it for a few seconds more, then drew X's at different locations. "So I want someone at these corners. They all need to stay in sight of each other, so that they can pass signals."

Each studied the drawing, his brow furrowing and thin mustache twitching some more.

"I'll have a man at Jacob's properties, just in case," Valentin said.

Each frowned. "What about me?"

"I need you traveling between those corners," the detective said. "The last thing we want is one of these characters falling asleep or deciding he's had enough and going home." It was a sly appeal to Each's sense of authority, and a way of placing him in danger.

"Can you help me?" Valentin said.

Each sniffed gravely and impaled a slice of sausage as if he was spearing the perpetrator dead in his tracks. "This fellow's as much as finished," he said.

TWELVE

Valentin walked in a little after five o'clock, having made his rounds and left messages for the men he would need for the night's work.

Justine greeted him curtly and asked if he was hungry. He told her he had taken a late lunch in the city, which irked her. She had been looking forward to not cooking his dinner and had to settle for serving cool looks and a colder shoulder. He got the message and kept his head down and eyes averted like a dog caught killing chickens.

It didn't make her feel any better. Beneath her anger at his foolishness was the return of an old fear from their years on Magazine Street when he ventured out after some evildoer. Wondering if this was the night that his fabled skills would fail him, or if he would just get unlucky and end up dead, leaving her alone and grieving. Along with the dread had come the secret, shameful notion that it would also bring a certain relief because she would never have to go through it again.

It was all the worse this time because he was nervous, too. He'd been out of the game for so long that he had to be wondering if he had gone soft working for the hoity-toity lawyers on St. Charles.

In any case, he wasn't the type to sit around fretting over it. She heard him moving about in the bedroom and pictured him opening the dresser drawer to retrieve his weapons: the Iver Johnson pistol in its oily cloth, the leather-wrapped whalebone sap that he tucked in the back pocket of his trousers, and the stiletto in the sheath strapped to his ankle. She had watched him perform the ritual a hundred times. He was always so meticulous about donning the tools of his trade that it reminded her of a priest at Mass.

She heard the drawer close and he was standing in the door-way, wearing the expression that told her his thoughts had turned to what was waiting twelve blocks away. Though he was ready to go, he waited to see what she would do.

What she did was treat him to a long look. "I guess I shouldn't stay up for you," she murmured.

"It's likely to take all night."

"And how long until it's over?"

"Not long. This one's a fool. Hell, Each almost caught him in the act." He paused, then said, "I intend to finish it tonight."

"You promise?"

Before he could come up with an answer, she had stepped into the bedroom and closed the door.

Valentin remembered reading how some wild animals could ma-neuver by smells that had been on the ground for weeks. And so it was for him with Storyville. Walking the streets, he happened upon landmarks, one after the next. He saw a familiar cellar door here and a hitching post there. He passed a storefront that hid a fencing operation and a laundry that stayed busy long into the night as an opium den. He could still locate loose bricks where contraband might be hidden.

As the sun was going down, he made a complete circuit of the front blocks of the District, ambling along Basin Street all the way to St. Louis Cemetery No. 2, then coming around on

Franklin to Canal. He covered Liberty, Marais, and Villere in this manner, with jaunts up and down the crossing streets of Iberville, Bienville, and Conti. It took up the better part of two hours, and when he was finished, he had a sense of reclaiming his turf. He had drawn Storyville about him like a well-worn suit of clothes.

At that moment Honore Jacob was making his rounds, letting himself be seen perched high up in the backseat of his Buick like some lord. Louis was driving and looking none too thrilled about it. He would have preferred a racier roadster over the heavy, slow phaeton, but it was better than a carriage.

At the father's direction, they passed all of their properties except for the line of cribs on Robertson, then made a final pass down Basin Street.

Louis's eyes flicked at the facades of the mansions, back in business without a worry in the world. When they reached the corner of St. Louis and the white walls of No. 2, he swung the big polished wood wheel, and they crossed the tracks to return to the French Quarter.

The car came to a stop on Royal, and Honore climbed down with some difficulty, instructing his son to take the Buick to the garage on the corner of Chartres Street.

Louis nodded, drove off, and once his father was out of sight, took a turn and made his way to the river and then along Decatur Street. At the intersection of Spain Street, he pulled to the curb and hopped down to the banquette. With the falling night as cover, he made his way two blocks up and stood across from the building with the number 627 on the doorframe. There was a light in the front window, and after a few minutes, he saw a silhouette pass by.

Justine wanted nothing less than to spend the evening thinking about Valentin prowling Storyville and was glad that Tuesday was the night she posed at the university.

She took another bath to wash away the day's sweat and put on a clean camisole and drawers under a day dress. She tied her hair into a long Indian braid and picked a boater from a peg on the wall next to the front door. Standing before the mirror, she was pleased by the image she presented, a young woman of color in common clothes. No one passing on the street would imagine where she was bound.

The day was fading as she stepped onto the banquette to begin a slow five-block stroll to the streetcar stop on Esplanade.

She sensed his presence before she saw him and so was not surprised when he materialized out of the shadows across the street. Without a word, she continued along the banquette in the direction of Elysian Fields, her only giveaway a quick sweep to make sure the street was empty of any nosy witnesses. And so it was, as Louis Jacob stepped into the street and closed at a gentle angle to intercept her.

By the time she reached the corner of Marigny, she decided she'd had enough of his gambit and turned around, surprising him. He stopped and raised his hands, and in the next moment his gaze raked her again from hips to shoulders and to face, which he found set in a frown of displeasure.

She wasn't about to break the silence and stood glaring until he said, "Excuse me," a weak entrée.

"What are you doing here?" she said.

"I'd like to offer you a ride."

Justine was confounded, wondering if somehow he knew of her destination. She watched him for another few seconds, then looked around deliberately. "Ride in what?"

"It's down around the corner," he said, and pointed. When she didn't move, he said, "Do you really want to spend an hour in streetcars on a night like this?"

His appeal to common sense caused her to laugh lightly. Before she could refuse him, he started backing away. "I'll go fetch it," he said. "If you want to wait for me, it will be my pleasure to carry you wherever it is you need to go. If not . . ."

He smiled his pretty smile and was around the building on the corner before she could stop him.

In fact, she didn't want to. Along with a girlish wish to be pampered, she considered the three rickety, rattling cars that would be required to get her to the end of St. Charles Avenue. And she was curious about the game this dandy was playing. He could no doubt bed younger, prettier girls if he put his charm to work. Or he could afford the company of an octoroon from one of the Basin Street mansions. And yet he had come buzzing around her . . .

She was caught in the glare of headlights as the automobile pulled up. The Buick sported a huge windshield trimmed in gold plate, like all the metal moldings and fixtures. The steering wheel was made of polished hardwood, and Louis's gloved hands lay on it easily. In one jump he was at her side and helping her up into the high seat.

"Where to this evening?" he said.

"St. Charles," she said. "To Tulane."

"Avenue?"

"University."

He didn't inquire why she wanted to ride all the way to the west side of the city and the venerated college with its green lawns, live oaks, and stone buildings. He simply nodded and put the transmission in gear.

Tall windshield or no, it was breezy at that speed, and she took a moment arranging her shawl to cover her throat and then patting her hat to make sure it wouldn't blow off.

She had never been one to care about wealth, having seen enough to know that it meant little except that a man had a certain knack for collecting money. Too often a gentleman was so intent on his riches that he cared nothing for anything else. Still, she was not immune when money was coupled with charm. This fellow Louis, at least six years her junior, was turning it on, all languid and flirtatious as he tried to snare her in a sweet trap. It was a ridiculous ploy that she could see, and yet she was riding across town with him like some debutante.

Lost in these thoughts, it took her a minute to notice that he had turned north instead of south along the river.

He caught her questioning look and said, "We've got time to spare," and before she could stop him, he had turned onto Basin Street.

They motored along the boulevard, passing the first of the mansions, the firehouse, French Emma Johnson's, Fewclothes Cabaret, and then the top of the line: Mahogany Hall, Countess Piazza's, and Antonia Gonzales's. (Did he slow down or was that her imagination?) She kept her gaze averted.

The Buick settled to a stop for the crossing traffic at the corner of Iberville, and she saw Louis gazing intently at the facade of Anderson's Café. The intersection cleared, he pushed the accelerator handle, and the car lurched forward. A minute later they turned into the steady flow on Canal Street, and then right again onto St. Charles. Neither one of them spoke until they crossed over Poydras, and Louis smiled and said, "Nice evening for a ride," all idle and innocent.

The trees had begun to shed their leaves, and as they drove along the boulevard, the big tires kicked up little tempests of red and gold that swirled beneath the streetlights. It was an entrancing sight, and Justine was dazzled.

It lasted only another block. Crossing Nashville Avenue, the line of trees and tempests of leaves gave way, and the old stone facades of first Loyola and then Tulane came into view. Justine directed Louis around the corner at Audubon Place. College boys strolling on the banquettes stopped to stare at the fine automobile, some no doubt noting that the driver was about their age.

She asked him to turn on Broadway and then stop at the corner of Plum Street.

"This is fine," she said, and lifted her skirts to climb down.

He hopped onto the running board and arrived on her side in time to lend a hand. With her elbow resting in his palm, he looked about the street and said, "Here?"

"I'm not going far," she said. "Thank you for the ride."

Louis studied her face for a few seconds, as if trying to read something there. She was giving nothing away, and he released her arm, tipped his hat, and ambled around to the driver's side.

Justine arranged her shawl and started down the narrow avenue. She didn't turn or even steal a glance back when she heard the sound of gears engaging and the Buick rolling away over the cobbles.

Having him deposit her on that corner was no ruse. Given the nature of her visit, she was required to arrive by a back street. Though not a secret, the class she visited was also not advertised in the catalog of courses. Only senior classmen were allowed to enroll, by invitation by the professor and with the permission of their parents.

As usual, one of the students was waiting on the winding walk to escort her inside. He held the basement door open and then accompanied her along the corridor to the professor's cramped office and workroom, which in turn was attached to the studio.

Professor Deville—a small, round, bearded man of seventy-one—had been a caller when she first arrived at Miss Antonia's. She had been surprised when he told her that he taught drawing classes at the university, and flattered when she saw how his artist's eye admired her figure. All the more so when he proposed that she pose for his master class.

During her first two visits, she sat on the stool in a camisole-like affair of thin, clinging silk called a "chippie." For her third session, she settled herself and then removed her wrap to reveal that she was naked underneath. To their credit, the young men gaped only briefly, then resumed their sober expressions. Though of course the professor was standing by, watching for juvenile mischief.

A young woman posing nude was a scandalous secret that the university officials chose to ignore. It had been going on for over three years, and no one had made them stop.

Professor Deville offered Justine the customary cup of tea, and they chatted for a few moments. The old man detected something distracting her this evening but was too much the gentleman to pry. When she finished her tea, he opened the door to the dressing room that was really just a large closet. She emerged a few minutes later, wrapped in a clean sheet and her feet bare, and the two of them passed through the door and into the studio.

The students were at their easels, looking serious. Justine stepped up onto the foot-high riser and settled on the cushioned stool that had been placed at its center. Deftly, she dropped the sheet from her shoulders. She felt the eight pairs of eyes roaming on her, inch by inch. If there was any lust in that hushed space, she didn't feel it. The young artists set to work and she relaxed.

They stopped at the half hour so everyone could stretch. She had just taken a seat again when she sensed something different about the room. With a shift of her eyes, she caught sight of the figure standing just inside the door. It came as no surprise to see Louis Jacob studying her with a fixed gaze, as if he was drawing her in his mind.

At eight o'clock Valentin arrived at Mangetta's to find Each pacing the banquette. The detective led him inside to the bar.

Frank greeted them with wide eyes, an opera buffoon. "Now he's out at *night*? There's gonna be trouble . . ."

Valentin bent his head to whisper in the Sicilian's ear.

Mangetta was dubious. "You think you're going to catch him that easy?"

Valentin shrugged. "He hasn't been smart so far. Just lucky."

The saloonkeeper looked unconvinced as he went about pouring two brandies. When he moved off to serve another customer, Valentin turned to Each.

"Are your people ready?" he asked. The response was one raised eyebrow and a curl of a mustachioed lip. "Just checking."

Out on the banquette, Valentin stopped to pat his pockets one more time before crossing the street with Each trailing along. He left the kid at the intersection of Iberville and Liberty and walked the rest of the way to Basin Street and Miss Antonia's alone. He found his man, a onetime prizefighter named Lyles, on the back gallery. They talked briefly, and the detective went inside to find the madam.

After a few minutes with her, he visited the three other addresses, ending at the one that was most in danger as the only property of Jacob's that had yet to serve as the scene of a crime. It was a small but tidy tenement house run by a woman named Marie Helton.

A former beat cop named Whaley was waiting. Valentin had found him some work after he got in trouble with the brass for helping him on a case. His police career was finished, so the detective sent him to a local ward leader who needed a right-hand man. Whaley never forgot the favor and was at Valentin's disposal whenever there was a need.

They hadn't seen each other in almost three years, and Whaley smiled with delight as the detective mounted the steps to the gallery.

"It's true, then." He grabbed Valentin's hand. "You're back."

"For now," the detective said.

They surveyed the street. Whaley was flexing his fingers in anticipation. "You think he'll make a try this evening?"

"I hope so. I can't be spending my nights out here."

Whaley smiled in the darkness. "Why? You got trouble at home?"

"I will if we don't finish this in a hurry." He knocked on the door.

Mrs. Helton was broad of face, bosom, and bottom, certainly hefty enough to take care of herself. She listened as Valentin spoke, her eyes shifting back and forth between the two men, and became indignant when the detective told her what she might expect.

"Son of a bitch better not come 'round here," she said, with just a bit of brogue in her voice.

"We want him to, ma'am," Valentin said, and then told her the rest of it.

The madam shrugged, then nodded in agreement and closed the door. Valentin shook Whaley's hand before descending the steps to the banquette.

He began another circuit of the District, mostly keeping in sight of either one of Each's corners, checking the faces of passersby. Among his skills was the ability to read a person at a quick glance. He knew that if he caught sight of a certain light there, he'd have his prey. He understood just as well that the chances of that happening were slight. There were hundreds of men in the District at that hour, and every one was a stranger.

Still, he had gazed into the faces of enough lunatics to recognize the signs. And they didn't include the demonic glare of the villains on the stage or in the moving pictures. No, the eyes of the deranged were electric with some unslaked fire or dead and distant, as if the human had moved out, leaving an empty husk that was still capable of bloody mayhem.

But so far it was the usual characters parading the banquettes: rounders who had just finished a visit with a favored girl and were heading off for a night of gambling; the nervous young men without sweethearts; older gentlemen who had almost per-

fected invisibility as they made quick trips from automobiles to
the front doors of bordellos; and finally, those dregs that wandered by like rags blown by a breeze. It was likely that Valentin's
man would be hiding in this last group, and so he scanned faces,
one after another.

He finished his first circuit in an hour without seeing anyone
suspicious or hearing a whistle of alarm. This was no surprise;
another sense told him that the killer wasn't there yet.

Justine half expected that Louis would be waiting for her, either
in the shadows next to the building or at the streetcar stop. Now
that he had surveyed her body, he might think he could possess
her in another way. It would make for an interesting evening.

But he was neither outside the door nor on the St. Charles
Avenue banquette. So she waited in the cool evening until the
streetcar rattled to a stop and climbed on.

Once aboard she peered out the back window. That she
didn't see the red Buick didn't mean there wasn't a part of her
that wanted him to be trailing her, more foolishness that made
her smile at her reflection in the glass.

She stepped down to change cars at North Rampart Street.
There was a faster route to the east end of the city, but she decided to ride by Storyville again. She could see between buildings
the turrets atop the mansions of Lulu White, Josie Arlington, and
Countess Piazza and knew that Valentin was at that moment
moving about the streets. She imagined him slipping in and out
of the falling shadows on the trail of a murderer.

In the next moment, she realized that it could already be
over. Valentin claimed the man was a fool, no match for the
skills of a seasoned detective. So he might well have finished it.
And there was always the chance that it was finished with a different outcome.

As the car left the District behind and crossed over St. Louis
Street, she caught a flash of bright red in the corner of her eye

and turned to the rear window. Whatever it was had disappeared, along with the lights of Storyville.

William Brown had packed his knife and his revolver and slipped out to make his quiet way down the back stairs to the street. He was winding his way to the end of the story, a relief. After this night his work would be done.

And then what? There'd be no going back to the hospital and its catalog of tortures. No, he would ride a train and disappear into the night. Wherever he landed, no one would know him, his history, nor even his true name. He would become a nobody.

He crossed into Storyville by way of one of the alleys, never using the same one. This time it was far to the back of the District, running between Claiborne and Robertson. The usual gangs of rats scrabbled in the dank hollows. Thirty paces on he came upon a man standing with a woman on her knees before him. When the fellow looked around, William averted his eyes and kept on.

At the end of the alley, he happened on another woman, this one with her back against the wall of a building, her petticoats hiked up, and her legs spread wide and head lolling as she pissed a drunken puddle in the dirt. She ignored him, too.

William was just about to take a step onto the banquette when he sensed something amiss. He stood still for a few seconds, leaned out, then drew back. Even though the traffic on the street continued to eddy, as men came and went looking for or after having a woman, his gut told him that something was not right.

Maybe it was the nights in the hospital ward with all those crazed animals on the prowl. Or that his brain lurked so close to his skull, allowing him to hear and see what others could not. Whatever the reason, every nerve was signaling trouble.

Poking his head from the darkness, he searched the street in both directions again. On the next corner, a street Arab lounged as if waiting for some rounder to whistle him up. But the kid didn't strike the right lazy posture and was not looking at the back of any of the houses from which a summons might come. Instead, he was facing the street and watching for something or someone—most likely, William Brown.

He retreated into the alley and found a place to hide in the recess of the rear door of one of the buildings. Wiping the sweat from his face, he waited for his mind to tell him what to do. He had been paid and had instructions. Tonight was the night, and then it was to be over. But then he heard that other grim warning: *Don't get caught.*

He thought about chancing a dash for the house. Maybe no one would spot him, and he could catch a victim and finish his work in a hurry. Or he could wait there to see if the sentry would give up and go away. He couldn't decide, and his brain ached as he slumped down and laid his head across his folded arms.

As he slouched, his thoughts wandered. Presently, he saw a pattern etched in light lines against a dark background begin to tilt and realized that he did not need to rush this business and get caught. Time and space were moving, fluid things. He had tomorrow night and the night after that one and he could take a different path through the streets, too. Just the slightest nudge to the design would throw whoever was stalking him into confusion and when that happened, he could walk in, do his work, and then escape for good. It could be just that easy.

With that thought in mind, he folded deeper into himself and fell into a doze.

As the hours dragged and the streets stayed quiet, Valentin made rounds to keep his men on their toes. Walking the banquettes, he heard not a sound nor caught movement to give his prey away. He guessed that the fellow might have seen one of the guards, realized what it meant, and bolted away.

Night sidled into morning, and with the first slate-tinted glimmers of dawn, he caught up with Each and told him to send his pals home. At Antonia Gonzales's he used the telephone to call Whaley and the others and ask them to be back at the same time that next evening.

As tired as he was, he decided to make one last tour of the District. The cleaning crews and other early birds were met by the sight of a solitary man stalking intently, peering into every dim alley as if looking for something he had lost. A wagon creaked along Conti Street and a faraway bell tolled half-five.

He left Storyville to walk the two miles back to Spain Street. He admitted to what he'd managed to park in the back of his mind: This might not be so simple after all. This crazy fellow with the pistol and knife was not going to walk into his waiting arms. The *fool* had been clever enough to make the Creole detective look like a dunce.

Hebert arrived as usual a half hour before the break of dawn. After twenty-odd years keeping the grounds at St. Louis No. 2, he treasured starting his days alone and at peace in the City of the Dead. There were no funeral parades trampling everything, no sightseers looking for the bier of this famed madam or that. For these brief minutes, St. Louis No. 2 belonged to him.

In all but the worst weather, it was his habit to bring his tin of coffee and pipe to one of the stone benches for a leisurely smoke and some reflection on mysteries of life and death. He knew others found the deep still within those whitewashed walls frightening, especially in that gray-shadowed hour between night and morning when ghosts were known to roam.

Hebert found the time spent with the departed citizens a balm to his soul. It was his private time and place. And so it annoyed him to see that some drunkard had decided to ruin the start of this day by slouching down to sleep against the cemetery gates. He fumed as he crossed the street. It was a good thing the gates were locked or the tramp would be inside snoring away on someone's grave.

Hebert drew closer. The sot's legs were stretched out before him, his hands rested on his thighs, and his head was pitched forward under a slouch hat.

The groundskeeper stepped up, kicked the sole of one of the shoes, and said, "Hey, there, fellow!"

In the silence that followed, Hebert, who knew about such things, realized that the man curled against the wrought-iron bars of the cemetery gate wasn't sleeping at all.

THIRTEEN

Justine came awake when Valentin crawled into bed. From the way he collapsed, rolled over, and dropped off without a word, she understood that the night hadn't gone as planned. He was still reeking of the Storyville streets, and, as if to avoid tainting herself, she pushed out of the bed and went off for a bath to start her day.

Once she settled into the fragrant heat, she began entertaining odd images, first of Valentin and then of Louis, and thinking about all the energy men spent on the hunt for a fight or a fuck. It brought a momentary flush of contempt for the lot of them.

And what about her? Hadn't she played her own part in the comedy? After the nightmare of her childhood on the bayou near Ville Platte, she had reason to despise men. So many of the sporting women she had known over the years secretly hated all of them and took their pleasure after hours from each other, though too often it was more with vengeance than love. She had decided long ago that turning her ardor in that direction would deny her nature. She refused to give her evil fuck of a father a victory over her.

Presently, her thoughts drifted back to Louis Jacob, and she spent a moment imagining a life of privileged ease before recalling that she'd tried it and failed. Though it was true that she could always play the role when it suited her, she wasn't the type to be owned.

Louis had brought something else to the table. Young, clever, and deftly handsome, he appeared to be enamored of her. She stopped for a moment to picture herself sitting high in the tufted leather seat of that fine automobile, in her best dress and Flora-dora hat, on parade along Basin Street . . .

She laughed quietly at this foolishness. Sliding down so that the water covered her ears, she closed her eyes, and for ten minutes Louis, Valentin, and the rest of the world disappeared.

Tom Anderson was up before dawn. Though one of his spies would have told him if anything had transpired overnight, he headed directly to the telephone. He called Billy Struve, but was unable to rouse that drunken fool. He thought to phone St. Cyr, then changed his mind and settled on one of his friends inside the police department. The officer reported that the only trouble in Storyville had been a brawl in Fewclothes Cabaret that was settled when one of the combatants was laid out by a nightstick. Other than that, there hadn't been a single call from the District.

Just as he was turning away, the bell gave a jangle that made him jump. It was his police spy, ringing back to whisper that a report had just that minute come in about a body found at the gates of St. Louis No. 2, of all places. The victim had been shot dead.

Feeling his gut sink, Anderson asked the copper to call back as soon as he could ascertain details. He dropped the receiver in the cradle and went off to dress for the day.

Detective Weeks decided it was best to get it over with and delivered the news as soon as Captain Picot walked through the door to the detectives' section.

"You'll want to hear this," Weeks said. "They found another body."

After what had appeared in the newspaper, the detective had been expecting an explosion of Picot proportions. Now he was astonished to see the captain's dour face relax. The olive drab eyes narrowed and that turtle mouth curved ever so slightly.

"Another body?" he said, sounding almost jovial. "Where?"

Evelyne came downstairs to find Malvina serving her husband his breakfast. The maid poured her a first cup of coffee.

"Did I hear the telephone ring earlier?" Evelyne said.

"No, ma'am," Malvina said in her flat voice. "Not this morning."

Evelyne wanted to ask if there had by chance been a message delivered to the door, but that would give too much away, and she'd already read the suspicion in Malvina's dark eyes. She wondered regularly if the maid and her lazy son were spying on her. More likely, Malvina knew something was amiss but hadn't learned any details. She was a sharp woman and would have made a good ally, except she was also a righteous sort who didn't abide anything that smacked of wickedness.

At that exact moment the maid spoke up, as innocent as a lamb. "What'll you be having for breakfast this morning, ma'am?"

Evelyne gave her a dour look and said, "I'll . . ." She brushed a hand through the air. "Just coffee for now." She started to leave the room, then realized she hadn't even acknowledged her husband, sitting frail and bloodless as he poked about his meager portion of soft-boiled eggs.

She said, "How are you feeling today, dear?"

Benoit whispered something she didn't catch. The enfeebled old bird could barely summon the energy to sigh. It didn't matter; they were all waiting for him to die anyway, and the sooner the better, as far as his wife was concerned.

Fresh from her bath and draped in an old kimono, Justine stood in the doorway and watched Valentin wrestle with sleep, pitching about and making sounds that had her thinking he was in mortal battle with some dream foe. He muttered, his brow pinched, and he clenched his fists. Then he let out a long breath, relaxed, and lay unmoving.

She made her way to the kitchen, with a detour to the front windows to peek out onto Spain Street. There was no red automobile in sight.

The telephone chattered noisily, and she gave a start and shot a vile stare across the room. It was ridiculous; the damned thing hadn't squawked in months, and they were now getting a call a day, each one delivering more bad news.

She picked up the receiver, listened for a few seconds, then thanked the caller and hung up. She wasn't about to wake Valentin. This bit of bad news could wait.

She was standing over the stove when she heard the bedsprings squeak and then water running in the bathroom. Valentin shambled to the kitchen doorway and stood for a moment as if he was a diner waiting to be seated. She took a cup down from the cupboard, filled it, and placed it on the table.

As he stirred cream and sugar into his coffee, she began slicing a potato into thin semicircles and then dropped the pieces into the sizzling frying pan.

"I didn't catch him," he said abruptly.

She glanced over her shoulder. "I figured that."

"But he was out there somewhere."

She poked at the frying potatoes. "They found a body," she said.

Staring, he put his cup down. "What?"

"They found a body early this morning."

"Where?"

"At the cemetery."

"At—" He was momentarily confused. "Which one?"

"Number Two. At the front gate."

"Who was it?"

"Some hobo, I believe."

Valentin sat back. "Oh." Then, "How do you know?"

"Mr. Tom called."

She turned back to the sizzling pan, leaving him to his thoughts. Once the potatoes had browned, she cracked two eggs over them and began to stir. She slid the mash onto a plate and pushed it under his nose. He regarded the food forlornly.

"Eat," she said.

"I'm not ver—"

"Eat." Her voice was firm.

Valentin sighed and picked up his fork.

The District was working up a buzz. No one knew what to make of the body that had been deposited at St. Louis Cemetery No. 2.

One of the coppers called to the scene was able to make a quick identification. As it turned out, old Hebert's first guess had been correct: The fellow was a drunkard, in this case a sot who went by the street moniker Stovepipe for reasons no one could ascertain. His true name was Timothy Smith, and he was a longtime fixture around the low-rent saloons on the east side of the old city. The cause of his death was a single gunshot wound to the chest.

By the middle of the morning, the coppers had roused a few of the other drunks who frequented the dives and learned that Stovepipe was a harmless sort who picked up day labor now and then and stayed in flophouses when he had a dime to pay. When he didn't, he slept in doorways. He had few friends and no kin that anyone could recall.

When the victim's long-unwashed body was delivered to the

morgue, a second wound was discovered, this one a bullet hole in the back of his left thigh, halfway between the knee and buttocks. Further examination revealed no marks cut into Mr. Smith's flesh.

Valentin learned this information by placing an anonymous telephone call to the precinct at Parish Prison and locating Officer McKinney. The copper delivered the essentials, and Valentin did him the service of getting off the line quickly. He had what he needed anyway. After he hung up, he went out onto the balcony and gazed south to the river, mulling over what McKinney had reported.

Men like Timothy Smith died every day, from the damage done by their drinking, from accidents, and from spats with knife- or pistol-toting rivals. It would be fair to assume that such violence befell this poor character. He had simply chosen the gates of the cemetery to slump down and die.

Valentin saw two holes in this construction. First, the bullet wound to the chest was a replica of those that had felled the other victims. The other one was the kind intended to bring a man to the ground.

The detective imagined the drunkard ambling along and some miscreant creeping up behind to snap a shot into the back of his leg. Once Smith crumpled to his knees, it would be easy enough to move around and put the fatal shot in his heart.

The second problem was the location of the body. There was nothing nearby that would draw the victim: no saloons, no flops, no back-alley slum of lean-tos where vagrants with no other place to go huddled, drinking whatever they could over open fires. Timothy Smith didn't belong there, unless he just happened to be passing that way.

That was all, though, and with nowhere else to go with it, Valentin turned his thoughts to his unfinished business with the law firms on St. Charles. Several cases had been left open, and he needed to deliver his last reports. So while Justine changed the bedding and dusted, he spent a half hour at their Camden desk, adding final comments to the paperwork.

When he left, he called in to let her know he would be back later. If she said anything in response, he didn't hear it.

As if he needed any more blows to his pride, Tom Anderson was not consulted before Chief of Police Reynolds, after a quick few words with the mayor, decided it was time to put more officers on the streets of Storyville. At least he was informed of the decision, which was something, though not much. It was not the chief himself nor even Captain Picot who delivered the news. Instead, a detective named Weeks showed up at the Café.

The King of Storyville didn't like Weeks the moment he stepped inside. The detective swaggered his way over the threshold, plainly annoyed at his role of messenger. He all but yawned when he greeted Anderson and then said his piece without preamble. The department was going to assign a couple dozen patrolmen and five or six detectives to the District until further notice.

Anderson listened to the policeman, caught the dismissive tone, and decided it was time to send a message back.

"Tell Captain Picot that they can order a damned army down here," he said. "It's only going to make things worse. And you can tell my friends downtown that as of today, payments of any kind to policemen assigned to the District will be suspended."

Weeks frowned dubiously, as if he wasn't sure Anderson still had the clout to make such a drastic change.

The King of Storyville noted this and said, "You understand me, detective? I'm putting an order out. Not a dime."

Now Weeks flushed in ire at being placed in the middle of this mess. What did he have to do with a spat between Anderson and the chief? Not to mention learning that the ten dollars or so that he collected every week on top of his pay was about to disappear.

Anderson was finished with the cop and snapped his fingers at Ned.

"Please get Lulu White on the telephone for me," he said. "Tell her I have something important to discuss." He then turned a cold gaze on his visitor. "Was there anything else, detective?"

Picot intercepted Weeks as soon as he arrived back at the precinct. The detective repeated what Mr. Anderson had said.

"The last part," Picot said when he finished. "You sure he said that?"

"Yes, sir," Weeks said. "That was it, all right. No more payments."

Picot sighed as if in regret. Privately, he was stifling a smile. Storyville was cracking apart, top to bottom.

"Well, then," he said, keeping his tone serious. "I'll need to report this right away."

Weeks said, "I won't say nothing about it."

Picot eyed him. "Tell whoever you want, detective. It's not a secret." He treated the junior officer to a sharp glance. "All right?"

"Yes, sir," Weeks said.

Picot dismissed him and ambled back into his office.

The phone finally rang and Evelyne took the call. After hanging up, she dressed in a huffing rush and called for the car. Thomas, sensing her mood and eager to get away without having to don the livery, hurried for once, and soon they were racing to the French Quarter almost quickly enough to please her. There was no time to stop at Mayer Israel's and be transformed, so she had him drop her in front of a china shop on Ursulines. When she stepped down, she told him to go park on the street alongside Jackson Square and she'd come find him when she was finished with her shopping.

If he found any of this suspect, he didn't show it. He was happy to be away from the house, more so to have the chance to lounge about the square with the fine automobile on display.

As soon as the Winton turned the next corner, she was heading for Royal Street, keeping her head bent and hoping for the good fortune to miss being recognized. She found some humor knowing that at the same moment any number of society women were in the Quarter and in the middle of their own mischief. Though she wasn't dallying with a secret lover. She was on a far more urgent mission.

Still, it wouldn't do to be noticed, and she was relieved to reach the gates of the house.

She found him in the sunroom, which was attached to the back of the house and framed on three sides with greenhouse glass and festooned with ferns. He was seated on the wrought-iron bench, looking much at ease, which annoyed her. Men of leisure—or those who pretended to be—frankly disgusted her. Perhaps because her husband, who had barely worked a day in his life, was now rotting away from the inside, a peeling back of his frail shell to reveal no substance underneath.

Louis was the same sort, mostly window dressing. Some people were blessed with an engine that drove them, and others lived to simply go along for the ride, mere passengers. A select few others, like her, were destined to drive the trains.

Louis turned his head in a practiced motion. She was in no way dazzled by his beauty. He wasn't a good enough actor.

She got down to business. "What happened last night?"

"Nothing happened." He shrugged.

"Did I hear about a man found dead at the cemetery?"

"There's plenty of those." He made an offhand gesture.

Evelyne reached down and grabbed one of his flawless cheeks in her fingernails. Louis let out a cry.

"Don't you play with me," she said.

He grunted, his teeth clenched tight, as the pain brought tears to his eyes. She held on long enough to leave scratches, then let go. He glared at her and rubbed at the spot where three welts had risen. He didn't look quite so pretty now, so brave, or very smart, for that matter. The young fool had no idea what she was doing. He still imagined that she was some rich woman playing a silly game. He was just as unaware of her plans for him after the dust settled.

He'd find out soon enough; they had more immediate business. "What about the dead man?" she said.

Louis let out a pouting sigh and said, "I don't know what happened. He was just some drunkard nobody cared about."

"That's right. So why did he end up dead in Storyville?"

"It wasn't Storyville," Louis said. "Not exactly."

Evelyne watched his face, especially his shifting eyes. She couldn't tell if he was just pretending to be a dunce or was really that dim. He was a fair liar and devious enough to blend truth with fiction. Which made her wonder if he was running a game of his own. She didn't think he'd dare, but then the world was full of lying scoundrels.

"All right, what else?" she said.

Louis rubbed his sore cheek for another moment to remind her what she had done, then began to smile in such a devilish way that she felt goose bumps rise on her arms and a twitch between her legs. She knew that look; he had good news for once.

Picot was careful about how he passed the information up the chain of command, simply requesting a moment of the division commander's time. At two o'clock he was standing outside the fourth-floor office.

He waited, dazzled by the stars and braiding on the uniforms that ambled by and the fine suits worn by the civilians who did a lot of business in the hallway alcoves, where no one could hear. He kept an eye out, just in case Chief Reynolds happened by.

The captain didn't know that the brass considered him half joke and half pest. No one liked or trusted him, and any time spent in his company was kept short. He was valuable only as a bull snake, allowed in the yard for his rat-catching abilities.

An officer stuck his head into the hall and summoned him. He found Commander York bent over a table, busily drawing pencil lines on a map, keeping busy being a requisite when hosting Captain Picot.

He barely glanced up from his work. "What's so important, Picot?" he said.

The captain, sensing that the senior officer prefer that he keep his distance, lingered at the door. "Sir, I sent one of my officers to pay a visit to Tom Anderson at his place of business," he said. "To extend the courtesy of telling him we would have extra officers in Storyville until the felon who's been committing the murders is apprehended."

The commander kept scribbling. Picot continued.

"Mr. Anderson told the detective he was going to pass the word that payments from the houses in the District were going to be suspended." He paused for emphasis. "Immediately."

York lifted his pencil. "I see." He pondered in what seemed an absent manner for a few seconds. Then he said, "Payments of those sort made to police officers are illegal. That means whatever Mr. Anderson threatens or does is of no concern to this department. But thank you for passing along the information."

Picot understood instantly. He muttered a thank-you, performed a slight bow, and backed out of the office.

Commander York stepped to his doorway in time to see Picot pass out into the corridor. Then he crossed directly to his desk to call Chief Reynolds.

The afternoon found Valentin arriving at the offices of Mansell, Maines, and Velline, his packet of files in hand. He stated his business to the secretary in the lobby. She accepted the files with one hand and handed over an envelope with the other. Valentin got the message: *Take your money and leave.* As he walked out, he allowed himself a glance down the long corridor toward Sam Ross's office. That door was closed.

A wave of anger swelled in the space of the hour it took the word to go down the line from the Café. As a matter of respect, Lulu White was informed first, by way of a personal call from the King of Storyville. She listened, dumbfounded, as Anderson explained that she was to cease paying tribute to officers on the beat and any other police official, all the way up to the chief.

To the madam's ear, he sounded odd, like a different person, and as he went about upsetting a system that had been in place for decades, she had to wonder if he was losing his mind. The graft was the oil in the smooth-running machine that was Storyville, insuring a basic level of order and protection. Tom Anderson had always been a generous patron. As a kid he had been a reliable police snitch, and his first saloon had served as the department's home away from home. Indeed, the very foundation of his empire had been his service as ambassador between the blue and scarlet worlds.

Now he was ordering a halt to the payments as a first salvo in a war, and it was on her shoulders to pass the word to the other madams. Before she could protest, he'd said his good-byes. She did not miss the way he had finagled her, appealing to her pride before dumping an onerous duty in her ample lap.

She selected a cigarillo from the box on her desk, fit it into her onyx holder, and struck a lucifer. The sweet tobacco always helped her relax and think.

She knew two things to be true: First, Anderson was making

a terrible mistake by starting a feud at a time when things were already going so badly; second, no matter what happened, that sweet-tongued, evil-eyed Josie Arlington and the vile witch Emma Johnson would waste no time blaming her for the debacle. She had always believed herself Storyville's second-in-command. Now she would pay for that conceit.

She stopped to wonder if perhaps St. Cyr could talk him out of it. But the Creole detective would have other things on his mind. He hadn't been able to get the first scent of the killer after a night of prowling. And another body had turned up, though apparently it was just some no-account tramp.

Her thoughts now turned to how things might play out for her. It didn't look promising, but who knew? The wild swirl of events could be a run of bad luck. It could also be a fiendish plan devised by the rare wicked intelligence. Then she tried to imagine who, except for the King of Storyville and herself, had such talents and could think of no one.

In any case, she had to leave it alone. If she didn't get busy calling down the line, Anderson would be pestering her to know why. She could hear the shrieks from the other madams before they began and thought it would be a good time to light up her opium pipe instead.

The five telephones in the *Picayune* newsroom were all placed on one long table that was wedged into a corner so that the reporters could take turns using them. In another year, they had been told, each of the scribblers would have his own set. On this afternoon a copyboy whistled and called Donald Packer's name. The reporter pushed away from his desk, crossed the room, and picked up the telephone on the end.

He listened for a moment. Anyone watching would see the startled look on his face shift to tense and then to relief that brought along a smile. He laid the phone in the cradle and hurried off to his editor's office.

The evening found Tom Anderson at his office window as the first of the Black Marias pulled to the curb at the corner of Basin and Bienville streets. The specially built Model T delivery trucks were usually reserved for those instances when multiple suspects had to be transported. In the wake of a brawl, for instance, or when the drunks were unloaded off the train cars coming back from the revelries at Spanish Fort and the other lakeside resorts. The vehicles were outfitted with bars on the back windows and steel eyes on the floor where the shackles placed on unruly passengers were attached.

As Anderson watched, the rear doors of the closest vehicle opened and eight patrolmen stepped down, donning their round-topped helmets and hitching their gun belts as they hit the cobbled street. Next, a police sedan pulled up and disgorged three men in suits—detectives from the precinct at Parish Prison.

The King of Storyville experienced a dizzying spike of alarm at the thought that he might at the moment be witnessing the end of his reign. Turning from the window, he went for his brandy, swilled one glass, and filled another. The sweet heat of the liquor calmed him, and he returned to his vantage point.

He observed the patrolmen and detectives huddling briefly, then fanning out like ants to mount their occupation of his territory. He imagined repeats of the scene on Canal, St. Louis, and Claiborne, and shook his head in dismay. The sick, sinking feeling in his gut was no joke.

A minute later his eye was caught by a familiar figure sauntering along from far down the line, and he felt his spirits rise again.

Valentin stopped to surveil the police activity from the opposite end of Basin Street, waiting until the police had moved off before he started walking again. Even then he used the cover of Union Station and the background of rolling trains to make his way to

Iberville Street, then crossed over to duck inside the door of Anderson's Café.

There wasn't much business, a dozen men playing faro at tables and three more sitting at the long bar. It looked like the end rather than the beginning of a long night. Crossing the tiled floor, he stepped into the back hallway and climbed the stairs to Anderson's office.

The King of Storyville was standing at the window, brandy glass in his hand. The setting sun cast his face in pale orange. He looked tired. Turning at Valentin's entrance, he gestured to the bottle and empty glass on the tray. The detective shook his head.

"Did you see the invasion out there?"

"I saw," Valentin said.

"It's my fault," Anderson said, then described his visit from Detective Weeks and the message he'd passed to Chief Reynolds.

Valentin started to smile. "That'll make everyone happy."

"Well, it's too late to back out."

Valentin said, "You know the word went right to Picot."

"Yes, I know," the King of Storyville said with a sigh. He tilted his head to the window at the scene beyond. "What are you going to do about all this?"

"I'm not going back home, if that's what you mean."

Anderson nodded gratefully and they stood in silence, at ease with each other, as they had so many times in the past. Before they drifted too far into their own thoughts, the older man noticed something and gestured with his glass. "And it's about to get better."

Valentin joined him at the window. Anderson pointed at the line of bullying clouds that were closing fast on the red-light district, bringing a gray sheet of rain.

"You still think he'll make a try tonight?" Anderson said. "With the storm, I mean? And all those coppers will be out. Your people, too."

"It'd be a hell of a trick," Valentin said. "The cops all over the streets will be a problem. But the rain will be good cover."

"So?"

"So, yes, I think he'll make a try. I would."

The King of Storyville treated him to a small smile.

"He can't control himself. He's—" The detective caught himself. "Either that, or . . ."

"Or what?"

"Nothing. Just a thought." He shrugged it off.

Anderson said, "You know if you go home and another one turns up dead, it will be on them."

Valentin said, "Yes, sir, I know."

Anderson shrugged. Of course, the Creole detective would be on the streets. He'd cast his lot and another dead man would be on his conscience, no matter what the King of Storyville said.

Anderson finished his brandy and Valentin made his exit just as thunder began to rumble over the river.

The rain came down hard for an hour before receding into a steady drizzle. Shapes scurried here and there, heads bent and umbrellas bobbing in the wet mist.

The patrolmen in uniform and detectives in their standard dark suits created such confusion with their milling about that the only way they'd catch the miscreant would be if he decided to step forward and identify himself. It was so chaotic that Valentin could have rolled a cannon up Basin Street unnoticed. Meanwhile, up and down the banquettes, the sound of falling water was punctuated by curses as coppers and civilians bumped into each other. Everyone was on edge.

The police presence was wreaking havoc with the scarlet trade as well. As if the rain wasn't enough, customers turned around and left by the dozens when they saw coppers peering at them. Madams and sporting girls found themselves having to vouch for regular visitors. More often, they watched helplessly as the men and their dollars turned around and walked away.

French Emma Johnson, the black witch of Basin Street, became so livid at the disruption that she closed up, canceling the evening's performance of the Circus and sending the pony, the girl who performed with him, and all the other attractions away.

Meanwhile Valentin roamed in aimless circles, feeling helpless and wondering which minute would bring word of another victim.

Long about midnight he settled into the doorway of a closed-down apothecary on the corner of Bienville and Liberty. With the whole world shrouded in mist, he drowsed for a few moments, then came awake. For long stretches nothing moved. Though he smoked rarely, he fished into his pockets for a cigarillo wrapped in dark paper and a box of lucifers. Stale as it was, the tobacco calmed him.

Looking out at a barren street that was curtained in fog and shadow, he pondered what he was doing there when he could be lying in a kind bed with his good woman. At best, the night would be wasted in a futile burlesque of police work. The killer he pursued could walk out of the drizzle at any moment and shoot another poor soul—or him, for that matter.

It had been a long while since such a glum mood had come upon him. It was as if one of the clouds overhead had his name on it and had begun weeping with woes that went back thirty years. But who didn't have a sad history? No one he knew. No one, save for the rich who floated above it on their magic carpets of privilege. And in the end even they could not escape fate's icy grip.

Thinking about it, he knew that what had landed him there was a life spent raging against the kind of fearful forces that had destroyed his family. Valentin had never despised evil with any sort of high-blown moral sense; rather, he had seen the misery it caused firsthand. Miseries that echoed down the years. And so he huddled in a doorway, waiting in the dark mist for an evil man who might be anywhere in the city or nowhere at all.

To shake off his funk he fixed his thoughts on something he could sort out.

He had been baffled all along by the killer's lack of a pattern. The fellow stepped out of the night to shoot a man dead, cut his flesh in one thin stroke, and then disappear.

Valentin had come across what seemed pointless killings before. They had all proved one of two things: Either the perpetrator was truly mad and his actions beyond logic or the caprice was intentional, pointing to some unseen hand—real or imagined—pulling the strings.

The detective now let his mind roam over what little he knew, and his thoughts began shifting back and forth between the oddities of the scenes of the crimes and the strange cuts on the bodies. After a few rounds, they began to meld into one.

The silence on the street deepened, and as if forming out of the rain, it came to him. It was so simple that he barked a loud curse, lurched to his feet, and started running.

Three blocks down, a form bolted out of the sheet of rain in such a sudden motion that Valentin snapped out his Iver Johnson, his finger on the trigger.

Each slid to a stop, threw up his hands, and yelled, "Don't!"

The detective forced his hand to stop shaking as he lowered the pistol.

"What the hell?" the kid said.

Valentin grabbed him by the shoulder, turned him around, and hustled him into the nearest doorway. "Right back there," he said.

Each brushed away the wet hair on his forehead. "Back there what?"

"That's where he'll take the next one. On that corner."

"How do you know?"

Valentin said, "You have the map?"

Each went digging. The paper he produced was only slightly damp. Valentin laid it flat on his left palm and drew with his right index finger. "That's how I know," he said.

They waited as the hours passed in near silence, coming to attention at every figure that passed in the dark and drizzle.

Valentin said, "We need to get away, in case he's still waiting." Each didn't understand. "He can't know I found him out. So we need to move."

"And what if he takes someone five minutes after we leave?" the kid said.

"Then it's that poor someone's bad luck."

FOURTEEN

The rain stopped just before dawn, and for the first hour of daylight, the cobblestones fairly glistened. The New Orleans gumbo of the odors of human and animal waste, sour rot, rust, smoke, and sweat had been blessedly washed north. It would all be back by day's end.

The talk of the morning was the night passing without another killing in the red-light district. Chief Reynolds wasted no time in crowing to the newspapers that it showed the kind of results professional police work could produce. His comments accomplished a double swipe at Tom Anderson.

That gentleman rose to the news, his relief tinged with a foreboding that Reynolds would now see fit to install a permanent police presence in the District, with the extra manpower and budget to go with it. It would be a dream come true for the chief and a nightmare for Anderson, who lumbered to the breakfast table in such a foul humor that he barely spoke a word to his wife.

Though his mind wasn't changed about the payments to the police. He made that clear when Lulu White, who was up especially early this day, called to ask what to do when the patrol sergeant came around with his hand out.

"Not a dime," the King of Storyville snapped. When the madam tried to protest, he cut her off. "This isn't over, Miss Lulu. It was just the one night, and it rained from dusk until dawn. A body could still turn up. So, no, ma'am, you don't pay. Nobody pays. Please pass the word."

He wasn't interested in a debate, and before the madam could utter another syllable, he clapped the hand piece into the cradle.

Valentin had dropped into bed and fallen promptly asleep, knowing what Tom Anderson did not, that the killer they all sought hadn't left another body.

He did not disturb Justine with his thrashing, and when she woke two hours later, she understood that the night had passed without disaster. The storm had taken care of that, and he'd be back at it when night fell.

William Brown had been unable to sleep or eat, and could only manage handfuls of the tepid water from the pitcher on the washstand to wet his throat.

He had stumbled in the back door long before dawn with the pelting rain soaking through his clothes and dripping off the brim of his derby. It took what seemed an exhausting hour for him to climb the steps to his third-floor room, where he sat in the dark as blue lightning flashed and thunder bumbled. He got up and paced, and then, hoping for some relief, stretched on the dirty mattress and dropped a hand into his trousers, only to find a limp and cold companion.

The face that peered back at him from the mirror looked like a victim's: drawn and grayish, the eyes a bleak green. The rain had cooled the streets outside, and yet he could not stop sweating. He found a stub of pencil and worked it until the lead was gone. After that he drew frantic designs in the air as he paced some more in the same pattern over and over.

Morning had arrived. At that very moment, he should have been on a train heading east, leaving New Orleans behind like a bad memory. Instead, he would have to wait out the day in that dank cell until it was dark again and then venture out and hope for better hunting.

Because he couldn't leave until he got the money he was promised and wouldn't get it until the last deed was done. That was the deal, and if he tried to run away, they'd catch him and put him back in that awful place, this time for good. He'd spend his years gazing out a window toward a river that would be beyond his reach forever. Such were the wages of selling his soul to the devil.

At that moment he decided that he would rather die than greet that fate, and be free, one way or another. The decision calmed him enough that he could close his eyes against the torments of the empty day and imagine another place far away.

Valentin didn't wake up until after two o'clock. Justine was out, and he rambled about their rooms, dazed after his first good sleep in days. Once his brain cleared, he began to wish the hours away so he could get back to Storyville and the one particular corner.

The morning and afternoon passed in a tense sort of truce. Chief Reynolds and Tom Anderson were at a standoff, and everyone seemed content to let their tempers cool. Instead of heeding Anderson's wishes that she spread the word, Lulu White prudently kept her own counsel and her mouth closed. Business up and down Basin Street was slow, even for the middle of the week, but that had been going on for some time. The men who happened by tried to pry gossip from girls who knew no more than they did.

The sky over the gulf was clear as far as the eye could see, and ship-to-shore and inland transmissions reported no approaching storms.

Afternoon trekked toward evening. This was the customary time for the professors to arrive at the better houses. These gentlemen, all Creole or Negro, would be treated to a bite of dinner in the kitchens before beginning a long night at the parlor pianos. But there was not enough money to pay them, either, so instead of donning their best suits for the Basin Street crowd, they threw on whatever was hanging and headed for various back-of-town saloons, where they pounded out rough jass and gutbucket tunes for nickels.

Justine arrived home at four o'clock to find Valentin picking over a cold plate of cheese, ham, and black olives. A glass of red wine was at his elbow. She didn't say where she'd been, and something about the distant set of her dark eyes told him not to inquire. It reminded him vaguely of those times in the wake of the Black Rose murders when she seemed to be another person, a stranger, in fact. That had been a result of her injury, and she always came around.

She did stop to ask him if he was going to want dinner, and when he told her he was fine with nibbling, she replied with such an absent nod that he wasn't sure she'd heard his answer before wandering into the bedroom.

He was distracted, too. After he finished eating, he stepped out on the balcony for the fifth time to scour the horizon for anything like a storm cloud. It appeared it would be clear into the evening, and he felt butterflies in his stomach, as if he was going at this for the first time. Some of this was the tension of knowing he could corner his prey at a particular place and time. The man was coming with a map laid out and a clock ticking in his crazy head.

From the bedroom he heard the springs let out a soft squeak and moved quietly back inside with mischief on his mind. When he got to the doorway, he found her asleep and curled away from him, and he let her be.

He'd had more than enough practice moving about without making a sound, and now he prepared in silence, careful not to wake her. Once he finished dressing, he collected his weapons. It was then that he sensed that she had woken up. She kept her back turned as she waited for him to leave.

Pushing the top drawer of the dresser closed, he made his quiet way out of the room. At that moment the police would be assembling for the ride to the red-light district. Each and Whaley and the other men would be heading that way as well, gathering before the next act.

Looking out his office window as the sun began to dissolve into twilight, Tom Anderson was surprised to see that Chief Reynolds had assigned less than half the number of officers that he had sent the night before. It gave him a worried start, and he shuffled through reasons for the change. Was the chief sending a message? Or did he decide not to push back at the King of Storyville? Perhaps he meant the smaller contingent as an insult of some sort. Or a signal that he could do whatever he wanted: big force, smaller force, no force at all.

Anderson's puzzling was interrupted when St. Cyr appeared in his doorway. He hadn't heard him on the stairs or in the hall. The Creole detective stepped inside.

Anderson rapped a knuckle on the window. "The coppers are back. But not as many this time."

"I guess you should have gotten them paid." When the older man snickered, Valentin said, "It's better for me this way."

Anderson studied him for a moment. "Can you finish it?"

Valentin said, "Yes, sir, I think so."

They met at Mangetta's. Over glasses of brandy, Valentin told Each and Whaley exactly what to expect. The kid and the ex-cop looked dubious.

"You sure he's going to be there?" Whaley said.

"Enough to bank on it."

"And he'll give up if he's cornered?"

"I hope he will. I want him alive."

"And I hope you shoot first," Frank said.

As hard as it was, Valentin decided to trust his instincts and keep out of sight. He sent Each and Whaley to their assigned places, one block down Conti, the kid to the west and the cop to the east. From there they would manage the men on the corners north and south. These last four would be able to see the remaining two men in the middle. So eight men could cover a mere four blocks. If Valentin was correct, the killer could not avoid being spotted.

He found a familiar hiding spot in a walkway between two buildings on Villere Street, just off the corner of Iberville. He picked the lock with ease, left the gate hanging open on its hinges, and settled just far enough into the shadows to be invisible to any-one happening by, as the minutes began their slow crawl.

William Brown approached from along the river, then turned north on Common Street. For two blocks he bobbed through the motion and chatter of New Orleans' Chinatown, and he felt the chink eyes watching him until he came out the other side of the odd cloud of sounds and scents.

The bells were tolling half past eleven when he slipped over Canal at Liberty Street. The District lay mostly quiet. He could see the lights from Anderson's Café two blocks down, and a pair of policemen standing on the corner, swinging their nightsticks in lazy arcs as they gazed down the line. He stood still and peered along the street ahead, waiting to see or hear anything worrisome. After a minute he began walking slowly, so as not to attract atten-tion and to make sure he'd notice any sound or movement, like someone's street rat sniffing a breath of air.

The house he wanted was near the intersection of Conti and Villere, and he fell in behind a pair of strolling gentlemen heading in that direction. The two stopped at several points to engage in animated argument before moving on, so it was slow progress through the streets, and the bells were tolling midnight when the pair veered off, leaving him alone.

He decided to make a loop in case anyone had been watching. They'd think him no one special; certainly not a man with murder on his mind. He bent his head and continued on, his footsteps barely sounding on the banquette.

Valentin had just struck a flame off one of the bricks when he heard a whistle from down the street. He poked his head out onto the banquette to see Each standing halfway down the block, waving a hand. He tossed the cigarillo into the gutter. A quick twenty strides brought him to the doorway where the kid had retreated.

"One of my fellows saw someone," he whispered. "Back by the alley runs through Conti to Iberville. Coming this way. He says this character don't look right."

Valentin gave a sharp nod and raised a finger to his lips. Each's man might have seen some Storyville dreg ambling about in search of a scrap of food or a drink. If nothing else, the word would get around and get everyone on their toes.

They found the kid who had spotted the intruder at the corner of Conti Street. He was short, skinny, and excitable, much like Each had been when he was still Beansoup. He was introduced as Black Jimmy, though his face was as pale as cotton.

Valentin asked for a report, and in a quick whisper Jimmy said he'd seen a man amble out of the darkness, cross Iberville Street a block north, and then slip along the banquette into the alleyway.

"What about him?" the detective whispered.

"He was hunched down." Black Jimmy ducked his head in a mime. "He wasn't lookin' left nor right, neither."

"Like he knew where he was going."

"Like that, yes, sir."

"He was wearing a derby, too." Jimmy glanced at Each. "Just like you said."

"You're sure about all this?" Valentin said.

"Yeah, don't you be making up stories." Each hitched his shoulders.

Jimmy said, "I saw, all right. The hat and everything."

Valentin addressed the kid. "You stay here and keep your eyes open. It could be nothing and the one we're looking for could move right in while we ain't looking."

Black Jimmy nodded, all solemn at the gravity of the order.

The detective turned to Each. "You get up to Robertson and come around that way. You see any of your people, have them close in a half block. I want the intersection covered on every side. But everyone's to stay the hell out of sight. Nobody moves and nobody talks."

Each hurried off as Black Jimmy faded into the shadows. Valentin stepped to the corner and poked his head around. The only person in sight was a fellow standing at the bottom of a set of steps talking with someone in an open doorway. Staying close to the buildings, the detective made his way to the mouth of the alley where Black Jimmy had spotted the man.

He stopped for a moment, then strolled across, stealing an offhand glance down the alleyway. That he saw no silhouette didn't mean that no one was lurking there. Once he reached the other side, he turned back and curled his body into a shadow just off the banquette where he could study the alley more carefully without being spotted.

The moon was down and the trees in the back gardens of the houses made a canopy, so that all light was shut out. He gave his eyes a few seconds to adjust and saw nothing like a human shape and nothing moving.

He waited for a full minute until he saw Each saunter across the Iberville end of the alley. Valentin grinned slightly. The kid

had tried the old trick of strolling past as if on his way somewhere, creating just enough of a stir to draw the attention of anyone who might be lurking in the dark. The detective took the
opportunity to slide around the bricks and into the shadow
under the back balcony of the two-story building. Each would
stop as soon as he got a few paces down the street and would
himself be hiding and waiting.

That's what they both did for a half minute. Valentin could
pick out a few more details in the purple darkness. Another half
minute passed and something moved.

The detective held his breath. Not something; someone. A
man in a long coat and derby had materialized from beside a tool-
shed at the back of one of the properties. The fellow stood very
still, took one slow step, then another, a thief's ruse that was not
unlike the one Each had just pulled, intended to draw out anyone who might be lurking. If some citizen appeared, the trickster
would act like he was relieving his bladder or pawing through
garbage.

Apparently satisfied he was unnoticed, this one crossed to the
other side of the alley in three quick strides and into the back garden of Jessie Taylor's house.

Valentin felt his heart thump, knowing it had to be the miscreant who had killed at least four strangers and then marked
their bodies. Though he could not see the man's face, could not
read his eyes or hear him speak, it did not occur to him that he
was wrong.

Now his mind shut down and his gut took over as if he had
thrown a switch. He knew that in ten silent strides he could be
on the man and putting a bullet through his temple. It would be
that simple. Then he would whistle up Each and Whaley, and the
three of them would drag the body into the street like a hunting
trophy.

But he wasn't an executioner, and so he decided instead to
drive this murdering fellow into the arms of the others. By now

Whaley would have been alerted and on his way and would know what to do.

Valentin first needed to let the man know he was there. It took only the slightest untoward movement, an intentional clumsiness that made a little cough in the gravel at his feet and brought the fellow's head around. A breeze came up and Valentin could smell him now, a familiar scent of flesh that was straining against unseen demons and clothes steeped in the same furious stench.

The man took a step forward and, when Valentin didn't move, took a step back. He stared for another moment, then made a sideways shift and passed through the nearest garden gate. The path around the house would take him out onto the Villere Street banquette.

Valentin, slipping through the shadows, caught movement and saw Each's gawky profile at the end of the alley. He pointed urgently to the south and then gave a sharp wave to get the kid moving. Each disappeared, and the detective went on stalking.

For his part, William Brown was in no small panic. Something was going wrong. Storyville had been quiet and still, just like the other times. He had been waiting to move in close to the house and lurk until a likely target appeared so that he could do his work and be finished. Then someone had come along to jerk him out of his dream. Not just anyone; this was a predator, too. He imagined eyes glowing catlike in the darkness. And now he was the prey. He felt the blood begin to race in his veins. *Don't get caught.*

The passageway was full of shadows and he took advantage, stepping quickly into the back garden of a house. He was moving away from where he was supposed to be, but that would have to wait. He found a pitch-black space below the back gallery of the house, and he crouched there and drew out his pistol.

Nothing moved as the minutes went by. Either the one stalking him had fallen as silent as a snake or he had gone away. After more minutes had passed, William decided to get to the street and use the light to his advantage, rather than squat there all night. *Don't get caught.*

From the shadow of a sycamore tree, Valentin saw the figure rise from beneath the gallery and creep alongside the house. He moved in as the profile was absorbed in the darkness of the cavern between the two houses, then stopped, sensing that his prey had done the same. Though he was in the open, he settled into a practiced stillness that rendered him all but invisible. He could do it so well that at times criminals had tripped over him before they realized he was there. He made himself into just another shadow.

The streets around the block were quiet; that was Whaley and Each doing their jobs. He heard a slight rustle of movement that could have been leaves falling to the ground but was the sound of the fellow moving again, either to try to finish his work or just run off.

Valentin circled around the other side of the house, picking through the narrow space a step at a time. All he needed was to stumble and twist an ankle or frighten up a cat.

When he came out onto the banquette, he saw the lone figure standing in the middle of Villere Street, halfway down the block. The fellow looked around as if searching for the correct doorway, and there was something jittery in his movements.

Valentin crept along, staying close to the houses. He knew that his men were standing in the dark of doorways and under balconies. At his signal they'd draw a web from four directions, hoping that when faced with such an array of force, the man would surrender. The shadows remained still as the detective stepped into the street, his hands out from his sides to show that he held no weapon.

The man in the derby, catching the sound of movement, turned around. Valentin stood fifty paces away, then forty. He held the fellow's gaze as if to mesmerize him, and it seemed to be working, as the stranger regarded him in return with a frank and not unfriendly curiosity.

Then, in a sudden moment, he seemed to come awake and realize where he was. He dropped a hand to his coat pocket.

Valentin said, "Don't."

A breeze off the river cut down Iberville Street to cross Marais, where it snatched the smoke out of the barrel of the Iver Johnson pistol and carried it away.

Once the shot echoed and died, it was quiet again. Each, Whaley, and the other men stepped from their lairs and closed on the intersection. Only one person was out of place: a character who hadn't moved from an opposite corner but stood calmly observing, as if the possibility of a stray ball of lead moving his way at a hundred feet per second didn't faze him at all. He was dressed like a gentleman in a good suit and wool coat.

Lying on the cobbles, William Brown let out a long tortured wheeze and, sounding surprised, said, "Jesus Christ!" He went into shock as the bullet had blown a bloody hole next to his heart.

Valentin fixed his eyes on the body that was sprawled bleeding on the cobblestones. The man's hat had come off and rolled to a stop a few feet away. His hand was clutching at the tail of his shirt and tugging feebly. He lifted the bloody cloth in a weak fist, and Valentin saw the edge of the scar, a red V pointing downward against the parchment-white flesh, and felt the chill of a primitive dread invade his bones. The grasping hand dropped, and the fellow let out what sounded like a sigh of relief before going still.

Valentin said, "Someone please call the police."

He heard a voice yell, "Drop the weapon!" and turned his head to see two patrolmen closing on him, their Colt service pistols held out before them. His own revolver was hanging loose in his limp right hand, and he knelt down to lay it on the cobblestones.

One of the cops holstered his weapon and quickly slapped cuffs on the detective, while his partner kicked the Iver Johnson out of the way.

"Everybody keep back!" the senior of the two coppers yelled. Once those on the scene had followed orders, the officers seemed unsure how to proceed. Word had come down some time ago instructing patrolmen to refrain from grilling suspects after serious crimes. That was the detectives' job. They could only address the basic information.

"What's your name?"

"Valentin St. Cyr."

"Address?"

"Six twenty-seven Spain Street."

"Age?"

Valentin had to think for a moment. "Thirty-nine."

The senior officer wanted to ask about the dead body lying a few feet away. Instead, he stood there with his gaze shifting between the handcuffed Creole and the victim. A few minutes passed as the onlookers huddled on the banquettes of the four corners. From the distance a siren wailed, and within another minute a police wagon pulled up and screeched to a stop.

Tom Anderson was roused from an edgy slumber by the maid knocking and calling that someone needed him at the front door. His gout had flared, and he lumbered into the foyer on tender feet, grumbling like a bear.

The kid they used to call Beansoup was standing on the gallery, all fretful. He was stunned to see the King of Storyville in a nightshirt, looking common and old.

"You're—"

"Emile Carter. They call me—"

"Beansoup," Anderson said. "No, it's Each, is that right?"

"Yes, sir."

"What's wrong?"

"It's Mr. Valentin."

"What about him?"

"Police got him in Parish Prison."

"What for?"

"He shot down a man on Iberville Street."

Anderson took a stunned moment's pause. "Was it the one he was after?"

"I think so."

"You *think so?*"

Each started to stutter an explanation when Anderson cut him off. "Never mind. I'll take care of it." He waved a hand. "You go on," he said, and closed the door. Each backed away, then trotted off into the night.

Inside, the King of Storyville found that the noise had awakened his wife, who now stood at the top of the staircase in her dressing gown.

She said, "What is it, Tom?"

"Go back to bed," he told her.

He sat down at the rolltop desk in his office off the foyer. His first call was to Parish Prison to ascertain that St. Cyr had indeed been arrested and was now confined.

"Yes, sir, they brought him in about a half hour ago," the jailer said.

The King of Storyville thanked him and broke the connection. He next asked the operator to connect him to Chief Reynolds's home.

The chief sounded sleepy and grouchy. "What the hell, Tom? It's the middle of the night."

Anderson bristled in turn at the chief's peeved tone. He could rightly argue that Reynolds might not hold the office if it wasn't for strings he had pulled. But this was no time to raise the point. He got directly to it: St. Cyr was locked down in jail, and the King of Storyville wanted him out.

Reynolds was irked by Anderson's gall, asking for a favor after the trouble he'd started over the payments from Storyville. After an irate few seconds, he said, "He's working for you again?"

"Not exactly."

"Explain that."

"Not now. Later. I'll post the bail if need be, but I want him on the street. Tonight."

"What's the charge?" Reynolds sounded testy again.

"He shot a man."

"Dead?"

"From what I understand."

"A *homicide*?" The chief's voice went up a notch. "And you want him out?"

"The victim was the one who committed those murders."

Even with this information, Reynolds hesitated. Time was, a chief of police would have snapped into action without a single word. John O'Connor had worked with him as a partner to keep the District safe and profitable. But O'Connor had died suddenly, and a model of crisp efficiency named William Reynolds had taken his place. Though he didn't sound so crisp or efficient at that moment.

Anderson hoped he wouldn't have to get nasty and drag out any of the dirt he had on the department, going back fifteen years. He had to consider if St. Cyr's freedom was worth that gamble. Thankfully, it wasn't necessary. With another grudging grunt, the chief said he would call down to Parish Prison and take care of it.

"I'll have him released on your personal bond within the hour," the chief said. "Send someone to pick him up at the back door. I don't want him on the street. And if I find out it wasn't self-defense, he'll be right back in there. Do we understand each other?"

Anderson rolled his eyes at the lecturing tone. "Yes, of course. Let's just get on with it."

Captain Picot could barely believe his ears and his luck. One of the men who had been hired to help St. Cyr happened also to be one of his spies and sent word back through the evening. Nothing much was happening, and Picot was hoping fervently that the Creole detective would sputter, fail, and go home.

That would have been satisfactory. When he received the news that St. Cyr had encountered a man in the middle of the intersection at Iberville and Marais streets and shot him dead, he was beside himself with joy. Even if he had cornered this particular killer, he didn't have the right to execute him. Storyville wasn't the Wild West, after all.

The captain had a late drink of whiskey to celebrate, then went to bed and slept like a baby. He was looking forward to waking up and paying a visit to the jail, just for the simple pleasure of seeing the Creole detective behind bars.

But by the time all this news had reached him, St. Cyr was already gone.

Valentin bribed one of the guards to send for Each. It didn't take long to find him; once he got back from delivering the news to Tom Anderson, the kid had kept a dutiful vigil outside the jail. He now hurried down the stairs and along the corridor to the cells.

"What's the word?" the detective whispered.

Each lowered his own voice. "They found a knife on him, too. Coppers are saying he's the one. They ain't very happy it was you shot him, though."

"Has he been identified?"

"Not that I heard." The kid regarded Valentin carefully, curious about how a man would act in the wake of a killing. As usual, though, the Creole detective's face showed little.

"I heard someone say Mr. Tom called Chief Reynolds and the chief is going to send the word to let you go."

"When?"

"Don't know about that."

Valentin considered. Even with Anderson putting on the pressure, if Picot had his way, he'd be there awhile.

"Go see Justine," he said. "Tell her what happened, but don't make it bloody. Tell her it's over, and that I'm coming home."

The detective waved him away, and he hurried back down the corridor.

When Each came knocking, Justine invited him in. He stayed out on the landing, all breathless as he recounted what had transpired in Storyville and where it had landed Mr. Valentin. Her brow furrowed as she listened, as if she was trying to decide if the news was good or bad. When he finished, she thanked him and closed the door, leaving him standing there.

The call came down at 3:00 A.M. The prisoner was released and escorted to the back exit, where Anderson's driver was waiting for him, along with Each and Whaley. They climbed into the Packard Victoria touring car and drove to Spain Street, where Valentin stepped down with a weary wave of thanks. The Packard rattled off into the night.

Justine heard the automobile pull to the curb outside, the mutter of voices, and the street door opening and closing. Slow steps ascended the stairwell. She unlocked the door and stood back.

He didn't look too bad for someone who had shot a man to death and spent half the night in jail. Before she walked off, leaving a cloud of anger in her wake, she said, "Mr. Tom says for you to call him right away." She closed and locked the bathroom door behind her, and Valentin heard the hiss of running water.

He found Anderson's telephone number and asked the operator to connect him. Anderson's drowsy maid answered and told
him the King of Storyville couldn't sleep and had gone to the
Café. He got the operator a second time.

Ned's creaky voice came on the line. "Who's there?"

"Ned, this is Valentin St. Cyr."

"Mr. Valentin. Y'all right, sir?"

Valentin was grateful. "I'm all right. Is Mr. Tom there?"

"He is," Ned said. "Stay on the line."

Ned's voice was replaced by Tom Anderson's. He got right to
the point. "The best thing you can do is get out of sight."

"For how long?"

"At least the rest of today. Maybe longer."

When Valentin started to protest, Anderson cut him off.
"This isn't over," he said. "Not nearly. You know that damned
Picot wants you back in jail. He can't put you there if he can't
find you." The King of Storyville let out an impatient breath.
"Do you have somewhere to go?"

FIFTEEN

Valentin crawled into bed and promptly fell asleep, his face sagging in exhaustion. Justine dozed as the gray hours of dawn passed into a cloudy day. The bells tolling nine woke her up.

She was troubled by the look in her eyes when she leaned close to the mirror above the dresser, little storms that foretold a drift toward melancholy. She didn't want to go down that path again.

So the drama of violence was finished, and yet she felt no relief that the murderer was dead and only a small amount that Valentin was safe. That he would be Storyville's hero again had nothing to do with her. He had tossed away a career, imperiled his life, and driven her to anger, choosing the risk of becoming a dead lion to carrying on as a live mouse. Though he had betrayed her, she knew she couldn't bring herself to do the same.

Instead of going home, Tom Anderson had Ned pour him a short brandy, and he sat at his usual table as the last of the stragglers ambled out the door. Sipping his drink, he wondered how in God's name things had gotten so out of hand. A murdering son of a bitch was dead—good news. Still, he knew in his gut that it changed little. Look at the way he had to beg Chief Reynolds for a favor, like he was some peasant.

It was another sign of a decline he didn't understand. Storyville was teetering and the next calamity could be the one that toppled it.

The King of Storyville sighed and sipped his brandy, considering that no empire lasted forever.

Valentin was up and lingering about when Justine came out of the bathroom, her latte flesh all fresh and sweet smelling and her hair hanging down in wet ringlets. Instantly, he felt a tug in his gut and farther south, too. She looked so beautiful, and it was not uncommon for him to catch her at such a moment and tease her into their bed. She would protest about getting all sweaty again but never quite refused him.

He knew better than to try that now. As she padded about, her black eyes broadcast a cool warning that was more lethal than having her stomping around yelling at him. Her distrust was a finger poking in his chest.

It was no time to be cagey, so he told her what Anderson had said on the telephone early that morning. It was another straw on a camel's back that was already sagging, and she shook her head balefully.

"I need to go somewhere," he said.

"Well, what are you waiting for?"

"Justine—"

A sharp look quieted him. She picked up a whalebone comb and began pulling it through her curls.

"I thought I'd take a trip to Jackson," he said.

She stopped what she was doing. "What for?"

"That morning Frank called? It was because King Bolden's wife was at the saloon and she wanted to tell me that Buddy had been speaking my name."

Justine said, "So? He lost his mind, ain't that right?"

"Yes, he —"

"Then so what if he's saying your name? Man's crazy."

"But he's never done it before. So I need to go, see what it's about."

She put a hand on her hip. "Why is it you do everyone's bidding but mine?"

He had to admit that she had him there. "I don't know," he said.

She took the frank admission and went back to pulling the comb through her hair. "You don't know much, do you?"

This was true, too. "If I don't stay out of sight, I could end up back in jail," he said. "So I might just as well go out there and see about him."

She gave him an absent frown, not really paying attention, and he wondered if she would be just as happy if once he left, he kept going. He tried to think of something he could say that would appease her and came up empty.

She finished with her hair and when she went to lay her comb aside, it tumbled off the vanity. Bending down to pick it up, her kimono loosened and he caught a glimpse of brown curves, a sight that all but reassured him that he was crazy to risk losing her. She straightened, turned away, and disappeared into the bedroom to get dressed. She didn't ask him when he was leaving or when he planned to come back. He went in search of the train schedule to find the time for the next local traveling to Jackson, home of the Louisiana State Hospital for the Insane.

Malvina called up the staircase that there was someone on the telephone. She was in the kitchen when the lady of the house appeared wearing an expression that gave her cause to narrow her eyes. The flesh on Miss Evelyne's face was infused with a rosy light, as if she had just finished a frolic in her upstairs bedroom.

She was positively breezy as she swept to the table, where Mr. Benoit was nodding over his oatmeal. Without even bothering to greet her husband, she devoured a plate of scrambled eggs, bacon, and toasted bread, drinking her coffee with noisy gusto. All the while she chatted away about nothing in particular, this neighbor and that, the wonderful autumn weather, and her plans for the day.

It was a strange, giddy performance, and Malvina wondered if her employer had gone soft in the head. She had heard stories from other women who worked as servants for well-to-do American families. Tales of love affairs, addictions, suicides, murders, and all sorts of other craziness. There was a hospital on Henry Clay called the Louisiana Retreat where dozens of wealthy citizens who could not restrain their urges were consigned, some behind barred windows. They had escaped justice for their deeds by being placed in a sanitarium.

Malvina studied her employer, knowing that beneath the facades of New Orleans' upper classes lay varieties of sin, madness, and corruption that would make John the Revelator sit up and take notice. The maid had long suspected Mrs. Evelyne of some special wickedness and was intent on vigilance, lest it be visited on her own blood.

Later that afternoon a mulatto attendant ushered Valentin into the large dayroom that he remembered from when he had first visited Bolden. Had it really been six years? With tall and narrow windows and a high ceiling, the room was like a cathedral, the afternoon light from the west casting swaths within which floating particles of dust glittered. There was also something sepulchral about the silence. Though the floor was populated by a variety of madmen, he heard no screams, shouts, or moans. Even those given to rants kept their voices down low, speaking in whispers, as if reciting prayers.

And there were many who spoke not at all, among them the lank-bodied black man in a loose, off-white shirt and black trousers who seemed to be searching for something. He traveled in a circle about the entire room, running his hand over every surface as if blind. Valentin remembered that, too.

A doctor had explained that it was not uncommon behavior for a man whose mind was unhinged.

"They want to touch something solid, something familiar," the doctor had explained in a quiet voice. "Otherwise . . ." He had shrugged, letting the words fade in the air.

Now Valentin and the attendant stood watching this meandering performance, one that the patient had repeated thousands of times. Presently, the mulatto said, "Good luck with him," and moved away.

Valentin crossed the floor, careful not to wander too close to any of the men. The attendant had warned him that some of them could snap into violence or dissolve into weeping hysterics if threatened. So he made a wide loop, but one that put him in his old friend's path.

Buddy approached and then moved around him with only the tiniest hitch, running water yielding to a rock. Valentin let him pass, turning halfway to watch his back as he padded off.

"Buddy," he said. "It's Tino."

Buddy hesitated, then stopped. He was still for a few seconds. Then he turned around. He didn't look at Valentin's face, instead directing his dark gaze somewhere over the detective's shoulder. He blinked hard three or four times, as if concentrating on a troublesome question. With his next breath, a sound rose from his throat and stopped, and Valentin realized that he had tried to speak, only to find his voice too rusty.

He swallowed and tried again. "Tino." His lips pursed as if tasting the name.

Valentin saw the nervous blink and shifted his own stare away, and in that moment they were back in their First and Liberty neighborhood, two shy kids meeting for the first time. The detective remained quiet because he didn't want to unsettle Buddy and because he didn't know what to say. He spent the moment musing on how much his old friend had changed, his back curling over and face going gaunt, so that he resembled the rendition of a saint in a stained-glass church window. Though he was only thirty-six, his wiry hair was tinged with new strands of gray. Yet he was still handsome, and Valentin could see shadows of the character who used to have back-of-town women fighting over him.

That was history. Who would believe, if they saw him now, that he had once set night after night ablaze with his riotous horn? That he had all but healed the sick and raised the dead with what came out of the bell of that silver cornet? That his delirious music and manic antics had gotten him worshipped and cursed from one end of the city to the other?

If he hadn't created jass all by himself, he had been the leader of the lunatic parade. But now that almost everyone was playing in that vein—and calling it *jazz*—he was mostly forgotten. The wild electricity that had animated him when he was Kid Bolden and then King Bolden, the shooting star of New Orleans music, was gone, like a tenant who had vacated the premises, leaving no forwarding address.

The years had eroded much, including secrets from their childhoods. When Buddy went away, the Creole detective lost one of his last connections to his past, and now and then he wondered if the reason he lingered in New Orleans was a furtive hope that some magic or voodoo would bring at least a few precious pieces back to him.

He doubted the poor fellow before him could brew such magic. Buddy looked like nothing so much as a poor soul who had been left along a road in some foreign land. Valentin could see him now struggling toward something and waited.

When he started to turn away, the detective thought he had lost him. But Buddy caught himself and his head came back around. Momentarily, he cleared his throat again and said, "Thought you were gone."

Valentin spent a moment startled at hearing the voice again.

Along with the gravel was a faint echo of music. Then he felt his face redden, thinking his friend was making a comment on his record of visits.

"I'm sorry," he said. "But when I did come out, you didn't—"

"No, no," Buddy cut him off, looking at and through him at the same time. "They said you were *gone*. Away from that place."

Valentin was puzzled. "What place? Storyville?"

Buddy's face pinched in frustration. Valentin, glancing about for someplace away from the other patients, noticed a vacant window alcove.

"Can we get over there?" he said, and began edging in that direction.

Buddy considered for a moment and then followed at a creeping pace. His eyes flitted as he reached out to touch the surfaces around him. Though now his fingers brushed the walls and moldings in an absent way.

They stood in the alcove, facing each other. To put his friend at ease, the detective made a point of leaning against the wall and crossing his arms languidly.

It seemed to work. Buddy relaxed enough to fix his own gaze out the window. Beyond the rice fields and the dirt ribbon of Highway 61 lay the houses of the dusty hamlet of St. Francisville and, farther on, the bright thread that was the Mississippi River buckled in a sharp curve. It was too far to see, ten miles or more, and yet he stared as if the whole landscape was laid out before him.

Valentin waited a few more seconds, then said, "This is about Storyville?"

Buddy was quiet for so long that the detective thought he might have lost him. Then he shifted his position and said, "They were talking. The two of them. And they said your name."

"The two of who?"

"The white fellow was in here. Him, and the one who come to visit him."

"A patient?"

Buddy's eyes, black and deep, moved to fix on Valentin's. "I heard someone say he went crazy and killed a man, so they put him in here. That one day, he was talking to the other one, and I heard. Then he went away again."

"What was his name?" There was no response, and Valentin sensed Buddy beginning to drift off. "Buddy?"

"What's that?"

"What was his name?"

The response came slower. "Whose name?"

"The white man," Valentin said, trying to hold his friend's attention. "The crazy one."

A sudden impish grin cracked Buddy's face. "Everybody's crazy in here," he said. "You see that sign outside? Says *insane* on it."

Valentin stopped to smile, then made another stab. "What did you say his name was?"

"It was . . ." Buddy hesitated, shrugged. "I don't remember that."

The detective thought for a few seconds, then said, "So he had a visitor?" Buddy nodded again. "And they were talking about me?"

The taller man nodded. "Said your name."

"You hear anything else?"

Buddy's expression turned fretful as he glanced at Valentin, then away again. "He was going to get out. And the other one say when that happened, he needed to go to the city. Said he had him some work to do."

"What work?"

Buddy was quiet for a long moment. "You know how I knew when it was all over?" he said suddenly. "When the hack that brought us here turned off the river road and I couldn't see it no more." He paused and when he resumed, his voice was dreamy. "Long as we were alongside the river, I figured we were fine. But when I couldn't see it no more, I figured I was bound for hell." He stared for a second, then leaned a little closer to the window. "It's out there somewhere, ain't it?"

Valentin looked. "What?"

"The river."

"It's pretty far off," Valentin told him. "But, yeah . . ."

"I know. I can't see it at all." Buddy pondered for a few seconds. "You know you can take it right down to New Orleans."

"I know."

"I bet that's what he did, then."

It took the detective a moment to realize he had jumped back to the original subject of the two men and their odd exchange.

"They wasn't up to no good." Buddy sounded a little tense. "That one spoke your name said when he got out, he was going to Storyville, and I could tell he wasn't up to no good at all."

He caught a breath, wearied by the speech. He took a step away, then changed his mind, and stepped back, his eyes narrowing into a stare that was almost familiar.

"What'd you do, Tino?" He cocked his head. "You shoot somebody? Another somebody?" He smiled, showing a hint of white teeth. "What was that first one's name? That nigger over in Algiers?"

"McTier," Valentin said. "Eddie McTier."

"You shot him dead." Buddy nodded, agreeing with himself. "And, what, now you done killed another one?"

Valentin didn't bother to question how Buddy remembered Algiers and McTier. Or how he guessed what had transpired with the man he had shot. It was luck or voodoo or some other something that came out of his mad mind. "That's right, I did," he said. "Last night. In Storyville."

"How many's that make?"

It took a moment for Valentin to say, "Three."

Buddy now eyed him wisely. "That why you're here?"

"I'm here because Nora told me that you said my name."

Buddy thought about that, then said, "Well, then, you come for the wrong reason."

Valentin was about to ask why that was when he detected the old Buddy reappearing, the dark eyes dancing as another white smile flashed. He said, "We played some *ragged* damn jass, ain't that right?"

Valentin recovered enough to say, "Yeah, Buddy, you sure did."

"Tore it up."

"All night long."

Buddy held it for a moment. Then his face fell by degrees into melancholy. "Now it's all over."

"People still play it," Valentin said. "Not like you, though. Ain't nobody ever played like you. And they call it *jazz* now."

"*Jazz.*" Buddy tasted the word. His gaze shifted once more, and again he fixed on the detective's eyes. "Don't you forget the way it was," he said. "Don't you forget none of it."

"I won't."

The stare drew away, turned inward, and went blank. Valentin felt that somehow a breeze had blown through the room, carrying his friend away and leaving him alone.

Buddy turned away to resume his travels, laying his hand on every solid surface as he made his silent way around the sunlit room.

Valentin found the attendant near the door and waited until the mulatto finished calming a slightly frantic patient before approaching him. Deftly, he slipped a coin into the pink palm. The attendant just as deftly made it disappear and with an easy smile said, "How can I help you, sir?"

"Did you have someone go missing from the hospital recently?"

"Go missing?" The attendant frowned. "You mean escape?"

"Or just leave."

"Not over here."

"What about in the white ward?"

"Only people I know of left over there was a man named Knox whose people took him home and another one name of Brown. But he died. That's all." He gave Valentin a sly look. "Why? Someone been telling stories?"

Valentin repeated Buddy's description of the patient and his visitor, leaving out most of the details.

"Ain't no murderers 'round here," the mulatto said with a gentle laugh. "They keep them types in the cage. But patients say things like that all the time. So the others'll leave them be. They go and make up all kinds of crazy shit. Say they the president, or Jesus, or something like that." He tilted his head in the general direction of the ward floor. "One time your friend there told me he was the one come up with jazz music. All by himself."

Valentin said, "That's true, he pretty much did that," and with a nod of thanks, he walked off, leaving the mulatto staring.

Valentin stood at the top of the driveway that curved downward from the broad stone veranda of the administration building, watching idly as a wagon filled with produce for the kitchen rambled through the gate. The gate swung closed, and the hack creaked as it rolled around the building.

Seeing Buddy for the first time in years had thrown his thoughts in a jumble. Though his old friend cut a figure that was beyond blue, it was at least a relief to know that his mind still had anchors, however small, and that photographs from a happier time remained in corners of his memory.

Valentin didn't know what to make of the odd tale of the two strangers—one a patient, the other a visitor—talking about him and Storyville. He knew it could be nothing more than a tangle of words, spoken or imagined, that got muddled up in Bolden's broken mind. The detective saw no pattern to it at all and no reason to give it any more thought.

As he started down the incline to catch the wagon to the station, he glanced back over his shoulder and wondered if he'd ever have reason to come back and see Buddy again.

The train pulled out as the autumn sun was falling and rolled to the southwest, picking up speed, then slowing and coming to a huffing stop at the Slaughter station. Two other passengers got on, drummers with their cases, looking worn out after a day's selling door-to-door.

Neither man would have the faintest clue about their fellow rider's last twenty-four hours. It was about this time the prior evening that he had been laying his trap. Before the night was over, his Iver Johnson .32 had claimed another victim, and the killer who had stalked the red-light district was on his way to the city morgue, the expense of a trial and hanging saved by the quick snap of a trigger. If Valentin wasn't a hero, he had at least done the District a service. He had been in jail, then set free, only to face Justine's wrath. He had made a trip to a madhouse to visit his childhood friend, maybe for the last time.

All that, and in less than one sweep of the clock. With any luck, things would be quiet when he got back to the city.

If only he could get some relief from the nagging, niggling worm that kept whispering that there was something more to Buddy's strange recollection. He gazed out the window at the flat landscape passing his window in the falling light. Could it really be coincidence that Buddy had begun speaking his name at the same moment he became embroiled in a case of multiple murder? It seemed unlikely, and yet all he took away from the hospital was shifting smoke.

The lights of another passing village flickered outside the window. Home was only two hours away. He could see no reason not to settle into the slow waters of his former life; except for the messy business about no longer having a job and the whirring tempest of Justine's anger, of course. Neither represented a permanent state of affairs. He slouched down and thought about how to manage those dilemmas until the squeal of air brakes snapped him out of it.

The train crawled into the station at Zachary. He sat very still for a few seconds, then got to his feet, hurried down the aisle past the two weary drummers, and stepped out onto the platform. The sign on the side of the terminal house said the next northbound train would arrive in thirty minutes. He sat down on the bench to wait.

The sun had gone down and the moon was rising over New Orleans. Evelyne Dallencort roused Thomas to carry her to the musical revue at the State Palace Theater on Canal Street. The young Negro had no sooner driven away than she turned to the doorman and asked him to whistle up another automobile for her.

The driver, a sober-faced mulatto, barely glanced at her, waiting for his instructions. She laid them out precisely and then dropped a Liberty half-dollar onto the seat next to him. He picked up the coin, threw the shift lever forward, and they were off.

She had him chauffeur her down Basin Street and then along Franklin, Liberty, and Marais. She took in the sights, making a busy list in her head. She spent an hour so engaged, and then told the driver to head south. In fifteen minutes the automobile came to a stop at the corner of Spain and Decatur and she sat quietly, observing one building and then the next, up and down both banquettes.

She then asked the driver to carry her home to Perrier Street and to take his time.

It was a dozen short miles back to Jackson, and Valentin walked the rest of the way to the hospital from the station rather than take a hack or jitney. In a fast forty minutes, he was standing in the darkness opposite the main building, quiet now that most of the staff had gone home, and scanning the horizon like a stalking cat. As he crossed over, it occurred to him that any doubt that he was back to his old ways was getting drubbed. He fell into his creeping habits as if drawing on familiar clothes.

Getting past the guard in the lobby proved easier than he expected. He was lurking between two of the columns on the veranda, working on a plan to sneak inside, when the doors opened and the guard stepped out and then to the edge of the veranda, where he stopped to light a cigarette. The face of the middle-aged white man was thin and drawn in the glow of the lucifer. Valentin didn't see a weapon; a front-desk guard wouldn't require one.

When the guard stepped off the veranda to enjoy the stars in the night sky, Valentin made a hushed trot to the door and pulled it open just wide enough to slip through. He quickly crossed the lobby to the corridor, then made himself part of the wall, in case the guard had been alerted by the swish of the door.

He waited for a half minute before poking his head out. The lobby remained empty and quiet. A few steps forward gave him an angle to the front window, and he could see the guard lolling in the same place, the tip of his cigarette an orange dot in the darkness.

He padded to the end of the east corridor and didn't find what he was looking for. Passing back across the lobby, he entered the opposite corridor. At the far end, he found a door with the word RECORDS painted on the glass. The lock was an old-fashioned type that he cracked by jiggling one of his skeleton keys for a few seconds.

He struck four lucifers before he found the drawer marked PATIENT RELEASES. The files were arranged by date, and he selected the first one, tagged as SEPTEMBER–OCTOBER. He didn't have enough lucifers left to be able to read through it, so he carried the file to the corridor and stepped out the exit to the north side of the building, taking care to block the door open with a stone.

The grounds were quiet and the lights in the windows of the wards glowed softly. At this time of night, staff and patients would be eating supper, which would be followed by evening recreation, then lights out by eight or so. No one was about, so Valentin leaned against the brick wall under the feeble glow of the bare bulb that was mounted over the door.

He flipped through the October releases and found eight files in all. He stopped at the fifth one.

The name written in the box at the top was "Brown, William P." Valentin read quickly through the essentials and found that Brown was from Merryville and had been committed by the Beauregard Parish sheriff. The reason for the commitment was a vague "Recommended by Court." Also noted in a box at the top of the page was the patient's assigned room: W-328.

Brown had been diagnosed as suffering from dementia prae-cox, a phrase that covered a vast array of mental disorders and meant the doctors didn't know what was wrong with him, other than a brand of insanity. There were a series of comments noting "some improvement" or "no improvement" over the months he had been a patient. The other notations were in the nature of "quiet" and "calm." Apparently, Mr. Brown had not been a problem for the staff.

Given that there was no notation of any illness or injury, the patient's death must have come as a surprise. He was transferred to the infirmary on the evening of September 29. He died two days later. Brown spent October 1, the final day of his life, at the State Hospital for the Insane. The last note read: "Body released to family for burial," followed by a pair of indecipherable initials.

Valentin closed the file and gazed across the grounds. Within three weeks after William Brown had died, five bodies had turned up in Storyville. A few days later, Valentin chased a deranged white man to the middle of a Storyville street and shot him dead.

The detective opened the folder to review the details. Brown's height and weight were listed as five feet six inches tall and 140 pounds. It certainly fit the man who had bled his life out on the cobbles of the Storyville intersection. It appeared that once Brown had been discharged from the hospital, he began a journey that landed him in the line of fire of the Creole detective's Iver Johnson pistol.

One more quick scan revealed nothing else of value, and he closed the folder. Pulling the door open, he peered along the still corridor, then stepped inside and made his way back to the Records room and returned the file to its drawer. When he poked his head out again, he saw the guard at the lobby desk, his feet up as he read a penny magazine. The detective made a soundless exit out the side door.

It was still quiet and he was crossing the grounds when he came upon the white ward, clearly noted by the large W high on the corner of the building. He circled around and noticed no activity behind the windows. The entrance at the end of the building was covered by a peaked roof, and just above it he saw a small window that had been left open a few inches. He made another quick scan of the grounds, then began a quick shinny up the post and onto the roof. The window opened with a soft squeak, and he was peering down a long hallway, the wood floors shiny beneath the electric sconces that were spaced along the walls.

He slipped over the sill and lowered the window behind him. The room numbers on the floor began at 200. He waited, listening for any errant sound, then started up the stairwell. Stopping to peek out the hexagonal window on the first landing, he viewed the lights of the dining hall. The doors had just opened to emit a slow parade of patients, accompanied by guards.

He didn't have much time. With a sprint up the remaining stairs, he hurried into the corridor and made a beeline for room 328, at the far end.

Three iron-frame beds were arranged on either side, with a small night table at each, and all but one dressed with sheets and a blanket and pillow. A patient sat upright in one of the dressed beds, watching the visitor with dull eyes. The man did not speak at all as the detective made a circuit of the room. Valentin reached the undressed bed and noticed something different about the wall behind the headboard. He stepped closer and peered between the rails.

By the slight shading, it appeared that the patch of wall had been freshly painted. Just beneath the fresh paint, someone had scratched the same design over and over, in near-perfect rows.

He straightened and turned to the patient, who had continued to watch him in silence.

"Brown?" he asked.

The patient cleared his throat as if unused to speaking and said, "He used to sleep there."

"Before he died?"

The man appeared puzzled. "Before they took him away."

Noise seeped into the hallway, and Valentin stepped out of the room just in time to meet the wave of patients returning from dinner. He was barely noticed in the hubbub and weaved through the bodies, down the stairs, and out the door without being stopped or questioned.

An hour later he was stepping off the platform and onto the late express train to New Orleans.

Louis was lounging against the sweeping fender of the Buick, smoking a Straight Cut, when she emerged on the balcony. She stood staring in his direction, so motionless she could herself have been a shadow. She lingered for a long minute, then stepped back inside.

Louis had flicked away his cigarette and was circling around to the driver's side when the street door opened and she appeared on the banquette. She looked up and down Spain Street before stepping onto the cobblestones.

He noticed that she was dressed well, with a long walking

skirt and shirtwaist and a shawl draped over her shoulders, pale silk embroidered with peacocks and fern branches.

As she drew near, he straightened, coming to attention like a servant. This gave her a moment's pause, and she laughed under her breath. He didn't say a word, simply opening the passenger side door and offering his hand to help her onto the running board. He closed the door and moved to the front of the Buick. The engine caught on the first crank, and he hopped nimbly behind the wheel, opened the choke, and advanced the spark until the twelve cylinders settled into a purring idle.

They rode back into the city the same way they had driven out on the previous Tuesday night, along the same streets, and in the same silence.

She didn't know where he was taking her. She also didn't know what he was after, though the simplest answer was the same thing they all wanted: the sweet prize nestling between her legs. Though he hadn't made any moves in that direction, and his gaze when he appeared in the professor's basement classroom was not carnal, only inquisitive, as if he couldn't quite fathom her, either. He had watched her face, and his eyes had roamed idly to her bare bosom. He slipped out as deftly as he had appeared.

She pondered these odd maneuvers as he wheeled the phaeton around Union Station, over the tracks, and onto Basin Street. She couldn't read a thing from his expression. He kept his eyes on the streets as he drove placidly down the line and then turned into the French Quarter. He steered the automobile along Royal Street. Just past Dauphine, he pulled to the curb in front of an old French house fronted by an iron gate and a courtyard. He shut off the engine.

She turned to face him and said, "Well?"

By the time he finally stepped off the train at Union Station, Valentin was drained, having spent the afternoon and evening in the bidding of others. Tom Anderson told him to get out of town and he did. Nora Bolden asked if he would go see her husband and he went. Buddy described overhearing two men talking about him, and he poked his nose into that business, too. All that was left was to go home to make amends with Justine, the one person he had yet to serve this day.

He walked out of the station and onto Basin Street in time to see a red Buick 10 chug by, heading down the line. He felt a momentary flash of resentment that he didn't have the use of such a fine automobile, but instead faced being stuffed into a rattling streetcar and hauled across town like so much livestock to be dumped at a corner from where he would have to hike another three tiresome blocks. Not knowing what sort of reception was waiting when he reached his front door; maybe none at all.

He stopped to gaze across the tracks at Anderson's Café just as the door swung wide for two sharp-dressed sports, and he caught sight of chandeliers glittering over a polished tile floor that was crisscrossed by paths of red carpet. The tables were filling up, and behind the chatter he heard a jass band tootling through a song that once would have been considered a felony in proper quarters. Now it was standard entertainment for well-heeled citizens who didn't seem to have a care in the world. It seemed the word had gotten around that the evildoer who had been stalking the District was dead and everybody could relax and have a good time.

The door closed again, and Valentin walked down to the next corner to wait for the Canal Line car that would carry him to the Elysian Fields car that would carry him to Spain Street, like any other common fellow heading home far too late after a long day's work.

He was all but staggering along the Spain Street banquette when he saw her approaching from the other direction. Behind her, what appeared to be the same Buick he had seen on Basin Street was pulling away. He was confused, but his brain was too frazzled to puzzle it out. He was just glad to see her, glad to know that at least she hadn't packed her bags and moved out.

They arrived at the street door, an encounter that swam in the wide window of the import office. Regarding each other carefully, they both waited for the other to break the silence. Without a word, Valentin unlocked the door and held it open for her.

Upstairs he was relieved to find that no notes had been slipped under the door. Justine wandered into the bathroom, and he sat down on the divan and took off his shoes, feeling as dull as a rock. She stepped out of the bathroom and directly into the bedroom.

He waited until she appeared into the doorway and said, "Are you coming to bed?"

The maid out of Josie Arlington's found him on her way home. He was lying on his back, his arms flung wide as if reaching to hold himself from falling into a pit, his dead eyes staring up at the starless blue night. Black blood had spread like a puddle beneath him.

She said, "Good lord almighty," and took a few steps closer. She had heard the talk going around the houses, and there it was, just like they said, a thin line scratched into the flesh of the poor man's brow.

She let out a low moan, then ran back the way she had come, calling for someone to help.

SIXTEEN

The telephone rang at Captain Picot's tiny house on St. Ann Street, and he sat up, blinking. Few people had his number, and he kept it out of the directory. He swung his legs off the bed and lumbered like a sailor on a pitching deck into his living room. Snatching up the handset, he grunted irritably, then listened. Within a few seconds, his sour face became a rubbery mask of delight.

He could barely keep from crowing his orders. "It's the six hundred block of Spain Street. He keeps rooms over an import office there. I'll be down in an hour."

He dropped the handset into the cradle. *Finally,* he told himself, *after all this time. I've got him now, goddamnit. I've got that son of a bitch St. Cyr, but good.*

This time instead of the telephone, it was a pounding of footsteps up the stairwell and then an urgent banging on the door. Valentin felt himself grabbed and wrenched out of the darkness by the sound of someone yelling his name, loud but muffled. With a groan Justine came awake, pulling a pillow over her head as he stumbled from the bed.

Now he could hear Each calling urgently and shivering the jamb with the force of his hand. Valentin jerked the door open.

"You got to get out!" the kid sputtered. "The coppers are comin'!"

Each gave it to the detective in a few quick sentences. Another victim had turned up, this one found lying out on Bienville Street, shot in the chest and cut, just like the others. William Brown was not the killer, and Picot had sent a squad to apprehend St. Cyr all over again. Tom Anderson wouldn't be able to come to his rescue. He was officially targeted for arrest, and the New Orleans police were minutes away.

Valentin gaped, stupefied by this news. Justine stepped into the bedroom doorway to listen, her face grim as she tied the sash of her kimono. Each was too unnerved to steal his usual hungry peek at her.

Valentin didn't waste a second, grabbing the kid by the shoulder, turning him around, and ordering, "Watch the street." He bolted for the bedroom.

Justine stood in his path for a moment, her face unforgiving. A brief second passed and she stepped aside. He dressed in a flurry, all but jumping into his de Nimes trousers, high-topped walking shoes, and work shirt. He came out of the bedroom to find that Justine had gone into the closet for his old railroad jacket, and he gave a nod of thanks, still avoiding her eyes.

Stuffed into one of the pockets was an old wool driving cap, and once he donned it, he looked like a common laborer.

"There's a car at the corner," Each called from the balcony. "I think it's coppers."

"It is," Valentin called back. There was rarely any traffic in the neighborhood at that hour.

In another minute or so, a second car would arrive at the other end of the block. Patrolmen, closing along the banquettes, would have him hedged in on all sides, including the alley in back, on their way to pulling a net around him. He could all but see Picot's grinning face and dirty hands behind the web.

Each was reporting a second car as the detective snatched up his sap and stiletto. The police had confiscated his Iver Johnson, so he dug out his ancient Colt Bisley model. Justine lingered at the bedroom doorway, her face cool and impassive. There was nothing for either of them to say. Valentin jerked his head, and he and Each raced to the kitchen and then out the door onto the back stairs.

Once the lock clacked, Justine spent a few seconds swallowing her anger, then stepped quickly into the kitchen and shoved a mop, broom, and sack of rice against the door. Turning off all the lights, she returned to the bedroom and slipped under the covers. Only then did she allow herself to curse Valentin St. Cyr.

The rear stairwell was the only way out. Mr. Perrault, the owner of the import business, had given Valentin keys to the first floor in case of an emergency. The detective and Each now hurried through the storage room and unlocked the back door, which opened onto a narrow loading dock. Stopping in the darkness, they could hear the activity from Spain Street: the gurgle of idling engines, muted chatter, shoe leather slapping on the boards of the banquette.

Valentin saw no one moving around the back lot. He grabbed Each's sleeve and led him across the alley as the silhouette of a copper appeared at each end. They dived into the shadows of the lot on the other side and crept around the building to arrive on the banquette in front of a closed St. Roch Avenue café.

Each was nearly shaking with excitement. Valentin whispered instructions for him to get back to Storyville. He was to stay out of sight until he got there, then let himself be seen.

"Where you going to go?" the kid whispered back. His voice was thin with strain.

Valentin shook his head and waved him away. Once he had run off, the detective cut a jagged path through the alleys to St. Ferdinand Street, then made a turn toward the river, losing himself in the jumbled maze of shipping warehouses, small factories, and shops for the outfitting of vessels that spread out for four blocks on the other side of the tracks.

Two detectives appeared at the door. They showed Justine their gold badges and raked her with cool cop gazes. The older, shorter one said his name was Weeks and introduced his partner as McKinney. They had a warrant for the arrest of Valentin St. Cyr on a charge of murder.

Justine gazed between the two of them as if she didn't understand. "He's not here."

"Where is he?" Weeks said.

"I don't know. He left."

"When?"

"Yesterday," she said. "He was on his way to Union Station."

"He say where he was going?"

"He didn't." She kept her voice and expression flat, and the junior officer was struck in that moment by how much she resembled the Creole detective. She wasn't about to give up anything, either.

"We're going to look around, then," Weeks said.

Justine stepped back. "Look."

The pair split up and covered the four rooms within a matter of minutes. While Weeks ignored her, she caught curious glances from the one named McKinney. It was he who poked around in the kitchen, then came out to report to the senior detective.

"Nothing," he said.

"Then he's gone." Weeks treated Justine to a cold glance. "And you ain't got no idea where he went?"

Justine shook her head. The senior officer gave her a harder look. "You know we can take you in as a material witness," he said.

Justine stared back, her eyes blank. "Witness to what?"

Weeks started to say something back, then stopped. After a moment's stiff pause, he said, "Just so you understand, he's wanted on a murder charge. It ain't no joke. So if you hear from him, tell him he needs to come in. Only way it's going to get settled. Otherwise . . ." He let it hang.

"Otherwise what?" Justine said.

McKinney spoke up for the first time. "He's a fugitive, ma'am. That means if he runs, he could end up being shot." He saw her eyes widen and said, "It'll be better if he comes in." He fished in his pocket and handed her a card. "That's got the number of the desk at the precinct on it. In case you do hear from him."

The detectives made their exit. McKinney gave her a polite nod before closing the door behind him.

Captain Picot was pacing in his office when Weeks and McKinney arrived back. Though it was the dead of night, he was dressed all natty, as if on his way to a wedding or some other formal affair. An astonished Detective McKinney realized that the captain had gone to this trouble expecting to make a big show of the arrest of St. Cyr.

Picot came to an expectant halt when the cops stepped to his door.

Weeks threw up his hands. "We missed him."

"You what?" Picot's olive-tinged face turned an angry shade of red.

"He was gone by the time we got there. We searched all the rooms. Nothing."

Picot slammed a fist down on his desk and papers went flying.

"We've got men all around the neighborhood," Weeks said, swallowing. "Maybe they'll nab him."

Picot rolled his eyes. "No, they won't *nab* him," he said. "He was tipped off, and he ran." After a moment's dark pause, he said, "Well, I guess that means he's guilty, then, don't it? As if there was any doubt."

He glanced at McKinney, as if expecting a challenge. The detective kept his mouth shut and expression blank.

"Did you bring her in?"

"Bring who?" Weeks said.

"His woman."

"Those weren't our orders."

"Well, they are now," Picot said. "Go back and pick her up."

The two detectives exchanged a glance. McKinney said, "We've got nothing on her, sir."

Picot treated him to a foul stare. "Did you hear me? And while you're at it, go ahead and put out an alert on that damn Beansoup character or whatever he calls himself now."

"'Each,'" Weeks said. "He goes by 'Each.'"

Picot said, "Him, too. Find him and drag his ass in. As soon as the morning shift comes on, we'll cover every house in Storyville. Let them all know that St. Cyr killed the wrong man and then ran away. Get the word out that anyone helps him will get trouble." He flicked a hand. "Go ahead, then."

The detectives filed out. Captain Picot turned to his window and stared out at his corner of the city, knowing in his bones that wherever the Creole detective had gone, he hadn't left town and likely wouldn't. Picot preferred it that way. The two long-time rivals—make that *enemies*—were going to engage again, another battle in a war that had been going on for the better part of ten years.

Picot had come close to snagging St. Cyr before, only to have him slither from his grasp like the snake he was. This time it was different. The Creole detective had slipped, an amateur's blunder that he never would have committed had he stayed in Storyville and kept his skills sharp.

He'd lost his edge working for those St. Charles Avenue lawyers and so ended up shooting the wrong man dead. Now no one could save him, not Tom Anderson, not the madams in their mansions down the line, not any of his old cronies. Unless he could perform some feat of magic, he was as good as done.

If he was smart, Picot reflected, he'd leave New Orleans and never return, losing himself in the great muddled morass of some other city or in some nameless hamlet far away. He wouldn't, though; he was bound to this place and would linger here, even if it brought him to ruin.

The only detail the captain had to sweat was where St. Cyr had gone to ground and how long it would be before he came out into the open, as he surely would, and into the clutches of the New Orleans Police Department. It could take a day or a month. The Creole couldn't hide forever, and they'd be waiting.

In those years every city in the land contained at least one jungle, a vile, filthy, and perilous warren that sane people knew better than to visit. Such neighborhoods were beyond the pale, festering like open sores on the fringes of decent society. Most often they were located near the water, convenient for sailors and other misfits arriving and dead bodies departing, and were too poor, dirty, and disease-riddled to serve as anything except dumping grounds for dregs. The denizens were the worst humanity had to offer: thieves, rapists, hopheads, drunkards, and killers, every one of them stupid or crazy, scrabbling in the muck to stay alive for another day.

Such an enclave had grown up at the south end of Charbonnet Street, below North Peters, in the small tangle of alleys that huddled against the levee, more an encampment than a permanent quarter. It fell into the gap between New Orleans and the town of Arabi, and in another five years it would be gone like a bad memory.

They called it Brown Bottom, and it was there that Valentin decided to lose himself for a while. Shadowy, scurrying figures were the norm, and he knew no cop would come poking around there without a small army of fellow officers.

Along the alleys were hovels that passed for rooming houses, one-story affairs that catered to sailors too drunk or violent to get regular work, which was saying something.

The detective lurked for a while between two of the buildings, just him and a crumpled body that might have been dead. Once the alley hit a moment of stillness and silence, he slipped to the other side of the street and rapped on a door. He paid a half-blind, half-drunk old hag a nickel and got a ragged towel and a key.

His room was at the end of a littered hallway, about the size of a large closet, with a pallet, a chamber pot, and nothing else. The walls were mapped with stains from the leaking roof, and the reek of urine and mildew choked him. He wasn't there for the accoutrements.

It wasn't the first time he'd spent a night in such digs, and he knew what to do. The lock was worthless, so he pulled the sack of a dirty mattress away and leaned the pallet against the door, propping it closed. He folded the mattress upright into the cleanest corner and sat on the floor with his back against it and legs outstretched. Justine had thought to drop an apple in his pocket before he went out the door, and he nibbled it as he pondered his situation.

In twenty-four hours he had gone from hero to fugitive felon. He wouldn't be able to hide for long. Though the only photograph of him was lying in the back of a drawer in Papá

Bellocq's studio, a police artist could come up with a good enough likeness. He could count on his face being in the hands of every cop in the city by morning. Once the word got around that he was on the run, anyone spotting him would sell the information for a dollar.

It would be easy enough for him to hop a freight smoking out of the yard behind Union Station. Railroad cops would be watching, too, but they couldn't cover every car. It would be the smart thing to do, except that he'd never be able to come back. His name would be forever tagged with the appellation of *murderer,* and for the rest of his days he'd risk being spotted, identified, captured. And what of Justine? What kind of life would it be for her?

Indeed, he was in deep trouble because he hadn't listened, hadn't respected her wishes. Why would she follow him down a fugitive trail?

His thoughts shifted and he recalled her approaching from the corner and the red Buick 10 slipping away in the background. He knew without asking that she had been riding in the car, and that it was the same one he'd spied on Basin Street. He had been too exhausted to ask her what it meant.

Maybe he should have stayed to find out, but from the moment he opened the door for Each, he knew his only chance was to run. Now his only choice was to stay and untangle himself from the trap.

If Justine thought her troubles were over when the two detectives walked out, she was mistaken. She drowsed fitfully and was roused within the hour by the clattering telephone. She came swaying out of the bedroom, wishing they had thrown the noisy device in the river long ago.

It was a gruff Tom Anderson calling again. He listened as Justine explained that Valentin had heard about trouble on the way and decided to leave. She was not happy about any of it and didn't provide any details.

"And he went where?" Anderson inquired, though they both understood that she wouldn't tell him even if she knew. She owed the King of Storyville less than nothing. To her, he was just another man wreaking havoc. He mumbled something about having Valentin get in touch, then clicked off.

She had just lain down again when the street door squeaked and footsteps thumped in the stairwell, followed by a hard pounding. Standing on her landing was Weeks, the senior detective from the night before, but this time accompanied by a beat cop in blue uniform and round-topped helmet.

"Captain Picot wants you at the precinct for questioning," Weeks said.

Justine recognized the name as an enemy's and considered arguing. She had nothing to tell him or anyone else. But putting up a fight would only make things worse.

"I'll need a moment to dress," she said.

From the bedroom she could hear them pacing around. They were likely wondering if she would try to escape out the back window and looked relieved when she reappeared in a plain shirtwaist.

Down on the street, they escorted her along the banquette to the corner, where a black Ford Model T with a New Orleans Police Department emblem on the door was parked. Weeks helped her into the rear seat, allowing his hand to linger on her too long. The patrolman started the engine, and they rolled off through the New Orleans dawn to a meeting with Captain J. Picot.

Each heard from one of his spies about the cops heading back to Spain Street. He arrived too late to warn Justine and had to duck into a doorway when the police sedan went by. He peeked out just in time to see the Model T round the corner, heading downtown, with her in the backseat.

Not that he could have done anything to help. The cops would be after him, too, thinking he would know where the Creole detective was hiding. Which, in fact, he did; or, at the least, had a fair idea. They had talked about it before, and Mr. Valentin had said, "If ever . . ."

Though it had been a long time ago, Each had never forgotten. He remembered almost every word of what the Creole detective had said over the years. Now he checked the street ahead, just as he had been taught, and when it was clear, he made his way out of the neighborhood and toward the river.

The cops brought Justine up the stairwell. The other detectives and uniformed officers stopped what they were doing and took notice. Low whistles followed her as she passed between the desks on the way to Captain Picot's office.

The captain, keeping his back to the officers and their quarry, gazed out on the dark streets. He had heard the stir outside his door and saw the visitors' reflections in the window glass, framed like a moving-picture show.

Once they arrived in the doorway, he took his time turning around. She was as exotic to him as a wild-blooming flower and made his gut churn to think that someone like St. Cyr claimed such a prize. And not just this one; Picot knew about others, one a lovely mulatto, another a black-skinned island girl, a third a young American lady from one of the better families on Esplanade Ridge. The Creole had enjoyed them and more, goddamn his soul. All sorts of women were drawn to him.

His quadroon was something special, though, and Picot could understand why she was the only one St. Cyr held on to. Though under medium size, she had a large woman's vibrant presence. Her eyes were round and black, and her nose was curved like a Jewess's. She had pulled her black curls back in an Indian braid. Beneath her cloak, her body was full and lithe, something a man could feast on for years, or so the captain imagined . . . He caught himself and straightened his shoulders.

There was more to the story. He held one of Justine Mancarre's deepest secrets, and all that kept him from using the rich morsel was that her man, that fucking Creole St. Cyr, had even darker knowledge about him. So while it was true that he and this young lovely were at a standoff, he still had some cards to play.

He had yet to meet her eyes. With a glance at the patrolman who had escorted her in, he said, "Go find a matron." The cop bowed out.

As a younger officer, Picot had taken his way with a share of the sweethearts and even wives of criminals he arrested. They were easy pickings for him. This indulgence lasted until a burglar named Duprez decided that his whore's honor was worth suicide and tried to murder the then–lieutenant second grade in broad daylight. It was good fortune that the patrolmen in Picot's company that day were crack shots, and Duprez ended up on the banquette, bleeding his life out through four holes in his chest. The last time Picot saw the wife was at Duprez's funeral parade, and her eyes were daggers. So he had her run out of town.

Since that time he had been more vigilant, taking advantage only of women who had no man to protect them. Even that had diminished as the years went by and his random cruelties began to eat at him.

That didn't mean he couldn't relish this moment. It was Valentin St. Cyr's woman standing before him, after all. He spent a moment picturing her undressed and at his mercy, then pulled his thoughts away from that scenario. If he abused her in any way, St. Cyr would come for him. Still, he could use the girl to his own ends; in this case, for bait.

She spoke up, poking into his thoughts. "Am I under arrest?"

Picot did look at her now, his brow pinching. "If you are, you'll be the first to know." He pushed some papers around on his desk. "Is there any point in me asking you where St. Cyr is at the moment?"

Justine said, "I don't know." She tilted her head. "I told the detective that."

"Oh, well, then I guess we made a mistake bringing you in." Though the captain's eyes widened clownishly, there was no humor in his voice. He saw the way she was watching him, prey to predator, just a little unsure of his power, and he felt a tingle in his bones. He had St. Cyr's woman, and there was nothing the Creole could do about it, having run away to hide.

When he looked at her again, their gazes locked and he saw that she was trying to read his thoughts. She was a sly one, all right, and had no doubt learned some tricks from St. Cyr. The captain remembered the other officers were standing by idly, surely wondering what the hell was going on. He quickly reverted to his officious posture, though his face remained flushed with agitation.

"Where's the damned matron?" he inquired to no one in particular.

"She's out there," Detective Weeks said.

"All right, have her park this one somewhere."

Weeks took Justine by the elbow to lead her out. Again, she said, "Am I under arrest?" She sounded like was losing patience with this foolishness.

"You ask too many questions," Picot said, and waved a dismissive hand.

He watched through the doorway as the matron, a trusty guard from the women's prison who wasn't more than twenty-five herself, directed her charge to the bull pen, a part of the room cordoned off by a low molded railing and set with chairs and a small table.

The captain wanted her to sit there and stew the rest of the day, if need be, and think about where St. Cyr might be, what he was doing, and if he was going to leave her to fend for herself.

SEVENTEEN

Uptown New Orleans woke Saturday morning to the news that the Storyville murders hadn't stopped after all. Another shot-dead body marked with a slash had been found on the streets, and the Creole detective St. Cyr had gone into hiding with a warrant out for his arrest in the death of William Brown.

The *Daily Picayune* and the *Sun* had already assigned reporters the task of wrapping up the story of the murderer Brown. The *Sun* was the bolder of the two and had someone tracking down St. Cyr for an interview by way of a young rounder who went by the moniker Each. But then the afternoon papers took a sharp turn with the lurid tale of a fresh killing in the tenderloin, a sure sign that something had gone terribly wrong in that part of the city, and that citizens should be on their guard.

Telephones had been ringing in parlors and foyers through the night as crabby men sniped back and forth. Chief of Police Reynolds's voice was trembling with anger when he finally got Tom Anderson on the line.

"You made fools out of the both of us!" he yelled.

"Calm down, Chief. We don't—"

"You had me put a murderer back on the street," Reynolds went on, rolling over him. "Now won't I have a hell of a time explaining that?"

The King of Storyville bit his tongue.

"Where is he?" the chief demanded.

"Where is who? St. Cyr?"

"Yes, St. Cyr. Who else? We have a warrant out on that Creole son of a bitch."

"I don't know where he is. He's not—"

"Don't you dare try to hide him."

Reynolds's tone was severe, as if he was dressing down some underling, and Anderson decided he'd heard enough. "I told you he doesn't work for me, goddamnit."

The chief took a step back to allow a moment of calm, and the two old heavyweights went to their corners. Momentarily, the King of Storyville said, "He's not my man anymore, Billy. It's different now. I helped him out because I couldn't believe he'd be so wrong about this man Brown. I still can't. But . . ."

Reynolds, standing in the study in his house in Carrollton, heard the odd note of defeat in Anderson's voice. The man sounded almost pitiful.

"Well." The chief was confounded. "If you do hear from him, he needs to give up. He'll get a fair trial. You tell him I said that." He lowered his voice as if there were other people in their respective rooms. "You know there's still bad blood at the department. The last thing we need is a 'shot while escaping' situation."

"He's not going to come to me," Anderson said with a sigh. "He knows I can't do anything for him. He's on his own." He paused for a quiet instant, then said, "Of course, he always preferred it that way."

The chief of police was mulling these last weary words when the line went dead.

———

Officer McKinney had been assigned the task of accompanying the victim's body to the morgue and working up an identification. He knew full well this was intentional, that Captain Picot didn't trust him and wanted him out of the way. The captain was as edgy as a rattlesnake when it came to Valentin St. Cyr, and alert for any sign of sympathy in that direction.

James McKinney had failed that test. Having become intrigued by St. Cyr from the moment their paths had first crossed, he had taken the time to learn that the detective had come from the uptown neighborhood around First and Liberty streets, had lost his family, and had later changed his name in order to become a New Orleans police officer. When that career ended badly, he hired on as Tom Anderson's man, responsible for the security of the red-light district.

He was a lone wolf and skilled investigator who had followed an uncommon path by working both sides of the law. The infamous King Bolden had been his best friend. He carried on a turgid romance with a onetime sporting girl named Justine Mancarre. He had been embroiled in several of the most remarkable cases in uptown New Orleans' recent history and had broken the Black Rose and jass murders, along with the Benedict killing.

McKinney understood that the brass cursed St. Cyr because he had embarrassed them time and again. Captain Picot in particular held him accountable for some unnamed offense. McKinney wondered what it could be that would inspire such bile. He was enough of a detective to know it was more than just two men who happened to despise each other.

Whatever it was didn't matter this day. He had been given an order to carry out, and while he had no love of dead bodies, he was curious to identify the victim.

The same two attendants—the dull and quiet one and his smaller, talkative companion—were waiting for him. They stepped into the alley and went about the business of unloading the shrouded corpse onto a gurney and maneuvering it back inside. The horse-drawn meat wagon rolled away, and Detective McKinney followed the two living and one dead citizen down the long corridor.

The attendants stripped the body, irked at having a copper standing by, which made it impossible for them to snatch any overlooked prizes from the clients: a watch, cuff links, now and then a few dollars in coin. So they stood aside, their arms crossed as McKinney went through the victim's clothes, finding nothing helpful, save for two calling cards with the same name and address printed on them:

Roland Parks
No. 1212 Perdido Street—2nd Fl.

Such cards could be found in many pockets. The lack of any profession generally meant that the holder didn't have one, other than day laborer, drifter, or petty criminal. Even gamblers carried cards, describing them as *Agents* or *Advisors,* whatever those titles signified.

So the casually employed Mr. Roland Parks had the prior evening left his room in a boardinghouse on Perdido Street and traveled to Storyville. Then, before or after visiting one of the houses, he was murdered, cut, and left where he fell, to be discovered some time later by a maid on her way home.

The policeman spent another moment with the victim's clothes. The bullet hole in Parks's jacket was surrounded by a corona of dried blood and a black residue. After he shuffled through the rest of the garments, he put them aside and turned back to the body. Parks was a common-looking white man, his face hitched in an expression of slight puzzlement, as if he, too, couldn't imagine why he had been marked for death.

"Your bad luck, fellow," McKinney murmured. The attendants exchanged a glance. The detective examined the wound, a hole the size of a Liberty nickel and the flesh around it bruised and stained. Taking the appearance of the jacket into account, he surmised that the weapon had been held dead against the body. No wonder Roland Parks looked baffled; a fellow stepped up to ask for a light or the time, and a second later he was dead. The cut on his forehead had a sloppy appearance, as if the assailant didn't care about getting it right.

McKinney straightened, closed his notebook, and put it away.

"All right, then," he said. "I'll see if I can find anyone who knew the man. Maybe there's next of kin. And if not . . ."

"Then we know what to do with him," the older attendant said with a smirk.

Evelyne spent extra time at her dressing mirror before she started her trip downtown. She could not remove the flush of excitement from her face or slow the thumping of her heart.

Every piece of her plan was in place. She had gone undetected, slipping through the undergrowth as sharply and slyly as a fox. Even when things went awry, she didn't panic, the sign of a true leader.

She tucked the last ivory pin in her hair and stepped to the window. The rain was drenching the cobbles of Perrier Street. She saw the Winton idling at the curb, the exhaust pipe billowing thin smoke into the afternoon mist. Though the top was up and the flaps were down, she could picture Thomas with his hands gripping and releasing the wheel and tapping his foot nervously, eager to get gone. He could wait a little longer. It was only the afternoon, and Evelyne wanted to savor the moment.

She accepted as simple truth that along the course of every person's life came an intersection grander than any other. The choice made at this junction would echo down the years to come.

She had reached such a crossroads, had made her decision, and so had drawn her fate.

The plan that had begun many months ago as a wicked diversion gradually bloomed as a strategy to be carried out. The District was coming apart. Evelyne recognized an opportunity and, rather than wait, helped it along.

Knocking down Tom Anderson had been simple. The King of Storyville was already tottering, getting older and weaker by the day. Lulu White and the other madams, Negroes and dagos and crude white women, could barely manage their mansions.

The only uncertain player in this rogue theater was Valentin St. Cyr. When Louis Jacob got around to bringing up the Creole detective, she was curious, then fascinated, at first enjoying a girlish thrill imagining the man. She went about ascribing to him a face and body, building a character out of the pages of a dime novel. When reality took over and she learned more, she was even more entranced.

She hired a copyboy at the newspaper to go through the files of index cards and bring her old issues with stories that mentioned him. She paid a clerk at City Hall to go into the police files and pull records that carried his name. It was New Orleans, and no errand was impossible if the money was right.

As time went by, she saw him as a potential enemy, the one person who might come to Storyville's rescue and wreck her plans. So she sought to draw him out and check him, and his skills were so rusty that he walked into her trap. It, and he, should have been finished, except that he managed to escape, and Evelyne realized that the man was her match. She decided it was time to present the Creole detective with his own special intersection.

It was another brilliant piece to be embroidered into a grand architecture created by her alone. She fixed it in her mind a final time, then turned from the window to make her way downstairs to the impatient Thomas.

Captain Picot stood at the front window gazing out at the dark city. The clerk called that Chief Reynolds was on the line.

"Jesus Christ almighty!" Picot groaned. He was sure the chief wanted to dress him down over losing St. Cyr.

He stepped to the desk and lifted the receiver gently to his ear. The chief laid into him, squawking like an angry rooster.

"What the hell is going on down there?" he demanded.

"Chief, we're doing every—"

"Well, you're not doing enough!" Reynolds's voice swooped. "What's your plan?"

"I'm putting additional officers on the street," Picot said quickly.

"That won't do it," the chief snapped with impatience. "We need more than that. This son of a bitch is thumbing his nose at us."

Picot allowed a significant pause, a signal to his superior. "We can close the net on him," he said.

"What's that mean?"

"We can start shutting down the District."

Reynolds said, "Good lord, Captain. Shut it down? Do you know what kind of a commotion that would cause? It would be chaos."

"We already have that, sir."

"No, we can't do it. There'd be too much trouble."

Picot understood: Too many important people had too much money invested. Not to mention the local diocese, full or part owner of at least a dozen properties in the District, by way of holding companies.

"I don't mean permanently," he said smoothly. "And I don't mean the whole place. We've been wanting to clean up that damned mess up on Claiborne and Robertson for a long time." He took another second's pause, then said, "We could probably close a couple more streets and no one would squawk."

He braced himself for the chief to shriek back that he was out of his mind and was quietly surprised when Reynolds said, "I don't know . . . I'd be stepping on some toes . . ."

Captain Picot understood that this meant Tom Anderson's. They'd be tangling with the King of Storyville himself. Tired as he might be, Anderson wouldn't let go without a fight.

Picot knew he was taking a big gamble, and if he lost, he'd be finished. He had no doubt that the chief would find a way to dump it all squarely in his lap.

"Where would the women go?" Reynolds inquired ruminatively, breaking the silence.

"Away," Picot said. "Let them be someone else's problem for a while."

After a vacant moment, Reynolds said, "Have you found St. Cyr?"

Picot, surprised at the change of tack, said, "No, sir, but we will. He'll be in jail before the night's out. I can guarantee that."

Of course, he had no idea if any such thing was possible; it was more important to placate the chief and worry about the rest later.

Reynolds took a pause, then said, "Don't do anything other than lock him down until you hear from me again."

"Yes, sir. Understood."

Captain Picot dropped the handset back into the cradle, thinking that no matter how long it took, sooner or later everyone got their due, even the likes of Valentin St. Cyr.

Once word of the latest murder made the rounds, business ebbed. A number of gentlemen who were in houses when they heard the news came up with excuses and cut their evenings short. Others who had regular Saturday-night visits turned around and headed back the way they had come. Some even stayed home and bedded their wives. It had the inklings of a disaster in the making.

Lulu White had watched the whole bizarre drama unfold from her Mahogany Hall parlor, first the murders, then the shooting of the suspect, and finally the twist that sent Valentin St. Cyr into hiding and put the whole of Storyville on edge.

Not willing to stand by and watch her place of business crumble into dust, she put on one of her best dresses and marched down the line to collect Antonia Gonzales and then Countess Willie Piazza.

The three madams made a formidable brigade on Basin Street, each with a security man in tow, a trio of bejeweled ships pushed along by heavier tugs. It was coming on to twilight, and they were all three done in their finest: long dresses, huge Floradora hats, ostrich boas, cloaks befitting queens in court. It was unfortunate that there were not more spectators to see them arrive at the doors of Anderson's Café with a full head of steam, leaving their roughnecks to loiter outside on the banquette.

The Café, like most drinking and gambling establishments, was off-limits to females except the better class of sporting women, meaning the prettiest of the octoroons. It had always caused a bit of rancor, more so as women began agitating for certain rights. Rather than fight it, Tom Anderson, in a stroke of inspiration, created a women's salon off the main floor, one with its own small bar and tables and effectively shielded from prying eyes by a heavy brocade curtain. It was into this lounge that Lulu White led the other two madams, as whispers of astonishment trailed in their wake.

Each had been hanging around the bar at the Café to see if he could pick up any word about Valentin, Miss Justine, and the coppers while he tried to decide what to do with the envelope that was stuffed in his pocket. He now stood by in wonder as the madams passed. With a curt word and an imperious twiddle of her gloved fingers, Miss Lulu sent him running to fetch Mr. Anderson from the upstairs office.

The women had barely tasted their champagne when the King of Storyville appeared through the curtained archway, pushing a smile before him.

"Ladies," he murmured. "What a surprise. And a pleasure."

The three feminine heads performed one nod. Countess Piazza and Antonia Gonzales smiled slightly. Miss Lulu treated him to a searching gaze, noting the flushed cheeks, tight brow, and eyes that seemed a little despondent. It was no surprise that he was feeling low after allowing such a mess to fester under his very nose.

And yet, even in the midst of mayhem, she knew he could still be a charmer, and so before he could befuddle her two companions with sweet talk and engaging smiles, she drove directly to the business at hand.

"What about Mr. Valentin?"

Anderson's grin fell; so there would be no idle chatter this evening. "He's in hiding. I don't know where, and I don't want to. The police have a warrant on him. He killed the wrong man."

"So they say. I don't buy it." Miss Antonia shook her head grimly. "None of this has been an accident, Tom. Someone's out to topple us. And this is part of it."

Though irked by the snippy tone, the King of Storyville understood that this was no time to indulge petty emotions or for forced jollity, for that matter. He knew as well as she what kind of trouble they were facing. It had been in the back of his mind that the killings of the past weeks might be more than just the work of a madman. Now the madam was giving voice to his suspicions.

He needed St. Cyr to muddle through it, but the Creole detective was out of service. It was all too wearying. At the same time, there could be neither a plea for sympathy nor false bluster before the six gimlet eyes.

"I don't exactly know what to do," he admitted.

"And you lost your right hand," Miss Lulu said.

He drew back a little, pursing his lips. "Valentin made a choice when he walked away, and he made another one when he came back. He got himself in this fix, and now he's no good to any of us. If he doesn't get out of the city, he'll be lucky to stay alive."

Lulu White kept her gaze fastened on her host. "You can't help him? Is that what you're saying?" The challenge in her voice and gaze were sharp, and Miss Antonia and Countess Piazza both dropped their eyes.

Tom Anderson returned the stare, though now his expression was merely thoughtful. He never got over what a remarkable woman she was. Though at times he swore she was crazy enough for the bughouse, she also displayed genius when it came to making money and was an expert player at games of power. Her failings were modest, and it had regularly occurred to him that if she'd been born a man, she might well be sitting in his place and probably doing a better job. Surely, she would have never let things get so far out of hand, with murder on the streets and his best man out of commission. Now she was laying down a gauntlet, pushing him to fix what had been broken on his watch.

"What do you want me to do?" he inquired in a subdued voice.

"You can't let the police get their hands on him," Lulu White said. "They'll lock him away in Parish Prison or kill him."

Anderson smiled dimly. "He can take care of himself, you know."

"They have Justine, too."

The three women and Anderson turned in Each's direction. They had forgotten he was there.

"Since when?" the King of Storyville inquired.

"Since this morning," he said. "She's been at the precinct at Parish Prison." He fidgeted for a second. "And they're looking to bring me in."

Anderson frowned blankly at him, then turned back to the table.

Lulu White said, "You understand that we can't make a fight without Valentin."

Anderson gave a petulant shrug of his shoulders. Lulu White sat forward intently and clasped her hands before her. The other two women at the table all but disappeared.

"Listen to me, Tom," she said. "You can't let this go or pretend it's just going to pass by, or we'll be finished."

Anderson's eyes flicked icily. Who spoke to him this way, like he was some schoolboy who had forgotten his lessons?

Shrewdly, the madam switched her tone to one brimming with sincerity. "You made Storyville," she said. "No one else could have done it." She launched a sweeping gesture to include the other madams at the table and then the entire District beyond the walls. "We could never have had our success without you." She dropped her arm. "But I swear, someone's out to get you. To get all of us."

Though flattered, the King of Storyville knew exactly what she was doing. Without fawning, she had left his pride intact. He stopped to consider with the brooding visage of a monarch. Momentarily, he shifted in the chair, his back straightening.

"You can tell the others. No one's going to destroy what we have here." His voice was firmer now.

Miss Lulu said, "We can't leave Valentin out there. We need him."

Anderson nodded slowly, pushed away from the table, then

rose to his feet and called to the waiter who was standing near the archway. "Bring the ladies another bottle of champagne." He regarded the madams one by one. "Thank you for the courtesy of this visit. Please enjoy your stay."

The waiter pulled back the curtain so he could make a regal exit. He crooked a finger, and Each found himself following the King of Storyville through a door and along the narrow back corridor that served as his passageway when he wanted to slip out of the building unseen.

They stopped near the door that opened into the alley. Anderson eyed the younger man and said, "What is it?"

"Someone else is trying to find him. And wants my help."

Anderson hiked an eyebrow. "Who?"

"I don't know." He went into a pocket and drew out the envelope of rich, creamy white. "I was on my way here when this fellow pulled up in an automobile and handed me this. To give to Mr. Valentin."

"What fellow?"

"Ain't never seen him before. Colored boy in a fine big Winton."

The King of Storyville fixed his gaze on the envelope, dying for a peek inside. He all but licked his lips. "Do you know where he is?" he said.

"I got a few guesses," Each said carefully. "The driver says he'll carry me to go to find him." He shifted nervously. "I don't know what to do about it."

"Go," Anderson said briskly. "Miss Lulu's right. If the coppers get to him first, he's finished."

Each swallowed, as if the import of being in the middle of this was just dawning on him.

"But you keep your eyes open," Anderson counseled him. "Use your wits. If anything feels wrong about it, get the hell away."

Each nodded and swallowed. As he turned to leave, the older man buttonholed him. "You tell him I'm on his side in this. Understand?"

Each said, "Yes, sir, I understand," and pushed through the door and into the alley.

EIGHTEEN

Another storm, the second in four days, had moved in from the Gulf and brought an evening of cool, drizzling rain. Windows glistened warmly, though with a forlorn light, as they peered down on near-empty banquettes.

With no word of St. Cyr's whereabouts, Captain Picot went back to paperwork as a way to take his mind off the quadroon sitting just outside his door. He could feel her presence, as if no wall of plaster and lath stood between them. Every now and then, he glanced up to see the matron escorting her to the ladies' toilet down the hall. She never looked his way, and he was sure that she thought of him as nothing but a dull and faceless weight bearing down on her.

He busied himself with some crime numbers the chief wanted. Boring work, but better than fretting the night away. He was penciling figures with a slow hand when Detective Weeks startled him by rushing in all out of breath.

"Someone spotted the son of a bitch!"

The captain almost leaped out of his chair and waved a hand. "Close the door! Spotted him where?"

Weeks pushed the door closed behind him. His eyes smiled as his lip curled. "Brown Bottom."

After a startled second, Picot cackled with glee and then clapped his hands. "I knew he couldn't leave. Brown Bottom? What the hell?"

The detective explained that over the last hours a whisper had gone from the mouth of a drunken old half-blind harridan to the gutter and then along the muddy street, eventually winding its way to a pair of officers on patrol a few blocks away on Frenchmen Street. The word was out that the coppers wanted St. Cyr, and that someone who looked like the Creole detective was holed up in—

"Looked like?"

"Who else could it be?"

The captain scratched at his chin eagerly. "Did you send a car?"

"They're on the way. Two of them. I sent those coppers on the beat, too."

"Good. That's good. You get down there and supervise."

Weeks, flush with success, took the opportunity to shift his eyes and lower his voice. "How do you want us to handle it?"

The captain understood. If St. Cyr was cornered in a place like Brown Bottom, "shot while trying to escape" could be one outcome. It had been a quick solution to problems in the past.

Picot considered, then with a twinge of regret shook his head. It was too dicey.

"If it is him, he goes back in a cell," he said. "I'll have them shackle him to the wall if I have to."

"And what if it ain't him?"

"Then keep it quiet. Understand?"

Weeks said, "I understand, yes, sir," and made a quick exit.

Justine was gazing morosely at the floor when she heard a small flurry of activity. Detective Weeks hurried into the hall. A moment later she felt a stare prickling on the back of her neck and looked up to see Captain Picot standing in the doorway of his office, gazing in her direction. He had his arms crossed in an insolent posture, and his thick lips were twisted in a faint smirk of a man who knew something.

She felt a stutter of fear in her gut. The cop had as much as told her that they had Valentin in their clutches.

He turned away and jerked a thumb. "We're done with her," he said in a tone that stopped just shy of a sneer. "Let her go."

The way he tossed off the order started her worrying again.

As determined as he was to buck up, Each found himself unnerved when he saw the Winton touring car idling one block back from the Café at the Franklin Street curb, its burgundy paint glistening and shimmering with beads of rain.

It had appeared on the street as the evening fell, coming out of the mist like some ghost ship, with the top up and side flaps down. The Negro in a tan duster pushed the flap open and called out his name.

Mr. St. Cyr had told him to always trust his gut, but this was deadly serious business and he was worried about making a mistake. He told the driver to wait down the street and ducked into Anderson's Café. He was leaning at the bar, fidgeting over a glass of whiskey, when the door opened and the three madams swept in. Within a moment he found himself caught up in the entourage and then standing by when Miss Lulu and the King of Storyville went eyeball to eyeball. He decided that he didn't mind waiting out their chess match to talk to Mr. Anderson. The King of Storyville had some steel in his voice when he told him what to do.

Now he came out the side entrance onto the banquette and looked up Iberville to where the Winton was waiting. With no time to hesitate, he strode to the automobile, put a foot on the running board, and climbed into the backseat. The driver kept his eyes straight ahead, waiting, and Each told him which way to go. The Negro gave a quick nod and made a U-turn, pointing them south.

Each had been such a regular part of Valentin's landscape for the better part of eight years that he had sometimes gone invisible. And yet he kept his eyes and ears open and learned plenty. Like the Creole detective's most secret hiding spots.

It took a half hour's scurrying along the river for him to locate the rooming house. He roused the blind woman and dropped a dime into her palm. She grunted directions, and he came tapping on the last door on the right.

"It's Each," he whispered.

Something moved inside. Valentin cracked the door.

"I got a car," the kid said. "Let's get the hell out of here."

The Winton emerged from the dirt alley and onto Alabo Street just as a police wagon was approaching down North Peters. The cop behind the wheel and the one in the passenger seat turned their heads in unison at the sight of the fine touring car, so out of place in that part of the city. It was too late for them to do anything. They had just bumped into the first of the alley's muddy potholes as the Winton raced off in the opposite direction.

The Negro driver hadn't looked around when Each and Valentin hopped into the backseat, and he now kept his eyes fixed on the street ahead. Once they turned onto St. Bernard, the tire and engine noise picked up, and the two men in back could talk without being overheard. Each explained how the driver had shown up on Marais Street on an errand from an unnamed employer.

"He gave me this to give to you," he whispered, and handed over the envelope. Valentin tore open the flap and drew out a single sheet of heavy notepaper with a message drawn in a florid hand.

Dear Mr. St. Cyr,

I wish to speak to you on a matter of immediate importance. I hope you'll honor the invitation. If, however, you choose otherwise, the driver has instructions to take you wherever you desire to go.

My sincere best wishes, E. Dallencort

"'E. Dallencort'?" Valentin studied the polite words, feeling the tug of strings being pulled from behind a veil. The author of the note knew somehow of his predicament and was offering him a hand out of his trouble. He understood that it could easily be part of an elaborate trap.

He leaned forward to lay a hand on the driver's shoulder. "Pull over, please."

The Negro swung the wheel without a second's hesitation, cutting onto Laharpe Street and steering to the curb. It was a good sign. One moment of hedging on the driver's part and the two passengers would have evaporated into the night.

The detective said, "Wait here, if you don't mind," and stepped down to the banquette, jerking his head for Each to follow. They ducked into the entranceway of a linen store that was closed for the night.

Each watched the detective's eyes nervously. "What's wrong?"

"Just go through what happened once more," Valentin said.

Each explained it again, taking his time. The driver had pulled up as he was crossing Marais Street. The Negro said his employer wanted to get a message to the Creole detective St. Cyr, and he was to help him flee the police, if need be.

Each had been clever enough not to gulp at the bait and instead told the driver to wait while he made his way to the Café to speak to Tom Anderson. So he was a witness to the tense encounter between Miss Lulu White and the King of Storyville, which he now related to Valentin as well. He said that Anderson had counseled him to take the chance and the help to find the detective.

"That's all," he finished. "The fellow was waiting down the street when I came back outside."

Valentin glanced away from Each's face, feeling a flush of shame at entertaining a notion that it might be a setup. But Each was as loyal as a mutt, and had neither the cold heart nor the dark cunning to commit such treachery. That didn't mean he wasn't being used.

Valentin read the note again, searching for something that might be tucked between the fancy lines. Who knew what lurked in the florid language? There was no time to ponder it. Each was already stealing tense glances at the street. It was time to move.

The Creole detective said, "Let's go see, then." He stuffed the envelope into his pocket, and they trotted through the drizzle to the waiting automobile.

Justine had decided to walk to Spain Street. Though it would take her a good half hour, she needed the time to think through the chaos that Valentin had brought down on her head.

They had been building a decent life until he had gone and wrecked it with his foolishness. Now he was on his own again, running from the coppers, a common criminal. How had the young cop with the kind eyes put it? *He's a fugitive, ma'am.* Which meant that if they caught him on the wrong corner, he might well end up dead. And for what? To pay a debt he thought he owed. Like the one he thought he was repaying when he went up the river to see crazy King Bolden. She could not for the life of her see the sense in any of it. Taken together, his actions added up to a hard slap that put her in her place.

She let her emotions have their way for a few minutes before forcing her thoughts on to practical matters. The rent on their rooms wouldn't pay itself. The money she earned posing naked once a week for eight college boys would not go far. So far, her only other skill had been providing company to men who were either wealthy or simply flush with winnings for a day or week or month. Valentin St. Cyr came along and changed her path. It would be a bitter pill if his troubles ended up driving her back to that life.

The thought gave her pause and brought Louis Jacob to mind. After so many years and so many men, she knew something of the male of the species. Louis's suave gambit was just another page from the catalog. For all his charm, he was just a little boy trying to play a man's game. Valentin would eat his dandy self alive.

She was still musing on Mr. Jacob and his pretenses as she turned the corner onto Spain Street and saw the Buick 10 parked at the curb, the paint shining ruby red in the glow of the streetlamp. She wondered for a moment if she had conjured him. Her next thought was that he didn't belong there at all.

Picot knew as soon as he looked out his office door and saw Detective Weeks shuffle in from the hallway that either St. Cyr hadn't been in Brown Bottom or that he'd been there and they had missed him again. He stared harder, his mouth setting.

Weeks had the drooping face of a dog expecting a beating as he edged up to the doorway. "Captain . . . ," he began.

"What happened?" Picot's voice was so brittle it almost cracked.

"He must have got tipped off," Weeks said.

"Do you really think so?" Picot mocked him. "I asked you what happened."

Weeks related the story of the burgundy Winton appearing out of the rain, and on Alabo Street, of all places.

Picot frowned, puzzled. "And St. Cyr was in it?"

"They couldn't see. The flaps were down. It was raining pretty good. He could have gotten out some other way, I suppose."

"No, that was it," the captain grunted. "It's just too damned perfect. He had someone helping him out. Probably Tom Anderson or one of the madams. Hell, all of them. And that fucking Beansoup."

"Each," Weeks said. "He goes by Each now."

"I don't care if he goes by Teddy goddamn Roosevelt," Picot snarled. "I guarantee he was in the middle of it. I thought I gave an order to pick him up."

"We couldn't find him."

Picot shook his head in frustration. "What about the automobile?"

"Burgundy Winton. Fine-looking touring car. That's what they said."

Picot rapped hard fingers on his desk. "All right, you call up the dealer first thing in the morning. See how many burgundy models they sold in the city. Couldn't be more than a few." He fell silent, brooding.

Weeks waited for a few seconds, then said, "Anything else, sir?"

The captain sat back. "I let St. Cyr's girl go home. But I want someone watching their rooms."

Weeks started to back out the door.

"Wait a second," Picot said. "Where the hell's McKinney?"

Exasperated, Justine said, "You shouldn't be here," and brushed past him. Out of the corner of her eye, she caught something moving at the far end of the street and turned her head in time to catch sight of a uniformed policeman crossing from one banquette to the other.

At the street door, she tried to put the key in the lock but found her hands trembling so much that it rattled. It was as if all the day's tension had somehow come to daunt that simple act. She just wanted to get inside and close the world away, only to find that she couldn't manage it.

Louis stepped to her side, wrapped her hand in his, and guided the key.

"There it is," he said.

She twisted her fingers and felt the bolt slide. "Thank you," she said.

Louis stepped back, waiting. Instead of pushing the door open, she turned to face him and saw his face cleaved by the light from the streetlamp, something strange in his eyes—something fearful.

She said, "What do you want?"

"I'm here to help you," he said. "You should know that."

She let out a curt laugh. "Help me?"

"You're in a lot of trouble."

"How would you know?"

He tilted his head slightly. "That policeman down the block? He's not after me."

"They're looking for someone," she said. "They think he's going to turn up here. But he's not."

"You mean St. Cyr."

She cocked her head warily. "That's right."

"I know the whole story."

She thought about this for a few seconds. "You and I didn't meet by accident."

"No, we didn't."

She wasn't surprised. He had been playing a game all along, but she was too tired to care. "Well, then? I asked you what you want here."

"I need to talk to you," he said. "It's important."

"Go ahead," she said. "Talk."

"Inside." He smiled, a freakish shadow of his former devilish grin. "You're alone," he said. "I can keep you company."

She almost laughed again at his show of disregard for the cloud of trouble hanging over her head, and Valentin's lingering shadow.

She watched his face for another moment. There was definitely an odd light in his eyes. Like he knew something . . .

Catching her gaze, he drew back uncertainly. "What is it?"

"All right then," she said. "Come in."

The Negro turned off Canal onto Magazine Street and closed on number 420, a building that Tom Anderson had once owned and where Valentin had for several years kept rooms. He had occupied the three-room flat over Gaspare's Tobacco Store, first alone, then with Justine, then without her again. It had for the most part been a good home. Now, with the upstairs windows darkened, it appeared empty and forlorn, and he wondered if anyone was living there.

Valentin glanced over at Each, who shook his head, no less puzzled at passing that location. The kid knew the address well, having spent nights on the overstuffed couch from the time he was a squirt. He recalled that there had been dark moments of mayhem in those rooms, but it had still been as close to a home as he had ever known. And now they had arrived back in its shadow.

As it turned out, the proximity was happenstance. The Winton slowed and drew to a stop a half block farther on at the corner of Poydras Street, across from Banks' Arcade, a hotel known for its fine dining room and elegant salons, but especially its fourth floor, a warren where for decades a fair share of the city's devious political and amorous intrigues had been conducted.

On the ground level, facing Magazine Street, a garden of stone sculptures, winding paths, park benches, and café tables lay mostly hidden from view by a brick and wrought-iron wall. In addition to the doors on the three sides, the building was fitted with a half-dozen private entrances. There had long been talk of a passageway under the street for those requiring the most extreme secrecy in their affairs.

Each nudged the detective, and then pushed back the canvas flap. He opened their door, and they stepped down to the banquette.

The Negro stuck his head out. "Room four-oh-eight," he said, then promptly engaged the gearbox and pulled away, swinging around the corner and into the darkness of the levee at the bottom of Front Street.

The two men stood on the corner for a moment. The detective said, "Four . . ."

"Oh-eight," Each said.

After a terse glance around the intersection, Valentin said, "What the hell. We're here. Let's see what it's about."

He led Each across the cobblestones to the covered walkway at the end of the garden. The soft drizzle provided extra cover as they wound along the brick path to a side door. They stepped over the threshold and into a corridor that was cast in the glow of electric lamps turned down low.

Directly on their right was a stairwell and they climbed the three flights without speaking. The door on the landing opened onto another corridor. Number 408 was the third door down. Valentin waved for Each to stay where he was. He listened for a moment, then inclined his head like a safecracker and knocked three times.

"Please come in." It was a woman's clear voice.

The detective hiked his eyebrows, a signal for Each to be on his toes, and turned the knob. They stepped inside, and the door closed behind them with a whisper of well-fitted wood.

They were standing in a small foyer that opened onto a large sitting room. A woman in a proper dress sat with a straight-backed posture on a divan that was arranged at a coffee table along with two button-tufted armchairs. Two electric lamps cast meek light, leaving her mostly in amber shadow. A tray with a full brandy decanter and two glasses had been placed on the table, along with a square box of light walnut.

"Please come in, Mr. St. Cyr," the woman said. She spoke his name with a perfect French intonation.

Valentin stepped forward into the archway. Noting that the invitation did not include him, Each hung back. The detective perked his ears for the faintest hint of another body on the premises. Unless someone was hiding in deep silence in either the bedroom or the bathroom, both to the right, they were alone. But then he was so on edge he might be missing something.

"You may have a seat," the woman said.

Valentin took one of the chairs. When the woman leaned into the muted light, he saw that she had striking features: dark haired, green eyed, full figured, and of regal profile. At the same time, the blades of probing light in her eyes and the curious tension in her finely planed face gave him pause. She was studying him in return.

Waiting for her first move, it occurred to him that in his old railroad coat and de Nimes trousers, he looked more like a workman who had come in to fix the toilet. He had forgotten to remove his hat and did so now. He spent a moment recounting the sequence that had in the span of a half hour led him from a filthy room in Brown Bottom to an elegant suite in one of the most storied hotels in the city. He knew it could still be a trap, and the police or a couple roughnecks could come bursting through the hallway door at any second.

The woman interrupted these thoughts. "My name is Evelyne Dallencort."

Valentin nodded politely and kept his mouth closed.

The woman paused, pursed her lips. "Does the name mean anything to you?"

"No, ma'am."

"Old French family. Very wealthy." She held up her left hand to show a ring studded with diamonds. "I'm a Dallencort by marriage."

Valentin didn't know what she expected by way of a response

and kept quiet. Evelyne, appearing momentarily irked, dropped her hand. Her eyes shifted briefly to Each, then back to the detective. "You won't want your friend hearing this conversation," she said.

Valentin turned his head slightly. Each got the message and retreated to the small foyer and one of the café chairs that had been placed there. The detective knew the kid would still pick up every word with his big ears.

Now Evelyne Dallencort leaned forward another few inches. Valentin did the same, closing the space between them.

"You have quite a reputation," the woman said. "And quite a history."

"How's that?"

"Starting out as a policeman. Then Tom Anderson's man. The Storyville detective. The cases you've handled. I've heard it all."

"I don't work for Mr. Anderson anymore," Valentin said quietly. "Haven't in some time."

"Well, I'm glad to hear that." She produced a smile that hinted at hidden meaning.

After a moment's pause, she reached out with a languid hand to pluck the cork from the brandy bottle and pour the two glasses full. She handed one to him and then sat back.

The detective took a grateful sip and felt the smoky liquor swirl into his stomach and head. He hadn't the faintest idea what Evelyne Dallencort wanted with him. He did know that he couldn't afford to dally with some silly rich woman who had decided to stick her nose into his troubles. His gratitude for the help escaping from Brown Bottom was giving way to impatience with any foolishness.

Abruptly, he said, "What can I do for you, ma'am?"

Evelyne wasn't about to be rushed. She took a long few seconds to sip her brandy before saying, "Let's talk about what I can do for you, Mr. St. Cyr."

Valentin all but huffed and rolled his eyes at this melodrama. "What would that be?"

"I can keep you alive, for a start." She treated him to a wise look. "You're in a bad way. The police have a warrant out for your arrest. For killing that fellow. What was his name—Brown?"

The detective paused, nodded. Evelyne Dallencort continued.

"For your information, Mr. Brown did commit those murders. So you shot the right man."

Valentin pleased her with a startled look. "How do you know?" he said.

"I know. We can leave it at that for now."

"Then who did this last killing?"

She gazed at him for an absent moment, as if she hadn't heard the question, then began tipping her brandy glass from side to side to watch the slow tilt of the amber liquid.

"It's quite a puzzle, isn't it?" she said. "Why were those men murdered in the red-light district? If it wasn't just some madman on a rampage, that is."

Valentin studied her more closely. She was acting coy, enjoying this sport, and it occurred to him that he was dealing with a type he had encountered in the past: women of means, bored with their upper-class lives, married to men who desired them only as showpieces who would tend to their homes, children, and social responsibilities in exchange for the wealth and privilege.

Eventually dabbling in opium and casual love affairs grew tedious, and they sought wilder escapades. More than a few were drawn downtown to the scarlet swamp of Storyville, with all its sex, intrigue, and violence. Some had ended up in the kind of trouble that would have landed any other citizen in Parish Prison. But they had the money, good names, attorneys like Sam Ross, and detectives like Valentin St. Cyr to avoid paying for their sins. They would scurry back into their castles, leaving misery in their wakes.

Valentin had seen it dozens of times, and he needed to find out in a hurry if Evelyne Dallencort was one of their number.

Now his ears were perked. The first errant slip of her tongue, and he and Each would be out the door.

"Mr. St. Cyr?"

He returned to the moment. "Ma'am?"

"I asked why you think those men were murdered."

Her expression was intent, and Valentin decided to indulge her and get it over with.

He said, "If it's not some lunatic, then it could be that someone has it in mind to make a problem that Storyville can't shake."

"But why?"

He mulled some more. "So it would look like such a dangerous place that no one would want to go there anymore."

Evelyne's green eyes fixed on him and she smiled absently.

"If that happened and business dried up, the authorities would have reason to shut it down for good," he said. "People have been trying to do that for fifteen years."

Evelyne produced a quick laugh that held a slightly frenetic note. "Oh, I doubt anyone would do anything quite *that* dramatic," she said. "Not with all that money over there." Now her eyes glistened and color rose to her cheeks. "Tens of thousands of dollars a week, isn't that correct? It's a river of gold. Not to mention all the political power that comes with it."

Valentin reflected on this curious speech, wondering how she knew the details of the scarlet economy.

The smile faded and her lips tightened in displeasure. "And all of it in the hands of Tom Anderson."

"Mr. Anderson has done very well with it," Valentin said.

"But he's not doing so well anymore, is he?" Evelyne said, her voice turning sharp. "He's old and tired, and the place has been falling apart in his hands. Don't tell me you haven't seen that. It's a terrible situation."

She posed with an imperious finger in the air. The hand came down to her lap. "Well, I plan to change that before he destroys it completely."

"Beg your pardon?" the detective said.

She paused to study him for a serious moment, then said, "Here's my proposition: I can give you the party responsible for sending Mr. Brown to commit those murders. The police will have nothing on you and you'll go free." She tipped her head in the direction of the foyer. "Your young friend will be out of trouble, too."

He stared at her, not sure whether to laugh or just get up and walk out. "I don't—"

"I'm not finished," she said. "If you wish, you can go back to work in the red-light district. I hope you will."

He had to make an effort to hold back the smile that was tugging at his mouth. "I'm sorry, I don't understand," he said. "Work for who?"

She tapped her breast as if it was obvious. "For *me*, Mr. Valentin."

Valentin was faintly amused, more puzzled. "Ma'am?"

"Anderson is finished," she said crisply. "He was failing already. These killings have broken his back. He should go, one way or another. I want him out. It's that simple. And I want your help moving him along."

The detective felt like snickering at this flight of fancy. She really was wasting his time. "Tom Anderson's not going anywhere," he told her.

Evelyne flipped a dismissive hand. "Not without being convinced, he's not. That's where you come in. You make him understand that his day is done. Thank him for his service and let him go on his way. How old is he, anyway? In his sixties? How much longer does he have? Does he really want to drop dead on Basin Street?"

Valentin spent a moment musing that it sounded like exactly what Tom Anderson would want: to spend his final moments in his beloved Storyville. He certainly wasn't going to just turn it over to some rich woman with a delusion about taking over. It was so preposterous that he felt a wild urge to laugh.

Evelyne Dallencort, by contrast, was dead serious.

"I'll let him keep his Café," she went on busily. "He built it, after all. But it will be one of many such establishments. Once things change on Basin Street, I mean. For the better, of course." She saw the look on the detective's face and began talking faster. "You must know that there's no room for a lady to make her way in politics, no room in any business, either. Tell me, where can a woman get anywhere, other than by spending her life on her back or her knees? Where in this man's world?"

"Ma'am, I'm—"

"In a place like Storyville, that's where. I can make a mark there. Better than any man. Even Tom Anderson. 'The King of Storyville.' Indeed!"

She drank off her brandy, poured a second glass, and sat back. "So?" she said after a moment.

Valentin said, "I'm sorry. Is this why you brought me here?"

Evelyne's tone turned cool. "It is."

"Then I'm not interested."

"Why not?"

"Because what you're proposing isn't possible."

Evelyne's eyes blazed with such quick anger that he wondered if it was possible that she had directed the murders of six innocent men as part of a plot to take Storyville away from Tom Anderson. Or if she might be part of a scheme devised by someone who did have such power. There had to be men who would be eager to take Anderson's place. Either way, he wanted no part of it.

"I'm sorry," he said, and started to get up from his chair.

Evelyne waited until he started to turn away to say, "What about your woman? Justine, is it? The sporting girl from Basin Street. Her."

Valentin heard Each's chair creak, then silence.

Evelyne said, "Do you happen to know where she is at the moment?"

The detective sat down again and, forcing himself calm, folded his hands and waited for her to continue.

"She's with an associate of mine," Evelyne explained. "At your address on . . . Spain Street, correct? Yes. The gentleman has instructions that if he doesn't hear from me by midnight, he'll kill her."

She either didn't notice or didn't care that Valentin's gray eyes had gone stony.

"You might have noticed him," she went on. "He drives a red Buick. He's been with her."

The detective's mind wound down and stopped cold. He heard a rustle of movement as Each started to come out of his chair. He dropped a hand to the side, signaling for the kid to stay where he was.

"If that's true, you're making a mistake," he said.

Evelyne stared right back at him, her mouth tightening severely. "Oh, it's true. And you're the one making the mistake. Don't treat me like I'm some fool, sir. I'm serious about this, and I'm not going to debate it. It's already gone too far. Seven people are dead."

She paused as if to let that fact sink in.

"Tom Anderson is old and in the way. Storyville needs new blood. So you and I are going to come to an agreement right now. Or your young lady will pay." She squared her shoulders. "And you'll end up in prison, and so will your friend in the foyer. Let's not forget about that. So think about what you're doing. And the choice before you."

Valentin couldn't tell how much of what she said was a bluff, except for the part about Justine and the dandy in the red Buick. That part he believed. It still didn't mean he could allow Evelyne

Dallencort the upper hand. Placing his glass on the table, he pushed his eyes at hers, a maneuver that was forward for a man of color. She looked startled; then her expression went blank, almost dreamy. It was a trick he had used before, a bit of hypnotism that rarely failed.

It worked on Evelyne Dallencort, who now held her brandy glass aloft in one hand while the other made an absent glide to the hollow beneath her throat, as if she was on the verge of a swoon.

"You really think you can do this?" he said in a low voice, holding her gaze. "You think you can just move in and push a man like Tom Anderson out?" He didn't give her time to answer. "He spent years building that place. He's not called the King of Storyville for nothing."

"Yes, yes," she said. "But now it's time for him to step down. It's been—"

"He's not going to do anything of the kind, ma'am!" His voice got louder, and Evelyne blinked in surprise. "They'll carry him out of there in his coffin."

A second went by and she broke the gaze. "Is that so?" She drew back and tossed off the rest of her brandy, the lines of her face hardening. "Is that what it will take?"

Valentin understood. Though she had quailed for a moment, she wasn't about to be seduced into a surrender. She had already gone too far when she directed the deaths of those men in the District. She had to know there was a chance she'd spend the rest of *her* life locked up somewhere if she backed away now.

It was strange. They had both fallen victim to the temptations of Storyville. The District had always been a seductress, drawing old lovers back and new ones in.

He didn't have the luxury to meditate on such notions. And Evelyne was getting impatient. "You know you really don't have a choice," she said. "Because it's going to come out the same way, no matter what you do. You understand that, don't you?"

She was watching him and waiting for an answer. He slouched back, feeling a sudden wave of weariness assail him. He was tired, so goddamned, god-awful tired of people who couldn't leave things be, the sort who had to have more and more to fill up the holes in their ragged souls.

Let them have it, he was thinking. *Let them battle over it. Let them raise hell right up out of the ground for it.* He had paid his fare a long time ago. But it wasn't so simple, as long as Justine remained in the clutches of the dandy in the red Buick 10.

"All right, then," he said, straightening. "What do you want me to do?"

From behind him, he heard Each let out a little gasp. Evelyne looked surprised, too, as if she hadn't expected him to give in so quickly. Her eyes narrowed in suspicion, and she said, "Do we understand each other? That one way or another, Tom Anderson will be out of the way tonight?"

He stared at her, then nodded.

"Because my partner is holding your young lady," Evelyne reminded him. "If I don't get what I want, he knows what to do. I'm giving you until midnight."

Valentin considered for a brief few seconds, then with a deliberate motion went into his jacket pocket, drew out the old Colt, and leveled it at her forehead. He hadn't used it in years, and though it felt odd and heavy in his hand, he held it steady.

"I'll do what you say," he told her. "But if she's harmed in any way, I'll kill you and your partner both. What's his name?" She stared. "What's his name, ma'am?"

"Louis," she said, her voice muted. "Jacob."

"You and . . ." He stopped. *Jacob.* Another piece of the puzzle fell into place.

Evelyne smirked with pleasure at his reaction. He removed her smile by pushing the barrel of the gun an inch closer to her brain. "Is that clear to you?"

She caught a breath, and now it was Valentin who was placated to see fear in her eyes. Apparently, she hadn't considered the possibility that he just might shoot her on the spot and solve the problem that way. He wouldn't, though; he couldn't. One killing had been enough. At the same time, he made sure she couldn't mistake the deadly look in his eyes.

"It's clear, yes," she said.

Valentin dropped his gaze and pocketed his revolver. Evelyne started breathing again and returned to business.

"Get to Mr. Anderson," she said. "Tell him what has to be done. Make sure he understands this is best for everyone. For him. For you. And for *Justine.*"

The detective bristled again at the sound of the name coming off her lips.

"And if he doesn't cooperate . . ."

"He won't."

"Well, then I suppose he *will* have to be carried out in his coffin, won't he?" Now she sounded snappish, an impatient woman who was used to getting her way. "But let's hold a hope that won't be necessary. And it won't be, if you handle it correctly." Her demeanor switched to brusquely animated. "You have until midnight to get a message to me that it's been arranged. You understand what will happen if you change your mind."

Valentin didn't bother to answer. Evelyne flipped up the lid on the wooden box and plucked out a card that bore the inscription 8955.

"That's the telephone number here," she said. "I expect a call from you." She smiled again. "And I have your telephone number on Spain Street, thank you."

Wordlessly, Valentin tucked the card in his pocket.

"My driver is waiting," she said.

The Creole detective shook his head. "Every copper in New Orleans will be looking for a burgundy Winton. We can find our own way."

Evelyne's eyes slid off him for a second. He moved away,

feeling her gaze follow him to the foyer, where he collected Each with a quick jerk of his head. The kid glared furiously, as if the detective had been transformed into some kind of monster. But he followed him out and closed the door behind them.

Evelyne waited until she heard their footsteps on the stairwell before calling to the man who had been hiding in the bedroom. She murmured his instructions and sent him on his way.

They didn't exchange a word during their descent of the stairs and the passage through the stone garden. Only when they hit the banquette did Each whirl around, his eyes alight. He opened his mouth as if winding up for a pitch when Valentin cut him off.

"Don't say a goddamn word." The detective was glowering. "I mean it."

Each wasn't about to keep quiet. "I'll talk if I want to!" he hissed back. "What the hell are you doing?"

Valentin cast a taunting eye his way. "You're the rounder, you tell me."

"You told that crazy bitch you'd help her push Mr. Tom out of the way," the kid said. "Or shoot him dead if he won't go." He was all but jumping out of his shoes. "After what she done? You're going to play for the other side?" He shook his head bitterly. "You can't just let it be? You gonna help her tear it down. And what about Miss Jus—"

In a blur of motion, the detective grabbed him by the collar and shoved him into a darkened doorway. He brought his face close and dropped his voice.

"You shut your mouth and listen to me, damnit. Her boy is tailing us right now, about a block back. Did you hear what she said? She's got Justine, and she'll send orders to have her killed if I don't go along." He released the kid's collar and stood back.

"So . . ."

"I'm not doing anything of the kind." The detective smiled coolly. "Don't worry," he said. "I'm not going to shoot Mr. Tom. Or anyone else, if I can help it."

The kid licked his dry lips. "I don't get it."

"The woman is serious, Each. She thinks she can take over Storyville. She's already arranged six murders. She's not going to give up on it now."

"She can't do that."

"Can't do what?"

"Take over Storyville. Run it."

Valentin said, "Why not?"

"Because . . . because she's a *woman.*"

The detective snickered. "You should read a little history. She got this far. She's knocked the District to its knees. Now she wants to push it over the edge. And she wants me to help her." He paused and wagged an index finger. "But this is as far as it goes. She'll never take Anderson's place. But not because she's a woman. She just doesn't have his talents. And I wouldn't help her, even if she did."

Each nodded, mollified. "What are you going to do about Justine?"

Valentin said, "Mrs. Dallencort won't dare harm her. As long as she thinks I'm doing her bidding, I mean. But if she finds out I crossed her—"

"Or midnight comes around."

"That's right," Valentin said. "Or midnight comes around. So we need to move."

They started walking again. Each hunched his shoulders and rolled his head, first one way, then the other.

"Don't 'round like that," the detective said. "You look guilty."

"I *am* guilty," the kid blurted. He looked so miserable that Valentin wished he could just send him away somewhere. That wasn't possible; he needed the help. At the same time, he couldn't risk having the kid fall apart on him.

He stopped walking. "Are you all right?" he said.

Each took a moment, then nodded and straightened his spine. "Yes, sir, I'm good."

"You keep your eyes open. Watch your step. Understand?"

"Ain't no coppers going to grab me."

"It's not the coppers I'm worried about," Valentin told him. "She might decide to send someone to kill the both of us."

Each said, "Oh."

They cut through the alleys east and north to Canal Street. In their common clothes, they didn't get any second glances as they approached the intersection at the entrance of Burgundy. Automobile and hack traffic made the streets noisy as the headlamps cut designs in the darkness.

The detective drew Each back from the banquette. "Listen to me," he said. "Picot won't miss a thing tonight. He'll have someone on every damn corner. And cops all over Storyville looking for us. I guarantee they've probably already sweated Mangetta and some of the madams. So just keep low."

Each nodded, all tense. "What do you want me to do?"

"Go to the Café and find Mr. Tom. Tell him about Mrs. Dallencort. That's all."

"What if he ain't there?"

"Then don't hang around waiting. Get out of there." The detective gave him a sharp look. "Whatever you do, don't go down the line. Go to Mangetta's. He'll take care of you. Just make sure you're not spotted."

Each came up with an impatient shrug.

Valentin's expression was severe. "This is no joke. It's the only place that's safe, so don't get caught in between. When you get there, tell Frank what's going on. Tell him I said to find Whaley and get to Spain Street. They'll know what to do."

"Okay."

"Don't trust anyone except those two with that part," Valentin said. "No one. Understand?"

Each stared for a startled second, realizing that *no one* meant Tom Anderson, too. So the detective was having doubts, maybe thinking that the King of Storyville had been playing a secret hand, as he had done so many times before.

"Anything else?" Each said.

Valentin mulled for a few seconds. The kid could see by the tension on his face that he was plenty worried.

The detective said, "If it happens that you do get picked up—"

"I won't."

"Just in case. Don't be a hero."

"What's that mean?" Each stared at him. "Give you up?"

"Me getting arrested won't be the end of the world. As long as I get to Justine before it happens."

The kid crossed his arms in a rude gesture, incensed. "What the hell makes you think I'd give you up?"

"You've never been in jail, have you?"

"I wouldn't, goddamnit!"

"All right, calm down." The detective smiled wanly. "Sometimes I forget you're not a boy anymore."

Each nodded. "What about Spain Street?" he said. "I mean, if that fellow's got Miss Justine . . . what are you going to do?"

"I'm not sure. The coppers will probably be sitting on the house. I still need to get over there."

"So maybe you better watch your step, too."

"I will."

The detective smiled and patted the kid's shoulder. It was such an uncharacteristic gesture that Each stopped his nervous fidgeting. Drawing himself up, he gave a serious wink, then stepped onto Canal Street, crossed over, and disappeared into the Quarter.

Standing on the dark corner, Valentin stopped to think about what a fool he'd been to let himself and Justine and Each get drawn into this. Instead of staying put and minding his own business, he came back to Storyville. Once he did, though, it was only because of King Bolden that he had any idea of what had transpired.

That didn't help Justine, who was now trapped in their rooms and at the mercy of a man with a gun in his hand. The thought sent him hurrying over to the other side, heading east toward Spain Street.

NINETEEN

It had been a long and troubling day, and yet Tom Anderson couldn't bring himself to go home and rest. Not with the tension that had cleared the streets outside and left the Café almost empty. Only a dozen or so men remained, most of them gamblers playing each other, since no suckers had appeared with bankrolls to be plucked. That also meant no audience to entertain, so the band members were hanging at the end of the bar, sipping Raleigh Rye and talking quietly among themselves, mostly about where they might find new work.

The lone bright moment during the evening came when the three madams set the place abuzz. The word had preceded the ladies' promenade down the line, and the noisy wake of curious followers had filled the place for the first time in weeks. There were whispers aplenty flying around about the meeting of the heads of state, some carrying the opinion that it could be their last.

After the madams departed, Anderson circled the floor, accepting greetings, slapping backs, listening with half an ear to the banter, meanwhile keeping one eye on the tables. The band had taken the stage and the Café glowed with electric light and echoed with jass music. For that short while, it was as if the clock had been turned back to a time when Storyville was alive, before St. Cyr went away, before business began sliding down, before some maniac started murdering people.

The excitement didn't last, because when the madams made their exit, most of the customers did, too. No one was inclined to linger, not with bodies dropping on every corner—or so the over-heated gossip had it. Soon, the King of Storyville mused gloomily, the decent whores would start wandering away to greener pastures, the mansions would end up in the hands of slatterns, and the general decay would turn his empire to dust.

They had all looked to St. Cyr to put a stop to it, but instead the Creole detective had ended up a fugitive with a price on his head, courtesy of that son of a bitch Picot. Another body could turn up on his doorstep that very night, and there would be nothing he could do about that, either.

In any case, with the circus gone, the big room had emptied out gradually, until by ten o'clock, it was eerily quiet. None of the few remaining customers could read Anderson's thoughts as he made his rounds. Though it made him feel low to see the place like that, his facade didn't flag a bit. As he headed for the door, he almost missed Ned calling him to the telephone.

He stopped and sighed tiredly. "Now who?"

"It's the chief of police, Mr. Tom."

Justine invited Louis to sit on the couch, and she arranged herself on the morris chair. He shifted about as if he couldn't find a comfortable spot, then stopped to ask abruptly if she had anything to drink. It was an oddly tense request, a departure from his usual suave poise. Which made her nervous and want him there even less.

Reluctantly, she said, "We have some whiskey."

"Whiskey?" He gave a quick nod. "Yes. That will be fine."

She stepped into the kitchen and took the bottle down from

the cupboard. Her eyes caught the glint off the blade of one of her good paring knives. She considered, then decided to leave it. When she returned to the front room with the short glass of rye in hand, she found he had opened the door to the balcony and now stood looking out over Spain Street.

She stepped up to hand him the glass. "Stay and finish that. Then I'd like you to go."

His eyebrows flinched, and he looked disappointed and a little angry. After a hefty sip, he smiled coldly. "Why?" he said. "Are you afraid he'll come home and find me here?"

Turning away, she said, "It's getting late. Drink your whiskey and leave."

She caught the rustle of movement and glanced over her shoulder to see the pistol hanging loose in his hand, but pointed her way all the same.

It didn't surprise her. He was a strange man, handsome as a picture, and yet she had sensed that he was little more than an actor playing roles, one after another. Now she wondered if his next one would include trying to take by force what he couldn't get with charm. It had happened to her, as it had to most women of meager means. Men had their way; but she had fought off better ones than he. She wished she'd picked up one of the knives.

She kept her eyes averted, lest he see what she was thinking. "What do you want?"

"I just need to stay. That's all."

"For how long?"

"Not long. A little while."

"You couldn't just ask? You had to draw a pistol?"

"You would have said no."

She nodded gravely. "That's true."

He didn't seem to know what to do next. Justine watched him as he thought for a moment, then stood up, leaned to the window, and peered along Spain Street.

"Are you expecting someone?" She hoped to keep him talking.

"*Someone?*" He produced the sly smile of a child with a secret. "Yes, I am."

"Who?"

He shrugged blithely. "You'll see soon enough."

Justine watched his face as he spoke the words and had to make an effort to control a tingle of fear.

"Please sit down," he said, keeping the pistol fixed directly on her heart.

One of the officers rapped on Captain Picot's door to tell him the chief of police was on the line. The captain snatched up the receiver.

"Yes, Chief?"

"I understand you have a damned army out hunting St. Cyr."

"Yes, sir, I do," Picot said crisply. "I'm sure he's still in the city, and he'll show up in Storyville, sooner or later. He's too smart to go back to Spain—"

"And then what?" Reynolds cut in.

"Then what?" Picot didn't understand. "Then we arrest him and throw him in jail for the—"

"I don't want him arrested and thrown in jail, Captain."

For a few crazy seconds, Picot wondered if the chief had just given him an order to do away with the Creole detective. In the next moment, he was stunned to discover that what Reynolds wanted was exactly the opposite.

"Pull your men off," the chief of police said in a clipped tone. "I want him out on the street."

Picot swallowed, tasted a bitter pill. "But there's a murder warrant out on him."

"Consider it lifted," Reynolds snapped back. "That goes for that kid who runs with him. What's his name?"

"Each," Picot said faintly.

"Him, too. Leave him be. So maybe we can get all this business settled tonight." Then, in an almost regretful tone, the chief said, "Jesus, how did it come to this?"

Picot had some ideas, but the chief would have no interest in his opinions, so he kept his mouth shut. He was too busy trying to think of a way to shore up a tumbling house of cards.

The pronounced silence caused Reynolds to say, "Do we understand each other, Captain?"

"Yes, sir." Picot's voice was hollow.

"Then see to it." The line went dead.

Captain Picot stared out the window for a grueling half minute before calling Detective Weeks into his office to inform him that the arrest warrant on Valentin St. Cyr had been vacated and that the Creole detective and his young friend Each were no longer identified as fugitives from justice. He waved his astonished subordinate out of the room, asking that he close the door behind him.

Thomas had only a vague sense of the machinery that had been grinding on around him, but it was dawning on him that it was bad news. Like his mama had always said, it was *white folks' business and none of ours.*

He could see in her eyes that she knew this time Miz Evelyne was up to no good, and it wasn't just some fancy man she brought indoors when she thought everyone except her poor, sick old husband was out. This was something else, something that caused Malvina to whisper a fierce reminder that he was by no means to get in the middle of anything that came out of that crazy woman's head.

But that's exactly what happened when his employer sent him first to Storyville to find a young rounder who went by the moniker Each and carry him to wherever he wanted to go. Which happened to be Brown Bottom, just about the worst damn corner of the city of New Orleans. He parked the Winton in front of a run-down shithole of a shack, one hand on the gearshift lever and the other on the accelerator handle, ready to fly away from that filthy warren at a second's notice. Doing the lady's bidding was one thing; getting murdered in some foul alley was another entirely.

Before anything happened, though, Each emerged with a stalking companion who kept his head down and his mouth closed. Thomas knew without asking that he was doing exactly what his mama told him not to do, and was now tangled up in some kind of awful, bloody business that was none of *his*.

Still, like too many young men he was attracted to trouble, and did what Miss Evelyne said. After the Creole and his partner reappeared from the Banks' Arcade building, he followed them on foot to Canal Street. That was as far as he went with it. His gut told him that things were about to get way out of hand, that maybe people were going to die this night, and that if he took another step, he'd be in too deep to get himself unstuck. He'd either be part of a crime of some sort or the victim of one.

So instead of obeying the rest of what the white woman ordered, he watched as Each crossed Canal into the Quarter and the other one lingered briefly before heading off along Decatur Street, then he turned around and started walking west away from downtown at a fast clip. He did not look back.

After the Creole detective and his partner left, and she'd sent the other one on his little errand, Evelyne spent some moments with bitterness twisting her stomach and tasting bile in her throat.

For a brief moment, she thought she truly had St. Cyr convinced, that he saw the sense of her arguments and agree that it would be best for everyone to go along. There would be no more bodies on the Storyville streets. The District's downward spiral would halt, and a new scarlet world would rise, as grand as the streets of light on the Continent or the willow quarters in Japan.

Then she caught a look in his eye and knew she'd been mistaken about him. He was good, as clever a man as she'd ever met, but she struck his Achilles' heel when she mentioned *Justine,* and just like that, she lost him. No matter what came out of his mouth from that moment on, she knew he'd be false. He had no intention of helping her push Tom Anderson aside—kill him, if need be—and assume control of those twenty square blocks.

Standing at the window and looking down on Magazine Street, she allowed her nerves to calm. She was not so foolish to have not prepared for such a betrayal. St. Cyr had been given his one chance and missed it. Too bad for him; she had others to carry out her plans. That they were not so clever meant they didn't have the wits to commit treachery.

Of course, St. Cyr would rush to Spain Street to save his woman instead of going to Tom Anderson to petition him on her behalf. He might send his young friend, but the police would be looking for that fellow, too, so there was a good chance he'd never manage to warn Anderson of what was coming. It wouldn't matter if he did. The King of Storyville's fate was sealed, as was that of Mr. St. Cyr, his quadroon Justine, and even Louis Jacob.

The Creole detective was the only one she'd miss.

But she had offered an olive branch, and he had spit on it. Now it would take more killings to settle the problem. This would be for the best, and she was sure everyone would understand that soon enough.

Justine and Louis sat in silence for long minutes as the clock on the wall ticked on toward twelve. She kept her eyes fastened on the carpet beneath her feet. She had no idea how close to an edge he might be and didn't want to take a chance on pushing him over it.

She spent some of the silent seconds cursing the Creole detective for what seemed the hundredth time. It was during one of these exercises that she decided to speak up.

"What about Valentin?" she asked.

"What about him?" Louis smiled indulgently, irking her.

"Do you know something or not?"

His eyes were lazy. "I know that Mr. St. Cyr has made an arrangement with my associate."

"Oh? Who would that be?"

"You'll find out soon enough."

"What kind of . . . arrangement?"

Louis was as pleased as a child with a secret to divulge. "He's been offered a chance to go back to work in Storyville, but not under Mr. Tom Anderson. He's finished over there. The red-light district will be under new management from now on." He sat forward intently, now like a drummer selling soap. "Anderson will be replaced, and it will be like it was before. When it was doing well." He cocked an eyebrow. "You remember. When you were working there."

She didn't understand and treated him to a dubious gaze.

"You can believe it," he said.

"You're telling me that Valentin is going to help your . . ."

"Associate."

"Help this person replace Tom Anderson?"

"That's correct."

"He wouldn't."

"Oh, he will. He has to. If he wants to keep you alive. You're his marker."

Justine drew back, frowned. "What's that mean?"

Louis was deliberate. "It means that he's trading Mr. Tom Anderson for you."

After a moment Justine smiled slightly. "Is that what he said? I mean, you heard him say those words?"

Louis recoiled slightly. "He said them. That's all you need to know." He tilted his head toward the telephone on its stand. "I'll be getting a call here before midnight, telling me whether or not it's all settled."

"And what if it's not?"

"If it's not . . ." Louis leaned back and turned his face away from her. "That would be too bad for you."

Each came around Union Station and stood alongside the terminal, peering across the tracks and Basin Street at the facade of Anderson's Café. Though it was a quiet night, he saw beat cops on the banquette, three on the two opposite corners, plus another fellow who stood in front of Hilma Burt's in a suit that fit so badly that he could only be one of Picot's detectives.

As he watched and waited for a chance to steal across the street, a third patrolman approached at a fast clip from the direction of Iberville Street.

With such a crowd of blue about, there was no way he could make a dash for the Café door or even manage to slip around the Bienville side to the rear entrance. He was considering how to best circle the District to get inside when he was startled by a loud whistle. Abruptly, the three uniformed cops directly across from him turned and hurried to join the detective and the officer who had just arrived from Miss Burt's.

For a panicked second, Each thought someone had alerted them and that they were about to turn as one to surround and grab him. He was taking a first step backward and out of sight when they did move, though not in his direction. Instead, the four marched directly up Basin Street past the Café and to Canal, where they rounded the corner, heading north.

Each poked his head out to see other shapes moving as the cops who had been posted down the line began strolling off. He waited another minute and then ambled unmolested across the street and through the front doors of the Café.

It was quiet, with no more than a handful of sports lolling about. One sharp sat alone at a table, playing solitaire, and he could hear the gentle slap of the cards.

He asked for Mr. Anderson and was told that the proprietor was in his upstairs office, but was expecting company directly. Each said he would wait, wandered away from the bar, and crossed the floor as if looking for someone he might recognize. There was a quiet game of faro going on at one of the tables, and he headed over to watch the action. By this time the bartenders had forgotten him, and he turned abruptly to make a dash to the kitchen doors before anyone noticed.

With no one dining, the kitchen was even more deserted. Each saw at a glance that the back doors were open and the cooks were standing on the dock, smoking and talking as they gazed up at the night sky. He cut through to the downstairs corridor and then up the stairwell to the second floor.

As soon as he reached the landing, he heard an angry snarl. Mr. Anderson was arguing with someone, and when Each didn't hear a second voice, he realized the King of Storyville was on the telephone. He didn't want to just stand there, so he made some noise along the hall before stepping to the doorway and reaching out to rap his knuckles on the jamb.

Anderson turned, glaring, then saw who it was and waved him inside. He turned back to cut off the party on the other end of the line.

"You tell His Honor the mayor that the game has changed," he snapped into the mouthpiece. "We're going to put things back the way they were, and that means St. Cyr, too. You tell him that if he wants to discuss it any further, I'll be right here. I'm not going anywhere."

He banged the handset into the cradle. He shot a look at his visitor. "Where's Valentin?"

Each hesitated, and Anderson's eyes narrowed. His mustache curved in a smile. "He tell you to keep it under your hat?" He waved a hand. "That's all right, son. As long as he's still alive."

"He is, yes, sir. But there's bound to be someone after him."

He swallowed. "He said to say that they're probably coming for you, too."

Anderson, grinning more broadly, said, "Is that right?"

In the next moment, they heard the creak of footsteps on the stairs.

It was slow going. The straightest route would have taken Valentin too close to the river and Brown Bottom and any coppers trolling for him down there. The police also knew he'd have to traverse the Quarter on his way to Storyville and through Jackson Square on his way to Spain Street. They'd be watching every street and corner.

But as he moved across town, he found the downtown streets quiet and didn't see a single patrolman. The pronounced silence was eerie, and he imagined coppers lurking in the shadows, watching him pass by so they could draw a net closed behind him. He was so sure of it that at one point he turned around in a sudden move—exactly what he had scolded Each for.

The bells of St. Louis Cathedral chimed 11:45 just as he crossed Esplanade. With no time to waste, he cut a bolder path directly down the Chartres Street banquette. Once he passed Mandeville and reached the intersection at Spain, he slowed, then stopped.

He had enough of a sense of the street to feel someone lurking, even when he couldn't see anyone. He detected no one lying in wait this night. If any cops had been there, they were gone now.

He could now spy his balcony from the corner and see the room light glowing through the French doors. Was that a shadow passing against the window? He couldn't be sure.

He had gone another twenty paces along the banquette when he saw the Buick 10 parked at the other end of the block, looking out of place with the red paint in full shimmer under the bleak streetlight. The automobile appeared to be unoccupied, and he knew in that instant that the driver was inside with Justine, perhaps ready to shoot her dead on orders from Evelyne Dallencort.

The church bells all over the lower half of the city had finished chiming their faint three-quarters. Within minutes his telephone would ring.

Drawing closer, he figured that the downstairs door would be locked, but he could crack that. He could also climb the balcony supports and get in that way. After that he'd be operating without a plan, except to move Justine out of danger. He pushed away any thought of what would happen if he made a mistake.

It didn't matter, because when he was thirty paces from his front door, he heard a rush of sudden noise: a doorframe slapping back, the breaking of glass, a harsh shout. His heart came into his throat and he started to run.

The fellow who appeared from the hall was a stranger, a wiry, dirty-eyed character, dressed in an old dark suit with a fedora pulled down low. When he reached the doorway, he drew up short, surprised to find not one man in the office but two. In his moment of hesitation, Anderson realized what was happening and started to grin, wide and devilish.

"Can I help you?" he said, and reached down to pull open the desk drawer that held his Aubrey Hammerless. Though he hadn't handled the pistol in years, it seemed now to jump into his hand.

Each meanwhile felt his feet move on their own volition as his hand swung to his back pocket for the whalebone sap he had stuffed there.

"What the hell do you want?" he demanded.

In the next second, the stranger drew his own right hand out of his pocket. It was empty. The King of Storyville raised the revolver, and Each walked him down.

"I said what the hell do you want here?"

"I have a . . . a message," the visitor said, blinking and stuttering. "It's for Mr. Anderson."

"Oh? What is it?" Anderson said. He was enjoying this.

The stranger's eyes shifted between the two as he gauged his chances. A dead second went by, and he muttered something that sounded like a curse, then took a quick back step to the doorway and bolted away. The nails on the soles of his boots clattered along the hall and down the stairs.

Each started to follow, but Anderson said, "No, let the bastard go." The kid stopped. "Don't worry, we won't see him again." He hefted the pistol for a second before dropping it back into the drawer.

"Well, god*damn.*" He let out a little laugh. "That felt good." He winked at Each. "You did fine, too." The kid chuckled in giddy relief.

The telephone rang as the King of Storyville was reaching for his bottle to pour them both a drink. He pulled the receiver to his ear, and Each saw the older man's smile fade as he listened. Anderson dropped the hand piece in the cradle.

"What's wrong?" Each said.

"Something happened on Spain Street," the King of Storyville said.

Justine was on edge, but she only grew truly frightened when the bells tolled the three-quarters and Louis lurched to his feet and started to pace. He wouldn't look at her as he went to fussing with the pistol. After five minutes of this fretting, he picked up the telephone and made two calls, muttering so she couldn't hear, but keeping the weapon fixed on her all the while.

Momentarily, his cheeks paled and his eyes went hard. She knew that look; he was bracing himself for something, and she had a good idea what it was.

Without turning her head, she gauged the distance to the door. There was no way she could get to it, throw the lock, and make an escape in time. The bedroom would be just as impossible, since she'd have to open the window, climb out, and then face a twelve-foot drop. All this went through her mind in the space of a few seconds. Time was running out. She couldn't just stand there and be a victim.

Louis moved away from the telephone and crossed to the French door again. Facing her, he took a step back onto the balcony, leaning a slight bit so he could search the street in both directions. He shook his head, his pretty mouth tightening into a grim line. She saw his chest heave in tension over what he was about to do.

In the next second, she was on him, throwing her body against his in a wild rush. His head came around and his eyes went wide, as she grappled with him, wrapping her arms about his in an embrace stronger than love.

Her sudden weight carried him back against the railing and for a second he was off balance, and she felt a spike of dizzying terror that they were going to pitch over together. Then he righted himself, but as he did the pistol tumbled from his hand and over the railing.

He let out a harsh grunt, and his handsome face contorted into an ugly mask as he struggled to get loose. He wriggled his arms in frantic spasms, and one of his elbows shattered a pane of door glass. The shards tumbled to the banquette.

Justine heard in his seething breath his rage over letting her surprise him and his panic over the terrible blunder of failing to finish her. Now she had turned the tables, and he flailed like a child throwing a tantrum. With a last hard jerk, his arms came free.

She felt his hands wrap around her throat and start to squeeze. She fought with all the more fury, while everything before her eyes turned red.

On the street below, Valentin came skidding to a stop, frozen for a second at the tableau of the two of them entwined on the balcony with the man's hands tight on Justine's throat as she flailed furiously.

He didn't feel the Iver Johnson in his hand, didn't realize he had aimed and pulled the trigger until the shot cracked and the pistol kicked in his hand. He saw the man's head snap and wobble. The choking hands came away from Justine's neck, and she lurched back through the doorway into the living room.

Louis teetered and then went over, a clumsy puppet, arms and legs at four different angles and head lolling like a ball on a string. The dull smack of soft flesh slamming into hard stone shot up from the street. Blood spurted from his ears, nose, and mouth and flowed in a black puddle. His eyes were wide open and staring at the rooftops.

Valentin pulled his eyes off the body and looked up to see Justine now standing with her hands gripping the wrought-iron banister, her face a mask of shock. She dropped her gaze to him, and the relief that flooded his eyes brought her out of it. She watched as he lifted a hand as if to reach her and took a weak step back.

"The police," he said after a moment. "Go in and call the police." She nodded and staggered out of sight.

Valentin crouched next to Louis Jacob. The dead eyes had settled on nothing. He was finished. Glancing around, the detective noticed the dark shape of a pistol and walked over to find a nickel-plated Colt .32. He left it lie.

The street door to the building opened, and Justine edged out, pulling her embroidered shawl tight around her. She stood on the banquette and stared at Jacob. Valentin moved to her side and laid an arm around her shoulder. Seeing the red marks that Jacob had left on her throat, he found himself unable to speak. She buried her face against him and began to sob quietly.

A police siren whined from the direction of North Peters, and a minute later the first car swung around the corner and bore

down, casting the Creole detective, his woman, and the corpse in
the street in a wash of yellow-white light. Figures descended from
behind the lamps, and Valentin was grateful that the first body to
emerge was that of James McKinney.

The policeman approached carefully. "Mr. St. Cyr?" he said.
"What happened?"

"There was an incident," Valentin said.

Justine drew away from him. "He had a pistol," she said in
a soft, though steady voice. "He was going to kill me. I knocked
it out of his hand. Then he tried to strangle me."

Valentin pointed and said, "The weapon's still in the street."

"How did he die?" the cop asked.

"I shot him from down here," Valentin said.

McKinney considered the marksmanship for a moment, then
said, "All right, sir. I'll have to make a report."

"There's more to this," Valentin told him. In a few hushed
sentences, he told the cop about Evelyne Dallencort, William
Brown, and the late Louis Jacob.

When he finished, McKinney said, "Where is the woman
now?"

"She was at the Banks' Arcade," Valentin said. "Though she
may have started for her home."

"We can send detectives to both—"

"No," Valentin said. "We should go. Just you and I."

McKinney mulled for a moment. "All right, sir," he said.
"But Captain Picot won't like it."

Valentin smiled dimly. "No, he won't."

The cop shrugged. "Of course, he doesn't like much of anything I do these days." He glanced around. "We're going to need
a car."

The words had barely cleared his lips when a Model T of no
recent vintage clattered over the cobbles from North Peters
Street. Whaley was at the wheel. Behind it came Tom Anderson's

gleaming white Packard Victoria. The King of Storyville sat on the right. Each was in the driver's seat.

"Take your pick," Valentin told the cop.

Evelyne heard the fracas in the background, the sounds of a struggle, a woman's voice in a cough of shock, some banging, a single gunshot, then silence. It was done. She sighed and waited patiently for Louis to come back on the line. Weak as he was, he would need time to settle himself.

She waited some more and heard the woman's voice, now faint and far away, and realized that something had gone wrong. A few seconds later the phone went dead.

Louis had failed, damn him. He had quailed and run; either that, or the quadroon had gotten the best of him. One way or the other, he was gone and St. Cyr and the girl were still alive.

Of course, the Creole detective would come after her. Forcing herself not to panic, she quickly rang the operator and asked to be connected to Anderson's Café. She perked her ears for the background noise signaling the chaos that would occur in the wake of the King of Storyville's murder.

Instead, a tired-sounding bartender came on the line. Evelyne's voice was trembling when she asked for Mr. Anderson.

With a yawn the bartender said, "Who shall I tell him is calling?"

She shrieked a curse, whirled around, and threw the telephone against the wall, bashing the plaster. Her gut churned sourly, and she ran to the bathroom before she soiled the floor. When she came back out, she had to hold on to the doorjamb to steady herself.

She stared out the dark window, seeing her careful construction shattering. She had worked so hard, planned so well! It should have been easy. Storyville had been there for the taking. Indeed, bringing Tom Anderson and his little kingdom down should have been simple. It was ripe for the picking, she would step in as its queen, send a shock wave from coast to coast, and reign supreme over a gold mine that would never be depleted, because men never tired of their carnal pleasures. How well she knew that.

Louis had found just the right man at the insane hospital. He saw to it that the mad fellow was released and his tracks covered. A hundred dollars of her husband's money well spent. The crazy character went about the killings, one by one, seemingly without rhyme or reason, just as she had planned it. Never knowing that he was on a suicide mission. She arranged for that, too.

She felt her way to the plush chair and sat down. All that brilliant strategy and now it was over. She stopped to remind herself that it had been a noble, fantastic adventure and her own private legend.

Now, if nothing else, she could still spend her days and nights going over the best moments: that instant when the stunning idea came to her; meeting Louis and finding in him a pliant servant; the murders without motive, one after another; and, finally, meeting Valentin St. Cyr face-to-face and recognizing an exotic creature, like herself . . .

She sighed deeply, shook her head in slow regret. So be it. Who knew, there might be another chance for her. All the great figures from history had risen from failures. Another golden opportunity could be waiting for her just down the road.

With that thought to cheer her, she got up to don her coat. It was late and she was ready to go home.

They were approaching the curb in Whaley's Model T when he caught sight of a figure exiting the building. Before the Ford had come to a full stop, Valentin jumped down from the seat and ran across the street. McKinney and Whaley followed a few seconds behind him.

The squeak of the iron gate swinging wide startled her, and

she turned to see the three men stepping through the portal and then fanning out: Valentin St. Cyr and two others, one short and one tall. She emerged from the shadows and came toward them.

"I'm looking for Thomas," she stated. "My driver. Have you seen him? I'd like to go home now."

"I'm sure he's gone," Valentin said. "He doesn't want any part of this. I don't blame him."

"Then he's going to hear from me," Evelyne snipped. "If he spent less time chasing the girls and more time paying attention to his—"

"Louis Jacob is dead, Mrs. Dallencort."

Evelyne stopped for a second, then gave a dismissive shrug of her shoulders. "That's no surprise. What happened?"

The detective said, "I shot him."

She mulled the news for a moment before saying, "He was a foolish boy." She glanced around with some impatience. "I still need to be carried to my home."

Valentin nodded toward Detective McKinney. "The detective is here to escort you downtown," he said.

"Downtown?" Her lips pursed. "I live on Perrier Street."

Stepping forward, McKinney said, "Please come with me, Mrs. Dallencort."

"What for?" She was getting annoyed.

"You're going to be placed under arrest."

"Arrest?" Now she laughed lightly.

"Yes, ma'am. For murder."

Evelyne glanced from face to face, and gradually the cunning light returned to her eyes. "I didn't murder anyone." She crossed her arms in a regal posture. "You have no reason to arrest me." She waited for a moment, then chuckled again, musically. "Murder? Who has proof of such a thing?"

The Creole detective stared at her. "I'll testify to what you said upstairs. And there was a witness."

She glanced his way. "Who would that be?"

Valentin understood. Each had heard only part of what she'd said, and who'd believe a rough rounder like him, anyway. In fact, who'd believe any of it? A society woman plotting a series of murders in order to take over Storyville? It made no sense. And he had shot dead the one person who could tie such a scheme to her.

The detective gave a slight shake of his head. She was nothing if not a clever woman. He glanced at McKinney, who was watching with a frown that said he didn't like what he was hearing.

Maybe Evelyne Dallencort would get away with it. It was likely, in fact. Still, Valentin wasn't about to let her toddle off to her nice home, and McKinney wouldn't be inclined to offer her the courtesy, either. Let her sweat.

Evelyne had given herself quite an escape hatch. And Valentin had done away with the one person who had anything on her.

He regarded her for another moment, then turned to the policeman. "There's a call box out on the corner," he said. "You know where to find me." He jerked his head at Whaley. "Let's go back to Storyville."

TWENTY

They were waiting at Mangetta's: Valentin, Each, Tom Anderson, Whaley, and the saloonkeeper, who kept the wine flowing and plates of provolone, prosciutto, and hard bread full. They'd been there for hours, and the night was creeping toward dawn.

Valentin would get up to use the telephone, then come back, shaking his head. "Nothing yet."

As he sat half listening to the others, it occurred to him that somehow he had known that once the dust settled, he'd land at one of Frank's sturdy tables. As the conversation went on without him, he felt as if he was seeing Storyville laid out before him with every detail clear to his eye, a street map in three dimensions. No, it was *four*; he could divine the movement through time over the hours and days since the trouble began.

When he tracked and shot William Brown, he had reached down for old nerve endings to help him on this way. Brown was easy prey, a hopeless, hapless, crazed fellow who had no idea that he was being sent out to kill and then die.

For his part, Valentin had been caught in a web that had been woven by Evelyne Dallencort. In all, eight men were dead and

Justine had nearly joined them. He shuddered privately for a moment, imagining what might have happened had the shot he fired gone astray. At the same time, he had a notion that he had somehow willed the bullet into Louis Jacob.

Frank was eager to hear more details of what had transpired. The detective wasn't inclined, so Each jumped in and, with some help from Whaley and Anderson, went through the night's adventure.

Valentin's thoughts drifted away again. He wondered how Evelyne had come up with her crazy scheme. At some point she met Louis Jacob, and they conspired to strike terror into the heart of the District. No one was safe. The target was Storyville and everyone in it. They had done a good job. It was true that no one had come as close to toppling the scarlet empire.

Anderson still didn't get it. Who was this woman and what did she want?

Coming out of his musings, Valentin said, "How much is Storyville worth?"

"What do you mean?"

"In a month how much money goes in and out?"

The King of Storyville paused, then said, "Almost a quarter of a million dollars."

There was a hush. The number seemed to take on substance and float above the table. With twenty square blocks of sin, it equaled three million dollars a year at a time when ten dollars a week was a fair salary.

The King of Storyville was unimpressed. He had heard the number before, written it out time and again, and bandied about by other men of importance.

"So she wanted her hands on the money?" he said. "Isn't she already plenty rich?"

Valentin said, "You know some people never have enough. And what she had was all her husband's money." He paused.

"And of course she wanted power over all the women. The mansions. The saloons and dance halls . . ." He smiled. "She said you could keep the Café, by the way."

"Well, that was generous," Anderson said. He shook his head in wonder. "So she thought she could take over just by killing a few men?"

Valentin said, "She probably would have murdered more to get what she was after."

"To prove that I couldn't control it anymore."

"That's correct."

"I suppose she was right." The King of Storyville sighed.

"What about her partner?" Whaley said. "What was his name?"

"Louis Jacob," Valentin said. "Honore's son. I don't know why he got caught up in it. Except that he was stupid. Or greedy."

"I think it had something to do with the father," the King of Storyville said.

"I wonder what he thinks of his son now," Valentin said.

Anderson gave him a sober look. "He's grieving over his death."

The detective said, "Mrs. Dallencort was going to get rid of him, anyway. That fellow she sent to the Café was probably going to go after him next. She couldn't afford to have him stay around. Not with what he knew."

"Our own Madame Lafarge," Tom Anderson murmured.

The men at the table produced blank looks, except for Valentin, who understood and smiled slightly.

"So where is she now?" Anderson said.

"McKinney took her in," Valentin said. "He wasn't sure what he could do, but he arrested her, anyway." He stared absently at the glass before him. "I think she'll walk free."

"I think so, too."

The men looked around. Justine was standing in the doorway with James McKinney, who was wearing a crooked smile.

"Delivery for Mr. St. Cyr," he said.

Valentin stood up. "You made a good trade."

He pulled a chair out for Justine while Frank fetched another for the policeman. Fresh glasses appeared before they were settled.

"What about Mrs. Dallencort?" the detective said.

McKinney looked toward Justine, allowing her to speak first. She described how she had been placed in a cell in the colored women's section. It was Picot's doing, and he claimed to be holding her as a material witness to a shooting. To her surprise, Evelyne Dallencort was placed in the next cell. But only briefly, until the police could make room for her on the white side.

"Or because Picot wanted to see if you two were somehow in cahoots."

Justine nodded gravely. "Yes, maybe so."

Valentin couldn't take his eyes off her. She avoided his gaze.

"At first, she didn't say a word to me," she went on. "She just watched me like I was something in a cage at the zoo. She did start talking, though." The men waited for her to continue. "It was women's talk. She asked me if I was the one who was 'intimately associated' with the Creole detective. That's how she put it." She shrugged. "A little while later, the officers came in and took her away. I think to question her."

"And let her go," Valentin said.

"That's right," McKinney said.

"So she just walks away now?" Anderson said. "There's nothing to hold her on?"

McKinney shook his head. "Not now, anyway."

"She's a clever woman," Valentin said. "She had it planned all along. It didn't work the way she hoped it would. But she made sure she had a way out if it came apart. And it did." He paused thoughtfully. "But she got close."

"I can't believe she thought she could pull it off," Anderson said.

"She saw Storyville as ripe for the picking," Valentin added. "Louis must have told her that you were done and that the District was falling apart and was going to get shut down unless someone stepped in. That would be like closing a gold mine."

"So she came up with this plan."

"And that's all it was until she decided to try it. Starting with finding William Brown."

Justine said. "Where did he come from?"

"Jackson," Valentin said. "The hospital."

She stared at him briefly. "Jackson? Was that why—"

"Why Bolden spoke my name. Why he wanted me out there. He overheard them say my name." He stopped to sip his wine. "They faked his death somehow. Moved him out and had the records fixed. Mrs. Dallencort would certainly have the money to bribe anyone who was willing."

The Sicilian said, "That one man did all the killing?"

"Not the last one. What was his name?"

"Parks," McKinney said. "I think the night after Mr. Valentin shot Brown, Louis murdered him. Probably Mrs. Dallencort ordered him to. Or maybe he decided to do it on his own. To up the stakes." He paused. "And it could be that he was the one who took care of the drunk they found by the cemetery. The one they called Stovepipe."

Valentin said, "That poor fellow was just in the right place." He drew a design in the air. "The wrong place, I mean."

"Was that a star?"

"He drew five-point stars like that everywhere he went," the detective said. "I saw dozens of them scratched on the wall in Jackson."

Mangetta said, *"Per che?"*

"That I don't know," Valentin said. "We'll never know.

Something he had stuck in his brain." He looked at McKinney. "Did you see the scar?"

The cop said, "It was there, all right."

Each looked between the two men. "What was there?"

McKinney said, "Mr. Brown had the pattern of a star cut into his torso. The doctor said it was an old wound. Probably happened when he was a child."

The explanation brought a moment of silence.

"So," Valentin said presently. "Louis would have told the woman about him, and she came up with the plan. Two houses form one line."

"And one cut," McKinney added.

"That's right. They decided to use Honore Jacob's properties to fill in the next ones. They could get the body into the first one with Louis's help. I don't know about the others. I mean, why involve his own father?"

"I suspect he despised him," the King of Storyville said. "Thought he was weak. The fool who let the family fortune go."

"And Mrs. Dallencort would have used that, too."

Anderson was incredulous. "I still can't believe she devised the whole plan."

"Well, she did," the detective said.

After a few moments' silence, McKinney spoke up again. "There was that fellow they found in the crib back on Robertson Street."

Valentin said, "That's right."

"He doesn't fit the pattern," the cop said.

"Then maybe he was practice. For him. Or her."

"I guess I still don't understand what she wanted," Each said. "Don't make no sense."

Valentin was about to comment when Justine spoke up. "She didn't want to have to live out the rest of her life as some rich man's wife," Justine said. "In his shadow. She wanted something of her own."

"She couldn't find a hobby?" Anderson quipped, and the men laughed.

Justine was serious. "She didn't want a hobby. She wanted a treasure."

Whaley eyed Valentin. "What I don't understand is why she dragged you into it."

Justine answered for him. "He was the only one who everybody in the District trusted. She probably found that out from Louis, too."

"But he wasn't working up here no more," Frank said.

"They knew he couldn't stay out of it," she said. "Not once the killings started."

Valentin noted the accusing tone in her voice and kept silent.

"She was going to draw him in, one way or another. And he took the bait." Now she looked at the detective squarely.

Valentin nodded and said, "Yes, I did."

"But in case he tried to turn the tables, she had Louis show up with his pistol and hold me hostage. He was supposed to get rid of me if Valentin didn't do his part. That was the plan."

Now it was Valentin's turn. "But first he had to pull *you* in."

She nodded. "That's right. And that's what he did."

The men waited for her to offer something more. She preferred to let them wonder.

"No, that's not what happened," Valentin said suddenly. "Did you set him up?" She started to smile. "Did you?"

"I'm not stupid, Valentin."

"I never thought you—"

"I watched you. And listened to you. For a long time." She regarded him with a distracted smile. "It was too easy. This fellow appears at the same time you're heading back to Storyville? I thought about that right away."

"So you . . ."

Her eyebrows arched on her latte flesh. "So I led him along. Let him think he might get his way with me."

The Creole detective dropped his gaze without asking how far it had gone. He had no right to the information.

"He wasn't that hard," she went on. "He had such a big head. He never had any idea that I was . . ."

"Playing him," Valentin said. She thought for a moment, then nodded. "To protect me."

"Well, I didn't know he was going to pull a gun," Justine said, and once more the table broke up in laughter.

Valentin gazed at her, then looked at Frank and shook his head in wonder. The Sicilian smiled and pinched his fingers in a familiar gesture of respect. Humbled, Valentin didn't know what to say.

Justine was watching his face, thinking her own thoughts. Now she rose from her chair and moved to sit in his lap, wrap one arm around him, and use the fingers of her free hand to raise his chin so she could look into his eyes. The others at the table drew aside for some small talk, letting them be.

After a little while, he murmured something to her, then leaned over to ask Whaley to bring the car around. When the Ford rattled to the curb outside, they stood and said their good-byes.

A hundred miles up the river and then inland another ten, Charles sat up in his bed, awakened by a vague dream. The ward was dead quiet, and he slipped from under his sheets and padded out into the corridor. The attendant who was supposed to be watching was slouched in the chair in his little office, dead to the world and snoring like a pig.

Charles made his way to the end of the hallway and the little alcove with the arched window. Though it was dark outside, a veiled moon was up. He could not see the river, but believed he could feel it out there in this hour before dawn. The thought and the image in his mind took him back to a room full of sound, light, and motion, a stage, and another window. He remembered how he put the bell of his horn over the sill and into the night and blew; blew so hard, some said, that they could hear him in Algiers, all the way on the other side of the river.

That had been long ago and far away, and now he felt it all slipping away from him, dissolving like paint in muddy water, but it was all right. Standing there, his sharp face bathed in soft moonlight, he thought of something else, and smiled.

Whaley drove off in the direction of Spain Street. Halfway there, Valentin tapped his shoulder and directed him south and west.

The Model T pulled to a stop by the levee. Valentin stepped down and offered Justine his hand. They began a slow ascent of the slope. Whaley called out, asking if they wanted him to wait. The detective told him to go on; they'd find their way home.

They stood atop the rise, looking out over the river as it flowed through the last minutes of the night. They could hear the quiet gurgle as the water lapped at the banks. A half mile or so off, a freighter drifted as silent as a ghost, with only the lights on its port and stern to define it against the inky shadows.

Valentin felt the warmth of her body at his side and started to say something, but it caught in his throat. Justine understood and allowed herself the smallest sweet sigh. She raised her eyes and stared into his as if she could read his thoughts. After a moment, she drew back, bemused.

"I didn't do anything with that boy," she said. "Did you really think I'd be that much of a fool? He was nothing." She stared more deeply. "And I would never do that to you," she said.

Valentin watched her for long seconds. Then he bent his mouth to her ear and whispered, "Marry me."